Praise for Somewhere Close to Happy

'This book is ⸻us and kind and funny. I fe⸻s, it made me f⸻rful w⸻ght

'A wonderfully written, funny and moving debut with an intriguing mystery at its heart. I laughed, cried and was completely swept away by Lizzy and Roman's story. Unforgettable'
Claire Douglas, author of *Then She Vanishes*

'I thought it was both a funny and heart-warming story . . . Louis's is a bold, standout voice in the women's fiction genre and *Somewhere Close To Happy* deserves to be huge'
Gillian McAllister, author of *No Further Questions*

'Honest and brave, *Somewhere Close to Happy* is a thought-provoking, beautifully observed study of love and real life, social issues and mental health'
Jill Mansell, author of *Maybe This Time*

'Oh my god, I LOVED *Somewhere Close to Happy*. It made me cry several times but was also really funny. It is so incredibly good'
Laura Marshall, author of *Friend Request*

Somewhere Close To Happy

Lia Louis

TRAPEZE

First published in Great Britain in 2020 by Trapeze,
an imprint of The Orion Publishing Group Ltd
Carmelite House, 50 Victoria Embankment,
London EC4Y 0DZ

An Hachette UK company

1 3 5 7 9 10 8 6 4 2

A CIP catalogue record for this book is
available from the British Library.

ISBN (Paperback) 978 1 4091 8416 4

Typeset by Born Group
Printed and bound in Great Britain by Clays Ltd, Elcograf S.p.A.

MIX
Paper from
responsible sources
FSC® C104740

www.orionbooks.co.uk

For my 15-year-old self. For holding on. For dreaming. For knowing good things would come to us one day.

You were right.

Twelve Years Earlier

In a moment, I'll open my eyes and wake up. I so badly want to wake up. Where is he? *Where is he?*

I knew something was wrong by lunchtime. I'd had no answers to my texts, and his phone, when I called, was going straight to voicemail. I knew. I knew from that moment.

'He never switches off his phone,' I'd told Ramesh desperately, shivering in the entrance of The Grove. 'C-call his social worker. Please. Do something – *anything*. Something is wrong, Ramesh, I can tell.' He picked up the phone, his eyes squinting, puzzled, then hung up, telling me she couldn't help. And nobody will. *Nobody* will help me, and I have asked and asked and pleaded, but they just keep saying he's fine, that he's old enough, that he'll be in touch, but they don't understand. They don't understand that I need to know he's OK. I need to know he's safe, and that his heart is still beating. Because Roman isn't anywhere. My best friend is gone. He has disappeared. And he promised me, so many, many times, he never would.

Chapter One

'They just called. He's a minute away.'

'A minute. Oh, god, did you hear that, Lizzie? Chris is a minute away.'

'Yes, I—'

'Shit. *Shit.* Bollocks. Oh, god.'

'Priscilla . . .'

'I can't breathe. I actually cannot *breathe.* Is everything ready? I mean, is it? Where's the big fifty balloon? And why are the spring rolls not on the buffet table, yet? I told Perry to put them out but he's probably too busy letching about the place to—'

'Priscilla, seriously. You need to chill.'

My best friend pauses, nods, and holds onto the inside of my forearms as if they are crutches, drawing in a huge breath, pink, glossy lips pressed together. Groups of party guests scurry past us to the living room, their shiny shoes scuffing and clip-clopping on the oak floor beneath us.

'Sorry, Lizzie,' she says. 'I'm just shitting it. Really shitting it.'

'I know, P, but there's really no need,' I tell her. 'Look around you. Everything's done, everything's perfect. The party's ready. All we need now is Chris.'

Priscilla smiles nervously and squeezes my arm. 'God,' she exhales. 'You have no idea how filled with nerves my belly is right now.' And I want to tell her that I do. I do, because my belly is the same, although it's for a reason she'd never believe; a reason that's sitting in my cardigan pocket as we speak, growing heavier and heavier at my thigh.

'You should be shitting it to be fair,' says my brother. He's standing beside me, looming like he always does, with a plastic cup of beer in his shovel hand. I roll my eyes at him.

'What?' he shrugs. 'I'm just saying, the bloke didn't even want a party. He might walk in and "shit it" all the way out the front door. Plus,' he smirks, 'the *elderly* aren't so keen on big dos, are they?'

Priscilla scowls up at Nathan, but there's a tiny smile on her lips. 'Oh, look, you're being an ageist bastard again.'

Nathan lets loose a roar of his buffoony laugh and gives a shrug. 'I'm just saying, even *I* know that your fiancé is not at all the surprise party type and—'

Nathan's sentence is cut short by Katie's elbow nudging him in his side. 'Oh, be quiet, you arse,' she tuts up at him, her hands moving to hold onto his arm now, tree trunk-like beneath her small, slim hands. She gives Priscilla a weary smile. 'Please ignore my idiot of a husband. Chris is gonna absolutely love it. *Isn't he?*'

'I'm joking,' laughs Nathan. 'Oh, come on, P knows I'm joking, don't you, P?'

Priscilla smirks, giving a flip of her middle finger.

'Deserved,' Nathan grins, but his words are lost as Seedy Perry Keilson – self-proclaimed 'brains' of this whole party operation – appears in the doorway, all ruddy cheeks, white teeth, and misogyny, and shouts, 'Positions, positions! Our main man's just parking up.'

At those words, all hell breaks loose.

Party guests speed from all over Priscilla and Chris's house, and there are so many more than I had expected tonight. This isn't the first party my best friend has held at her house – dinner-party perfect with its white-walls, high ceilings, and jars of flowers and candles in all the right, Pinterest-precise places – but never before have I seen its rooms as crammed with bodies as it is now. There are shoals of them, rushing in from the kitchen, squeezing through the dining area, stumbling in from the patio, giggling, chattering, drinks sloshing in hands. And the guests are just as immaculate as the décor. Hair tumbles and shines, sitting neatly atop heads, pairs and pairs of elegant feet glide in elegant heels I'd walk like a constipated bridge troll in, and there are sleek, razor sharp suits at every turn. You can tell I arrived on a whim – in a gust of wind – from one look at the creased straight-from-the-ironing-pile dress I'd slung on in my desperate panic to get out, and this morning's make up, which has sweated off after a long day in an airless office with my boss and his hairdryers for sinuses.

I am not meant to be here. I wasn't prepared to come to a fiftieth birthday party tonight. But then, I wasn't prepared for the letter that was handed to me as I left work either, and the sudden desperate overwhelming need that followed after I broke open the seal, to be anywhere else, except in my flat alone with it pulsing in its envelope. I tried. I did. I made a cup of tea, put on my pyjamas, and picked up the phone to order Chinese food, trying to carry on the way I do every Friday night. But I felt sick. I couldn't dial, or swallow, or even *think*, so instead I paced. Paced and paced – the way you do when you're waiting for vital news – and nibbled my fingernails until they were raw, all the while staring at the letter across the room as if it were a bomb that could go off

4

at any moment, as if someone might be watching me unravel like this, as a result of their sick joke. And I just couldn't stay. I had to get out, get to Priscilla. Because she'll make sense of it, unearth the logical explanation. Nothing's a big deal to Priscilla. She is 80% steel.

'I've always liked the idea of a surprise party,' muses my brother, as we shuffle together at the end of one of the lines of guests. There are rows and rows of us in Priscilla and Chris's lounge now, like concert-goers squeezed together in the standing zone. 'Just the thought of everyone stressing, sneaking about in their droves, all for me . . .'

'*Droves*,' I say.

'What?'

'Nothing,' I shrug. 'Just you know . . . *droves*. It's a very confident thing to say.'

Nathan puffs up his chest and nods once.

'For a common estate agent.'

Katie laughs, and chuckling, Nathan opens his mouth to speak, but we're pushed against by even more filing, squishing-together guests, and he misses his chance. We're arm-to-arm now with Nathan's huge frame squashed against the wall, his head next to a canvas print of Priscilla and Chris in front of Sydney Opera House. Chris looks waspy in a pastel blue shirt, his razor-sharp jaw peppered with grey stubble, and Priscilla shines like the bright lights behind them. I'd once thought that the beaming elation Priscilla wore on her face after the almost-glimpse of Mr Dunmow's crotch she got on our year ten trip to Walton-on-the-Naze could never be replicated. Priscilla had fancied him since year seven, and when he'd jumped into the sea with the rugby boys and his trunks had begun to fall down, Priscilla had grabbed my arm beside me on the shore, gasped like she'd just spotted Jesus walking on the horizon, and said, 'I saw pubes! I saw skin!' and the look on her face was unrivalled, concentrated happiness. Then she met Chris, three years ago, and ever since, she has been wearing the same shining, 'can't-believe-my-luck' smile that she had on her face on that windy Essex beach.

Her face is stretched into her token constipated fake grin now though, over by the lounge door with Perry, one of Chris's business partners and oldest friends. His arm is around her, squeezing her into his side, like the big seedy, smarmy snake that he is, and he is no doubt telling her, as if talking about a reliable used car, that if she had wanted an older man she should've gone to him first.

'Come on, come on,' he bellows, hand hovering over the light switch. 'That's it, party people, in your positions.' Then he grins with eyebrows waggling so much that I expect the tinkling sound of a xylophone, and he says, 'Anything from the Kama Sutra suits me, ladies of the room.'

I usually avoid parties and dos of all kinds – always have. Especially when the likes of Seedy Perry Keilson are floating about in them, but anywhere is better than home, alone tonight. Even here, at a party full of black tie wearing, hair like spaniels, sixty-year-old pervs shouting shit about the Kama Sutra. At least here, I stand a chance of drowning out the questions rapidly filling my head. They've been sprouting one-by-one, then two-by-two since I read those words inside the envelope; like weeds, weaving, wrapping around my brain, taking root, blocking out the light.

Nathan looks down at me. He's huge, my brother. It's always seemed ridiculous to me that he plays golf. He'd be much better suited to the tug of war or pulling along trucks with his ear lobes like those men on TV. I tell him this often.

'Alright?' he smiles.

I nod.

I'm not. I can barely move. We are all squashed and huddled together, packed tightly in lines like boxed cigarettes, and my head is pounding with anxiety. I've never fared well in crowds or confined spaces. They make me panic and turn the oxygen around me into thick gloop. I just want to talk to Priscilla, alone. I need to show her the letter. I know I'll feel better once I do. I tried to show her when I arrived, after she'd finished squealing with excitement that I'd actually turned up, then telling me over and over that I looked so pale, I was 'practically bloody see-through.'

'I'm OK,' I said. 'I just . . . can we talk somewhere?'

'Course. Liz, are you sure you're alright?'

I told her I needed to show her something. She ushered me inside.

But then Perry and his ridiculous, flammable quiff had interrupted on his way to the kitchen, booming and smarming about me being late and arriving after the half-past-seven threshold, and how I'd get a 'bloody good seeing to' if I ruined the surprise of the party, and after that, everyone seemed to conspire against us. There were people everywhere, all of whom seemed to want to speak to Priscilla, and when it was announced that Chris was on his way home, the whole brimming houseful launched into an over-excited panic, a beaky woman I didn't recognise asked Priscilla over and over why she and Perry hadn't hired the 'drink staff' she'd recommended, then Nathan and Katie came bounding over, shocked to see me, full of excited smiles and questions. I gave up. I'll wait until the excitement dies down. I'll wait until after Chris arrives. The whispers making their way slowly through the crowd like a Mexican wave now, tell us he is in his car, parked up, on the phone.

'Here, meant to ask,' says Nathan, ducking his head, a stray wave springing loose from his gelled, mousy curls. 'Are you around on Sunday?'

I give a shrug. 'I should be. Why?'

'Katie and I are venturing back up *into the loft*.' Nathan says the last three words in the way someone would say 'Monster Mash' and laughs. 'Dad's hoping to move out of the house when he's back from Menorca so I want the loft clear before he goes. That way he can take stuff with him while we've got the rental van. Makes sense.'

'But why do you need me?'

Nathan's brow furrows. 'Um, because there is loads of your stuff up there?'

'Still?' I ask. 'You dropped round two bags of crap last week.'

Nathan shrugs. 'Not my fault teenage Lizzie was a hoarder. Dad said there's a box up there full of your CDs, and one with just your pencils and paints in, and that's only what he can see sticking his head up there—'

'Oh, just chuck it all, Nate.' It's hot in here, so bloody hot, and as I turn my face away and look over my shoulder, I meet the staring eyes of a stranger who is so close, she's practically nuzzling my hair. Oh, I wish Chris would hurry up. The walls feel like they're closing in on us all.

'Chuck it all?' asks Nathan. He ducks closer again, lowering his voice. 'But what about photos and stuff for . . . I don't know,' he shrugs, hand in his pocket, beer to his chest, 'for memories?'

'But it'll just be junk.' Heat pounds my face, and all I can see is heads and backs and shoulders. I step onto my tiptoes to get a view of Priscilla, for a hint as to when this'll all be over. She's nervously looking at her phone, still squeezed into Perry who is mouthing something to someone far behind me.

'Maybe just pop in?'

'Nathan . . .'

'Just take a quick look, so I know what's junk and what's not. There's loads of Mum's stuff, too, and to be honest, I could do with a—'

'OK, *fine*,' I cut in, mouth dry. Nathan's lips press together. 'Fine. I'll pop in.'

A voice from behind shushes us then, and I raise my eyebrows at Nathan as if to say, 'your fault.'

'Sorry,' he grimaces. Then after a breath and a sip of beer, he ducks again and whispers, 'Lizzie, are you alright?'

'Me? You've already asked,' I say, widening my eyes, and putting my finger to my lips like a school child. 'I'm fine.'

Nathan nods. 'I know, I know. Just that . . . you weren't gonna come tonight, were you? Usually, we wouldn't be able to prise you out of your flat on a Friday night for love nor money.'

'Changed my mind.'

Nathan nods once but carries on. *Of course he does.* Thirty-one years into life, and my big brother is still utterly incapable of taking a hint. 'You're just acting a bit . . . weird.'

'Nathan, we're currently being squashed into what can only be described as a mass grave,' I whisper, 'so, yes, maybe I am acting a bit weird.'

And then there is darkness. Pure, sudden darkness, as the light switch is pushed. The room fills with low, excited giggles and more hushing, and Nathan doesn't say anything else. Divine timing. That's what it's called, isn't it?

There's the jingle of keys, a click, and a bang. Chris has let himself in and closed the front door behind him.

'Priscilla?' Chris calls through the house. 'Only me.'

We all stand still and silent in the darkness. It's disorientating. I can see nothing, besides dancing navy blue and black fuzz, like at the beginning of an old video tape before the film starts, and my brain is racing; more and more weeds continue

9

to sprout, weaving into the gaps that are usually filled with visual distractions. I think about the letter. I think about his words, scrawled on the page. My brain runs over and over them, like a tripping record. '. . . where none of this ever happened.' '. . . where none of this ever happened.' *This.* None of 'this'. What does 'this' mean?

Someone's chest presses into my back. I can smell breath and onions and too-strong aftershave. I am working my arse off here not to tear from the room into a wide, open space to swallow down fresh air.

'Hiya!' Chris calls through the house again.

Silence. I close my eyes and breathe deeply, stuffing my hand into the deep woolly pocket of my cardigan. The letter folds under my fingers and crackles in the silence.

'Shhhh,' someone says.

It's real. It must be, if it rustles, if a room full of people can hear it.

My heart thump-thumps in my throat. He mentioned Sea Fog in the letter. God . . . *Sea Fog.* I thought I had forgotten about it, but actually, I don't think I've passed a caravan without looking for its name ever since. That bucket of rust – safety and freedom, and a reminder of how trapped we were, all rolled into one – must be hidden, but anchored in my mind somewhere, like it was anchored to that driveway. Until the day it wasn't.

'Priss?' Chris calls through the house, his voice close now, on the other side of the door. 'I know you're here. Your bloody phone's in the kitchen . . .'

The handle squeaks; the lounge door swings open. Someone snaps the light switch.

The room floods with blinding light. Everyone erupts.

'Surprise!'

December 4th, 2005

Dear Lizzie J,

Somewhere in the universe there is a life playing out where none of this ever happened and wherever that is, we're happy. We're driving Sea Fog for miles and miles to where there is nothing but sea and our brains are clean slates and we're just happy. We're finally free.

That's the only thing that's getting me through this nightmare, J. Thinking of that place, and hoping one day we'll get there. Or somewhere close.

I thought I'd know what to say if I started writing, besides I'm sorry. But I don't. I've tried, I've tried so hard, but I don't know how. There are no words for what I have done.

Please know you deserve more than this. You deserve the whole world.

Thank you. For every minute.

I'm sorry. I am so sorry.

Roman x

'Roman. This is . . . this is from *Roman*?'

Priscilla opens her mouth to speak, but no words come out. She swallows, the letter still open in her hand. Her other flies up to her forehead, as if pressing to check for a fever. Gradually, her hand drifts down to her cheek.

'Lizzie . . .' she utters. Then she pauses again, glancing back down at the letter. 'Bloody hell. I mean – *where* . . .' Priscilla trails off.

I sit down on the bed beside her. It creaks under our weight. She stares at me, dark, feathery eyelashes slowly batting.

'Where did this come from?' Priscilla's hand is pressed against her chest now, where her heart is. 'And DDC, what's that? This logo printed at the top.'

'Headed paper, I guess. I don't know, P.'

'Two thousand and *five*. Jesus,' she says. 'December. That's . . .'

My heart heaves against my ribs. I nod. 'The day he disappeared.'

Priscilla blinks down at the letter, her lips parted. 'But why now? Where's it been? Lost or something?'

'No idea. Just turned up at Dad's with the rest of the post.'

'Today?'

'Yesterday. Katie brought it into work this morning on her way past. It didn't get to my desk until I was leaving tonight.'

'Jesus,' she says again.

'I opened it on the tube,' I tell her. 'I think I knew. It was the handwriting.'

We look at each other in the dim light of Priscilla's bedroom, our chests rising and falling, silence between us, as music, laughter, and chatter from the party below thumps through the floor.

'Bloody hell,' says Priscilla again into the silence. 'How do you feel?'

I shrug. 'I don't know. Slightly sick actually. Confused. A bit sad. Seeing his name again, saying it—' The words get stuck in my throat. I really don't know how I feel. Besides knotted on the inside; veins and bones and tissue and heart twisted together in a ball in my chest.

We sit in silence again. Priscilla stares at a spot on the ceiling, then at the floor, then back down at the letter in her hand. '*Shit*,' she mutters. 'Mad,' she says, over and over, picking up the envelope beside her on the edge of the bed and studying it, back and front, turning it over in her hand. She smiles, her manicured finger is pressed on the post mark. It's dated two days ago.

'Reading,' she says. 'So, what, Roman's in *Reading* now? All those years and he's a couple of hours away?'

'Who knows?' I say. 'He could be anywhere, P – could've *been* anywhere.'

Priscilla beams down at the envelope and letter, one in each hand. 'This is amazing, really. I mean, if you really think about it.' Priscilla shakes her head in disbelief. 'What're you going to do?'

I fold my arms across my body. My pulse hammers in my throat. 'Nothing.'

'*Nothing?*' says Priscilla, her eyes snapping up to look at me. The sudden burst of sound, such a contrast to speaking so softly over the humdrum of the party below, makes me sit up. 'Sorry, babe, it's just . . . don't you want to know?'

I lift my shoulders to my ears. 'But know what? It was years ago, P.'

'I dunno,' she says, quietly. 'To find out why you got this now, where it came from, what he *means*?'

Heat flashes across my cheeks. 'P, we were teenagers when he wrote this. *Kids.*'

Priscilla's brow furrows. 'But this isn't just a *kid*, is it, Lizzie? This is Roman. Like . . . actual, real, Roman.' She studies my face for a second, but I'm not even sure I'm breathing. My head is rushing with blood. I am frozen; stunned, I suppose, by all the questions, by the memories, trickling in, slowly, one by one. 'And now you have this,' carries on Priscilla, 'you could probably trace this back, or at least try. Look, we know it was stamped in Reading, so maybe we could call the sorting office—'

'I don't think so.'

'But you could just find out where it came from,' says Priscilla. She's turned now, so she's looking right at me, eyes wide and glinting with excitement, beside me on the bed. Like she's hatching a plan, and she wants me on board. 'It was only sent *two* days ago . . .'

'Yes, but written twelve years ago,' I say. 'He's a man now, Priscilla. A grown man, probably getting on with his life and, knowing Roman, living in some sort of weird yurt in some tribal village with wolves for friends, and playing his bass. He probably hasn't a clue this was even lost.'

Priscilla looks at the letter in her hands, her eyes narrowed, as if looking for a detail she might have missed. 'But how can it be lost if it was only just posted?'

I swallow. 'I – I don't know.' My arms are pricked with goosebumps. That's the thing that's jarring, that's what playing on my mind, apart from the meaning behind the words inside, apart from wanting to know why he was sorry. *So* sorry, in fact. The idea that it was sent two days ago purposely. By him.

Priscilla brings her arms around herself and looks at me, sadly.

'Bloody hell, P,' I say, my voice shaking. 'I really thought that you would . . . I don't know, tell me it was cute, reminisce a bit, and then tell me to chuck it or something. That it's been years, and how spooky, and how *weird*, now let's go and have some mini crab cakes and watch Perry dance to Ricky Martin.'

Priscilla laughs. Light catches in her eyes, the colour of burnt sugar. 'It is cute,' she says. 'And it is spooky. But you can't chuck this, babe. You can't just *leave* this.' She places her hand on mine. 'I don't really know what any of this means, but . . . there must be a reason you've got this now – today – all these years later.'

I shake my head.

'Lizzie, you could even find him—'

'*Priscilla*,' I say.

She stops. We stare at each other. I take the letter from her hands and push it back into the envelope. She watches me, biting the corner of her lip. Eventually, she nods.

'Nothing,' Priscilla says, her shoulders deflating. 'Fine. *OK*. Nothing.'

'Nothing,' I say.

Chapter Two

Three boxes. That's all my childhood whittles down to. Three cardboard boxes, the tape crunchy and curling with age, and a shoebox of keyrings that I collected from every holiday and day out we had from about the age of six. All tat; plastic boats, enamel shapes of countries and counties, dusty teddy bears too big for keychains really, but each one carefully and meticulously picked out. Each one with its own story of a moment in time.

'So, hang on a minute,' Nathan had puffed, this afternoon, creaking down the steps of Dad's loft ladder, a split bin bag of dusty clothes bundled in his arms. 'You have just dumped a box full of perfectly good oils and pastels, but you're going to keep . . . that?'

'For *memories*,' I told him, squeezing a squeaky plastic pig keyring in his face.

He'd smirked, dumping the bin bag on the landing, next to a line of boxes and an old ironing board. 'See, if you'd left me in charge, I'd have binned those and kept the paints and pencils and stuff.'

I shrugged. 'But you can get paints from anywhere. I could never buy or collect all these again.' I looked down into the shoebox held against my stomach. 'I can tell you where I was when I bought every single one of these.'

Nathan cocked an eyebrow. 'Go on then,' he said. 'The squeaky pig.'

'Easy,' I said. 'Oakwood Farm with you, Mum and Dad. Dad got reflux from the scone in the farm café and she told him he was fat and killing himself with dairy and they didn't speak for the rest of the day.'

Nathan laughed. 'And uh . . .' He fished about in the box, chains jangling. 'This one? This bear thing.'

'Alton Towers with Priscilla and her parents. We were fourteen.'

'Is that one a . . . rose?'

'*Peonie.* Some urban botanical garden place in a dome. Suffolk, I think.'

'With Hubble,' Nathan stated, incorrectly, more than asked, dusting his top down with his hand, and I swallowed at the sound of my grandad's name.

'No,' I told him, lowering my voice. 'Dad. Two weeks after Mum left him and he went a bit mad and kept taking me to weird places because he couldn't bear to be in the house with all her stuff.'

Nathan raised both eyebrows, as the sound of Dad's feet began to pound the stairs. 'Bloody hell, Liz. Your memory's a Tardis. I don't even remember when I last took a shit.'

'Right,' said Dad, breathlessly, as he'd reached the top of the stairs, hand rubbing the side of his big tummy, as if kneading out a stitch, 'car's full for the tip. Lizzie, did you still want a lift home, darlin'?' As Dad helped me gather up the last of the boxes, he stopped at the top of the stairs and said, 'And it was last night, Nathan, when *Britain's Got Talent* was on. You took so long, poor Katie had to wee in a bucket.'

I hadn't planned to open the boxes. I was going to slide all three of them to the back of my wardrobe, drape them with an old winter coat and save them for another day, for when I was ready – whenever that'd be – but when I sat cross-legged by the wardrobe after Dad dropped me home, boxes stacked beside me, I saw a glimmer of orange through a loose flap of cardboard – the amber of an old college prospectus. 2005. I pulled it out, scraps of old drawings and doodles scattering from its pages like a switch had been pressed on a fan, the want to open it was like a hand, shoving me. Now, I sit staring at it, my hands carefully, peeling back the layers and layers of memories, one by one, as thunder rumbles outside, and a cup of tea turns cold on the carpet next to me.

I remember packing this box; tearing photos and papers off my bedroom walls, pulling every piece of evidence of The Grove, of him, from every crevice and shelf, and pushing them deep, deep down. It was January, 2006, a month of nothing but grey skies and howling winds. I remember the intense need for it all to go away as I packed. I remember my eyes, swollen and gritty from weeks of crying, and holding that gift in my hand one last time before I buried that too – the strong, heavy book wrapped loosely in the crinkled black tissue paper it came in, its gold gift tag still attached, still waiting to be used. And I remember the disc – the CD I made in a hurry, dragging over folders of conversations, hundreds of them automatically saved over one year, and picking and choosing what was worth saving; what would be most important to Future Me. The me who would one day unpeel the wrinkling tape. The Lizzie James who would know the answers to all life's questions and be strong enough to look back.

I find the CD easily now, between the pages of my old art book – front cover stamped with a sticker that says 'Lizzie J, group B' – and balance it on the end of my finger. 'Lizzie laptop' is scrawled on it in black marker in my sixteen-year-old self's handwriting. I stretch over to my bed and pull my laptop onto the floor with me. I slide the disc into the tray.

Thunder rumbles, like a grumbling monster outside in the humid night. The air is so dense this evening, it's like breathing static electricity.

The computer whirs, and I'm seconds – millimetres – away from ejecting it now, throwing it back in the box, taping up the lid, and shoving it – shoving everything – back to where it was. Hidden. Forgotten. But something in me wants to open it; a part that's been lying dormant for twelve years and has been roused since opening Roman's letter on Friday. I can't stop thinking about it; about him. Us. That year.

The computer fan silences and there's the soft crunching sound of the computer's gizzards. The folder opens. And there it all is, as if it's been waiting all this time. Everything worth saving.

I scroll and scroll. Music, school essays, photographs – mostly of bands, some of me, razor-cut bob, thick fringe, and eyes smudged with an awful lilac eye shadow I thought looked fabulous, all taken with a digital camera pointing into my dusty bedroom mirror. Then I stop, cursor hovering over a folder. The ends of my fingers sting with the urge to slam the lid shut, but I click twice, and for a beat, I don't think it's going to work, corrupt with age or something, but then the screen turns white. It stutters. 'Roman' opens.

This PC/D: Lizzie Laptop/Roman/
Roman signed in on 29/09/04 21:54

Roman: Did you know that otters are actually aggressive arsewipes?

Lizzie: um . . . no?

Roman: Yep. Watching a documentary and they're proper sick dickheads.

Roman: Just telling you. In case it ever comes up on your GCSEs.

Lizzie: hahaha

Lizzie: "Who are the biggest dickheads in the animal kingdom? Please answer and explain below . . ."

Roman: and/or arsewipes*

Lizzie: sorry. course. and/or arsewipes*

Roman: Think I might announce it to the group tomorrow.

Lizzie: I dare ya.

Roman: "I sit before you, a changed man after a week of discovery."

Lizzie: hahahaha

Roman: "For I unearthed the groundbreaking fact that otters are dark dark shits who would never survive a day in the court of law."

Lizzie: pissing myself.

Lizzie: shit! think I just woke my dad up.

Roman: Good.

Roman: :)

Lizzie: :)

Lizzie: not sure even that announcement will beat the giant ball sack that girl painted today in art tho – that was real bravery.

Roman: Jade. She's a lifer like me.

Lizzie: the girl with the white hair?

Roman: Yeah, the one who drew the bollocks.

Roman: Good word that . . . bollocks :)

Lizzie: bollocks :)

Lizzie: didn't realise Jade was a lifer btw. She seems OK . . .

Roman: whereas I'm quite obviously NOT?

Roman: :P

Lizzie: haha, you know what I mean.

Roman: Yeah. Jade talks a good talk. She's strong.

Roman: But nobody goes to the grove for nothing Lizzie J.

Roman: not one of us.

Lizzie: I guess not.

Lizzie: well unless you're just a misunderstood genius miles ahead of his time . . .

Roman: Who knows a lot of crap about ruffian otters.

Lizzie: yep

Roman: and has the devastatingly handsome smile of a fallen archangel.

Lizzie: errrrm . . .

Roman: and the rippling physique of a Greek warrior.

Lizzie: ok now I haven't a clue who you possibly could be talking about.

Chapter Three

'Ludicrous. Absolutely bloody *ludicrous!*'

'Gail, please, I think we should discuss this.'

'Last year you had us dress as nurses. Nurses! And you had the cheek to say it was to raise awareness of the flailing NHS. Yeah. Course it was. As if you give two hooeys.'

'Gail . . .'

'No, Tim. No. OK? Just *no*.'

Priscilla and I stand peering out of the sliver of the open door of my unnecessarily tiny accounts office. My boss, Calvin, is standing behind us watching, enrapt like me and Priscilla, as Sad Gail Travers, the saddest and most barbaric of all Fisher and Bolt Stationery's sales reps, tears Tim Bunting, the sales manager, a brand spanking new arsehole. Gail's outbursts happen often, although concealed deep in here, in this doom-filled shoebox of an office, I usually miss them and have to relive them vicariously through Priscilla at lunchtimes. Not today, though. And today's is a humdinger. Not quite a chinned-Gerry-in-the-warehouse humdinger, but it's up there, and it's the sort of distraction I have been holding out for this week. A little nod from the universe that all is still well.

'Tim must've sent the email,' whispers Priscilla, her cheek squashed against mine. Calvin looms behind us, the Very

Serious Gossip-Abhorring Accounts Manager mask that he wears is dangling at his chin.

'What email?' he asks.

Priscilla shrugs. 'He wants our department to dress up in school uniform on Friday. You know . . . for charity.'

'And?' says Cal.

I slowly look upwards. Calvin is staring out across the office floor, face screwed up, mouth gaping; it's his 'I forgot my bloody glasses' face. He left them at home this morning. His wife, Eva, called to tell him she found them on one of the twins' highchairs and somehow, it turned into an argument about the horrendous way in which Calvin had parked the car last Wednesday, and the fact he kept her up last night because he has nostrils like a lawnmower.

'Well, Gail thinks he's a pervert,' Priscilla continues, 'so she's dead against it, of course.'

'A *what*?'

'A pervert, Cal,' I whisper. Priscilla nods and goes to take a bite of her sandwich, but stops, when her mobile phone bursts into song on my desk. She straightens and goes to answer it.

'Well that's rubbish, that is,' Calvin flaps. I look back up at him. He's shaking his whopping meathead and his mouth is a hard, appalled line. 'Tim Bunting isn't a pervert, of course he bloody isn't.'

'I didn't say it,' I tell him. 'Gail did. Although, to be fair, such an accusation doesn't exactly shock me.'

'Well, he isn't,' Cal tuts. 'He has a wife, Lizzie. He has kids.'

I snort a laugh. 'Oh, well in that case, he *must* be innocent. Just like all those prisoners with wives and kids, all those murderers and savages . . .'

Calvin pushes off from the door frame and shoves his hands in his pockets. 'She's hardly an upstanding citizen herself, though, is she?' He sits down at his desk. 'She nuts people in the workplace, chins innocent men trying to earn a crust. She deserves the sack if you ask me.'

'And thankfully, Cal,' I say, turning back to look at him, 'nobody is.'

Cal smiles, picking up something that looks like a gigantic pastry brain in both hands. I have never seen someone handle pastry the way Cal handles it. It's like he's cradling glass, or the breast of a beautiful woman. It was one of the things Priscilla told me about him before my first day here, six years ago. 'You'll never meet a man more in love with the notion of eating. You wait until we have a board meeting with free cake. He almost climaxes.'

'Well,' chews Calvin. 'Nice to see the back-chat is back.'

I laugh. 'Me? Did it ever leave?'

I look past Calvin to Priscilla, who's on a spare chair at the end of my desk. She's talking in a low voice into her phone and her hand is over her ear, her face is turned away from us.

'Ah, I dunno,' Cal shrugs. The enormous ham and cheese croissant is inches from his mouth. Gary, our clammy, bumbling, lone IT guy, brought it in for him at the start of our lunch break, and neither had said a word when he'd placed it down. Calvin had just looked up at him, watery-eyed, and Gary had sashayed off. They're unlikely friends, really, Calvin and Gary, although I guess people used to say the same about Priscilla and me, at school. But there is one common interest that keeps their relationship ever-spiced: baked goods. Both are obsessed with pastry and specifically, the tray bakes Hiking Sarah often brings in. 'You've just been quiet lately,' Calvin carries on. 'Even more so this week.'

'Have I?'

'Mmm,' he munches. Behind him, Priscilla hangs up. She stares at the desk for a moment unblinking, her hands, one on top of the other over her phone on the desk. I bet Chris's ex-wife Mandy's been on the phone again. She rings Chris a lot, harping on about how Chris doesn't discipline their daughter, Summer, enough on the weekends, and nothing irritates Priscilla more. 'You've been a bit . . . what's it they say?' Calvin says. '*Away with the fairies*? Somewhere else. You know. Not your usual self.'

Priscilla looks at me then, at the sound of those last words, as if someone called her name. Her glassy eyes search my face.

'Well, I am *fine*, Sir Meathead.' I clear my throat, turning to look back out through the gap in the door. 'Now, I'd appreciate it if you would shush. Sad Gail has just brought the Suffragettes into this and I won't hesitate to kill you if you make me miss it.'

The truth is I haven't been anywhere for the last few weeks – not away with the fairies, not anywhere else. Nowhere. I've just been here, living solely in my own head, which feels like standing in a dark tunnel of a thousand chattering voices, talking a thousand words a minute, overlapping, urgent, each voice trying to be heard. It's exhausting. *I'm* exhausted. I'm not sure when it started. Maybe it was turning twenty-eight that did it – my 'scary' age, the age that always seemed miles into the future, the time when I'd be brave enough to be exactly who I wanted to be. Maybe it's Dad, moving in with his long-term girlfriend, Linda, and moving out of the home my childhood played out within; the rooms slowly transforming as things are sold, or thrown away, or moved out. Maybe it was those boxes; all those drawings, books, *plans*, and the hope that was attached to it all – the world that was waiting for us. Or maybe it was all of it, finally coming to a simmer. And now there's the letter, of course – Roman's letter – landing in the centre of it all, causing everything to boil over and spill over the edges. It's the questions more than anything I think, getting heavier the longer they sit there unanswered. The whys, the wheres, the hows. My mind is brimming with them, bowing with them, like rain-filled tarpaulin, and as hard as I try, I can think of nothing else besides Roman Meyers. Nothing besides The Grove and that year. Roman's letter, lost, that somehow made its way back to me too many years too late; too late for any of it to have any meaning now.

On Sunday night, I sat staring at the hundreds of instant messenger conversations on the disc, scrolling and scrolling, watching them drift up the screen; these tiny little windows into *us*. Roman and me. Talking. Frozen in time. I'd scanned over a few at first, lump in my throat, scared to read too much, but then I couldn't help but stop to take in the words. And as I read, I felt him coming to life again. I could hear his voice, as if there was a tape playing, could remember how his arm felt, heavy and strong over my shoulder, and how we'd sit, like that, in Sea Fog, squashed together, legs up on the flimsy vinyl-wood table, talking, singing, eating chips, and praying that when the time came for me to open the narrow caravan door to go home, we'd find that we'd somehow missed the end of the world, and we were the only ones who remained.

'S'cuse us, Liz, out the way.'

'Uh?'

'Chop, chop, out the way, *excuse et moi*.' Cal taps on the top of my arm with the back of his hand, which clutches a piece of paper.

'Cal, no,' I say. 'You can't possibly think of going out there. Gail's still on one.'

'Don't talk daft.' Cal pulls open the office door.

'But it's an unsecured area,' I say, pressing my hands to my chest. 'Keith just went over to use the photocopier and Gail actually mistook him for a predator and snarled at him, with *all of her teeth . . .*'

'I need to speak to Niall,' Calvin chuckles, jaw still chewing a mouthful of croissant. 'He's going at one, I need to catch him before he leaves.'

'But think of Gerry's nose,' I whisper, frantically. 'It still looks like a beef tomato and it's been weeks since she chinned him . . .'

Cal walks out.

I look round at Priscilla and grin. She bursts out laughing.

'It really does look like a beef tomato, doesn't it?' She pulls open the lid of her lunchbox. 'How's Tim doing out there? She disembowelled him yet?'

'Unfortunately not, P.'

'Shame.' She tilts her Tupperware box towards me. 'Brownie?'

'If they're the ones you make with sweet potato and all those seeds—'

'Nope,' smiles Priscilla. 'Made with all the bad stuff.'

I join Priscilla over at my desk. We eat our brownies in silence, occasionally narrowing our eyes and nodding at each other in agreed ecstasy at the dense slabs of sticky deliciousness in our hands. It reminds me of those times we'd raid the school cafeteria of all the custard doughnuts the loose change in our blazer pockets could buy, and eat them on tables in empty form rooms at lunchtime, talking about what we'd become and who we would be, and what we imagined certain teachers looked like with their pants off.

'Was that Chris on the phone?' I ask, not looking up from scrolling through eBay.

'Mmm? Just now?'

I nod.

'Yeah,' Priscilla sighs and leans back in her chair. 'It was nothing. You know, just . . . a disagreement.'

I pause and look over at her.

'Oh, I dunno.' Priscilla lifts her bony shoulders to her ears, chewing slowly. Her eyes drop to her lap. 'Being a step-mum to a fourteen-year-old at twenty-eight. It's hard sometimes, Liz. Most of the time I feel way out of my depth and like I'm just not cut out for the whole thing – mood swings, messy bedrooms, homework, karate classes . . .' Priscilla waves her hand in the air, as if she's batting away a fly. 'Anyway. It's nothing, really. I just told Chris that this morning – that it's too much for me sometimes, a teenager to parent when I don't even have a child of my own yet. Not to mention the drama of Bandy Mandy and her blaming us for every bad grade, every bit of bad behaviour, and well,' Priscilla sighs, 'I may have accidentally said it in the style of a tactless motherfucker.'

I laugh at that and Priscilla breaks into a smile – her lips are a deep plum colour today. I don't know how she pulls it off. I think if I walked in with lips that colour, Cal would sound the alarms and drag Boring Jeremy from marketing in for first aid assistance.

'He was just ringing with an olive branch,' continues Priscilla, fiddling with the piece of brownie between her thumb and finger. 'You know Chris. Hates arguing.'

I wrap my hands around my mug of tea. 'I'm sure he gets it, though, Priscilla. Anyone would. He finds it hard enough at the moment, and he's her dad.'

Priscilla nods. 'He does,' she says, breathing deeply. 'I'm lucky. I know that.' Then she straightens in her chair and says, 'And what about you?'

'Me?'

'Yeah. Are *you* OK? You know, since Roman's letter and everything.'

I nod, so hard, that what feels like a ball is shaken free and rolls around in my skull.

'Yes,' I lie, turning back to my computer and opening my emails. 'Fine. I mean of course I've been thinking about him and I've read it probably five hundred times now but . . . it is what it is, isn't it?'

Priscilla smiles and bows her head in one nod. 'Yeah. I suppose.' She dusts the ends of her fingers of crumbs and leans back in her chair, phone in hand. I take the last bite of brownie and glance at my screen. A new email from my brother, like I get most Thursday afternoons. Today he's asking me to get some biscuits on my way to Dad's later. 'Dad says nice ones. M&S or something?'

'Lizzie,' says Priscilla. I nod, fingers tapping the keys. When she says nothing else, I look at her. She's staring at me, nibbling the corner of her lip. I stop chewing.

'What? What is it?'

Priscilla pauses and puts her phone down on the desk. She straightens it with her fingers then looks up at me.

'I found something.'

'Mmm?'

'To do with Roman.'

I can't swallow. The brownie sits in my throat, a disintegrating lump. She stares at me, waiting for a response.

'I know you said you didn't want to, Liz, but—'

'*Priscilla* . . .'

'I know, I know, but I couldn't help myself,' she says, fanning her hand at her face, the way people do on films, when they start to cry or accidentally touch something disgusting. 'You know what I'm like, Lizzie, I'm like a fucking dog with a bone with stuff like this.'

I raise my eyebrows at her, but I can't speak.

'But it's driving me mad. I haven't been able to stop wondering about it. Have you?'

I hesitate, but eventually, shake my head. Priscilla smiles gently.

'So, I Googled DDC, 'cause those letters in the logo at the top of the paper are really bugging me,' she says, leaning forward, forearms resting on the desk. 'And I got nothing, Lizzie. Zilcho. It's too vague. I mean, there are a billion companies called DDC – IT places, clothes shops, building firms, *people*. DDC could literally be anything.'

I don't react. Because I already know. I couldn't not search for it myself. The headed paper Roman's letter is written on has a logo made up of the letters 'DDC' in gold-brown at the top, but nothing else – no address, no phone number, nothing. I don't know what I was expecting or hoping to see, but still I found myself typing the letters into a search engine, little sparks of hope drifting like embers from my fingertips as I typed.

'So,' Priscilla continues. 'On the envelope there's a stamp, isn't there? A tree in the bottom corner.'

I pause, furrow my brow. 'You mean the recycled paper logo?'

'Yes,' she says. 'Well, no, see it's not a recycled paper thing. I thought it was too, but when you look closely, it's a pear tree, and the trunk of the tree is actually a fish.'

I don't say anything. I just watch her; her eyes the shape of mint leaves, the apples of her cheeks always taut, and her perfect, perfect skin. I remember that being one of the first things I noticed about Priscilla – after her ridiculous cackle, of course; her flawless light brown skin, always smooth and glowing. Nothing like my typical teenage skin was. Dry one day, and as greasy as lard the next, and where foundation went to clump, gather, and die.

'I thought it was weird when I saw it. That's why it stuck with me,' rambles Priscilla, the pad of her index finger swiping and tapping on the screen of her phone. 'So, I went a bit Sherlock Holmes, had a search, and that's when I found out it isn't just any fish. It's a trout.'

'Right?'

'And this came up.' Priscilla flips the phone over to show me the screen. And there it is. The little bottle green tree logo at the corner of the envelope Roman's letter came in. The exact same.

Priscilla stares at me for a moment, then her lips slowly lift into a smile. 'So, I kept delving.'

I can hardly bear waiting for her to speak. She is dancing around the words as if they are burning coals.

'And it was easy, really, once I'd found that.'

'*Right?*'

'See, once I'd found—'

'Priscilla, for Christ's sake,' I blurt, 'can you *please* just spit it out?'

'I found an address, Lizzie,' she says. 'I think I've found where Roman's letter came from.'

Roman: I'm still laughing.

Lizzie: i'm not! i'm mortifed.

Roman: Why!?

Lizzie: because she was so rude to you. i'm sorry Ro.

Roman: I honestly couldn't give a shit, it was hilarious.

Roman: And don't say sorry. Your auntie Sharon's a knobber but that's not your fault.

Lizzie: hubble chucked her cake in the bin when she left.

Lizzie: he was angry, i could tell. he said for us to go there again after the grove tomorrow. if you wanna?

Roman: Oh no, not her amazing pineapple cake! :o :o :o

Roman: And cool. That's nice of him. Thanks :)

Lizzie: she really believed you when you said you'd never seen a pineapple before.

Roman: Well that's the thing about us kids who live on council estates. We only eat spam and Findus pancakes. A pineapple could be anything to us ;)

Lizzie: I think I died when you put it to your ear and said hello?

Roman: hahahahaha

Roman: Just a shame she snatched it off me before I could do something else with it.

Lizzie: lol. I do not want to know.

Roman: Mind out the gutter J :)

Roman: So I'll see you in the morning?

Lizzie: yep.

Lizzie: and come to hubble's with me after for dinner?

Roman: It's TEA. :P

Roman: But course. I'm there. Let me know if Shall's coming. I'll bring her some Special Brew.

Chapter Four

My brother leans against the kitchen counter, his mouth a gawping 'o'.

'What?' he whispers. 'What's the big deal?'

'I just can't believe you didn't mention they were coming.'

'I forgot. End of story.'

'But you know, Nathan. You have always known to tell me when Auntie Shall is anywhere near the vicinity, to warn me, so I can you know, not come, or get Norovirus or something equally awful—'

'Well, I didn't this time. Get over it.'

'No, I will not *get over it*, because I don't actually believe for one second that you forgot.'

'I do,' says Nathan, crunching a chocolate finger in half and shrugging. The kettle rumbles beside him as Katie rushes about, lining up mugs on the countertop. 'Because guess what, Lizzie? Humans forget stuff sometimes. And shock horror, call the fucking papers, I am human.'

It's Thursday evening, and like every Thursday evening, I am at Dad's for dinner. It's something Nathan, Katie and I have been doing for about thirteen years now, ever since Mum left Dad and the chaos and heartache of everything simmered down. It was something Dad seemed adamant on doing after his dad died, too. I guess we needed a new constant – something to rely on again, like Hubble always was – and since then, that's how it's been. Occasionally it's Linda too, Dad's girlfriend, but mostly it's us four, a tray of steaming, homemade lasagne, a dish of crumble, bundled on the sofa watching rubbish soaps in the honey-glow of Dad's lamp-lit living room. And that's where we should be now; watching EastEnders, snuggled on the sofa, passing bourbon creams around and discussing Max Branning's life choices as if they are those of a dear friend. We're not though, and that's because sitting in the next room on the sofa instead, is Dad's soft wally of a brother, Uncle Pete, and his wife – uppity, sour-faced Auntie Shall who treats me like I am somewhere between a puzzle she wouldn't dare begin to solve, and a Harry from *Harry and the Hendersons* type character – someone of sub-zero intelligence, who is experiencing human family life for the first time. They're here because they have an announcement to make apparently, which may have piqued my intrigue for a second had they not made approximately 7654 'announcements' in my twenty-eight-year-long life. Their last one was made over lunch at The Toby Carvery, and it was the news that Uncle Pete was getting a vasectomy.

'Well, this is certainly a surprise,' says Auntie Shall as I place down a plate of M&S shortbread on the coffee table. 'I didn't realise you'd be here.' She's standing in front of the television, hands clasped together at her lap, as if she's about to give a sermon.

'Didn't you?' I settle down onto the two-seater next to Katie. 'But I'm here every Thursday.'

'I know that, sweetheart, I know that. But I thought we might've *missed* you, what with it being gone eight o'clock and everything. I know you like to get yourself home, that's all I meant.' Auntie Shall tuts, and looks at Katie, rolling her eyes, as if to say, 'sometimes I think there's only you and me left.'

Auntie Shall always wanted another daughter, and growing up, I always felt my presence was a reassurance to her; to be thankful she never fell pregnant again, because she might've had a stroke of bad luck and had a second, strange buffoon like her poor brother-in-law did. Then Nathan started dating Katie in year eleven, and it was like someone had presented Shall with the second daughter she'd never had. Shall loves Katie – marvels at her, as if she is a nineteenth century antique teapot – and is always far too familiar with her, stroking her fine, blonde hair, or flashing her secret, knowing looks that seem to bewilder Katie, who barely sees her from one week to the next.

'Well,' I smile, leaning forward for a biscuit. 'You're stuck with me till at least the watershed, I'm afraid. I'm a bit of a party animal these days.'

Auntie Shall smiles a tight smile back at me and says, 'Well, as I said, it's a nice surprise.'

Moments later, we're all gathered in Dad's living room, bowls of snacks and cups of tea scattered about the room like ornaments. There's something very sitcom-like about this scene; all of us sitting on armchairs and sofas, looking awkwardly at one another, Auntie Shall in front of us as if she's about to perform a one-woman play. She dances nervously now, her long, lean legs, hopping from one foot to the other, and her eyes, which are clumpy with electric-blue mascara (Auntie Shall never left the 1980s) darting around the room, from the clock on the fireplace, to each one of us, smiling every now and then, in the way a teacher does before assembly begins. We're rarely all in the same room like this. Even when my parents were together, Dad would visit Shall and Pete at their detached new-build around the corner on his own most Sundays, and Mum would breathe the sort of sigh of relief you do when you've been given the all clear on a full blood count when he'd leave without asking us to go with him.

'Should you—' starts Uncle Pete, nervously.

'*Wait*,' growls Auntie Shall. I stare at Nathan. The corner of his mouth twitches, and he disguises the smile creeping on his lips by taking a sip of tea. Pete looks around at us all, smiling, apologetically, shamefully, as if he would rather be in the centre of an erupting volcano than here, watching his wife wordlessly stare and huff at her watch.

Then, the doorbell rings.

'Oh, thank god,' exclaims Auntie Shall, her hands flying up to her chest. 'I would have bloody burst if I'd have had to have waited any longer.'

She dashes to the hallway, and we hear her before we see her – neat, elegant giggles, part-birdsong, floating down the hallway. My cousin, Olivia.

She appears at the door, beaming – her natural state – and holds a hand up in a wave bashfully at her side. 'Hi, guys!' She's buttoned up to the neck in a floral rain mac which glitters with rain. She looks like she's just stepped out of a Joules catalogue. 'Gosh! It's raining cats out there.'

There's a chorus of hellos, and Dad gets up to kiss her. He's sweating, of course. Dad always sweats when we have guests. He does relay laps to the kitchen, trays and bowls of biscuits and pretzels and slices of cake instead of a baton and doesn't settle until every surface of the living room resembles a tapas bar.

'Go on in, Olivia.' Auntie Shall gives her a shove. 'Go on. We are all about to die of anticipation.' Olivia walks into the room, and Auntie Shall dances behind her, all bouncy heels and tippy-toes – she's practically juddering, fit to burst with excitement.

Olivia takes off her coat and lowers herself on the armchair.

'No!' squeals Auntie Shall. Olivia jumps as if she has squatted on a gaggle of scorpions. 'Don't sit down!'

'W-why?'

'Not at a time like this, Livvy. Not now.'

'Mum, I—'

'They're waiting!' Auntie Shall whispers, motioning with her hands, as if doing breast stroke, to all of us, the audience, mugs-in-hands, biscuits-in-mouths, awkwardness oozing from our pores, all on the edge of our seats, waiting to hear the news. News I was sure, up until about sixty seconds ago, was something to do with Shall moving from Avon to Kleeneze, or Uncle Pete announcing a newly-discovered calling for the world of sadomasochism after stumbling upon a website on ball clamps. But since Olivia arrived, I'm pretty sure I know what it's going to be.

'Right. So. OK.' Olivia takes a breath, puffing out her cheeks. 'I'm sure you've seen on Facebook that David and I have recently been to Goa. We had the most amazing time, we really did.' She's beaming. So much, I fear her head might explode and throw out golden confetti. 'Oh, it was the trip of a lifetime, it really was. We saw things we never dreamed we'd see, we did things we never dreamed we'd do and—'

'We've got an announcement to make!' swoops in Auntie Shall with an excited leap. Katie squeezes my foot under a cushion. Uncle Pete sighs, like a pool toy, deflating.

'*Mum*,' Olivia tuts, but quickly papers over her irritation with another beaming grin. 'But yes. Mum's right. We do.'

Then, silence. We wait. Until from behind her coat, Olivia lifts her left hand as if in slow motion. The ring on her finger is huge and glittering. She wiggles her fingers, just like they do on the movies.

'We're getting married!'

Like a switch being yanked, there's an explosion of '*Ohhhh!*'s from us all, as Dad jumps up – well, as much as his chubby little legs allow – and envelops her in his arms. Nathan stands, like someone who has been called on stage, slowly, brushing creases out of his shirt, smiling, saying, 'So, you're joining our club then, Liv?' and Katie is kissing Shall and Pete on both cheeks and grinning, 'Congratulations to you all. I am so happy for you.' And then there's me, standing awkwardly in the unofficial waiting-to-hug-Olivia queue, frozen to the bone at the mere idea of kissing Auntie Shall's sour cheeks. I've never hugged Uncle Pete or Auntie Sharon in my whole life. Am I supposed to now? Do I squeal like Olivia did? What am I supposed to say after 'congratulations'? Plus, the last time I congratulated Olivia – which was on her graduation day – Auntie Shall leaned in and said, hand on my knee, 'See, this is what your dad wanted for you. But . . . well, you can't say we didn't try, can you?'

I turn to say something to her, but she is crying into a tissue, emitting greyhound-like howls, tears painting turquoise waves under her eyes.

'I've got some Buck's Fizz in the cupboard,' announces Dad, making for the living room door. 'I've been waiting for an occasion.' But Olivia grabs his arm and stops him going any further.

'There's actually something else, Uncle Charlie,' she says. Dad stops. The room freezes. 'We've already booked a venue and set a date. And it's this autumn—'

'November. Like us! Like me and Pete!' cuts in Auntie Shall again, from beneath the balled tissue. 'Father Jonas even moved a church event for her, Charlie, just to fit her in, the same church we—'

'Sharon, love,' Uncle Pete huffs, 'come on, let Livvy speak.'

Shall snaps her head round. Pete looks so small, so feeble, hunched on the sofa, among us all on our feet, as if he is just inches from disappearing forever, never to be seen again, into his polo shirt.

'Oh?' snaps Auntie Shall. 'Oh, I *am* sorry, Peter.' She has this way of speaking to Pete when she's annoyed. It's the way

39

a horror movie murderer speaks as they circle their victims who hang like cows in a slaughterhouse – slow, cocky, and almost affectionate – right before they cut out the spleen. 'I am just excited, that's all. I am *excited* about our beautiful daughter's news. Is that OK, Peter? *Is it?*'

Uncle Pete looks down into his coffee, as if contemplating diving into it, into another world, where a land full of fishing, bomber jackets and happiness awaits him, and says nothing else.

Olivia continues. 'It's November. November the 26th.'

'It's a Saturday. One o'clock,' chimes in Auntie Shall again.

'Oh, wow,' says Nathan. 'Blimey. Nice one.'

'David's nan isn't very well, and we just thought . . . why wait?'

'Absolutely, my darlin',' says Dad, pulling Olivia into his huge round belly for another hug. 'Fantastic news.'

'Congratulations,' I say over the hubbub, but nobody hears. The words are dry on my tongue, and I can feel my heart sinking slowly. I have no idea why. 'Congratulations,' I try again, but Auntie Shall has taken Olivia's arm now and she's whispering to her. She passes her something. I can't see what it is.

'Er, Katie?' grins Olivia, Auntie Shall giggling at her side. 'I hope you're free.'

Beside me, Katie's face glows pink. Everyone turns to look at her. 'Um. W-well, of course.'

'Good.' Olivia steps forward and holds something out in her hand. It's a wooden puzzle piece with a tag hanging from it. I can't make out what it says, but when Katie takes it, her olive eyes widen. 'Say you'll be my bridesmaid!' Olivia's face explodes into a grin – rows and rows of clamped-together straight, white teeth – and lets out a long, high-pitched squeak. Before Katie can say a word, Olivia throws her arms around her.

Shall is crying again, quivering to Dad, 'It says my wedding won't be complete without you, Charlie. Isn't that clever? Isn't that lovely?'

But then silence falls over the room like a veil.

Dad, Nathan, and Pete are looking at me, and from me, to Auntie Shall, to Olivia, to their feet, and to me again.

'Oh. Oh, god.' Olivia drops her arms from around Katie. Her hands fly up to her heart, one on top of the other. 'And gosh, of course, you too, Lizzie.'

My drooping heart picks up its speed. 'What? Oh erm. No, no, don't be silly, it's fine.'

'No, come on,' says Olivia. She glances at her mum quickly, but her smile doesn't falter. She strides forward and drops to the floor, searching around in the tiny little tribal-printed saddle bag beside the armchair. 'Ah. Um. I'm sure I have another.' She rustles and digs about for what feels like ages, muttering as she does. 'Oh. No. No, it seems I don't have another puzzle piece. But you must, Lizzie. You must be my bridesmaid.'

I shake my head, and laugh a slightly hysterical, high-pitched laugh. My face is as hot as fire, my ears, sizzling like steaks on the sides of my head. My whole body feels like it's being pulled downwards, like the ground is a magnet. Sinking. It's embarrassment. Sadness. A feeling of utter inadequacy. All rolled into one. 'Oh, no, don't be silly, Olivia, honestly, it's—'

'No! Don't even think about saying no!' Olivia squeaks. 'Seriously, Lizzie. How could I not have you, my only female cousin in the James brigade? You simply have to say yes. *Say yes.*'

I open my mouth to protest, but then she squeals again and pulls Katie and me into her with both arms. Our heads bash together at her chest, as Dad, Nathan and Pete start clapping and cheering around us, as if this is a football game at the end of an American movie and I, the pathetic, knock-kneed underdog, have just scored the goal to secure us the state championships.

I am cringing. No. I am beyond cringing.

I am *mortified.*

I have never wanted the ground to fizzle away and suck me into its roaring hot chasm of nothingness as much as right now. I can still hear them though, above the clapping, cheering and squealing: Auntie Shall's stark, annoyed, panicky 'Olivia? Olivia?'s.

'This is going to be so fun!' Olivia gushes, bouncing up and down. 'So much fun!'

The tray in my hands is piled high with empty boxes of chocolate fingers, plates of posh jam biscuits without their creamy halves, empty mugs, and half-empty glasses of Buck's Fizz. Making my way down the hallway, I hear Olivia dictating the web address of a wedding dress shop to Katie in the next room, and Pete telling Nathan about the new fishing tackle shop in the high street, and how Jimmy, the owner, has a voice like Frank Sinatra and should go on *Pop Idol*. I've busied myself most of the evening, helping Dad with the tea-making, nominating myself to be the one to wash up the dessert bowls, refilling glasses, and nodding along at the dresses and flower arrangements Olivia has been swiping through on her phone as I've swept by with dirty crockery and fresh drinks. Because I can't shake this feeling of plummeting, of deflating, and I don't want to sit still long enough to feel it. Olivia is getting married. My cousin – younger by five months and six days – is *getting married*. The ultimate grown-up thing to do. She has found the person she wants to spend her whole life with. Just like that. She's done it. She's found him, and it took her twenty-seven years to be sure of such a thing – just a few months shy of the amount of time it took me to learn what APR means and that no, actually, I don't like parsnips. Olivia is going to be a bride. A wife. She's been to Goa. She's slept in a hut in a rainforest, and she griddles asparagus for dinner out of choice. She owns a food processor, buys actual framed art for her walls, and would likely break out in hives at the sight of the Blu Tack stains and posters on my living room walls. Because she's an adult. She is going to get married. Olivia will be someone's wife – someone's *Mrs.* And where am I? Besides being asked to be someone's half-arsed, last-minute, because-she-feels-she-has-to bridesmaid. Besides being somewhere that feels like nowhere.

The kitchen door at the end of Dad's dark hallway is ajar, creating a perfect line of warm, syrupy light on the carpet. I pause by the door, tray rattling in my hands, and push out my foot to nudge it open. Then I freeze.

'I appreciate it, Shall. I really do,' I hear Dad say on the other side of the door, his words almost whispers.

'Mmm.'

'I think she's very happy to be asked.'

'We were only meant to have the four bridesmaids,' says Auntie Shall with a huff. 'Olivia wasn't expecting her tonight. She didn't mention Lizzie at all before this evening. But she's kind, is Livvy – too bloody kind.'

'Liz is always here on a Thursday,' says Dad. 'And they're cousins, Shall. I think it's a nice idea.'

'Mmm. Yes, I suppose they are.'

Then there's a moment of silence, a clatter of cutlery being picked up from the draining board, the sliding open of a drawer, and a loud nasal sigh from Auntie Shall.

'Just make sure . . .' she huffs. 'Make sure she doesn't, you know. *Mess things up.*'

'Of course she wouldn't. Lizzie would never.'

'Well you say "of course" as if she didn't completely ruin my—'

'That was a long time ago, Sharon.' Dad's voice cuts through the silence, his words clipped. 'She was a kid.'

Auntie Shall clears her throat. 'All I ask is that there is no funny business this time. No drama. This needs to be a happy day for Livvy.'

43

Dad sighs. He says nothing else.

'I mean it, Charlie. If she ruins my Livvy's big day like she did mine – like her and that . . . *boy* did – then she'll know about it. I can promise you that.'

I make an excuse and leave Dad's as soon as I've dumped the tray down in the kitchen and lined up the champagne flutes in the dishwasher. I barely get to the top of the road before I'm typing out a text to Priscilla, thumbs pummelling the screen.

'Changed my mind. Let's do it. Let's go to the address you found. Are you free Saturday?'

Chapter Five

28th February 2005

'So, this wedding you've invited me to . . .'

'It's not a wedding.'

'Oh shit, apologies. The *vow renewal ceremony*.' Roman grins as if he's just said the most ridiculous thing in the world. 'Do I have to wear a suit? What's the deal, when you're marrying the same dude again?'

'I dunno. I don't think so. Just smart, I guess.' I pull a big, round sliver of sliced tomato from my chicken sandwich. Roman jerks his head.

'I'll take it.'

I pause. 'The tomato? It's so soggy and gross.'

'Looks perfect to me.' He opens his mouth, and leans back on the bench, arms crossed and hands under his armpits. 'Come on. Hurry up.'

I love how he says 'up'. *Op*. I like it almost as much as when he says 'bath', or the way 'foot' and 'cut' rhyme when he says them.

'God,' I laugh, leaning over and dropping it into his mouth, the way a zookeeper might feed a dolphin a sardine. He clamps his mouth shut and chews. I stare at him. 'You're gross.'

'What?'

'Your mouth really is ridiculously big, isn't it?'

'Oi,' Roman laughs, flicking out an arm and shoving my leg with his hand. 'It's all in proportion, thanks very much.'

Oddly, Roman's mouth was the first thing I mentioned about him to Priscilla, when I'd had my first day at The Grove – well, his smile, anyway; all white teeth and pink lips, the top one so perfectly bow-shaped, it's as if it'd been painted in one perfect flowing stroke. 'It's like a Mick Jagger mouth but not at all disgusting or elastic-y,' I told her on the phone, about a week after I'd started.

'Probably a rubbish kisser, then,' she said. 'All spit and licking 'cause his tongue's blatantly the size of a swimming float.'

I told Roman that the next day. He howled with laughter and said, 'Priscilla should try me out. Me and my swimming float are renowned in this town.'

Beside me, Roman stretches, and slumps down even further on the bench, the wood grey with age and years of rain. His long legs are straight in front of him on the path and crossed at the ankle. He's wearing black Doc Martens and the laces are bright red. He doesn't dress like anyone else I know. I've never seen him in jogging bottoms or pristine white designer trainers, like Nathan or the boys at school. 'So,' he yawns, 'are you gonna be wearing the whole meringue-y bridesmaid thing?'

I shake my head. 'No, it's sort of flouncy and yellow. A horrible yellow. Like mouldy mustard yellow.'

Roman looks over at me and screws his nose up. 'Like *catarrh yellow?*'

I put my hand over my mouth to stop chewed sandwich flying from my lips and snort a laugh. 'Yeah. Catarrh yellow's pretty accurate.'

'Jeez, what a liberty,' Roman grins. He turns his face back towards the sun, the back of his neck resting on the shabby slats of the wooden bench and closes his eyes again. His thick dark eyelashes are the colour of old copper in the sunlight.

'Yellow, eh,' repeats Roman. 'Your Auntie Shall definitely has it in for you.'

I nod. 'She's only doing this for Dad, though,' I tell him. 'She'd have never had me as a bridesmaid if it wasn't for him. She's trying to cheer him up. Show him everything is normal or something. Prove a point.'

'What point?' Roman asks, the spring sun beating down on his face, his eyes still scrunched closed. I always imagine painting the line of his profile when he lies like this. It would be a perfect line of peaks, lines rising and falling, like the tracing of a slow heart rate on a monitor.

'That there's nothing to it,' I say, eventually, squishing the fresh white bread between my fingers. 'That I'm lying; that if I can put on a dress and walk down an aisle, then I'm fine. Then there's no need for all this. For The Grove, for the doctors . . .'

Roman's face turns towards me at those last few words. His scrunched eyes open. 'That you're lying? She said that?'

I shrug. 'I heard her saying to Dad that he should call my bluff, put his foot down—'

'So, we all lied to get here?' Roman says, brow furrowing, eyes flashing. 'Because being here is, what, preferable?' Roman shakes his head, a muscle in his jaw pulsing. 'She really has no idea, does she? No idea how tough it is being here. No idea how far you've actually come, what you're going through . . .'

A mass forms in my throat at the sound of those words, and my nostrils sting – the threat of tears. They come so easily these days, especially when someone is being nice to me, when someone cares. And Roman does.

I can't reply. I fiddle with the crust of the sandwich in my hand and stare at it as if I'm doing an intricate cross stitch I can't take my eyes off.

Roman watches my face for a moment, but then he straightens, suddenly, as if someone has asked him to sit up, don't slouch. He sits tall and straight on the bench beside me now, legs wide, shoes flat on the cracked concrete. 'So. I have a tux,' he announces, clearing his throat and pulling out a packet of cigarettes from his inside pocket. 'Two actually.'

I blink. '*You* have a tux?'

'Two,' repeats Roman. He smiles widely, biting his tongue, tapping the end of a cigarette on the box in his hand. 'Yep. One black, one white, motherfucker.'

I burst out laughing. It's sudden, comes out of nowhere. It's his face; his stupid, dorky face. The giant smile, full of cheek, and those blue eyes, always flashing with something – as if he knows something you don't, and behind his eyes is where it's hiding. And 'motherfucker' did it too, I admit; the way it sounds in his accent. *Motherfockeh.*

'How the hell did you end up with two tuxedos?'

'Same way you'll end up with a catarrh yellow dress hanging in your wardrobe soon,' Roman smiles, cigarette between his lips. He lights it on the first go and takes a drag. 'So, you can take your pick, Lizzie J. Black or white?'

'Black,' I say.

'To match the colour of our souls. Good choice.'

I smile. The Grove stares back at us from across the road; its angular lines like a disapproving frown, and the white-painted metal-framed windows, set with glass that looks as though it would rattle if there was even a slight tremor, look like a row of mirrors with no reflection. It was built in the late forties, apparently. It used to be a small, village infant school, then a drop-in clinic. Now this. I wonder if it's always looked so unremarkable. I wonder if it's on purpose, so it doesn't stand out, and doesn't bring any attention to itself and to the people inside it.

After a while, Roman stands up, squashing the cigarette under the heel of his tatty black boot. 'Come on. It's almost one.'

I groan and squint up at him. The way he's standing in front of the sun makes it look like there're sunbeams shooting from his head.

'Come on,' he says again, holding out his hand. 'Stat.'

'Jobsworth.'

Roman smiles and pulls me to my feet. A crisp breeze swirls through the maple trees lining Lambourne Avenue, making the sound of distant waves. 'Just keeping you in check,' he says. 'Someone's gotta.'

'But I don't want to go back.'

Roman smiles, sadly. 'I'm afraid you have to go back, Lizzie J,' he says, putting his heavy arm over my shoulder. 'It's the only route out of this. But . . . least I'll be there.'

Chapter Six

'Turn back.'

'No.'

'Seriously, Priscilla, I mean it. Abort. Abort mission.'

'This is just your nerves talking.'

'No, no, it isn't, P. This is logic talking. This is normal me talking. This is actually ridiculous. I mean if you really think about it, this whole thing is absolutely bloody *ridiculous.*'

'Lizzie,' says Priscilla, her hands wrapped around the steering wheel. 'I am not allowing us to come this far and turn around again. We're almost at the Dartford Crossing and we've only just cleared all that god-awful traffic.'

'But I have a bad feeling. In my tummy. Like . . .' Priscilla sighs as I ramble, the corner of her mouth twitching a smile. 'Like we shouldn't be doing this, we shouldn't be going all the way to this random address we know nothing about. I mean, it is mad, isn't it? Really mad.'

'Yeah, OK, it is mad.' Priscilla flashes me a look over the tops of her sunglasses and looks back at the stretch of road ahead. The icy air-conditioning blasts through the vents on the dash, making her hair dance as though she's on a misty, whispery perfume ad; a perfect metaphor if ever there was one for how bloody cool and irritatingly relaxed she's been about what she is simply seeing as a little adventure on a Saturday morning. 'It's *really* mad,' she carries on. 'But going there is all we have. We tried the number from Google and it's dead. All we're going to do, Liz, is take a look. A quick drive-by and home again. We'd kick ourselves forever for not doing this if we didn't bother at least *trying* to find out where that bloody letter came from while the iron's hot.'

'Oh, god, I feel sick.'

'Nerves.'

'No, Priscilla, I mean it. I feel like I'm gonna poo myself and puke all at the same time.'

'*Neeeerves*,' sings Priscilla again, and I desperately want to slap her.

I am nervous. Terrified, actually. The unwavering confidence that overwhelmed me after overhearing Auntie Shall had dissipated about five minutes into this journey. I thought I might wake up this morning and change my mind; regret the rash decision to go to Kent, to the trout lakes and pear farm – the home of that stamp – but I didn't. Instead, I woke up determined. I woke standing taller than I had in a long time, as if held up by the anger about it all; Shall's words, Dad trying to defend me the way you would someone that committed a shameful crime, all the unbearable things that stepped out from the shadows of my mind since opening Roman's letter. He sounded so desperate, so sorry – *why*? I owed it to him. I owed it to Roman not to ignore his letter, regardless of how late it found me. That's how I felt until the car began drawing further and further away from home, anyway. I owed the person that dragged me back from the edge.

But now, I just feel terrified. I'm scared I'll find him. I'm scared he won't want to be found, least of all, by me. I'm scared I'll find nothing.

'Lizzie?'

'Mmm?' My eyes are closed, my hand clasped around the handle above my head, as if I am on a rollercoaster, holding on for dear life.

'You haven't shit your knickers, have you?'

'Fuck off, P. My stomach might explode.'

Priscilla laughs. Her laugh is a cackle – a 'dirty' laugh. It's always been the same. I remember the way it stopped me in my tracks the afternoon we first met: Homework Club, age twelve, her there for detention, me, because it was my go-to hiding place. I said something, she cackled, in the middle of slicking on raspberry lip gloss, the teacher hissed at us, and I wondered for a moment, if it was a total and utter piss take. It's just that sort of a laugh. Infectious and unapologetic. Just like Priscilla.

Priscilla pops two fruit pastilles in her mouth from the bag on her lap and says, 'You won't shit yourself, you know.'

'And how do you know exactly? Cal had that sickness bug and came into work last week.'

'Oh, it isn't a *bug*,' tuts Priscilla. 'If it's a bug, then I am Ian Botham. It's nerves, that's all. Simple nerves. I think you forget how well acquainted I am with your bloody bowels.'

I stare at her. 'Do I?'

'Every P.E. lesson,' Priscilla says, 'you'd say you had cramps, that you felt sick, felt ill, like you might be getting a bug or the beginnings of food poisoning or dysentery or blah blah blah . . .'

'P, look, do you have a mint or gum or anything peppermint to actually *help* me here?'

Priscilla stretches an arm over and pulls open the glove box. She hands me a pot of chewing gum.

'Every P.E. lesson,' Priscilla continues, pausing to look in the rear-view mirror as she moves over into the middle lane, 'especially cross-country running, you'd be pale – like deathly pale, and you'd be promising me that your bowels would likely explode over us all. Do you remember, Lizzie? All those years, every lesson the same, until we actually got out on the field.'

I nod rapidly, though I still want to slap her. Of all the memories of me this woman holds dear, it's this she remembers with clarity.

'And then before every date you had with Ricky Gardner at work last year,' says Priscilla. 'Every single time, and well, you never ever have shit yourself, have you?'

I look over at her. She raises her eyebrows at me and gives a victorious shrug.

'Well. Thanks for that, Priscilla,' I say, resting my head back on the seat and raising a thumb. 'Romantic story.'

'You're welcome,' she nods. *Ricky Gardner.* You can always trust Priscilla to dredge up things I'd rather forget – her brain is a recycling bin of all the moments I have erased from my own. It's not that I regret dating Ricky. It was just a total waste of time. He'd started work at Fisher and Bolt last year as a temp on the sales team. He was shy, well-spoken, wore round, trendy glasses, and had a smile that made his eyes glitter. He asked me out three times before I agreed, and we'd had a nice time – such a nice time, there was a second date, a third, and a fourth. It's just a shame we never got to date five. After spending most of our fourth date eating cheesy chips and kissing in a booth in a dark, trendy pub in Soho, he held my face, told me he loved my mouth when I smiled, and then said, 'Guess what I'm thinking about. Go on'. Cheesy chips, I'd guessed. How Slater from *Saved by the Bell* likes his eggs? 'Nah,' he grinned, eyes drunken slits. 'I'm thinking of you, on your knees . . . sucking off that waiter over there. I bet you would, wouldn't you? I can tell. Always the quiet ones. Always.' I walked out when he stumbled off to the loos, shocked – but not shocked enough to forget to ask for the almost-full bowl of cheesy chips to be wrapped up in a doggy bag for me to take home – and within a week of ignoring each other at work, his eyes always averted to the floor, he left. For greener pastures. For pastures littered with 'quiet ones' eager to blow random bartenders, I expect. He was my first date in three years. I've not had one since. Haven't wanted one.

The rest of the journey passes in an anxious blur, with Priscilla looking over at me, grinning excitedly every time the Sat Nav gives us a new instruction, and now we're off the motorway, winding down country lanes, meandering through higgledy-piggledy villages, getting closer and closer to the address of the farm, it's every few minutes.

'Shit,' Priscilla grins, reaching over with her spare hand and grabbing my wrist. 'Six minutes, babe!'

We wind and wind for what feels like ages on the last mile, swaying, stopping and starting, as tractors and cars squeeze past, and people riding horses trot by. There is nothing here. Just stretches of leafy emerald land, sandy cornfields, and wedges of thick, dark forest – the sort of places you imagined as a kid that witches and bears lived. What would Roman want with a place like this? He dreamed of travel and cities and adventure, counting the miles between us, and home, until the figures doubled and tripled and quadrupled. We both did. We saved for it, counted down the days until we could go after it together – that was our plan. He had nowhere else to go; no family. He was trapped – stuck with his mum in a boring town in Herts, stuck at The Grove, stuck in 'the system'. Why would he have come here? It's the middle of nowhere. There are no train stations, no shops, no bus stops. It's even been ages since I saw a house. And suddenly, this trip feels outrageous – *ludicrous,* as Sad Gail would say. We are grown women chasing a white rabbit into the middle of the countryside on a Saturday morning when we could be – should be – doing anything else.

'In one hundred feet, your destination will be on your right.'

Priscilla lets out another excited squeal and I can't respond. I swear my heart beats must be visible from the outside.

Then, I see it: the logo. The tree tunnel ends, and there it is, as a backdrop on a white sheet of a sign, the edges bordered with overgrowth, bottle green letters spelling 'Broxton Farm'. Beside it, is a dusty, dirt-track road, and an open metal gate.

Priscilla pulls in and stops in the entrance. The engine is running, and other than its soft chugging, and the distant tweeting of birds, it's silent here.

'You ready?'

I turn to look at Priscilla. 'I don't know about this.'

'We don't even have to get out,' she says. 'See how you feel. But, remember what you said Thursday night, Lizzie. What's the alternative? To ignore it? To never know?'

Yes, I want to say. Yes, let's go with the alternative and never know, turn around, and go home, where I can shut all the curtains and stay holed-up until Monday morning.

But Priscilla is already pushing her foot down on the accelerator and we are easing forward, down the track.

'We'll just take a look,' she says, the car swaying, rocking on the uneven road. 'See how we feel, see what we find . . . and, of course, see *who* we find, too.'

Broxton Farm is abandoned. A still, silent circle of shabby barns and barren wooden shelters, all empty, except for the odd rusty looking spare engine part or pile of rubble. My heart filled with relief but sank with disappointment all at once as we drove in. But then we saw the house, set back behind a cluster of overgrown spruce trees. It's the sort of house that demands a double take. Layers of gingerbread brick, a spray of wild yellow flowers climbing around the front door and to the upstairs windows, all of them set in black lead, with diamonds on the glass. Each window has a window box, too. Empty, but striking, painted in midnight blue. A chocolate box cottage, that's what Priscilla called it.

I raise my hand to the peeling front door.

'Go on. Hurry up,' whispers Priscilla, jiggling about on the spot. 'Knock.'

'I just need a minute.'

She eyeballs me. 'You told me to make you. Literally minutes ago, you told me if you chickened out—'

'P, I know what I said, I just mean I might need to take a—'

Priscilla reaches her hand up quickly to the brass knocker and knocks twice. She raises her eyebrows at me. Sweat pricks the back of my neck. It's just a knock at a door – that's all it is. But it feels like more than that. I feel like we are pelting a bee's nest with rocks; tampering with something that shouldn't be disrupted.

There's silence. A moment. Then a man's voice, calling out to someone inside. My head whooshes with my heartbeat. Something clatters on the other side of the door – a latch. I haven't even thought about what I'd say if it's Roman who answers. The thought makes my stomach turn.

The door opens in one swoop.

It isn't Roman.

It's a man; tall, skinny, with greying hair, darkened by combed-through gel. His cheeks are marked with deep set laughter lines, and his eyes squint as he looks at us.

'Now, you certainly don't look like Richard the property surveyor.' He chuckles. 'How can I help?'

He's posh. The sort that says 'ghastly' with oodles of 'gaaaaah' and probably reads the *Financial Times* on the loo while shouting stock prices through the door.

Priscilla's eyes fix on me. She clears her throat – a prompt, a nudge to speak.

'Er,' I wobble. 'I um . . . we may be barking up the wrong tree completely here, but we're looking for someone. An old friend from um, school. I think he used to live here.'

'Or still lives here,' adds Priscilla, hopefully.

'Right.' His voice lifts at the end of the word, as if it's a question. 'And who is it you're looking for?'

I launch the first rock. 'Roman.'

'Sorry?'

'*Roman?*'

The man's face barely flickers.

'Roman Meyers,' I say this time, and louder, clearer, hoping the surname jogs something, but he is doing what I hoped he wouldn't. He is shaking his head, his mouth a hard line.

'No, I'm sorry, girls,' he says. 'I'm afraid not.'

My shoulders deflate. Disappointment and relief again, both wash over me. Priscilla looks at me, then back at the man.

'Could he have been a previous tenant or—'

The man shakes his head before Priscilla can even finish. 'This farm has belonged to the same people for fifty years. There have been no recent movers, or previous owners or anything similar, I'm afraid.'

Just like that, the palpable excitement that had been buzzing between us, even amongst all the anxiety, like electricity, fizzles, as if a kill-switch has been yanked. But I smile at the man.

'Well, thank you, anyway. Sorry for disturbing you. I suppose it was a long shot.'

'The thing is,' interrupts Priscilla, 'he sent us a letter, this friend. And the envelope had your logo on.'

The man straightens in the doorway. A breeze floats through the house and to the outside; a swirl of earthy aftershave and freshly brewed coffee. 'Broxton's logo?'

'Yes.' Priscilla nods at me. 'Show him the envelope, Lizzie.'

I want to ask Priscilla what the point of this is but refusing would be embarrassing now that he's staring at me, waiting. I dig about in my bag and slip it out of the inside pocket. As I hand it to him, a woman's voice, posh and raspy, calls through the house. Echoing heels on wooden floor follow.

'Michael? Are you— who is it?' She calls through the house. 'Richard Farrand's just called. He's cancelled. Says it's too—'

She appears in the doorway, stopping mid-sentence as she sees us. Her golden eyes widen but she smiles, closed-mouthed, at us. She's petite, with short, wavy, dirty-blonde hair which is combed back over her head. She wears a chunky gold and green-stoned necklace, and a cerise pink blouse, with ruffles at the front. Her chest is tanned with old sun and covered in freckles.

'Hello,' she smiles, tightly. We say hi, but she doesn't look at us. She is staring down at Michael's hands where the envelope is.

'These girls are looking for someone, darling.' Michael doesn't look up when he speaks – he is still studying the logo.

'Oh?'

'They say they received a letter from this old friend of theirs.'

'She did,' jumps in Priscilla. 'My friend. Lizzie. She got the letter.'

The woman looks up at me for a beat, and nods once. She looks back down at Roman's letter.

'Look at this, Helen,' continues Michael, his voice dropping in volume, as if just to her. 'The envelope has a Broxton logo on it.'

Helen bends to get a closer look at the envelope. She takes it from his hands. 'Gosh, I . . . can't remember the last time I saw an envelope with that stamp on.' Her eyes are slits as she brings it closer to her face. Then she looks up at me, quickly, as if I called her by name. 'Who is it you're looking for?'

'Roman,' I say. 'Roman Meyers?'

Unlike Michael's, Helen's face flickers. Her hand flies up to her mouth. 'Crikey,' she mutters. 'Goodness, I . . . yes. *Roman.* Gosh.' Michael is looking at her now, but Priscilla's eyes are burning into me. I am frozen – feet bolted to the ground.

'That was . . . well, it was a very long time ago. Before you.' She gives Michael a quick smile and looks back down at the letter. The thumb and finger of her other hand squeeze her bottom lip. She looks up at me. 'Roman is my cousin. Second. Twice removed, something like that.'

Electricity again – a spark, dancing in my tummy.

'Although, I regret to admit that I've not seen him in many years. Eleven. Twelve, maybe?' Helen says years like 'yuuurs'. 'He stayed here for a few weeks, couple of months at most. My mother took him in – fostered him, if you like. I was working in Sheffield at the time, at the university, and—' She stops, dusky-pink lips parted, as if she's just realised mid-sentence that we are perfect strangers – as if she's realised she could be saying too much, to the wrong people. 'So, you said Roman was an old friend of yours?'

'From school,' chimes in Michael. Helen's brow crinkles and she folds her arms.

'Actually,' I cut in. 'It wasn't really school. It was . . . instead of school. It—' My cheeks and ears pulse with heat. Helen watches me. She nods gently. 'I met Roman three weeks before my fifteenth birthday. A couple of months before his seventeenth.'

Helen nods again, just the once, and the corner of her mouth lifts in a gentle smile. It's a sad smile. The type I haven't seen in years but was given to me all the time back then and made me feel as small as the tiniest speck in the universe.

'Yes,' she says, 'we aren't an exceptionally close family as it is, but well, Lindsey is totally estranged, sadly.' Lindsey,

Roman's mum, blinks into my mind, for just a second. Pale. Sad. Shrinking. 'Nobody sees her. It's been like that for as long as I can remember. But Mum kept in touch. She tried with her, really tried.' Michael folds his arms across his chest, and watches Helen. His brow is furrowed. 'That's how Roman came to be here. Mum visited, and they'd had the most dreadful argument, she and Lindsey, and she left. But she came home and was so worried about Roman, you know. A young lad, living in such an environment with such people, and with the problems he had.'

She looks to me, as if hoping it makes some sort of sense. I feel rigid, like you do on a winter's day, outside in the wind, with no coat on. But I manage to nod.

'She offered him an option, I suppose. A *refuge* if you like. She was like that, Mum. Loved to help. She and Dad fostered a lot of children in their time. They only managed to have me, you see.' Michael reaches down and squeezes her hand. Helen's golden eyes are shimmering now, and she's looking right at me, waiting for a reaction and I realise I have been staring at this woman, barely blinking, barely breathing ever since she started talking, the wind knocked from my sails. I'm not sure why. It's not like I thought Roman disappeared from the bubble in which we lived for a tiny lifetime together and then just ceased to exist. But it was hard to imagine he went on existing – that he was even real at all. But he was. With every word this stranger speaks, that's what it means: Roman was real. *We* were. But there is no slotting of the puzzle pieces that I'd hoped for, no settling in the stomach. If anything, I feel even more unease now, and it's creeping in like night the more I run over her words. 'In such an environment', 'with such people'. *Who?* Things were hard. They were. And his mum, not a mum at all. But Roman had nobody, not really. Except me. Except Hubble.

Priscilla lets out a noisy sigh, the way someone does after holding their breath for too long. 'See,' she glows, 'we *haven't* just chased a white rabbit across the M25.'

'Well, you're certainly on the right track,' says Helen, softly. A phone rings inside the house. Michael excuses himself and goes to answer it. 'I'm just sorry that I can't really help you any further,' Helen carries on. 'All I know is that he went to London after he left us. Was just after Christmas. It would've been 2005. Friend picked him up.'

'Really?' says Priscilla.

Helen nods. 'He was never going to stay long. Not much here for a boy of his age. Well, *man*.' She ducks her head to look at me. She's smiling that smile again – sad, the head a fraction to one side, eyes downturned at the corners. 'You look rather spellbound, there.'

'Sorry,' I say. My palms are cold and clammy at my lap. 'I suppose this is just a bit weird for me. It's been years.'

'You were close.'

It doesn't sound like a question, but I bow my head in a nod. 'We were best friends. Him disappearing was sudden so, this is a lot to take in . . .' I trail off.

'I'm sure,' says Helen.

Then I ask her. It tumbles out of my mouth. 'Why did he leave?' I ask. 'I mean, how did he seem? Did he mention— do you know if there was a reason?'

A breeze thick with the smell of rapeseed whips my hair into my face, and attempts to slam the door of the gingerbread house. Helen grabs the side of the door and stands in front of it.

'I didn't see a great deal of him. Just when I'd come up and visit Mum. He was . . .' she pauses, as if considering her words, 'in a bad way. Exhausted. *Broken*, I suppose is the word. Gosh.' Helen blows out a breath. 'I know that's a bit of a downer, but, well, you learn to spot things when you're around youngsters in foster care all your life. And Roman, well, he needed a fresh start. All the trouble he was in, a mother like Lindsey . . .'

Helen doesn't finish her sentence. Her last words just hang there, in the air, as thick as the floral heat we stand in, but she's watching me, eyes misty and narrowed. Hubble used to say my face was a weathervane – that when I was sad, my eyes were black clouds and my face was full of shadows, but when I was happy, I shone 'from the toes up'. And I obviously look how I feel; like someone whose heart has plummeted – suspended, high with hope, and then dropped, suddenly, to the pit of my stomach. It was 'broken' that did it.

'Well, thank you so much, Helen,' says Priscilla, clasping her hands together like a door-to-door salesman. 'You've been such a big help.'

Helen brings her shoulders up. 'I'm not entirely sure that I have.'

'You have.' I force a smile. 'Honestly. Thank you. And your house is beautiful.'

'Stuff of dreams,' Priscilla adds.

Helen smiles. 'That was all Mum.'

We say goodbye, and Helen watches us walk to Priscilla's car before she goes inside. We sit in silence for a moment, windows wide open.

'He told me once,' I say into the silence, 'that he had a "posh" side of his family somewhere. But I admit if someone had said "Roman's cousin" to me I would've expected, I dunno. Liam Gallagher, Jim Royle . . .'

Priscilla laughs. 'She was lovely, wasn't she? Very *equestrian*,' she says as she starts the engine and we sit for a moment more. Quiet, mumbling radio chatter floats through the speakers, and I watch as a plane passes overhead. My heart rate gradually slows. It reminds me of those times in the beginning, when Priscilla would sit silently beside me on the school field, waiting until the panic passed through me like a wave, not saying a word, not staring at me, not touching me, but there. Strong, calm, accepting; never leaving my side.

'You OK, Liz?' she asks now, letting out a long breath.

All I can manage is a nod.

'Shall we go for lunch or something?' Priscilla pulls the sunglasses down from the top of her head. 'Mull all this over, talk, eat pudding.'

'Haven't you got to get back for Chris? You have Summer this weekend, don't you?'

Priscilla looks at her lap and shrugs.

Then we hear her.

'Hello! Girls!' It's Helen, sprinting on her tiptoes across the driveway. 'Sorry!' she calls. 'I thought I was going to miss you.' She gets to the car, and crouches, leaning into the driver's window. She hands Priscilla a piece of paper. It's torn from an address book, the types that have pages with descending tabs for each letter. The page is 'M'.

'We're sorting through Dad's study at the mo. There's paper everywhere, it's a living hell. Anyhoo, Mike thought he'd check when he went inside. Out of curiosity, I suppose . . . and he found this in the address book. Mum and Dad used the same one for years and years.' *Yuuurs.* She sucks in a deep breath and laughs, her hand pressed against her chest. 'Ran from the upstairs,' she chuckles. 'So, look, there's an old address and a number for Roman on there. I have no idea how old the number is, it might be utterly hopeless. But well, it's something, isn't it?'

'Thank you, Helen,' I say. 'I really appreciate it.' Priscilla folds the page into her lap, as Helen smiles across at me. She pauses, and for a moment, I don't think she's going to say anything, but then she says, 'December the nineteenth.'

I pause. 'Sorry?'

'Dad took Roman home on December the nineteenth,' she says. 'For a funeral. I remember because that's my birthday. I turned up here for celebrations, just family, a few friends, dinner. And they both got caught in the most dreadful traffic and missed it. The dinner, I mean. Dad had taken him, gone to see a friend nearby, and gone back for him a couple of hours later. Then on the way back, an accident on the motorway, a wheel bearing, snow . . . I can't remember now. But I do remember that. A funeral. And Roman in a suit.'

My heart stops.

'I don't know if that helps you. I hope so, somehow. It always seems so sad to me, estranged friends.'

Helen stands back on the gravel, arms folded, watching us drive away. As soon as we're out of sight at the gate, Priscilla stops the car.

'Hubble's funeral,' I say quickly, and she nods.

'I know,' she says.

'He wasn't there, though, Priscilla. He definitely wasn't.'

'I know.'

'I mean I— I'd never have missed him. It's . . .' I don't finish my sentence. Can't. My arms are rough with goosebumps, my limbs tingling again. Adrenaline rushing in, a nudge to run from danger, from all of this. I waited that day. I waited and waited, believing he would be back to say goodbye to my grandad, the only man who was there for us when everyone else fell away, despite everything, I believed that he would never leave me alone by that coffin. I looked for him everywhere. He wasn't there. He never showed.

'Well,' says Priscilla, holding the torn page in between two fingers. 'Shall we see what the paper says? See if he's living in a city of yurts?'

She unfolds it. I can see the first one. It's in bold blue felt tip. 'Roman London' and a scribbly address, but there's a strike through it, in faded pencil, and then it's circled, with a line leading down to something else, which is circled, hard, more than once.

'This is the phone number she mentioned, I guess,' utters Priscilla. 'There's a date. *As of zero three slash 96.* So, as of March, 1996, I suppose. And a name. Frank Matias. Roman is written next to him in pencil and . . . Cardiff.'

I sit up. 'Frank?'

Priscilla holds up the page. 'Yeah. Here. Frank Matias.'

I take the page out of her hands. I want to see it with my own eyes.

'What, Lizzie? What is it?' asks Priscilla. 'Who's Frank Matias?'

Chapter Seven

22nd September 2004

Roman and I stand at the top of Hubble's driveway. It's warm today, with dandelion seeds drifting on the breeze. They kept getting caught in my hair and on Roman's baggy beanie hat as we walked home from The Grove, stopping for Dr Pepper and chips from the Chinese takeaway, and taking the shortcut through the park to Hubble's. I can't face going home. Not after this morning with Dad, blaming me yet again, for something Mum should be here to clear up herself. I would rather be anywhere else today – at The Grove, with Roman, as quiet as he's been since this morning, walking the streets, even school. Anywhere.

Roman holds a leafy branch of the rosemary bush at the edge of Hubble's perfect square lawn, between his fingers. 'I'm sorry,' he says, 'that I didn't say anything in group earlier. When you were upset.'

I lift a shoulder to my ear. 'You don't need to say anything.'

Roman twists the leaves between his thumb and fingers and brings them to his nose. 'You know I understand,' he says, looking at me quickly, then at the ground. 'That I get it, don't you? I mean, it's different, I know. With my mum it's completely different, but I understand, J.'

'Course,' I reply. 'I know you do.'

Roman smiles gently, a flash of white teeth. His lip is busted and risen slightly on one side. I haven't asked him why. The last time I did, his cheeks flashed red and he couldn't look at me, and I don't want to embarrass him again. But it worries me. 'It's just . . . the stuff about your dad. It's rubbish. Really rubbish.' *Stoff*. 'And I felt like I didn't have anything to say to you today, to make you feel better. Because I don't know mine.'

I look up at him. His eyes drop to the floor. 'Have you ever met him?'

Roman shakes his head. 'No. I know nothing about him, really. Well, apart from that he's a total lowlife.'

'A lowlife?'

Roman nods. 'Yeah. Knocked my mam about and that. Could've killed me,' he stops and sort of laughs – a scoff, 'and I even know the bloke's name, but—'

'Could've *killed* you?' The words blurt from my mouth, before what he said even registers.

Roman looks at me, blue eyes flashing, before they drop to the concrete again, and I know he wishes he'd never said anything. 'Left a tonne of smack next to my cot in reaching distance,' he says, his Adam's apple bobbing. 'I was eighteen months old. Mam legged it with us, then.'

I barely speak, just his name and a sharp intake of breath. His words feel like a punch to the gut. My hands are up by my cheeks, fingers pressed into the skin.

'But it's fine,' he says, quickly, as if he's worried he's upset me. Like he needs to get to the good part, for *my* sake. 'He's nowhere to be seen. He's in prison, last Mam heard, and he's called a couple of times, trying to talk to me but . . . it's fine, Lizzie. I don't remember. Not a single thing. In my mind, it's like he doesn't exist, so, it's fine. Really. It is.'

I shudder. Shame creeps over my skin and I screw my face up with embarrassment. 'And then there's me,' I say, 'moaning and crying about my dad and that's nothing. Nothing compared—'

'*Nothing?*' Roman says, his eyes fixed on me now. 'Lizzie, of course it's not nothing. What your dad did to you, to your brother, to your mam – it was grim. It hurt people. And I dunno. Pain is pain. You're allowed to feel what you feel.'

'I'm sorry,' I say, and he just shakes his head, and laughs, 'You say that too much.'

A breeze sways the shrubs bordering Hubble's lawn. A neighbour a few doors down turns on a power hose. He looks up at us quickly, double-taking, and I watch when he goes back to spraying the terracotta brick of his driveway. Mostly because I suddenly can't bring myself to look at Roman. He's looking at me, though, all the time.

'Well,' he stretches, 'as always, it was a pleasure, Lizzie J.' I glance at him, and he reaches a hand to my hair now. His eyes squint, fixed on mine, and the corner of his mouth twitches a tiny dot of a smile. I freeze, as the tips of his fingers touch my cheek. Neither of us say anything. My skin is jelly.

'Dandelion seed,' he says, softly, his hand brushing my face as he flicks it into the breeze. He clears his throat. 'You in tomorrow?'

I nod stiffly. 'Yep. Sure am.'

'Cool.' He straightens and takes a few steps backwards. I hear Hubble's front door squeak open behind me. Roman lifts a hand in a wave and looks past me. 'Afternoon, sir.'

'Hello, Roman,' calls Hubble from the porch. 'And how are we today?'

'Good, thank you,' nods Roman with a smile. 'And how're your potatoes?'

I glance over my shoulder to see Hubble, hands in pockets, smile, wide but mouth closed, as if it amused him a lot more than he wants to let on. 'Coming along,' he says, with a nod.

'Should have some ready next week. You'll have to come for dinner.'

Roman smiles. 'Cool,' he says. 'Thank you, sir.'

Hubble nods again, just the once, and says, 'Less of the sir.' He turns and goes inside, leaving the door ajar.

Roman looks down at me, hair in his eyes. 'Your grandad's a ledge, d'you know that?'

'I know. Shame his son's a bit of a cock.'

Roman laughs and takes a few steps backwards, readjusting the rucksack strap on his shoulder. 'His granddaughter got all the good genes,' he laughs, and I can't help but laugh too; it warms me through, like treacle. And then the words jump from my mouth, disobediently. He's a few paces away when I ask, and I don't know why I do. Maybe because I'm nosey. Maybe because I desperately want to know everything about him; about all the things that make up Roman Meyers, my newest, dearest friend. 'What's his name? Your dad.'

Roman stops, an unlit cigarette stuck to his lip, on the busted side. He takes it out between two knuckles. 'Frank,' he says. 'Frank *Matias*. Spanish, apparently.' He laughs, eyes raised to the sky for a moment, as if it's amusing – pathetic, even.

I open my mouth to speak but can think of nothing to say.

'Speak to you online later, yeah?' he smiles, and I give a quick nod.

'Yeah. Speak to you later.'

Chapter Eight

'What are you trying to say?'

'Nothing terrible, Calvin, honest. Just that, well, I'm not entirely sure linen suits you.'

'It's hideous, Lizzie, just tell him. He looks hideous.'

'I wouldn't say he looks *hideous*,' I say. 'You just look . . . I don't know. As if you belong on a Benidorm beach buying fridge magnets or something. As opposed to, you know, running an accounts office in Camden Town.'

Calvin looks down at the fawn-coloured linen trousers he's wearing, as Eva nods once, victoriously. Eva, Cal's wife, works with us twice a week, where she does nothing but bicker with Calvin while disinfecting surfaces with antibacterial wipes as if me and Cal do nothing but sit in our own faeces while she's away.

'See,' she scoffs. 'Ridiculous. You look ridiculous, Calvin. Not someone in a position of power. Not someone who people *respect*.'

I duck behind my computer to hide the grimace stretching across my mouth involuntarily and continue working my way down the long list of outstanding invoices printed on a piece of A4 on my desk. Calvin Ellis 'in a position of power' is the thing that did it for me. The only power Cal would be suited to would be if an island made solely of egg custard tarts was discovered and they needed a king. Still. The trousers aren't that bad, but then I don't suppose it would matter if he was standing in a full blown, expertly-fitted Armani suit, complete with a shimmering six-pack beneath. Eva rarely says a nice word about her husband. I often wonder how they managed to have actual child-creating intercourse twice without it ending in Calvin having his head bludgeoned to bits. Priscilla reckons they have angry sex where they shout insults and marital disappointments at each other as they go, which to be fair, seems far more plausible than cuddling and Dr Hook albums.

It's Thursday – five days since we met Helen at Broxton Farm – and things have been at a bit of a standstill since. Frank Matias's phone number is a dead line. Nothing but a long, harsh bleep; a heart, flatlining. It was a long shot, a number so old, but I would be lying if I said it hasn't made me lose faith. I called it on Sunday, after spending almost twenty-four hours hyping myself up to do it, practising what I would say as if rehearsing lines for a play. I tried, Priscilla did, we even tried at work, but every time we were greeted with the same long, cold, dead beep. Then we called the sorting office – Priscilla's idea – and a woman had answered, her voice sing-songy and helpful, all 'no problem' and 'I'm sure we can help with that' and we waited, pen poised on paper. But then she passed us onto a man – her 'supervisor' – who as good as laughed us off the phone, making a joke about being able to dust envelopes for fingerprints. Priscilla though, remains fiercely undeterred and excitable, and spends lunch hours and evenings speculating, or showing me obscure Facebook or Twitter pages that could be Roman but turn out not to be. 'Leads' as she calls them. She's really quite taken with this detective lifestyle. She's started calling me Watson both in emails and in real life, and she called me at ten o'clock the other night as I sat in the dark watching an old episode of *The Office* asking if Roman had ever been known as 'Cassius' as there was a bloke on Instagram who has his 'exact nose' except he had a different name and was currently hiking in Venezuela.

'I feel like Sherlock Holmes,' she said, afterwards. 'But you know. Reincarnated.'

'Well, you have to be dead to be reincarnated,' I said.

'What?'

'Well, they never actually killed him off, so . . .'

Then she cackled down the phone – that infamous dirty laugh. 'Oh, babe,' she laughed. 'He's dead. Dead as a dodo. Died bloody years ago!'

'Priscilla, Sherlock isn't real.'

'Well no, course, not *now* he isn't, he's bloody dead,' tutted Priscilla. 'Now, babe, open up Twitter and put in this name.'

And while Priscilla may be coursing with a level of adrenaline only Inspector Morse could empathise with, I have spent most of the time since Thursday cocooned in the flat in baggy clothes, eating beans on toast, watching lost memories unravel like ribbons, and leaping from wanting to tut and laugh at the ridiculousness of it all – of chasing a white rabbit to a farm in bloody Kent and bothering innocent postmen at work – to staring in the face the worries that have grabbed me by the lapels and won't let me go. I'm worrying in a way I haven't in so long. It's in the way I'd worry back then, about Roman at home with his mum, about myself, about what would become of my family with its fresh cut right down the middle; Mum living in ignorant bliss with her toy boy, and Dad barely fit enough to look after himself, let alone us. It's the sort of consuming worry that seeps into everything, like drops of ink in water, gradually clouding your world. I can't concentrate. I can't stop thinking about *everything*. About that box of old crap from Dad's loft. About that book wrapped in black tissue, its pages blank and still waiting, patiently, inside. About Hubble, about Roman, and those last few days before he disappeared. I'm replaying them, over and over, just like I would back then, until the circles I run in my mind kick up dust and nothing is clear. His dad. His awful, awful dad. He'd just turned eighteen. They were going to help him get a flat after he left The Grove, move out of his mum's, start afresh, and the money we had . . . it was into triple figures. We were getting there. He counted down to that birthday. We both did. But he left – he chose then to run away. Why? What happened that was so bad – that he was *so sorry* for – that the only option he felt he had was to disappear?

'So, I think we've established that Lizzie also disapproves of my wardrobe choices today.' Cal cuts through my thoughts. He's standing by the printer, and his hand is running up and down his lineny thigh.

I blink out of the trance I'm caught in. 'W-what's that?'

'My trousers, Lizzie.'

I look down at them again. 'Er, well, I would just say that linen *is* a fickle beast in that it doesn't hold any sort of shape so maybe that's why—'

'Oh, a fickle beast, indeed.' Eva makes a 'hmm!' sound in her throat and carries on scribbling on her desk. 'They're going into the bin as soon as you get home,' says Eva. 'Honestly, the second you walk in the door I'm tearing them off.'

'Oh?' smirks Calvin, sitting back down at his desk, pulling at the knees of the material as he does. 'That almost sounds sexy, my gorgeous wife, I'd be careful what you're saying.' He tips his glasses down his nose and looks over the top of them. 'Tell me what else you'll *tear off*.'

At that moment – the precise second my libido shrivels inside me and dies a death – Boring Jeremy from marketing, with his criminally beautiful arms, walks in, notebook and pen in hand.

'Hiya,' he says to Calvin.

'Oh, hello, Jeremy!' jumps in Eva, chucking down her pen. She sits up straight and grins widely. 'How are you? I haven't seen you in for ever!'

He smiles. 'Yes. It's err, been a few days.'

Eva fancies Jeremy. I mean, we all do a little bit. He's very handsome with his dark curls, sharp jawline, and it has to be said, the most beautiful, muscular arms in the human race. They're huge, and so hard, that he once tripped in reception and as his arms fell to the ground, they made a clanging sound, like metal poles being dropped in a ballroom. It's just a shame he's so boring and serious. Eva doesn't seem to care, though. She lights up when he comes into the room and notices the tiniest of things about him, from new nose hairs to new shirt cuts.

'Oh, look, you've got new shoes!'

See.

'Oh, h-have I?' Jeremy's eyes drop to the ground. 'Oh, yes. I bought these a few months ago but I forgot about them.'

Eva bursts out laughing and Jeremy looks pleased that his anecdote has hit the spot, and continues to tell Eva the reasons he forgot all about his new shoes. I tune out. Cal raises his eyebrows at me over the top of his monitor and continues typing.

'So,' smiles Eva, with a clap. 'What can I do for you, Jez?'

Jez.

'Actually, it's Lizzie I'm after.'

Eva's smile fades, as if he's rejected her for a cha-cha at a school dance. She looks over at me and says, 'Oh. OK, then.'

I stop typing. 'How can I help?'

'Two things.' He frowns down at the notebook in his hand. 'Strawberry Moons.'

'Sorry?'

And for a minute I think it's poetry. For a minute I imagine he's describing what he thinks it might be like to kiss me, under a pink sky, him in a bronze body plate, the light of the moon illuminating our faces. But then he says, 'Louisa's leaving celebration tonight at Strawberry Moons. I'm trying to get numbers.'

'Oh. I can't,' I lie, 'I wish I could, but I actually have plans with my brother tonight. We're . . . going to the cinema.' I'm not. Me and Nathan haven't been to the cinema together for at least a year. I just don't like going to work dos. I don't like Louisa, either. She reminds me of all the nasty pieces of work I went to school with and spent five years avoiding in classrooms at lunchtime – the type to insult your new haircut or outfit, or slag off your 'fattening' lunch, but then cover it over by telling you they're only saying it because they're being 'a mate' even though, most of the time, they can't remember your name. There's at least one in every office and every school. There wasn't one at The Grove, though. Perhaps we were all too exhausted with our own lives to consider reviewing someone else's. Perhaps because it was a place so many of us went to *escape* those people.

Jeremy scribbles something down in his notebook. 'Right. And will you be coming to Newport?'

I look at him blankly.

'The annual summer work trip. Twenty-sixth of August. We'll be meeting at the Newport offices, staying one night, and this time onto Bath the following day.'

Ah. Yes. The annual summer work trip. When every singleton and/or party animal at Fisher and Bolt (UK and Germany offices) travel by coach from across the country to some poor, unsuspecting town, get drunk and/or naked and/or off with each other.

'*Oh*. Oh, no.' I shake my head. 'No. But thanks.'

Jeremy shrugs. 'Well, you'll be missing out on a stellar itinerary.'

'I'm sure. Really not my thing, though,' I tell him, but I really want to ask him why he's bothering. Every year, Jeremy and his boss Graham arrange it, and each year, Jeremy tries to make it a respectable little mini break with drinks, National Trust sites, and continental breakfasts, and somehow, every single time, Graham manages to turn it into an 18-30s event with added syphilis, and returns home to find his belongings turfed out, yet again, by his wife.

Jeremy scribbles something down. 'I thought as much,' he says. 'I just thought I'd ask. You should think about it, though, Lizzie. Our first stop is Newport Cathedral.'

'Perfect,' chuckles Calvin. 'Free holy wine for Graham to pickle his bloody liver in.'

And as Jeremy grimaces so awkwardly that his jaw practically dislodges, Priscilla appears in the doorway, face flushed, and from nowhere, as if shot from a cannon.

'Hi,' she says, taking a deep breath, her eyes widening as if she wasn't expecting our little Shoebox of Doom to be full of so many people. 'Um, Lizzie, can I—'

'I was just telling Lizzie,' Jeremy cuts in, 'that she should think about it. What do you think, Priscilla?'

Priscilla raises her eyebrows. 'About what?'

'The work trip. She could share your room.'

I blink. Priscilla is *going*? I open my mouth to speak, but before I can say a word, Priscilla swoops in. 'Um. Yeah. Sure. Sorry— Lizzie, can I have a word?'

Calvin looks over his shoulder at her, eyebrow cocked.

'It's work,' she says to Calvin. 'Tim needs her to look at . . . something.'

Calvin shrugs and says with the face of a defeated man, 'Right-o,' and goes back to his work. He can't be bothered to argue today. He only knows Priscilla will then escalate the matter and say she needs me because of periods or tampons, like she would when trying to get me out of Mr Greenwood's Geography class, and he'd rather live in blissful ignorance that women piss only dried flowers and pressed apple juice.

We walk through the office, Priscilla leading me straight past her desk (and Tim's, as expected) and she says nothing until we're out in the corridor, in silence. 'So, I think I've found out why the number doesn't work,' she says, barely a space between her words. 'Frank Matias's,' she says. 'I've just had a sales meeting and we were all given some new accounts to look after. Two of them are in Wales. One in Cardiff. Totally different area code to what we have.'

My heart thumps. 'Right?'

'So, I asked Adrian, he's been here since time began and is a literal dinosaur,' Priscilla says. 'He couldn't work it out at first. Said it can't be a Cardiff number, that we'd got it wrong. But he grabbed me as he was going to lunch. He said he thinks it's an old area code.'

'Old?'

'Yep. Defunct. Some big number exchange thing happened ages ago. 0181 and London codes changed to 020 and Cardiff . . .' She trails off, handing me a Post-it note. 'If you change the 01222 bit to that . . .'

'It'll work?'

Priscilla shrugs, her mouth stretched into a grin. 'Hopefully,' she says. 'So, shall we try it?'

'He's dead.'

'Sorry?'

'He's dead. Frank. Frank's dead.'

'Oh, gosh. God, I'm so sorry, I didn't realise—'

'Mmm. Update your bloody databases.'

'Oh, no, I don't have a— I'm not selling anything.'

'Mmm.'

'I . . . well, see, I'm not actually looking for Frank Matias.'

'Then why're you calling his bloody widow and asking for him when he's been in the ground almost ten years?'

'I'm r-really sorry. I'm actually calling because I'm looking to get in contact with his son.'

'His son?'

'Yes. I'm looking for his son, Roman. We're old friends and—'

'*Roman*? No, no, no, no. I don't know where you got this number, but I suggest you remove it because he doesn't live here now and won't be back.'

'Ah. OK, sorry, I do have old information, I'm afraid, but that's all I have to go on. Do you happen to have a forwarding address or a number or—'

'Did you not hear me, lovie?'

'Yes, I—'

'I just said he *isn't* here, he won't ever be, and I have no idea where the hell he is and don't care to know, OK? Alright? You listening?'

'S-sorry, I just— I'm just trying to find my friend, I really didn't mean to disturb or upset anyone—'

'Listen, love, I'm not interested in anyone that's got anything to do with the waster, OK? It's done. We're well shot of the robbing nutjob, so don't you be ringing this number again, alright? You understand? Hello? Are you still there?'

This PC/D: Lizzie Laptop/Roman/
Roman signed in on 20/01/05 23:03

Roman: Hey. You're on late J.

Lizzie: can't sleep. dad's still not home yet. Nathan's asleep
in his room. tried calling my mum. she was out somewhere
loud n couldn't talk.

Roman: You ok?

Lizzie: I don't think so :(

Lizzie: I just feel so sad. sad and lonely.

Roman: I'm sorry you're sad :(

Lizzie: everything's so messed up. this house doesn't even feel
like my home anymore Ro.

Lizzie: it's dark and cold and silent and always a fucking mess.
& Mum and Dad are off doing these things they've never
done before. my mum is in bars on a Tuesday night and I
don't even know where my dad is. actually. bet I can guess :(

Roman: I wish there was something I could do.

Lizzie: I don't trust them anymore. I feel like they've been lying
to me and Nate our whole lives or hiding these whole other
versions of themselves or something. I don't even know
them.

Lizzie: I'm just so lost Roman.

Roman: :(

Roman: I wish I could fix this for you.

Roman: But we will soon. I promise you. On my life.

Roman: We won't even pack. We'll get behind the wheel and
drive Sea Fog for miles and miles and just keep going.

Lizzie: wish we could just go now.

Roman: Only 17 and a half months to go. College first.

Lizzie: that sounds like forever.

Roman: I know. But it's not. Plus £54.60 in the plant pot now. Added another tenner :P

Lizzie: :) that's made me smile.

Roman: And you can trust me J. I promise you. With everything. You can. I'm hiding nothing. There are no other versions. Just me.

Roman: Tall twat with the big gob.

Lizzie: and swimming float tongue.

Roman: RENOWNED swimming float tongue cheers.

Lizzie: and I do trust you.

Lizzie: more than anyone.

Roman: :)

Roman: I'm watching a program about aardvarks by the way.

Lizzie: course you are.

Roman: Did you know their bollocks are INSIDE their bodies?

Lizzie: wow. it really is always balls with you isn't it?

Roman: Always.

Roman: What else is there?

Chapter Nine

'Hello, darling. It's Mum. Just calling you again, seeing how you are . . . *again*. Wanted to hear your voice. I made a vegan cushion today at the centre, we had a woman come in, and the whole time I could hear you in my head, laughing away at me. I thought of you the whole morning. I'm always bloody thinking of you. Why didn't you come with Nathan and Katie for dinner on Sunday? I was sad, darling, I was. Call me back when you get this. If you ever listen to it, that is. Miss you, Lizzie.'

Katie blows out a long, noisy breath, her blushed cheeks puffed up. The wine glass in her dainty hand looks like a fish bowl. Red wine rocks gently inside. 'Wow, Lizzie,' she utters. 'So, this woman, his Dad's widow. She was definitely referring to Roman?'

'Yes,' I nod. 'I asked for him and that's when she launched into it. Said all those horrible things, called him a waster . . .'

'And a robbing nutjob.' Under her blonde fringe, Katie's brow furrows. 'That's a really horrid thing to say, isn't it?'

I run my fingers down the stem of my glass. 'I know. And the way she said it, Kate. I can't get it out of my head. She was so angry.'

A waiter drifts by the table, eyeing the glasses in front of us. He smiles as he passes.

'C-can I see it?' asks Katie, leaning across the ring-stained wooden table, her voice dropping, and nose wrinkled, as if she's telling a secret. 'The letter. If you don't mind, of course.'

I reach down to the handbag at my feet and pull it out of the inside pocket that's become its home over the last few weeks. I place it down on the table in front of her. Katie picks it up, as if it's delicate lace, her eyes narrowed in concentration. If there is one word for my sister-in-law, it's neat. She's petite, her features in perfect proportion, and everything she does is gentle and measured, like a nurse. I still remember the way she would knock gently on my bedroom door when we were teenagers, the way she'd pad in quietly as if she weighed nothing and settle down a sandwich or bowl of soup. She'd ask softly if I was OK, if I needed anything, and on the bad days, she'd hug me. Wordlessly, but there. Katie is calm. She always has been. She's probably never tripped over in public, or walked into a patio door, or had the runs on a date and made up a dead relative for an excuse to leave halfway through the starter. It simply is not her style.

'Just don't mention it to anyone,' I whisper.

'Course not,' she whispers back. 'Can I?'

I nod.

Katie reads the letter, and I find myself instinctively looking over my shoulder, to the restaurant's heavy, brass-rimmed glass door, to check for any sign of a fast-approaching Auntie Shall, Olivia, or the other bridesmaids. It's our second meeting, to help Olivia decide on her top three dresses before she makes her final selection. But there isn't anyone there.

It's almost a week since I called Frank Matias's phone number – a week since I got an earful, from his widow, Pam. Pam Matias. Priscilla had Googled the phone number after I'd spoken to her, and it had led us straight to her Facebook page – a cake making business run from her house in Leckwith, in Cardiff, and one photo of Pam, the Venomous Widow; short and auburn-haired, at least fifty-five, with leathery tanned skin, smiling on the balcony of an exotic-looking hotel, somewhere. Voices rarely match their owners, but she was almost like I'd imagined, though I wasn't expecting someone quite so pruned. I sent her a message on Facebook while at work. It was the day after we'd spoken, and her voice – the anger, the snarling, the words she had used – made me want to explain properly. I was sure she had the wrong person, heard the wrong name. It was a short message, apologising profusely again (though I'm still not sure what for), and asking if she had any contact information for Roman. Hoping she would see my inconspicuous, smiling Facebook photo and I don't know. Perhaps, realise I don't look the type to bring trouble to her telephone. But she hasn't responded yet. I'm positive a reply is never coming.

'Bloody hell,' says Katie, turning the letter over in her hand. 'I've gone all cold.' She lays the letter on the table in front of her, and with her gaze fixed on it, she picks up her glass and studies it. I wasn't going to tell her – tell anyone else, in fact – but this situation is growing and swelling, taking up so much of my reality that not mentioning it to someone like Katie – someone that genuinely cares – would feel like lying. Sitting opposite her, my head pounding with questions, the letter smouldering in my bag, the weight of all this bearing down on my shoulders, saying nothing, would've been harder than saying it all out loud.

'I feel like . . .' Katie squeezes her chin with her thumb and forefinger, her eyes still on the letter. Her short, square fingernails are a perfect, neat fawn. 'I don't know. This headed paper.'

'What?'

'I feel like I recognise it,' she says.

'Really?' My pulse twitches in my throat.

'I dunno. Which school did he go to?' She looks up at me. 'Before The Grove, I mean.'

'St James's.'

She shakes her head and grimaces. 'I don't know. Maybe it just reminds me of something else.'

'We Googled it,' I tell her, rubbing the tops of my arms through my top – they are rough with goosebumps. 'Nothing. Nothing substantial, anyway.'

Katie sits back in her chair and takes another mouthful of red wine. 'How're you holding up?'

I shrug, giving a slight smile. 'OK, I suppose.'

Katie leans in, eyes softening. 'How are you really, Liz? Honestly?' she asks, quietly. 'I've been a bit worried since we talked at your birthday dinner. And I know you told me not to, but I have been. I just didn't want to keep on. You know . . . *prying*.'

The second she says those words, tears form at the edges of my eyes. I shake my head. 'I'd be lying if I said this whole thing hadn't raked up old memories, made me feel even more lost than I was feeling, but . . . oh, I dunno.' I fiddle with the edges of the napkin under my glass. An eighties ballad wails through the restaurant speakers. 'Twenty-eight was my scary age, Kate. By twenty-eight I thought I'd know exactly where I was meant to be, what I was meant to be doing – *who* I was meant to be. And realising that you aren't even close on any of them. It's frightening.'

Katie nods gently. The light, silvery chain at her neck glistens in the light. 'But does anyone even know what they're supposed to be doing?' she says. 'I'm almost thirty-one and I'm not totally sure I do.'

'But you've done a lot, Kate. You went to uni, you're doing all this amazing stuff at the charity and that is always what you wanted. You travel, you *do* things, you've got Nathan—'

'But you could meet someone if you dated,' says Katie, eyes widening with enthusiasm. 'I told you Nathan's friend Liam fancied you when he met you at my thirtieth and he is *really* lovely.'

'Katie, it's not about meeting someone,' I say. My heart is beating hard in my chest, embarrassment creeping up my body. 'It's . . . do you remember the course I enrolled on? The art diploma. When I was sixteen.'

Katie nods. 'At Ware college.'

'Yeah,' I say. 'Well, I found the prospectus. In the box Nathan gave me from the loft. And the second I saw it I could hardly bear to—' The words jam in my throat, as if catching on something. I drop my voice to a whisper. 'I remember how much I wanted that, Kate. It was everything. I was going to take back control of everything; show everyone. Work hard, pass and then off I'd go. See places. Learn more. *Teach.*' A tight laugh of disbelief escapes my lips. 'And . . . I quit. Before I even really began. Thinking I'd try again the next year, and the next year, and the year after that. And I didn't. All because I was scared.'

'But you'd been through so much, Liz. You were grieving,' cuts in Katie. 'Hubble died, then your best friend disappeared—'

'I'm twenty-eight, Kate,' I carry on, my voice louder, clearer now. '*Twenty-eight years old.* A grown woman. And when I opened that box, I realised . . . I'm still waiting. Still waiting to be ready. Still waiting to feel brave enough to start.'

Katie reaches across the table and holds my hand. 'Lizzie,' she whispers. 'You're twenty-eight, not one hundred and eight. If you want to do something, you absolutely can.'

I shake my head. 'I don't even know what that's supposed to be.'

Katie brings her shoulders to her ears. 'Well, what about college?'

I look up at her and laugh. 'Katie, I'm not bloody Billy Madison. Sitting there among teenagers with my lunch box on a tiny chair, trying to be *down* with the kids . . .'

'I'm deadly serious,' she laughs. 'At the charity, we often help place people on courses, and honestly, these days, Liz . . . there's a course for everything, on evenings, even at weekends, and for all age groups.'

I glug a mouthful of wine, gulping away the tiny spark of something that ignited in my tummy as Katie spoke, and give a smile. 'Is there one called How to Tame the Auntie that Wishes you'd go Fuck Yourself all the way to Saturn?'

Katie smiles and gives a shake of her head. 'You can do it, you know,' she says, gently. 'Whatever it is. You're strong enough, and brave enough. Even though you think you aren't.' She pushes her hair behind her ears and looks across the table at me. 'Back then, everyone treated you as though you were this . . . alien. But all I saw was this really strong person. I wouldn't have coped with what you did, Liz. I *definitely* wouldn't have coped with being taken out of school and put in somewhere like The Grove.'

'You would have,' I say, my voice wobbling at the edges.

Katie's eyes glitter in the golden spotlights above us and she shakes her head. 'I remember your dad and even Shall telling us we weren't to mention him, after he disappeared. We had strict instructions that we don't do this, don't say that, *don't talk about Roman because it's bad for Lizzie to keep bringing him up.*' Katie scoffs a laugh. 'As if you were this tiny, fragile, weak little thing that couldn't even take hearing his name. After everything you'd already dealt with. And I remember thinking, *You really have no idea, because Lizzie will cope, regardless. She's strong, and she will cope and come through*

86

it, as she always has, because that's who she is. And you did. You did, and you have.'

I can't speak now, and I bring the heels of my hands to my eyes and catch the stray trickle of tears. I manage a smile and bring a hand flat to my chest. It feels like a tight ball of fire is crackling there. Strong is something I have never felt. Strong has always been something I wished I was.

'Gosh.' Katie clears her throat and brings the corner of a napkin to her eye. 'What're we like?'

'Quick,' I sniff. 'Let's stop with all the emotions before Shall catches me crying and rings Dad to report me.'

Katie laughs, dabbing the pads of her fingers on her cheekbones. 'OK. So. Roman. Where were we? The address. What about that other address? The one that was crossed out.' The music in the restaurant has changed to something upbeat almost as if the waiters sensed we needed a mood change, and Katie drains the last inch of wine in her glass.

'It's a Hackney address,' I tell her, swallowing to clear the thickness in my throat, 'a flat, I think.'

'Hackney's not far.'

'I know, but it's old info, isn't it? Like, twelve years old.'

Katie gives a shrug. 'But I guess if that's all you've got.'

Then she looks past me and smiles, and before I can turn, bony hands squeeze my shoulders.

'Enjoying your drink?'

I turn around. Olivia's radiant, rose-blushed face, greets me. She's smiling, but her wide eyes and puffed up chest tell me she's at least a tiny bit irritated.

'Oh, hey!' I smile.

'So, you've both started without us, I see.'

Katie is stuffing the letter in the envelope. 'We were super early,' she says, putting the letter on her lap and shuffling her seat closer to the table.

'Why?'

'It's just a few stops away from work,' I start, but Olivia cuts in.

'We were waiting outside.' She slips off her thin sleeveless cardigan and drapes it over the back of the chair beside me. The other bridesmaids circle the table, smiling and lifting their hands in greeting, sitting down, picking up the drinks menus. Olivia is waffling, about waiting outside, about sweating in the heat, about being 'seconds away' from taking her phone out to call us as if it would have been a huge inconvenience, because she was worried.

'Sorry,' I say. 'We just thought instead of waiting for half an hour, we'd come in and have a drink. I didn't realise—'

Olivia nods and gives a quick smile. 'It's fine. You got us a good table at least.'

'Well, certainly one that'll freeze us all to death.' Auntie Shall appears in a fluster, her eyes skyward, eyeing the air conditioning vents as if they might be seeping tear gas. She leans down and kisses Katie on the cheek. 'Hi, darling.' Then she looks at me and gives a small smile, and says, 'You're in trousers, Lizzie. You're always in trousers.'

I nod and look down at my jeans. 'Indeed I am.' Auntie Shall has always made a point of mentioning the fact I nearly always wear trousers. Ever since I betrayed her and wore a pair to Olivia's graduation. 'I said *dressy*,' she'd whispered. 'You're not a bloody boy.'

A few moments later, a waitress comes over and passes us all menus. Auntie Shall asks us all what we're having and then manages to push us all to the final page of the menu – Light Bites – a page that would be utterly depressing if it wasn't for the desserts section at the bottom.

'Katie, look,' I laugh, reaching over and pointing at the last item on the dessert list. 'Gooseberry crumble.'

Katie's eyes widen and she chuckles, her hand at her mouth. 'Oh my god, we *have* to have it. If only to disrespect it in the way it deserves.'

'Can you imagine Hubble?'

'What's that?'

I shake my head at Auntie Shall. 'Nothing,' I say. 'Just Hubble loved gooseberry crumble, and he had a full-on row with someone at the allotment once who said that gooseberries in a crumble had to be the biggest disrespect to the fruit he'd ever come across and—'

She looks away, down at her menu, as if I wasn't speaking at all. Olivia and the other bridesmaids are still looking at me.

'And?' grins Olivia, eagerly.

I blink, taken aback by Auntie Shall's ardent rudeness – the way her back went up, like the pricks of a porcupine – but I carry on. 'He erm. He was so angry about it. Kept going on about how his Mimi made the best gooseberry crumble, and that this guy was quote a "lumbering thicko", and he was telling us. Me and—' I stop. All eyes are fixed on me. 'Roman,' I carry on. 'He was telling me and my friend. And then Katie and Nathan arrived and I remember Nathan asking us over and over "what's happened? what's happened?" thinking this bloke must've done something *terrible* because of how angry he was.'

'Honestly. Over gooseberry crumble,' jumps in Katie. The bridesmaids are laughing, politely. Olivia is smiling, but vacantly, almost embarrassedly, and Auntie Shall is holding the menu so close to her face, she looks as though she's hiding from someone.

'Anyway,' says Auntie Shall after a moment. 'Are we ready to order? I think I'm having the salad.'

The evening goes by slowly, as bridal magazines and Pinterest boards are passed around. I grin. I nod. I pick out favourites, and gush, and pin, and fold over edges in magazines. But I feel as though I am buzzing, unable to sit still, and that every moment spent here is wasted. Because the want to keep looking now feels stronger than ever. A want that has attached itself to me and has its own beating heart, because the more I talk about him, out loud, out in the open, in the present day, the more real he becomes, once again. What was it he did, that he had no words for? Why did he disappear, then, when we needed each other the most? I want to know everything. I want all of my questions, after twelve long years, answered.

Chaos swirls through my head the whole night. Roman's words, Auntie Shall's face, Olivia's sinking shoulders, at the mention of his name, and the conversation I had with Katie. 'I remember your dad and even Shall telling us we weren't to mention him.' I replay those words over in my head, like a jumping record, anger bubbling beneath my skin. Sure, Dad wasn't keen on a seventeen-year-old boy like Roman – someone with his background, his problems, the scruffy clothes, the smoking, the painted nails I always caught Dad eyeing as if they were concealed weapons. But he never deserved to be a dirty, unspeakable secret. Roman was never something to be ashamed of. I loved him. He saved my life. Not them. None of them. But Roman did. Every day.

And more than anything, now, I want to – I have to – find Roman Meyers.

Chapter Ten

1st March 2005

'Sweetcorn or leftover beef casserole?' Hubble had asked, face straight, bent over the chest freezer.

'Um. Sweetcorn, please, I guess,' nodded Roman, nervously.

Hubble had smirked then, amused, and threw the bag over to him. 'Keep it on for as long as you can,' he said, before strolling out of the kitchen and saying to himself, 'Well, bang goes me sweetcorn fritters.'

We're sitting in Hubble's living room on the velvety two-seater that my late step-nan, Mimi, had hated, Hubble in the armchair, all watching *Coronation Street*, the heavy drapes keeping out the late winter draught, and only a lamp in the alcove lighting the room. All in silence. All eyes fixed on the wooden-framed TV in the corner.

'Tell you something. That bloody Tyrone gets on my wick,' Hubble grumbles. 'Wet as they come, that one. Dumb as mashed potatoes.'

Beside me, Roman laughs. Hubble turns at the sound, looks over his shoulder at him. He smiles ever so slightly and looks back at the screen.

'Dunno why you're laughing,' he says. 'He's one of your mob.'

Roman looks at me, drooping bag of thawing sweetcorn pressed to his knuckles. My stomach tugs at the sight. He won't say what happened, he never does — just that he and Ethan got in a 'scuffle' with 'some lads' in the park. A scuffle. Ethan Sykes doesn't strike me as being someone that has a 'scuffle', a word that sounds like a clumsy, accidental misunderstanding, all arms and legs and a kicked-up cloud of cartoon dirt. 'Am I as wet as they come, then?' Roman asks. 'Am I as dumb as mash?'

Hubble chuckles, not moving his eyes from the television. 'No. I meant, a northerner. A *Mancunian,*' he adds in a horrendously bad mock accent.

Roman laughs, adjusting the bag on his hand, and says, 'Not bad, Hubble,' and I see Hubble smile. It's his proper smile — the one that shows the straight bite of his dentures and turns his cheeks tight and pink. He really likes Roman. Dad doesn't. Neither does Auntie Shall or Uncle Pete. Even Nathan doesn't seem keen, and I don't know why. But Hubble does. There's something lovely about someone you love, liking someone else you love; seeing just what you see. It fills you up. Makes you feel proud. Validation that you found a good person in the world, all on your own.

The room falls quiet. All of us gaze at the television, and every now and then, I steal glances to my left. Roman's eyes squint when he concentrates like he is now. He chews his lip at the corner when he's worried — something he does every time he looks down at his hand. I really wish he wouldn't hang around with Ethan. He says they're friends, but I can't see how. Ethan is nothing like Roman. He isn't kind. He doesn't want good things for the world, or for himself. Maybe it's the smoking they have in common, or the having nowhere to be at night. Both lonely. Both in need of a friend. 'We hang out, have a chat, a joint,' Roman had said, once. 'Just, you know . . . only sometimes, when we've nowhere else to go.'

The credits roll, and Hubble turns the shrill wail of the theme music down a few notches.

'Nah,' Hubble groans, almost as if to himself. 'You're not wet, my boy. A wally, sometimes, maybe.' He gets up, pulling his trousers at the knee, straining as he does, the way someone does when they're stretching first thing in the morning. 'You know, messing about with idiots you have no business being around, staying out too late. That's called being a *wally*.'

Roman blushes and looks down to his lap.

'But not wet, no. Not dumb,' Hubble carries on. Then as he passes us on his way to the kitchen, he looks at us, and says, 'You're way too smart to be that. Both of you are.'

Tingling heat pricks my heart, at those words, the way feeling slowly comes back to your hands after you've been sitting on them for too long. Roman ducks his head to the side and looks at me, his eyes glassy, the colour of the sea.

'Now,' calls Hubble from the doorway, 'who wants something to eat? I've not seen either of you touch food in the last three hours so don't even think about saying no. Just don't ask for sweetcorn. We've sold out.'

After we eat beans on granary toast while sat on stools at Hubble's breakfast bar, Hubble and Roman in loud, back-and-forth conversation about aliens, politics and old record players, I stand at the porch door. Roman, who's done up to the neck in a tatty black parka, stands opposite me in the dark on the driveway.

I hold onto the door, the wind pricking icy needles into my skin with every gust.

'Go on, J,' Roman says, stuffing his hands in his pockets, his words making clouds in the air. 'Go in. It's absolutely freezing.'

'I don't want you to go home,' I say, quietly, almost hoping my words get lost in the wind.

The corner of Roman's mouth twitches. 'Me either,' he says. 'I never do when I come here. Or when I'm with you.'

'Let me ask if you can stay again—'

'No.' Roman shakes his head. 'It's late.'

'So?'

He shrugs and looks at his feet. 'I should see my mam.'

Why? I want to ask. *Why?* She doesn't care. Not like I do. Not like me and Hubble do. He'll be lucky if he can even get in his own front door. Last week when he left Hubble's at this time, she'd put the latch on and he had to sleep in Sea Fog, on the driveway. In minus five. He was so cold, he was shivering when he knocked for me the next morning, his lips grey, and I made him detour with me to Hubble's. Hubble made him take a hot shower, then drove us both to The Grove so we weren't late, stopping at Greggs to buy Roman two bacon rolls for his breakfast. I hate the thought of that happening again. Seeing him like that, so pale, so cold, so vulnerable, but still showing up despite it all. If he's here with us, he's safe. He won't freeze to death in the night or have to clear up his mum in the bath again. He won't be pushed outside, to Ethan. To god knows what he does when he's with him.

A gust of wind whips through the air, and my shoulders fly up to my ears, my jaw clenching. 'J, go in,' insists Roman, stepping backwards and pulling his rucksack onto his back. 'Go get warm. I'll text you in the morning.'

'When you get home,' I say, teeth chattering. 'Message me when you're home, in bed, safe.'

Roman smiles, embarrassment flashing in his eyes. 'Course.'

'If you need to, you can come back here and—'

'I'll message you,' he says. 'Thank Hubble again for me.' Roman pulls the furry hood up over his wild curls. 'Now, seriously, go in, Lizzie. I need to get moving. It's so cold, I can't feel my bollocks.'

Roman doesn't sign in on MSN, but twenty minutes later, my phone vibrates. A text. It just says, 'Sweet dreams, J x'. Nothing else. When I turn over in bed and close my eyes, I imagine

Roman warm, and safe, and in his bed, by lamp light, shut away from the freezing cold, from the darkness, from smoke and the echoing laughter in the black of the park, beyond the garden fence. Then I imagine he's on the floor, beside me, on the blow-up mattress, blankets up to his chin. I imagine reaching out for his hand and holding it, tightly, across the bedroom floor. It's the only way I manage to fall asleep.

Chapter Eleven

'Hey, Liz, it's me, P, all the way from sunny Newport. Well. Actually, I have no idea where we are now. Me and Becks are on a train. Where are we? What— I think I keep breaking up. Am I bre— I have no idea. This is a voicemail, I keep forg— So, we've been there ten minutes, we're all in this lovely restaurant and Graham orders two shots *each* for everyone and then throws a hissy fit when me and Becks are like, "it's Saturday morning, dude, Jesus Christ." So, we decided to leave them all to it and go shopping. Becks knows it 'round here, she grew up nearby. God knows what I'd do if she wasn't here, I really shouldn't have— I think my phone keeps cutting out. So yeah, we're on the train, the both— and we're going t— *Yep!* Can you believe it? Maybe I'll even see her. I'll look for an old dragon! That's Becks giggling. I'll see you Monday, but I'll call— *end of message.*'

104 Edgar Fields. It sounds nice, like a little country nook surrounded by sweeping green landscapes, the sound of tractors, cows and silence. It sounds romantic even; like it could well be the address of one of Mr Darcy's holiday homes or something. But Edgar Fields is none of those things. It's made of

concrete and the sharpest lines. Most of the windows and doors are blocked up with sheets of brown metal, and from up here, on the sixth and final floor, the ground below looks like a waste land; an almost-empty, pot-holed car park, and the grassy area at the entrance, a sea of rusting washing machines, split open bin liners, old scaffolding, and the ripped, filthy chairs of a car's backseat. It's nothing like the other blocks on this estate. They looked homely – lived in. This is practically barren.

It isn't the first time I tried to come here.

I tried yesterday. I even got as far as leaving the flat, to go to Dad's, to pick up Katie's car, address in my pocket, postcode locked and loaded, but then I stopped dead on the corner as I turned to leave my street. Panic rose in my chest and my throat, and the smell of Saturday morning bacon sandwiches wafting from nearby houses made me sick to my stomach. I couldn't go. Today felt different, though. It's the sort of clean-slate, blue-sky of a late August morning that makes you want to tear open the curtains, throw open the windows, and be spontaneous. The perfect sort of weather for running away, Roman used to say. And I think that's why I woke up and decided to go, before I'd even eaten breakfast and given myself a chance to talk myself out of it. Nothing under a sky as blue, a world as beautiful, can be frightening.

The top floor, where I am now, looks very much like all the others, but it's the loudest, most alive-feeling floor yet, despite the boxed-in doors and bars at the windows. It's the booming music that does it. It's the sort of music Hubble used to tut at, before saying, 'I can't understand a bloody word they're saying.'

'Why's it matter?' Nathan would say.

'Why does it *matter*?' he'd exclaim, pointing his knobbly finger. 'You go and listen to some music in Taiwanese then, if understanding what they're singing about isn't important.' Then when Nathan would look blankly, he'd say, 'See.'

Hubble. Lovely Hubble. Sometimes I find it hard to believe he's not here anymore but at the same time, I can't believe he ever was; until he was gone. Just like that. On that cold concrete, alone. Sometimes, I wish I still believed the lie Dad told me – that he had the heart attack in his own home, surrounded by his own things, in the warm. I believed that was the truth for two years, until Uncle Pete slipped up one day. I think Dad was too worried to tell me at the time – to tell me it was outside, in the freezing cold, Hubble still dressed in the suit he'd worn to the vow ceremony – in case it had undone everything, and I had spiralled even more.

109. The numbers are descending. Just five more doors and I'm there, at Roman's old address. 108 is numberless and boarded up with wood. The next flat is without a number, too. Both its window and door are blocked with metal sheeting. At the bottom of the door there are letters jutting out, stuffed there by an optimistic postman. I look over my shoulder, then bend and pull a letter free, to check the name, just in case. The envelope curls as I pull it. A burst of laughter comes from the stairwell and I jump back, almost falling on my arse. Am I doing the right thing? Roman doesn't even live here anymore. Well, that's just going by the light, almost could-be-accidental pencil strikethrough on Helen's dad's address book page. But say if he does? Say if this is where Roman – the boy I loved – made a life? Maybe he came back here after being thrown out by that nasty cow on the phone. Maybe this is where a family member of his lives? Or a friend I never knew. They might be able to tell me where to find him now.

I stand up straight and look down at the Thames Water envelope in my hand. 107. Not his name. Two more doors. I keep on walking.

106: a pair of muddy boots on a threadbare, green doormat.

The music is louder now. Much louder. I'm getting closer to it.

105: Boarded up. The music is booming.

104.

I'm here. Roman's old address. The music is coming from inside. The brass numbers and knocker are blistered with rust. There is a white plastic doorbell with a grey button in the centre above the lock. It looks new.

My hands are sweating now. It's the music, I think. It's harsh and computer-y, a mess of fast drums and sound effects. Well, going by the music alone, Roman definitely doesn't live here now. If he did, it would be The Smiths blasting out or The Scorpions. And for some reason, the music is the thing putting me off knocking, above all else, and I know it's stupid. As if listening to loud, brash music makes a person unsavoury.

I raise my hand to the door. I glance left and right. There's a man, at the top of the stairwell, just by the arched entrance to the sixth floor. He's tall, black, handsome, with a record bag on his shoulder, open and full of papers. He's on the phone. And he's watching me. He's the first person I've seen the whole time I've been here – ever since I pulled up. Clocking me looking, he hesitates, and smiles, quickly, just a glimmer of one, not breaking the conversation he's having on the phone. He disappears out of sight.

I raise my hand to the door again, seconds before it flies open in front of me. A man, pale with a ring in his nose, wrapped up in way too many layers for late summer, flies towards me.

'Whoa!' he shouts, halting. 'Jesus, fuck—'

'Sorry,' I say. 'Sorry, sorry, it's just . . . I was about to knock, I'm looking for some—'

He's gone; rushes straight past me, hands in pockets, head disappearing into his coat, right in the middle of my sentence. He takes a quick glance over his shoulder at me before he gets to the stairwell and disappears. Something deep down is telling me to forget this now. I can't shake it. It's a dread, creeping up my body. Nerves, maybe, or a gut instinct.

But there is still someone inside. I saw someone, as the door flew open, for just a moment. A man. Tall, leaning against the wall, at the bottom of the hallway. Just a silhouette.

'Hello?' I call out. The door is ajar and it moves under my fingertips. 'Anyone home?'

I knock now, and as I do, the door opens a little more. There's the man at the end of the hallway – I can only see his profile. He's facing into another room. His hair . . . it's shaggy and messy on his head. Like Roman's. As daylight fills the smoggy hallway with daylight, he turns and begins walking towards me.

He's smirking when he gets to the door. 'Alright?'

He's tall, but with a skinny, pointed face. His eyes are perfect circles, and underneath are yellowy bruised bags. He is nothing like Roman.

'Hi,' I say. 'Sorry to disturb you—'

He holds up a finger to stop me, and disappears. After a moment, the music is turned down, and he appears again. He's scruffy, this bloke. The Adidas top he is wearing is creased and baggy, the tips of his fingernails are lined with dirt. Mum would say he needs a good scrub.

'I dread to think how long it's been since that back saw water,' she'd whisper if she was here now. 'And I suppose he has a poor girlfriend who has to touch him. I expect she can't go down there without a bloody snorkel.'

The guy smirks. 'Sorry about that.'

I really don't like the way he's looking at me.

'Sorry to disturb you,' I try again. 'I have this address. For an old friend and . . .'

He nods, eyes drifting down across my body. I pull my cardigan tighter around myself.

'I'm just wondering if you know him.'

'Yeah,' says the man, looking back up at me and chuckling. 'I know him. I know anyone if it means you wanna come in.' He steps towards me – a big stride, over the threshold. I step backwards. All I can think about now is could I run fast enough? Could I get down the steps before he caught me?

'It's fine,' I say. 'Wrong flat.'

I turn, but he steps in front of me, and says, hands up at his sides, 'No, no, come on, love, I was joking. *Joking.* Crap joke. Who're you looking for?' His accent is strong. Scottish. He's stopped smirking but he's wearing the sort of expression where he looks as though he may burst into laughter at any second.

'Roman,' I say.

'Roman who?'

I hesitate. 'Meyers.'

He pauses, eyes narrowing. He throws a look over his shoulder. 'Mate. Come here!' My heart lifts with hope. But as quick as it starts, it droops. A man with long hair and a short, ginger beard joins him at the doorstep. He nods at me. It isn't Roman.

'She's looking for someone,' says Smirky. 'Roman.' I hate the way he says his name. As if it's amusing.

'Hey, I can be Roman,' says the guy with the beard, smiling. I can smell the alcohol from where I stand. 'Come and have a drink, we'll see if we can find him.'

'No, thanks,' I say, and I step back, a massive stride. I want to tell them to go fuck themselves. I want to rush off, run back to the car. But I'm almost worried they'll run too. So I say, 'Thanks for your time,' and turn and walk away.

But Smirky steps over the doorstep, and then his hand is on my shoulder. Then: another voice – a man's bellow.

'Hey! Craig!'

Smirky drops his hand from my shoulder and holds his arms out at his side. 'Heeeeey, it's Munkers!' he shouts. It's the guy who was on the phone in the stairwell.

'What're you playing at?' he says, walking at speed towards us.

'Er, having a laugh?' says Smirky.

'Looked like it,' growls the black guy – *Munkers,* as Smirky called him. 'Run along back inside, eh? Go on. Sod off. Leave this woman alone.'

Smirky – *Craig* – goes to open his mouth.

'Do you wanna be a nuisance to strangers? Do you? Or do you wanna be a decent human being? 'Cause I thought you'd already made that choice.'

Craig's smirk falls from his face. He pauses, staring at me, as if in shock that I exist at all, then shrugs and storms past us, into the flat. The guy with the beard has already gone.

The black guy turns to me. 'I'm Nick.'

I say nothing.

'Are you alright?'

I nod, my heart is hammering in my throat.

'He was just trying to get a reaction,' he says. 'No excuse, I know, but between you and me the guy's a massive twat. One poke and you'd have knocked him down like a sack of spuds.'

I am shaking now – adrenaline, I suppose – and all I want to do is get to the car and burst into tears. This feels hopeless. A series of winding routes, each leading to a dead end. I look at the guy and I nod. 'Cheers,' is all I say, and I turn to leave.

'You sure you're OK?' Nick calls after me, but I don't stop walking.

'Yeah,' I call. 'Fine.'

But he's caught up with me. He stands at the side of me. 'I'm in social care,' he says. 'I work for a charity.' He pulls his jacket to one side – there's a plastic pass around his neck.

He holds it between his fingers. I stop. The pass has a .org. uk website address printed on it – it's small but looks like it's called 'Free to B' – beside a photo of him, an ID number, and his name: Nicholas Munk.

'Just in case you thought I was an accomplice of ol' silly bollocks over there,' he laughs, but he's watching me with concern; as if I'm something that might collapse at any moment. 'You're shaking. Do you think you should take a minute?'

I shake my head. 'I'll be alright. I just wanna get out of here.'

I still can't get my breath. My words come out in short bursts.

'Then at least let me walk you out. Those stairs are concrete, and there's hundreds of them. I used to work in risk-assessment. A wobbly person and those steps . . .' he pauses, and grimaces. 'Well, I wouldn't forgive myself. And I'm not sure your bones would, either.'

My head spins. 'Um. OK. Fine.'

Nick and I walk without talking for the first two flights of stairs. My stomach lurches at the smell of piss. It's putrid, and at the moment, everything feels more intense than usual. Every sound is loud and alarming, every colour, illuminated. The shock of it all; of all of this.

'Think lovely thoughts,' laughs Nick, trotting down the stairs beside me. Then, as we descend the fourth flight, he says, 'Can I ask what brought you here? Totally fine if that's too personal a question.'

'I shouldn't have come,' I tell him. 'It seemed like a good idea.'

He nods. 'Was surprised to see someone, to be honest. It's being demolished soon. They're rebuilding. Most have moved out.'

'I'm trying to find an old mate,' I tell him. 'This is the only address I have. But I think it's old. Years old.'

'Was he an ex-con?'

I stop on the steps. When he sees I'm at a standstill, he stops too, a few steps further down, his eyebrows raised, lips parted.

'What? No. No, he wasn't an ex-con.' Then I notice his face. His mouth a tight curve, eyes downturned at the corners – the same face Helen wore at Broxton Farm. *The smile.* The sad, pitiful smile. 'Why do you ask that?'

'Because that's what number 68 and 104 are, here. It's shared housing for ex-cons.'

'Ex-cons? As in . . . people who've been in prison?'

Nick nods, twice. A bow really, his eyes widening slightly as if to say, 'What else would I mean?' My hand grips the cold handrail. I think of Roman. I think of that place, those men. I think of prison, of cells, of how much he hated the idea of being trapped; that nightmare he used to have, of being locked in. Then I think of us. Looking up at the clouds, pointing out swifts and kites, us on that beach, his hands holding my arms, counting with me, till the panic stopped, the laughing until we cried, cocooned together in Sea Fog, running through the town in black tie, him crying in that hospital bed. God, that hospital bed. My heart heaves against my ribcage. It's unbearable. All of this. It's too much.

'It was a dry house for a while,' says Nick. We haven't moved from the steps. I can't. It's like someone has sliced a knife through me and I'm deflating. 'Place for recovering addicts. Then we had the new rehab centre open. That was about fourteen, fifteen years back now. Then it became the housing for ex-cons. When was it your friend—'

'Not as far back as fifteen years.' As if addiction would be better – as if it would be preferable.

'Right.' Nick nods again – that sad bow. He watches me. There's silence between us for a moment. There is water drip-dropping somewhere, and distant sirens.

'Sorry,' I say. 'I just wasn't expecting that. I don't understand any of this.'

'Never easy,' he utters.

After a moment, I straighten. We start walking again.

'I always say this place is a stop gap, between your mistakes, and the rest of your life. So, hopefully this place is long behind your friend. Ex-cons either—'

'*No.*' I stop. We're just one flight from the ground now. 'I don't— I don't think Roman was an ex-con.'

Nick says nothing, and brings his hand up to his stubbly chin.

'I know that's probably what everyone says and I sound really naive, but . . . he would never steal, or hurt anyone. He was a good person.' Silence, again. 'He was better than anyone. He had this heart, and . . . he was just a good person. Better than good. Better than all the people I ever knew. I think maybe the address was a number out or a mistake or something . . .'

Nick smiles, the skin at the corners of his eyes crinkling as he does. 'Look, I don't doubt there's a possibility it could be wrong information. But I've known many good men go into those flats,' he says, softly. 'In fact, most are, at the core, beneath it all. They just take a wrong turning, make a poor decision. Then they need to get back on track. That's what we provide, and sometimes, that's all it takes.'

'And other times?'

He hesitates and takes a deep breath. 'Other times, it doesn't matter what we say or do or help them with. They've made their minds up.'

'They re-offend?'

He nods once. 'Or . . .' He doesn't say anything else. He just raises his shoulders to his ears, and I don't want him to say any more. We stand on the step, halfway down. There's just the sound of our breathing, and that dripping of water, and I wait, as my heart slows from a gallop to a trot.

'And what about Craig?'

'Sorry?'

'Craig. Twat upstairs. Is he a good man?'

Nick laughs, rubbing his chin. 'Ah,' he says. 'Well, I've seen worse pull their finger out, put it that way. So, who knows?'

When we get outside, Katie's car sits welcomingly on the concrete. There's a black car parked beside it, a 'Free to B' sticker on the side of the door. Nick's car. I can't hear the music now, or the sirens; just distant traffic and the wind, through trees.

'There're places online that have a registry of everything. Names, cases, convictions, all that. Not all, but . . . you might strike lucky.' Nick grimaces. 'Perhaps, wrong choice of words there.' He ducks to look at me. 'You OK?'

'I'm fine. Thanks for walking me out.'

'Anytime,' says Nick. 'Good luck, yeah? And no more knocking on strange doors. You never know who you'll find.'

'Babe, it's me again, Priscilla. Remember me? Your best friend who went to that bloody work trip and should've never ever gone because Graham is the worst drunk in the whole frigging universe and I want to bathe in holy water just because I *observed* it. God, you're crap at answering your phone. I'm almost home. You need to ring me back as soon as you get this. I mean it. Please?'

This PC/D: Lizzie Laptop/Roman/
Roman signed in on 22/03/05 23:57

Lizzie: hey.

Roman: Hiya

Lizzie: where have you been? you been out dog walking with Ethan again?

Roman: No. Offy in town. Phone's dead. Sorry.

Lizzie: the offy? why?

Roman: Came home, found Mum passed out, 3 bottles of vodka and a bottle of wine in her handbag.

Roman: She's been out robbing agauin.

Roman: again^

Lizzie: roman :(

Lizzie: are you ok?

Roman: Sort of.

Roman: Took them back. Dude at the shop was cool about it. Shook my hand, gave me 15 quid to say thx . . .

Lizzie: that's shit Ro, I'm sorry :(

Roman: It's ok. Kipping in Sea Fog tonight. Can't be arsed with her when she wakes up and finds them gone. Only just got signal so if I sign out it's not me it's my net :/

Lizzie: it's so cold. do you have loads of blankets?

Roman: Yeh lots. & a oil heater thing I found in the loft. Made the hot water bottle you got me too :)

Lizzie: I wish you could just sleep here.

Roman: Me too.

Lizzie: Dad's asleep and Nathan is at Mum's. can't you climb up my drain pipe?

Roman: I wish.

Roman: Wait . . . that was a euphemism wasn't it?

Lizzie: NO!!!!

Roman: Oh.

Lizzie: lol! shut up.

Roman: Haha. Sorry. Too easy.

Lizzie: nob.

Roman: Silver lining is we've got a 5er for the pot. Would've been another tenner but we needed stuff. Loo roll and milk, pasta for my tea . . .

Lizzie: ok Jamie Oliver :D

Lizzie: seriously tho, you don't have to explain. you should have it all.

Roman: Nah. Rather give it to Operation Sea Fog :) plus . . .

Roman: I bought you something.

Lizzie: did you?!

Roman: Just a little something for college. Wrapped it and stuck a tag on and EVERYTHING :P

Lizzie: that's so lovely <3 thank you :)

Lizzie: I've gotta get in first tho.

Roman: You will.

Roman: Then there'll be no stopping us.

Lizzie: counting down the days . . .

Roman: Me too J. One at a time.

Chapter Twelve

'Sesame orange chicken, vegetable spring rolls, prawn pancake rolls, prawn *and* mixed meat pancake rolls, beef chow mein, pork chow mein, chicken chop suey . . .'

'Wow—'

'Sweet and sour chicken balls, sweet and sour *pork* balls, sweet and sour chicken Hong Kong style . . .'

'Is that in the light batter?'

'Yes, Calvin. A light batter and served in the sauce.'

'Well,' says Calvin, 'I must say, mate, this definitely sounds—'

'On to sundries. Steamed beef dumplings, steamed vegetarian dumplings, chips, fried in groundnut oil . . .'

Gary, Fisher and Bolt's scruffy IT guy, and Cal's unlikely BFF, stands in front of us with a crumpled piece of folded lined paper, and with small rounded glasses on the end of the nose of his enormous beardy face, he reads from it. Cal is sitting on his computer chair, lounging back, his eyes fixed on Gary, as though he's watching a marvellous opera.

'Could you at least look as though you're working, please, Lizzie?' he'd said about fifteen minutes ago as I'd stared into space, and willed away the hours until home time, when I could crawl back into bed and pull the duvet over my head and stay there until morning. 'Gary'll be in in a minute and I don't want it getting back to Lenny that you spend work time Googling things and emailing Priscilla.'

'Why is Gary coming in here exactly?' I grumbled.

'He's going to be looking at my Outlook.'

'Right.'

'And he's tried that new Chinese buffet in Stratford. Says he wants to show me the menu.' I thought by menu, he meant an actual menu, which he would just hand to Cal after fannying about with his email and grunting a bit, and say, 'Nice place to take the wife. I recommend the sweet chilli beef, and to dine before seven.' But no. This is Gary – Gary and his soul of batter and heart of fondant potato. There is no menu. Just a handwritten list of every food and accoutrement available courtesy of his own fair, hairy hands, and it's being verbally delivered. Calvin looks enrapt though; as if he's listening to Wordsworth, and he is quite sure he is the cloud. I sigh, loud enough that he might get the message (he doesn't) and open my email. It's not that I don't love Chinese food. In fact, it's one of my favourite things in the entire world, normally, and listening to a menu, especially read by Gary and his unintentionally-comedic ways, would be a highlight of my day. But I'm in no mood. No mood for food, no mood for laughing, no mood for anything. I'm teetering – on the edge of tears, on the edge of just jumping up and walking out the door.

Because everything feels odd.

Everything seems flat and colourless and as if everything and everyone is just moonlighting as themselves, and they're really something else beneath the surface. I imagine this is what stepping through to an alternate reality is like. Everything's there, the world looks the same, everything in its place, as it's always been, but it's just not quite right. Something is off, something has shifted. Nothing feels true. And unease, like this . . . feels like an old friend. It's been a while since I've felt it this strong. It's always there really, a dulled, weak version, thanks to the tablets that have kept it that way for years, now; the edge of something I know would try to engulf me if given half the chance, ever blunted. But I can feel it today, fighting to become more than just a shimmer; to be a wave, of helplessness, of random, gratuitous dread, that crashes over me and knocks me to the floor.

'You'll become addicted,' Dad told me when I came home from seeing the doctor, age eighteen, a prescription bag held tightly in my hand. 'You got off them once, you don't need them again. You'll never know how to be happy without them if you're not careful.'

'Well, the doctor doesn't agree.'

Dad had let out a scoff of a laugh. 'He wouldn't, would he? Quickest way to get you out his office and onto the next one is to chuck you happy pills.'

'But they might help me, Dad.'

'Or make you worse.'

'Well,' I told him, pushing down the want to shout at him, to ask him what was worse than being unable to start college for the second time, or being unable to hold down a simple Saturday job because of this *thing* he seemed adamant on curing with pep talks and new clothes. 'Stay tuned. You'll soon find out.'

Twelve weeks later, Dad waved Priscilla and me off at Ashford station, our bags packed for France, our Eurostar tickets in hand, and he held me for much longer than usual.

'I'm so pleased,' he said into my ear, his voice thickening with tears, 'to see my girl smiling again.' He has never mentioned them again. Not negatively anyway.

'Liz?'

'Hm?'

'Popping to Greggs for lunch. Want me to get you anything?'

I shake my head. 'No cheers, Cal. I'm going out at one. With Priscilla.'

'Oh. Oh, that'll be nice.' He rocks slightly on his heels as if he is contemplating asking me something else, but he doesn't. He just nods, says, 'Alright. See you in a bit,' and dashes off, leaving with Gary, the pair of them chatting madly, bouncing as they walk from the office.

I close the door of the Shoebox of Doom when Cal leaves – less likely to attract anyone wanting to come in with accounts questions – and I want the peace.

I open my email. There's one from Martin, our German director, one from Jeremy – photographs from the work trip, as well as a link to them and a password to gain access, and two from Priscilla – one is a reply to an email I sent her earlier, asking why she was late in again this morning and didn't answer my texts last night.

From: Priscilla Greene
To: Lizzie James
Date: 28 August 2017 11:57
Subject: No subject

Morning babe. Sorry I didn't text you back last night. (Bit rich coming from someone who was begging for you to call them back I know, but nightmare night, nightmare morning. Chris and me. Another row.)

Can we go to Princess of Wales at lunch? I know it's a walk but I want somewhere quiet away from work. I need to talk to you. 1 still OK?

For a moment, I feel like I'm going to burst – explode into chunks of woman with anticipation across this pub, all over lunching workers and pint-drinking builders on breaks. This always happens when she has news, good or bad, or she has to talk about something she'd rather not; speaks nothing but pure bollocks, prolonging the misery and/or excitement. We cover the consistency of pub chips, how long it took her to put her eyelashes on last Saturday, the smell on the Northern Line this morning, and what exactly work's cleaner, Martha, found in the loos last Friday morning that made her cry then send a very cross email (poo apparently, on the floor, in the cold light of day. Gary, I guess. Priscilla agrees).

'So . . .' P looks over her white wine spritzer at me, and smiles. I admit I'm relieved at the smile. The bags under her eyes today, another argument between her and Chris, and her rare make up-less face had me leaning towards bad news. But she's smiling widely – teeth showing and every-thing – so it has to be good. Something *funny* about the work trip, like Jeremy dancing on a table with a carnation between his rock-hard buttocks, or Graham going missing before being found drunkenly dangling his balls over the continental breakfast selection in the hotel restaurant in a dress that wasn't his own.

'I went to Leckwith,' she says. I blink. 'You probably guessed from the voicemail that—'

'What?'

'The one I left on the train. I said I was going to Cardiff to a shopping centre—'

'*What?* You didn't – you kept breaking up.'

Priscilla stares at me over her glass, eyes wide. There's a beat – a moment of silence between us at that round table – of shock, of disbelief, before I lean forward, head pulsing, my hands shaking as her words sink in, and say, 'You went to Roman's dad's. As in . . . Pam's? Dragon, bitch-from-hell, *robbing nut job* Pam's? Are you for real?'

Priscilla starts to laugh. 'I know it's mad. But . . . how could I have not, Lizzie? We were right there. We were shopping and I was telling Becky, just that we were trying to track down an old mate and she told me to put the postcode in my phone, because Cardiff is obviously a massive fuck-off place and . . . it was just a couple of miles. Before I knew what I was doing I was booking a cab—'

'My god, Priscilla.' I am speechless. I wasn't prepared for this. I thought it'd be gossip, a little work-related secret or something, and then I'd tell her the news, all about Edgar Fields. But *this*. I can barely speak. 'And was she . . . d-did she speak to you?'

Priscilla nods. 'I mean she didn't want to, but I was nice Lizzie, I really was. I even made Becks wait a few houses down so it didn't feel like an ambush or something, but as soon as I mentioned I was your friend, she just kept saying Roman was long gone and she knew nothing, so stop bringing trouble to her door. Trouble. I was standing there with an M&S all butter Madeira cake, for God's sake. *Trouble.*'

'You bought a cake?'

Priscilla shrugs sheepishly, glass in hand. 'I guess I was preparing for a best-case scenario. That she'd open the door, invite me in—'

'But she didn't?'

'God, no.' Priscilla shakes her head. 'She was a cow, babe. *Total cow.* Slammed the door in my face after a minute or so, but . . .' P leans forward. 'Did you know Roman has a half-brother?'

I can't help but gasp. 'No.'

'Well he does. Matt.'

'Matt?' I shake my head. 'He never mentioned—'

'He wouldn't have known back then,' says Priscilla. 'But he's lovely. Bit nervous, but really lovely and *really* Welsh.' Priscilla laughs, lightly. 'I was turning away, door slammed in my face, and this guy comes out, and well, you'd never know because this guy – he looks nothing like Roman. Like, he looks like a foot, Lizzie. An actual human foot. But he says he's Roman's brother, Matt. *Half-brother.*'

'Priscilla, I can't actually digest the fact you went to her house let alone that there's a half-brother.'

Priscilla looks down into the drink in her hands. 'He said Roman turned up three weeks after his dad was diagnosed with pancreatic cancer. Roman got a year with him. Matt says he's sure it was Roman that kept him going so long.'

My chest feels like it's been wound tight, like a bobbin. 'That's . . . God, that's terrible.'

Priscilla nods. 'He didn't go into too much detail. Just said Roman had arrived in an absolute mess – had been living with some mate in London, that he'd got into some stuff—'

'Stuff?'

Priscilla shrugs. 'Dunno,' she says. 'But he said he came at the right time. That he'd got his dad all wrong, that Frank had been trying to make contact for years, but Roman coming meant they'd worked through all that before it was too late. He said they were really close in the end, and Matt loved having him around. Big brother and all that.' A waiter with a tray of food walks by our table, and I am grateful, for the first time in my life, that the plates of steaming food aren't for us. I don't want Priscilla to stop speaking. 'Anyway, when he died, he left Matt a load of money to be released when he was eighteen, and . . . Roman got everything else. And he had loads, Lizzie. Garages, two houses, a business, a flat up north somewhere.'

I can't find the words. My mouth is just hanging open, and I'm staring at Priscilla. The image of Roman's dad – a penniless, violent, imprisoned junkie, with no hope, no care – bursts, like a balloon in my mind. 'Jesus, so that's why—'

'*Robbing nut job*,' Priscilla nods. 'Pam took him to court and everything. Matt says Roman was great throughout, tried to half it, because he didn't want to accept it all. But she didn't want to split it or allow Roman to have any of it, so the courts were involved. He won. But Matt says he still signed over half, gave them the house, and left. And that was it.'

Relief and sadness wash over me. He'd have been barely twenty-one when faced with such things. But of course he still signed it over. Roman was kind and had a heart that was good. And he still is those things, that person I knew. But then what caused him to be so desperate that he had to go there? What pushed him into that? To Edgar Fields, to his dad. 'Does he know why he left? Does he know where he is?' I ask Priscilla, eagerly. 'Are they in contact?'

Priscilla inhales, her chest puffing up. Her eyes fix on mine. 'He—'

'Here we go, guys.' A waitress stands at our table, two large white plates in her hands 'Chicken wrap and chips, with a side salad?' Priscilla nods with a quick smile, and the other plate, a mound of amber-coloured pasta is placed down in front of me. The waitress says something about sauces, tells us to enjoy our meals, and speeds off towards the bar.

I wait for Priscilla to continue but she's opening out her napkin and staring at the food in front of her. I haven't moved.

'So? Does Matt know where he is?'

Priscilla looks up at me and rests her hands in her lap. 'No,' she says after a beat. 'Pam made him promise that he wouldn't see him anymore. He says he misses him every day. But they do talk, sometimes. Secretly. He calls Matt on his birthday, every year without fail, and sometimes on Frank's anniversary.'

'He must know where he is, then? Some sort of idea—'

Priscilla lifts a shoulder to her ear and deflates. 'He said he thinks Roman travels around a lot. He said he once called him and it must've been a payphone, as when he started to run out of call-time, a foreign recorded message came over the line. He didn't recognise the language. He said numbers are usually withheld, and he thinks it's for his mum's benefit, 'cause Roman always calls their house phone, and—'

'So, he's never managed to get a number off him?' I ask, eyes narrowed. 'Maybe he lives abroad, then. He always wanted to live in—'

'It's not always withheld,' says Priscilla, quickly. 'Matt said when he called a couple of years ago, he did 1471 and there was a number. When Matt called him on it a few weeks later, a woman answered. She said he wasn't there anymore, but she could give him the number to get a *form* if he wanted to visit him.'

I stare at Priscilla. 'What?'

'We don't know, babe,' she says. 'Matt said he didn't understand, and asked her what she meant, and then she got really cagey. Said she'd get Roman to call him when he was back but he didn't until months later, and when Matt asked him, he said the woman was someone he was seeing for a while, and he had no idea what she could've been on about.'

Bile rises in my throat. A form. A visitor's form. Prison. Re-offending, like Nick said. I can't get my breath. Roman in prison. The two things together – him and the mere notion of prison – feels disorientating and unreal. No. How could he have been in prison? What would he have done? He would never hurt someone, he would never purposely do something *criminal*. Unless . . . he would. I knew him at seventeen and eighteen. I didn't know him at twenty-seven, twenty-eight and twenty-nine. I don't know him as a grown man.

'Lizzie? Are you OK?'

I shake my head. 'A form,' I say. 'It's just . . . say if he's in jail, Priscilla? I went to . . . at the weekend, and—' I swallow down the fuzzy ball forming in my throat, stifling my breath. 'He could be in prison. Could've been—'

'No,' says Priscilla, hands shooting across the table. They land on mine and she squeezes tightly. 'Liz, no. He isn't in jail. Hey, deep breaths, yeah?' Priscilla grabs my Coke bottle and straw. 'Have some of this.'

Priscilla watches me take a sip. The pub pulses and warps around me, and everything is suddenly too loud, too much. I close my eyes. He'd hold my shoulders, sometimes, when this happened when we were together, and I'd shut my eyes and listen to his voice. It helped more than most things did. He always anchored me back to earth, like nothing else could. Roman looked after me. He was the only reason I got up in the morning, walked against the grain of the crowds of kids on their way to school – *normal* school – and turned up at Grove House, as The Grove was officially known. 'Special school' as Auntie Shall called it more than once. 'A day centre' as my social worker called it, 'for kids like you. With *behavioural issues*. Those, you know, struggling with mental health among other things.'

That never felt right, either. I behaved just fine, my whole school life. It was my anxiety that began behaving on my behalf, like a drug that caused sporadic movements, making it hard to study, to listen, to get out of bed when the alarm went off without vomiting, without feeling as though the walls of every room around me were going to collapse. 'The Grove' is what we always called it, Roman and I. It never felt like a school, or a day centre, or like anywhere I'd ever been before. Looking back now, I'd call it a safe-haven. I'd call Roman the same, if a person can be such a thing.

'All OK?' whispers Priscilla.

I nod. Tingles, like soft sunshine, creep up my spine and across my forehead, as the panic starts to pass.

Priscilla straightens in her seat and picks up a chip. She holds one out to me. I take it and nibble the tip of it off.

'Look, he isn't in prison,' says Priscilla, chewing slowly. 'At least he wasn't eleven weeks ago. Matt's birthday. He called him again. And this time, he got the number.'

My heart stops. Eleven weeks ago. That's close. So close. And for a moment, it's like only time is separating us; like this is a time machine movie and I've been missing him by years, and now we're getting closer – now, we are only weeks apart.

'Wow,' is all I manage, breathlessly.

'Sherlock reincarnated.'

I open my mouth to reply as she holds out another chip. 'Yes, I know he wasn't fucking real.'

Priscilla and I laugh – a hysterical burst; a release of adrenaline leftover from the unbearable electric panic that just raged beneath my skin. Priscilla pulls out her phone and holds it between us, the screen pointing towards her chest.

'I've got the number.'

'Really?'

Priscilla grins now. 'Liz, it's a local Hertford number.'

'*What?*'

'And I Googled it – I was going to wait until I saw you and do it together but—'

I can't wait. I snatch the phone from Priscilla's hand. She waits, watching me with wide eyes. But I am frozen, staring at the address on the screen, and the photo on the listing Google is giving me – the angular fifties building, metal framed windows; windows that look like they might rattle if there was a slight tremor, just like those on a rickety old bus.

It's The Grove. Roman was calling from The Grove.

Chapter Thirteen

3rd June 2004

'Remember, guys, this Friday it's Darren's last day at the centre, so we'll be having a special lunch. Just some nibbles, some—'

'Vodka?' grins a girl with a shock of white-blonde hair, adjusting the collar of her shirt which is buttoned to the neck. She sits like Nathan does, bent over, tartan-trousered legs open, elbows resting on her knees, her hands together in the middle.

'No, Jade,' says Ramesh with an amused eye roll. 'I'm afraid you'll have to cope with Dr Pepper and some lemonade.'

'Shame,' Jade smirks. 'Could do with getting pissed.'

Everyone in the circle laughs. So does the guy from earlier, the one that was hunched over the railings, watching, smoking, when I was crying outside with Dad. He stands leaning against the pastel blue wall now, arms folded, hair falling over his eyes. He's really tall. Six foot two, maybe three. His legs are super long. He looks at least nineteen. A youth worker, probably. My social worker said they have lots of volunteers.

'Groups are up on the wall,' carries on Ramesh, arm outstretched. 'Group A have art with Cassie, Group B are with me. Thought we'd do some reading this morning. And as usual, guys, there will be one-on-ones all day. Times, again, are on the wall.'

A couple of the kids nod. The rest don't react, just listen. There must be about twenty of us. Nobody seems to be as nervous as me, but then some have barely lifted their gaze from the floor.

'Matty and Martine are going to be around all day in the break room so you know where to find them if you need them—' Ramesh stops, as someone utters something I don't catch. I just hear the end of it – something that sounds like 'this is bullshit' from a large boy with ginger freckles opposite me. He eyes me for a second from hooded lids, from my feet up to my face. I want to be at home. I want to be with Hubble. I want to run away.

'Ah, Sammy, come on guy,' sighs Ramesh, hands clapping together, 'we can do better than that this morning, can't we? It's a nice day, the sun's shining . . .'

'Yeah, well, I like it when it's pissing down,' says Sammy, sarcastically.

'You're only saying that now because you cut off all those gorgeous locks you had,' says Ramesh, smiling. 'I remember the panic before, nicking all our brollies, *oh sir, oh sir, it'll ruin me gel.*'

Some of the kids laugh. Sammy tries not to join in but smiles down at his lap, his cheeks blotching pink. I don't laugh. I can't. My eyes are fixed on the cowl-like brown carpet, and I'm trying to concentrate on keeping my heart beating. I'm trying not to lose it, to not jump up and cry, 'I can't do this,' before running out of this place. Running and not stopping until I'm miles from anywhere. Because I don't know how this place will help the way my school say it will. I don't know how anything will.

'OK then, guys,' Ramesh says, loudly, clasping his hands together, 'let's have a good morning, yeah?' He turns, shoving his hands into his jeans, as the group begins to disperse, everyone knowing exactly where they're going and what the procedure is, and he spots me, here, shrinking on the chair.

'Ah, um . . .' Ramesh scans the room quickly, looking over his shoulder. 'Hey, *Mike*, my man with the cracking locks.' He puts his hand on the shoulder of a boy with long blond hair and a perfect centre parting who is rushing purposefully across the room, rucksack over his shoulder. He freezes, eyes wide with irritation. He has deep set dark eyes and a big nose. A strong nose, that's what Priscilla would call it, if she were here. And god, I wish she was. So much, that it hurts me, like a fist squeezing my heart. I'm really scared. I'm scared without her, without a single face I recognise. I wonder what she's doing right now, if she's missing me in our maths lesson. I wonder if any of the other kids have noticed, if they're talking about me, if they're laughing that I'm here, at a school for weird kids, for 'scummy kids' as Auntie Shall said to Dad last night. I wonder if Priscilla will get used to me not going to school. OK, my attendance has been rubbish lately, but she might make new friends and forget all about me now I'm here all the time. I doubt I'll be hard to forget. She's probably relieved to be without me; cramping her style, embarrassing her . . .

'This here is Lizzie,' Ramesh continues, turning to me, as I stand from the chair. 'She's new. Do you think you could show her to the wall, show her where to go, tell her all the tricks of the trade—'

'I can't,' says Mike, giving me a weak smile, that's hardly there at all. 'Gotta go with my social worker and Martine—'

'Ah, course!' says Ramesh. 'You're off to school today, aren't you?'

Michael gives a nod and a heavy shrug. 'Yeah.'

'Sorry, mate. Go on, you carry on.'

Ramesh turns to me, as Mike trudges off, the chain on his baggy jeans jingling like shackles. 'Left my brain at home,' he smiles, gently. 'OK there, Lizzie?'

I nod. I lie. I feel sick to my stomach.

'Right, well I was gonna pair you up, but it seems you'll just have to tag along with me, I'm afraid. You're in my set first, so—'

'I'll do it. Well. If you want someone with *cracking locks*.' It's the guy. The tall, smoking guy from outside. The one with the blue eyes. The one with the weird boots and scruffy hair. He stands about a metre away from us, shoulders square, bag over the left one, chest jutting out. 'If you want,' he says, smiling a little at Ramesh, and not looking at me. He has an accent. Northern. Manchester maybe.

'Brilliant, thanks, mate,' says Ramesh. 'So, this is Lizzie.'

The doorbell sounds at the entrance; a shrill bell-like chime. All three of us peer over our shoulders. A woman stands on the other side of the glass door with a black, leather bag and a beige mac with a belt at the waist.

'Ah.' Ramesh makes a start for the door. 'Show Lizzie the wall, the rooms, where she's got to go for lunch, the loos, that sort of thing. Think you're in the same set today, actually. Lizzie, we'll check in later, OK? Shout if you need anything at all . . .' Ramesh trails off as he sprints to the door, giving a quick wave to the woman through the glass. Then there is an awkward moment of fizzing, thick silence between me and the boy with the eyes. His hands are stuffed in the pockets of his black jeans, and he looks over his shoulder at Ramesh. He watches for longer than necessary. We both do, to delay speaking, I suppose. Then he turns to me and smiles. His lips are full and very pink for a boy. I find myself looking at them, unable to meet his eye, then I quickly look away.

'Do you wanna hang that up?' he says.

'Sorry?'

'Your jacket,' he nods. 'D'you wanna get rid of it? It's hot in here. There's a cloakroom.'

'Oh,' I swallow. 'OK.' I know there's a cloakroom. Ramesh showed me on the way to his office this morning, but I was shaking so much, I couldn't bear the thought of having it taken off me. It smelled of home. It smelled of the detergent Mum always used.

'I'll show you,' he says. 'It's by *the wall*, anyway.' He says 'the wall' as if the name is amusing and he grins as he says it. He jerks his head, hands still stuffed in his pockets. 'Over here.'

I bend to pick up my bag from the floor and I notice my hands are striped with deep red grooves from how tightly I have been holding the cord at the waist of my coat. I loop my bag over my shoulder, and the boy raises his eyebrows, as if to say 'ready?' and we start walking. Neither of us says anything as we cross the floor to 'the wall', and I wonder if he's regretting offering to help. He must be. I can't speak. I don't know what to say to him – to anyone here. I feel as though I have nothing in common with any of them, that they'll realise that soon enough, and I'll be lost here too. Just like I am at school. A broken brain in amongst a sea of functioning, normal ones.

'The wall,' says the boy, clearing his throat. We've reached the other side of the lobby. And it really is just that; a wall, papered with a huge sheet of green, bordered with a white strip of wavy corrugated card. It looks just like a school wall display. 'So, um, this is where we see where our groups are today, which classes, where to go and all that.' He pushes a finger onto a piece of paper pinned with red and blue drawing pins. He has a silver ring on. Just a plain thick silver band on his index finger.

'It's Lizzie yeah?'

'Yeah.'

'J.'

'Sorry?'

He smiles and taps the paper with 'Group B' written at the top.

'That's what's down here. Lizzie J. I dunno why, but they always put our surname's initial. As if there's three hundred of us and seventeen different Lizzies. I quite like it, though. Makes us sound like rappers.'

I smile. A proper smile, not just out of politeness.

'You're with me then,' he says, tapping a name on the paper, right below mine.

I lean forward to peer closer. 'Roman M,' I say, and he pulls his mouth into a tight line and nods once, like a bow.

'Yup. That's me. Lizzie J and Roman M, with Ramesh in the library.'

I nod.

'With the lead pipe.' He ducks his head as if he's telling me a secret. 'One I hope he chooses to smack me over the head with if it's 'how does this poem make you *feel*?' again.'

I make a sound in my throat. The beginning of a giggle, and he grins at me from under his hair. It's scruffy. Wild, brown waves that point in all different directions, like he's just got out of bed. He's handsome. Weird, Priscilla would say, eyeing his black boots and obscure T-shirt. But handsome.

'It's pretty simple,' he says, pulling a hand through his hair. 'We come in, we get stuck in whichever classroom our group's in . . .' I like the way he says stuck. *Stock*. 'And then if you have a meeting with The Mads, it goes on here.' He taps his finger on another piece of paper that says 'One-to-Ones'. 'That's when you'll go with one of the counsellors who are more nuts than we are and they do a shitload of nodding.' Then he stops and studies my face, pink is blushing his cheeks. 'Not saying that means— I mean, *I'm* nuts. That doesn't mean you are—'

'I am,' I say. 'I mean, I have to be, to be here, right? *Nuts*.'

Roman's face breaks into a wide smile. 'Then, great,' he laughs. 'We've got something in common.'

Roman shows me to the cloakroom next, and I hang my stuff up on a peg next to his.

'What're you searching for?' he asks as I rifle through my bag, my face pulsing with the fluster and shame of trying to find my pencil case. It's things like this that floor me these days. Tiny, pathetic things that swell and grow bigger in importance than they should ever be.

'Pens,' I wobble. 'I . . . I can't f-find my—'

'You don't need one,' he says calmly. 'They supply it all. You just need yourself. We're privileged here, Lizzie, don't you know.' I like how he says my name. I like that he makes me feel normal. *Warm.* Although my veins are still surging with nerves, my hands have stopped shaking and sweating, and I'm breathing a little easier now, walking beside Roman down a long, musty-smelling corridor. The Grove reminds me of a clinic, a school and a youth centre all rolled into one. The floors are carpeted with that horrible thin, scratchy brown carpet you find in classrooms, and the double doors, bookending the corridors, look as though they belong in a hospital. But then there are the huge, proud displays of artwork, and photos, and posters, on every wall. There's even graffiti and pool tables and drinks machines. But beneath the sombre quietness, are the distant sounds of ringing phones, muffled voices, typing, and printing. It's not a big place, but large enough to get a bit lost in if you don't know your way around. I barely remember my way back to the entrance.

'Landscapes. That's what you need to think about,' a Scottish, female voice speaks as we pass an open, wooden door. 'Is there a special place you can think of? A house, a place by the sea you've always wanted to be . . .'

Roman looks down at me. He really is so tall. 'Art,' he says as we pass. 'It's pretty cool. You draw whatever you want, paint, sketch, whatever. They've got some cool stuff in there. If you like art, anyway.'

I nod.

'You like it? Or you're just nodding?'

I laugh, nervously. 'I like it. I draw, paint sometimes . . .'

'That's cool,' says Roman. 'Which school do you go to?'

'Woodlands.'

'I know some kids there. Do you know Deano Williams?'

My heart sinks at the mention of that name. Deano Williams is a vile bully; the leader of a gang of brash, confident, good-looking wankers in my year. I don't know why it surprises me that someone like Roman knows him, but it does.

'Yeah,' I tell him. 'He's in my form.'

'Oh yeah? Yeah, he's a massive twat,' laughs Roman, shooting a look at me. 'A massive twat for a tiny little person with tiny little legs, and a tiny little charred soul. *Probably*.'

And at that, I burst out laughing. So does Roman, and when we get to the doorway of the library – which is really just a room with books in (but then to quote Roman, 'that's literally what all libraries are, right?') – we are both still laughing, cheeks taut and flushed.

'Ah. Delivered her back to us safely, I see,' says Ramesh, handing out books to rows of students, chattering amongst themselves.

'Course,' says Roman.

'Good. Come and take a seat.'

Roman holds out his arm in front of him. 'After you, Lizzie J.'

'Thanks . . . Roman M.'

Chapter Fourteen

'Good evening, The Grove House Day Service, Charlotte speaking, how can I help? Hello? Hello, is anyone there?'

I can't do it. I just can't bring myself to speak. If I ask for him, and she says no, there's nobody there called Roman, then what? Hopes dashed, another wild goose chase to another number, to another address where he *won't* be; my elusive, disappearing, was-he-ever-real friend? Because he's never there, is he? And surely fate, the universe, Buddha, whoever's in charge, isn't going to make it so easy, and so cruel, that he's been ten minutes away, where we used to be, all along. And if I ask for him, and she says yes, this Charlotte woman who keeps answering The Grove's phone, what then? 'Hi Roman, it's me, Lizzie, after twelve years. How the devil are you? Got your letter that you wrote over a decade ago when I was a mere child. Where did you go? Why did you up and leave? After all those months of saving up, of planning our escape, what happened? PS: are you a dangerous criminal now?'

No. I don't want the first time we speak to be on the phone. I want to see him. I want to know it's really him I've found, after all these years, by looking right at him, in his eyes. I've contemplated emailing Ramesh – he's still there. It says so on the website. But then, if Roman is there, at The Grove, working on the next desk or frozen in time, drawing cocks in Art Therapy, like some sort of psychological Benjamin Button, I don't want the first he knows about me trying to find him coming from an email, and from someone else. And if he is just around the corner, then why hasn't he tried to find me? I would be so easy to find. Embarrassingly so. I haven't moved from the same town I was born in. I shop at the same shops. Order food from the same Chinese place. I haven't moved a muscle in twelve years. Why hasn't he found me? Because he's never wanted to? But then, why the letter? These are the sort of circles my brain has been running in; round and round until I'm dizzy. Priscilla says I'm scared. Maybe she's right. Maybe I've finally stopped to digest all this, and I *am* scared, and who can blame me for not wanting to step back in time to a year where everything fell apart?

The shrill, bleep of my flat buzzer blasts through my thoughts. I freeze under the heavy blanket on the sofa. It's a Tuesday evening at seven. I don't ever get guests, certainly not ones that don't call or text, warning me first, anyway.

Buzz. Buzz.

I pad over to the phone by the front door. The blanket draped around my shoulders drags along the carpet. 'Hello?'

'Lizzie, it's me. Can I come in?'

My shoulders sag with relief. I hold down the button to unlock the heavy entrance door below and unlatch and open my front door. I stand and listen as her clip-clopping heels climb the two flights of stairs. She's grinning as she gets to the top of the steps. Then her face drops.

'Oh dear,' she says. 'You've not got another cold virus, have you?'

'Hi, Mum. And no, I haven't—'

'Did you take those B vits I gave you? I had John-George start taking them . . . you know, the new instructor I hired at the centre? Well, he reckons his liver has *regenerated*. All thanks to B vitamins. His doctor was bloody flabbergasted.'

'I'm fine.'

Mum takes me in her arms. She smells incredible, and her hair is blow-dried to within an inch of its life. 'Of course you are, darling. Shall we put the kettle on?'

Mum glides around the kitchen as if it's an ice rink and she's a gifted skater, and within minutes, she has filled the dishwasher and made two cups of tea – hers, lemon green tea, and mine, strong, with milk, and probably just the one sugar hoping I won't notice the lack of the second.

'It is OK, me dropping in like this, isn't it, sweetheart?' Mum holds the tiny paper square of her teabag in her fingers and lifts and dips a few times. She has carried a small box of lemon green tea bags in her handbag for as long as I can remember – back when green tea had to be ordered from a mail-order catalogue. 'I was at a training thingy in Ware – a *moxibustion* course – and I had to drop some bits in to Nate and Katie, and I was sitting in that house, remembering the way you'd toddle about the place, thinking *oh, I miss my baby. How is she? Why hasn't she called me?*' She cocks her head to one side and raises an eyebrow.

I shrug, bringing my mug to my lips. 'I did try calling you back on Monday, on the train home.'

'Did you?'

'Clark said you were teaching a yoga class and he'd get you to call me back but—'

Mum fans her hand and shakes her head. 'Oh, that's as good as leaving a message with the toilet brush, Lizzie.'

'I know, but if you'd actually *text*—'

'It's bad for you,' she says, manicured, ringed fingers, enveloping the mug at her lap. 'I don't want to read bloody messages from you, I want to hear your voice, and better than that I want to see you.'

I look down at my lap. 'Sorry.'

Mum pauses, her lips lifting into a smile. 'I just miss you, darling, that's all.'

'And I miss you.'

Mum then snuggles back on the sofa – lean legs bent underneath her, the edge of my blanket over her feet – and talks non-stop about the news, her holiday to Sri Lanka in December, how banana facials will 'reclaim' my skin as if it's an old sideboard abandoned in an M&S car park, and how her neighbour's daughter went to Australia and came back with a man named Garth who is 'very handsome, despite the dreadlocks and the occasional questionable odour' and who makes the most 'darling' carvings out of scrap wood.

'Australian men are very free-spirited. Generous lovers, too,' Mum says now, as I try to hook out a fallen custard cream from my mug. 'Have you ever considered going to Oz, one day, darling? You know, when you eventually *do* travel.'

I cough a laugh. 'Whenever that'll be.'

Mum smiles. 'It can be whenever you want it to be,' she says. 'I've always said, if it's the money, I will happily loan you—'

'It's not the money.'

Mum watches me, and after a beat, reaches down to her handbag and pulls out a large bulky envelope. 'Here,' she says. 'From Katie.'

'What is it?' I take the heavy envelope from Mum's hand. It bows with the weight of it.

Mum raises her mug to her lips, watching as I pull out a thick wodge of papers. The creamy, clean smell of glossy paper hits me.

'She said she did a bit of research,' says Mum, excitedly. 'That one – the blue brochure – they have an open day next week. She's noted down the times, look. On that Post-it.'

Three of them. Three thick, shiny college prospectuses – snapshots of young, excited-by-life faces on the covers, each with neon-coloured sticky tags, bookmarking pages inside. I stare down at them in my hands. Eventually, I pick up the first one and flick to the place marked by a pink sticky bookmark. 'Access to Higher Education, Art and Design' is highlighted in yellow. There's a photo of a young woman with glasses and a concentrated, happy gaze on her face, paintbrush to canvas, beside a description of the course. I remember envisaging myself as a girl like that. Getting signed off from The Grove, finishing my GCSEs at school with the rest of the kids, and going to a place where I could draw, paint, make things, bring ideas to life every day, blend in with everyone else. I'd look like that girl, I thought. I'd be immersed and relaxed, my brain full of nothing but ideas and excitement for what was ahead of me. No fear. No crippling sadness. Just hope, and plans of where Roman and I would go when I'd finished; when the plant pot was brimming with money we'd saved from Roman's dog-walking and the over-generous, guilt-money Mum would chuck me when we saw her. All the places we'd see, when Roman had passed his driving test. Who we'd turn out to be once we were free of everything. Once we were better. Once we were old enough not to be prised apart, like we were sometimes, banned from seeing one another, frowned upon, like defects. The reality, of course, was nothing like that. I had barely drawn a single picture before it all ended, and I had quit. It was as if a curtain fell. Hubble died. I broke in half. Then Roman left. Nothing mattered after that.

I shut the cover and move the books to the coffee table.

'I didn't realise,' Mum says quietly, after a moment, 'that you were thinking about studying.'

'I wasn't,' I say. 'I'm not.'

'No? Katie said you talked about—'

'*She* did,' I say, swallowing tea. 'Not me.'

Mum breathes in. 'She's only looking out for you, Lizzie. She loves you. She knows how much you're wasted in that office job and how talented—'

'Well, it's none of her business,' I cut in. 'It's none of anyone's, Mum. It's my life. I'm not asking anyone else to live it, am I?' Mum's eyes narrow sadly, and instantly, I regret saying those words. I don't mean it, of course I don't. Katie is one of the most important people in my life. She's excited, that for the first time in god knows how long, I might be stepping out of my tiny bubble, towards things that have been waiting for me all along. 'Sorry,' I say. 'Sorry, Mum. It's just . . . I don't know where I am right now. Plus, I told her it was too late for me to do anything like that.'

'Oh, Lizzie,' Mum laughs. 'You aren't about to say that to *me* of all people surely.' Her hand flies in the air, as if swatting away a fly. '*Me*, your mother, who went to college at forty to learn how to be a personal trainer, and again at forty-two to become a yoga instructor, and then again at forty-five for business studies, and *again* . . . well, just now, actually, to study sodding moxibustion of all things. I'm fifty-six, Lizzie. Fifty-fucking-six.'

I look at her and snort into laughter.

'Bloody twenty-eight, and it's *too* late,' she mutters. 'If it's too late for you, then god only knows what it is for the likes of me.'

I run my finger around the handle of my mug in my lap. 'But you've always known what you wanted to do, Mum,' I say. 'You never stopped wanting it. For as long as I can remember, you loved exercise, and helping people, and . . . avocados.'

Mum laughs and cocks her head to one side.

'I remember you directing an aerobics class in the lounge once for other mums, and I must've only been about five. You were never going to do anything else.' I look over at the brochures stacked up on the table. 'Me? I've never really wanted something like that.'

Mum pulls her mouth into a tight line. 'Yes, you have,' she says. 'Did you forget all those hours you'd sit with Mimi, drawing those fabulous little people you were so good at, telling me how you'd be just like her one day, drawing, and showing people how it was *just putting lines in the right places.*' Mum shakes her head. 'Your dad and I couldn't even hold a pencil, yet you . . . you just could. Thank god for your step-nan really, or you'd have never got half the things you got for your birthdays, we were clueless. Mimi sorted that. Bought most of the art shop on Galley Road. And you loved it.' Mum stops, lips pressing together. 'Do you remember the blueprint you drew? Of your future art studio.'

Mum smiles and I feel my cheeks pulse with heat. 'I was ten.'

'So?' Mum sniffs and gestures towards the coffee table. 'I remember you being sixteen, too. The day you got onto that course. You were the happiest I think I've ever seen you.'

I can't look at Mum now. It's the mention of Mimi. It's the mention of being sixteen, and that day I blew open the door to what felt like my future, when I got into college. When I started.

'I remember,' I say, but the words get caught in my throat and are barely there.

'And I know you still draw. We get the cards every birthday and Christmas and they are just . . .' Mum doesn't finish her sentence, but instead holds her hand at her chest and closes her eyes for a moment. 'Sometimes, we just get stuck,' she says, gently. 'I should know. I was before your dad decided to

– well, it gave me a wake-up call, that's all. Made me realise we get one life, and it's nobody else's responsibility but ours, regardless of what we've had to deal with.'

I nod, still looking down at my lap.

'I'm not telling you what to do, darling,' Mum says, her eyes fixed on the brochures again. 'But . . . never be too afraid to live the way you actually want to. In my experience, it's never as frightening as you think it'll be, and nobody really gives a toss about what you're doing as much as you think they do.' Mum gestures over to the brochures. 'No harm in taking a look some time, is there? Katie was good enough to get them for you.'

I look up at her. 'No,' I say. 'There isn't. I'll take a look.' And I mean it, I think. The irritation that I felt when I first pulled them from the envelope, dissolved a little as Mum spoke, and now there is nothing but that tiny spark flickering in my belly, again.

'Good,' says Mum.

'This doesn't mean I'm going to Australia, though,' I tell her, over my mug. 'And to be honest, if Garth's sculpting brother is out there waiting for me with his *questionable smells*, then I am happy to rule it out for ever.'

Mum bursts out laughing and puts her hand on my leg. 'Oh, darling, you do make me laugh. You're so like me.'

Mum and I watch soaps together with more tea and slices of toast and Marmite, like we used to, and despite myself I feel safe beside her; content for the first time in a while. When Mum first left us – me, Nathan, and Dad; her family – something was lost between us. She was my mum. The only woman in the world I was supposed to trust, wholeheartedly, a person who was meant to love me in a way no other person ever could, protect me – and she left me. Like I was part of the furniture of an old house she'd grown out of. Like it was no big deal, like it was *expected,* after what Dad did. She called every day, of course, voice wobbling, asking us to live with her and Clark, her new boyfriend, as if it was just a case of packing a bag and starting again, but I couldn't leave Dad. I couldn't leave Nathan, or the house I'd known since I was six. And she didn't deserve me – us. That's how I felt. That pull in my stomach towards her died when she walked out that Sunday afternoon, as I sat at the kitchen table, alone, her cup still warm from the last tea she drank with me in that house. I muted it. Pulled it from the root. I just haven't realised it's been trying, over the years, like a flower through a crack in the concrete, to grow again. To bloom. Tonight, it has. I guess, because I let her in. I let her be Mum to me again, for just a moment.

Mum leaves at half past eight. She stands in the open doorway, the cream tartan shawl she always brings out at the whiff of autumn slung over her shoulders, handbag hanging in the crook of her arm.

'We've been invited, by the way,' she says, 'Clark and I. To Olivia's wedding.'

'Wh— really?'

Mum nods, amused. 'Can't actually believe ol' *Shall* has allowed it. But then me and Livvy often chat on Facebook. I am her auntie. Or *was,* for thirteen years.'

'I can't believe it either,' I blink. 'Are you going to—'

'God, no. I can't be in the same building as your father.'

My heart sinks as I stand there looking out of my front door, a draught circling my ankles. I don't know why. It's not like I'm surprised. I suppose it would just be nice to have Mum there, to see me in my bridesmaid dress, to spend the day with all of us under the same roof, for once. To have Mum not act like it was just hours and not over thirteen years ago that she checked the savings account outside Morrisons and came flying home in a hysterical rage.

'Anyway, remember what I said,' says Mum, pulling her shawl closer at the chest and shuddering. 'Don't take any crap from this whole bridesmaid thing. They're lucky you even agreed again after Shall's bloody vow circus. Honestly, that woman has no right getting on her high horse—'

'Mum.'

Mum, fussing with a clump of tassels that are caught on the zip of her bag, looks up. 'Yes, darling?'

'You remember Roman, don't you?'

And I don't know why I tell her. It just feels right that I do.

Mum's face doesn't flicker. She doesn't look down, or away, the way Dad does when I bring him up, or the way Olivia and Auntie Shall do. Mum just smiles. 'Of course. Why?'

I gaze down at the brown, scratchy doormat beneath my feet. 'I'm trying to find him.'

Mum's sandy eyebrows lift. 'Really?'

I nod again. I don't tell her about the letter. I don't say anything else, and for a moment, there is silence between us, until Mum asks, 'Have you got very far?'

'I've been round the houses a bit, but I think I know where he might be now.'

Mum's eyes soften. 'That's wonderful, darling. He was . . . he was very important to you. I know I wasn't really around then and—' Mum stops, swallowing. 'But he kept you going. It was just a shame it ended like it did, but he had a lot going on, didn't he? I remember Nathan telling me about that mother of his.' Mum grimaces and gives a shake of the head. 'Well, keep me posted, won't you? I mean that.'

'Course.'

Mum cuddles me and steps backwards.

'Can't wait to hear what he's like now, what he's doing, how he *looks*.' She stops at the top of the steps and gives a little wink over her shoulder. 'I love a romance.'

'It's not a romance,' I laugh, but Mum isn't listening. She's starting down the stairs with a wave and a blow of a kiss. I say goodbye, and start to close the door, but she stops on the steps. I freeze. 'And remember,' she whispers, through the banister, 'next time Auntie Shall gets all high and mighty and Mrs *Moral Bloody High Ground* with you, remember that she once posed in knickers and suspenders for *Reader's Wives* in the eighties and made it very, very clear she liked it up the . . . well. *Aris.*'

I open my mouth. No words come out. Mum raises her eyebrows and says, 'Bye, darling. Now close the door. There's a terrible draught.'

This is your booking confirmation for your appointment on 17 OCTOBER 2017 at 17.45, with STEPHANIE AKENZUA in Careers Advisory. Thank you for choosing Borough of Camden College.

Chapter Fifteen

28th October 2004

'I stay in here a lot.'

'Overnight?'

'Yeah,' says Roman. 'Not so much in the winter. It gets so cold that you practically die.'

'Does your mum know?'

Roman laughs and slumps down on the narrow, brown flock sofa bordering the rickety caravan walls. 'No. Yes. Who the hell knows? Either way she doesn't care. Even if I am in the front garden, stealing the electricity through the garage.'

I tell Roman I like it – Sea Fog – this tiny metal caravan anchored to his driveway, and he says he's glad, and he's only sorry it doesn't have a driver car at the front like a motor-home so he could drive us to the sea. We spend the rest of day inside it, playing music through Roman's laptop, and eating cereal and bowls of crisps, and tea made from water he boiled on a portable camping hob in a saucepan that looks two hundred years old. As he boils and stirs, I watch him, loping about the kitchen, too tall for such a tiny space, and imagine we are travelling across the country, and have just pulled up at some picturesque roadside in Cornwall, with nothing but sand dunes and cliffs and turquoise seas around us. I imagine us as a couple. I imagine us as friends, on an adventure. I don't know what feels better.

'I think something's going on with Priscilla and Ethan Sykes,' I tell Roman as he sits beside me holding two small mugs, covered in orange seventies flowers, full of steaming tea. He hands me one. Rain batters the caravan, and from inside Sea Fog, it sounds like we are being soaked by waves. 'She's acting weird with me. Has he said anything to you?'

Roman shrugs and shakes his head. 'Saw him Saturday. He just said he likes her.'

'As a mate or . . .'

Roman laughs, stretching his arm along the back of the sofa. 'More. *Obviously*.'

'Why obviously?' I ask, irritated. 'What, he *must* fancy her 'cause he's a boy, she's a girl and they hang out all the time?'

'Like us?' Roman asks, small smile on his face, his eyes not drifting from mine. I look at him, waiting for him to laugh. He doesn't. I look away.

'I- I just . . .' I stutter. 'I wish she wouldn't go there, that's all.'

Roman sips and looks down into his mug. 'Why?'

'Why?' I look up at him then, my brow wrinkled. I can't help it. 'The guy's a . . . he's a dickhead, Roman. He terrorised our teachers at Woodlands, and he's always knocking about with that big gang, and they're just . . . *wrong'uns*. Hubble says he sees them most nights from his bedroom window in the park and they're always causing trouble—'

'So, I'm a wrong'un?' Roman slowly looks up at me. His fingers with the nails painted blue through fingerless gloves, hold the mug inches from his lips.

'No. You're not in his gang,' I say. 'Are you?'

Roman brings a shoulder up quickly. 'But I hang about with him sometimes.'

I look at him. 'And I wish you wouldn't.'

'What, you want me to stay home instead?' Roman laughs tightly, straightening, his eyes flashing. 'Eat my home-cooked dinner, sit on the sofa with Mum watching the telly, help her with the dishes, tell her all about my *awesome* day, like she gives a toss?'

'I- I don't mean—'

'No, course you don't,' he snaps. 'Nobody ever does.'

I freeze. I feel like I'm going to cry. 'Ro,' I start, my voice tiny. 'I'm sorry, I didn't mean it like that, you know I understand. I just . . . I . . .'

'No.' Roman takes a deep breath, eyes closed. He leans in, breathing out noisily through his nose, touching my arm. 'No, I'm sorry, J. I didn't mean to snap at you. I would never mean to, I— he's a mate, Lizzie. He texts, he calls, he cares about what I'm doing, and OK, if I'm clearing up my mum's puke and he calls and invites me over the park then, yeah. I'm gonna go.'

I stare at him, but eventually I nod. Because he's right. Where's safer? Where's less lonely? In a house with his drunken mother, clearing up her mess, like a glorified carer, or at the park with a gang of boys, up to no good, who see him as one of them? A regular seventeen-year-old boy.

'I'm sorry,' he says again. 'You didn't deserve that.'

'You don't have to explain anything. I get it.' I put my hand on his. He bows, rests his lips against the skin of my knuckles. Goosebumps prickle my arms, like spitting rain drops.

'I don't deserve someone like you,' he whispers, breath hot against my hand.

'Don't talk daft.'

He looks up at me. 'I don't, J. Not even close.'

We say nothing else for a while. We just drink tea, listening to the rain, and the rumble of cars that go by, and I steal looks at him, and try to remember what life was like, back in June, before I met him, before I knew he even existed. I can't. Life before Roman seems clouded.

The rain slows, the sun creeps out from the clouds, and we finish our tea. That's when Roman sits up, eyes fixed on the misty window. It's his mum, giggling up the path with a man who has his arms around her waist, his lips on her neck. Roman stares at the floor. It's the same guy we saw last week. The one Roman despises.

I take our mugs to the kitchen, just for something to do while the air is this thick, this awkward. I rinse them with an old Coke bottle full of water.

'Do you ever just think that your life is one big mistake?' says Roman, cutting through the silence. 'That . . . you're not actually meant to be *here*, but somewhere else?'

I look up from the kitchen counter – mugs wet in my hands. His eyes stare forward, his back straight against the back of the sofa.

'Your grandad, Hubble. He said something last week when I was waiting for you on the drive,' Roman utters. 'About chances you don't take, paths that you end up on, because you said yes to this, no to that, and how everything can change – your whole *life* can change – just by choosing a different option.' Roman swallows. 'And I've been thinking about what *that* Roman's doing. The Roman whose mam chose not to drink, not to chuck her life away.'

I don't move, eyes fixed on him.

'And I reckon that somewhere in the universe, in some alternative life, *that* Roman is part of a massive, big family. Loads of brothers and sisters.' Roman smiles, a tiny glimmer of one, his eyes not moving from the ground. It's as if he can see it, right there, playing as if on a screen. 'And he's happy and he's at college with a buff-as-fuck girlfriend and a mum and dad that go 'round Sainsbury's with a trolley and eat dinner at a table, and go to Homebase at the weekend or something.' Roman laughs, giving a shake of his head. 'And *that* Roman drags his feet, moaning because he's bored, 'cause he just wants to be at home, or with his friends, *real* friends, that go to the cinema and don't knock about in parks. 'Cause his mam and dad would never allow that. They'd be too worried about him doing that.'

I can't speak. I don't know what to say. He looks smaller, somehow, in this moment. Vulnerable. Child-like. I put the mugs down and cross the floor to sit beside him on the sofa. As I sit down, close to him, hip to hip, he puts his arm around me and pulls me to his chest. I close my eyes to stop the tears. Because it's such a lovely idea. *That* Roman is such a lovely idea – the Roman I know, but truly happy, and in a life he deserves. And now I can't stop thinking about the other me – the other Lizzie, at school like all the other kids, coming home to homework, instead of Dad in bed, cowering and crying; instead of Mum speeding away from the drive, car bursting with new suitcases, the tags still attached, leaving the remnants of her family along with the bin bags of old rubbish she doesn't want anymore. I think about my brain not being against me. I think of happy, safe, contented Lizzie, where nothing – absolutely nothing – is falling apart.

Roman sighs, shakily. There's a long pause, and we listen for a moment, to the fading voices and trudging footsteps of passers-by, to cars, and the wind that's picking up. Roman rubs my arm, his hand smooth and warm, and rests his chin on the top of my head, his breath against my scalp. We talk about our other lives, playing out right this second; about family holidays, and summer barbecues, huge Christmas trees and Christmas dinner tables so long, that you need to bring in the garden tables and chairs to fit everyone in. We talk about our futures, playing out somewhere in time and space. I talk about paying McFly to play secret concerts for me, about trips to blustery beaches, for fudge and chips in paper that sticks to the soggy ones, about drawing cartoon strips and greetings cards in a studio at the bottom of my garden, while a hot husband that looks very much like Christian Slater brings me bacon sandwiches and love notes written on napkins. Roman talks about bonfires, and lines of bookshelves with a ladder, and shotgun midnight trips to the beach for ice cream in waffle cones. He talks about freedom, and France, and having a dog – 'someone to love him in all of his ugliness,' he says, and I want to tell him that I already do.

'Maybe,' says Roman, softly, lips against my hair, 'one day we'll work out how to jump to that place,' he says. 'Visit.'

'That sounds nice,' I mutter, my cheek against his chest. 'Do you reckon we still meet? In that other place; the life where you go around Sainsbury's with a trolley and have a *buff* girlfriend?'

Roman laughs, his arm squeezing me tighter to him. 'Are you joking?' I can't see him, but his voice is thick, and I'm sure there are tears on his cheeks. 'Try to stop us.'

I nuzzle closer. The sun outside dims like a dying bulb, and winds tremble the caravan. But we're safe here. Safe, from it all, in our tiny metal bubble.

'Whatever happens,' whispers Roman, 'wherever we end up, when we're older and free from all this . . . I know that somewhere out there, there we'll be.'

'In Sea Fog,' I say.

'Far away,' says Roman. 'Somewhere where there're no people, and it's just sea for miles and miles. *And* a wraparound porch.'

'And your wood-burning stove.'

Roman laughs. 'And my wood-burning stove. I promise you. If I can get there, that's where I'll be.'

'Deal. Meet you there.'

Chapter Sixteen

The Grove is quiet, save for the odd distant ringing phone, which makes it so much easier to hear my own heart, thumping in my ears. This feels unreal. Like I've woken in a dream. It's barely changed. The straight-backed, itchy chairs still sit in a u-shape as you walk in the door to the lobby, the area where we would squish and bunch in the mornings, some of us still with our coats and bags on, as Ramesh or Cassie took the register. In the first week I sat as far from anyone as I could, sitting on edges, or choosing to stand, my hands wet with sweat, but after that, I always sat beside Roman, our legs becoming more and more squashed together as the weeks sped on, him playing with the keyring dangling from my bag, and me, sneaking looks at the perfect inverted arc of his nose, trying to work out if I fancied him or just adored him, like I did Priscilla. Roman and The Grove were the only constants in my life, back then. I may have woken every morning to a silent house and an empty fridge, Dad still in bed where he'd likely stay until lunchtime, and panic creeping in like smoke, but as I sat alone in the dingy, messy living room, watching the minutes tick until eight o'clock, a part of me was hopeful. Because I knew it'd be waiting for me – The Grove, unremarkable but safe. Roman, standing at the entrance to the park, cigarette burning, clothes mismatched, face breaking into a smile as he saw me. Happy I was here, to see another morning.

I stand, feet still on the ground now, and take in the room – a room I know every inch of. Why here? Was he visiting? Does he work here now, mere minutes from my flat? You hear of that, don't you? People estranged from their parents or siblings or friends, people searching for missing loved ones desperately, who end up discovering they have been living just minutes away, probably passing each other, missing one another by seconds, year after year, but not seeing them because you're not looking; you're not tuned in this close to home. You never expect them to be living in the world right in front of your eyes.

Footsteps. Heels on stark, thin carpet – the same carpet, brown like a monk's cowl – getting closer. It was Charlotte who buzzed me in – the same voice I kept hanging up on yesterday. She was friendly, but hesitant when I told her I was hoping to talk to Ramesh, an old friend. But then I don't suppose it's very often she gets a knock from someone who isn't a frazzled parent or social worker.

The clopping footsteps get closer, and within seconds, a woman rounds the corner; pretty, mixed race, with a warm smile and square black-rimmed glasses.

'Hello, there,' she says, and holds out her hand. I shake it. My palms are icy with nerves. 'You're looking to talk to Ramesh?'

I nod. 'Yes please, if that's possible.'

'Sure. He's on a call at the moment,' the woman says, 'but you can come and wait outside his office. I'm Charlotte.'

I nod again, stiffly. 'Thanks.'

Charlotte gestures for me to follow her with a turn of her head, and she begins walking but my feet won't move. I cannot walk down the corridor knowing I could walk right into him, like I used to. If he's here, if he works here, I need to know now so I can ask for him and not just spring up in front of him.

'Excuse me, does Roman work here?' The words come out loud and rushed.

Charlotte stops. 'Sorry?'

'Roman,' I say. 'Do you have a man here, named Roman?'

Charlotte shakes her head. 'I'm afraid he's not around now.'

'But he was?'

Charlotte nods again and looks quickly at a dangly silver watch at her wrist. 'He did a workshop. Think he was only here a week, maybe two. Couple of months back?' Charlotte eyes me, a flash of worry passing over her face. I realise my lips are parted in a slight gawp, my eyes wide. 'Is he a . . . friend of yours?'

I don't respond other than something that tries to be a nod.

'Ramesh should be finished soon. Come and take a seat.'

The familiar smells, the sounds of footsteps that don't echo, of voices behind closed doors, make my legs wobble. Then I hear him. Ramesh. Muffled, but voice exactly the same as I remember it. Charlotte seats me at the end of the corridor on a black padded chair outside Ramesh's office, a room we once used for one-to-ones. He didn't really have an office when we were here. He shared the tiny reception admin office with Cassie and Ian, the caretaker-stroke-handyman who would answer the phones when they were both in classes, shovel hands mucky from working in the gardens or decorating. We never had a Charlotte, who sits behind a white modern desk inside a tiny room opposite Ramesh's and has bookshelves and a computer with a large screen, with the door pushed to. The Grove looks cleaner, shinier. But smaller.

I listen to Ramesh chatting behind the closed office door, and look up, when at the end of the corridor, a girl in high-waisted jeans and a cropped white T-shirt, rushes to a class-room a few doors down. I catch the tail-end of someone talking about *Othello* as she opens then closes the door behind her. I am there. I am hurtling backwards to those classrooms, those therapy rooms with Roman, with Ramesh, as if on a rollercoaster. I feel as though every cell of my body is made of electricity, banging and fizzing as they collide under my skin. I remember everything so clearly. The day I started. The penises Roman painted in art. The lunches on benches, the syrupy smell of Dr Pepper and Wispa bars. The rain, the blistering sun, the laughter, and the tears that told the stories – so many of them, told to the empty space in that loose, scatter of a circle in group therapy. The time Jade and I planted potatoes in the vegetable patch and sang Abba songs, before she punched Mitchell G in the face for calling her a 'fuckin' she-male'. (She broke his nose. He cried.) The day we made bread, the day a dance teacher came in and none of us wanted to do it, but by three o'clock, were all dancing a messy routine to Destiny's Child with silver canes, Roman and the two Toms in feather boas and trilbies. The days of sudden empty chairs, of leaving lunches. The day Cassie told me Roman was in hospital and I cried so much, I was sick in the staff loo. The day I left to go back to school and had to say goodbye . . .

The door opens beside me, in one swoop. I jump, look up. And it's him. It's Ramesh. The man who helped me build everything, slowly, back together again, painstakingly, one brick at a time. He stands, staring at me. When I smile, his face slowly explodes into a grin.

'Oh my god. *Lizzie!* Lizzie James!'

I rise to my feet quickly, and as I do, I put my arms around him. It's involuntary, like seeing an old friend, and I suppose that's because it is; he was once one of my only friends. He envelops me in a tight cuddle, and I remember the last and only other time he did this – the day Roman disappeared.

He stands back, bringing his hand to his open mouth.

'I- I mean, I . . .' He laughs again. 'I really am speechless here.'

'You look the same,' I tell him. 'And I am *loving* the whole silver fox thing.'

I'm trying to keep my composure, keep up the smiling, with-it, 'I'm better now' Lizzie James facade. But every inch of me is trembling, inside and out.

Ramesh holds open his arms. 'Come in,' he says. 'Sit down. Talk to me, tell me everything.' I step through to the old therapy room – Ramesh's office – the walls within which I used to unravel. He calls through to Charlotte to bring in some tea and water and closes the door.

'Gosh,' he grins. 'Lizzie James. I've been waiting for this.'

There is silence between Ramesh and me. After the initial pleasantries are done – the 'so, how've you been's and the 'what have you been doing with yourself's, and after we've reached forward to the tray of mugs and settled back into our seats, sipping our tea, there is silence. Ramesh looks at me over the rim of his mug.

I don't know where to begin. I have so much to ask, so much to say, but it's like when something is too full. It gets jammed. My mind has no idea where to start. Everything from twelve years ago, the letter, Edgar Fields, him turning up – supposedly – to Hubble's funeral but never actually showing, the 'form', all I have learned, *everything* just sits in one giant mass in my mind.

Ramesh leans forward, putting his mug on the desk, and rests his wrists on the counter, his fingers knitting together. He has a lovely face. Warm eyes and a warm smile, and skin that looks impossibly young when he is clean-shaven. But he must be at least forty-one or forty-two now. I vaguely remember a thirtieth birthday when we were at The Grove.

'I'd ask what brought you here,' he says, 'but I think I know.'

'Do you?'

He smiles, but it doesn't meet his eyes. 'Roman.'

I nod. I wait for him to say something else but he doesn't. 'I got a letter from him.'

Ramesh's dark eyebrows raise, and his eyes brighten. 'So, he finally reached out?'

'It was from twelve years ago. Dated the day he disappeared.'

I slide the letter out of my handbag and push it across the table towards him. Ramesh hesitates but takes it, unfolding it with his long fingers.

'Am I OK to read?'

I nod, and he studies it, slate-grey eyes crinkling at the corners as he reads to the bottom. It's the same look of concentration – a sort of full immersion – he'd wear when he listened to us. When we'd ramble and rant and sob and purge, everything from the inside, out. He always listened with everything he had. 'Wow,' he says, blowing out a long noisy breath. He folds it neatly back into its rectangle. 'So, this is all you've had?'

'Yeah,' I tell him. 'I mean, I've done some searching of my own, trying to track him down after I got this. That's why I'm here. His brother said he called him from this number – from The Grove.'

Ramesh nods, lips pressed together. 'Bet that was a shock.'

'Hearing he'd been here? Yes.' The mug is hot against my hands, and I realise I am squeezing it hard, as if holding on for dear life. I place it on the table. 'Massive. I guess when he left I put him miles away – seas away, lightyears . . .'

'Sure,' Ramesh says, rubbing his stubbly chin. A gold band on his ring finger glimmers in the light. 'Roman and I stayed in touch. I got a phone call a few months after he left. He was quiet, quick to get off the phone, but I remember all he asked was if you were OK, and course, I told him . . . you weren't.'

A flash of hot betrayal sears my chest. I remember the flurry in which I stormed in to Ramesh that day, the desperation in my voice, the wanting to grab him by the lapels and shove him in the tiny office, make him call Roman's social worker, the police, *anyone*, to help me find him. He was so calm, so relaxed, it infuriated me. 'After that,' Ramesh continues, 'I didn't hear for a while. He rang to tell me he was living with his dad; said they'd reconciled and he seemed happy. Then his dad passed away.' Ramesh studies my face for a moment, waiting for a reaction. I nod, to tell him I already know. 'He calls every so often, to check in, but a year or two can pass between calls. April was the first time I'd seen him since he was about twenty-three. He's only visited a couple of times.'

'So, he was here? A few weeks ago.'

Ramesh nods. 'He called, wanting to volunteer again. I was overjoyed. Having someone here of his age who's actually been where they *are* . . .' Ramesh pulls his mouth into a hard line. 'It's huge for the kids. With mental health facilities like this, unity and stories of recovery, they can be so helpful and healing, as I'm sure you remember.' Ramesh smiles at me, and a slow warm tingling travels over my skin. It's a comfort – empowering – to have someone talk about something that's seen as a quirk, a mood, something to 'pull yourself out of', as exactly what it is: an illness. Something to be healed and treated. 'So, he came down, helped us with a two-week music workshop we were doing. There was a lot of—'

'Morrissey?'

Ramesh laughs, grimacing. 'Afraid so. Which stemmed a heated political debate, which of course, he revelled in. He was very popular with the kids. They loved him.'

'I bet.' I gulp away the ball forming in my throat.

There's quiet between us now – silence, except for the ticking of a clock, and the distant whirring and clicking of a photocopier machine. Ramesh sips his tea, but I can't bring myself to drink. I feel sick. I can't shake this feeling of unease. The atmosphere is thick, like smoke, and I find myself holding my breath, worried about what he knows, and what he might say, but at the same time, desperately wanting the words to pour from him.

Ramesh breathes deeply. 'I really did want to talk to you, Lizzie, to tell you that he hadn't just disappeared. That he was OK. But . . . it was difficult to know whether to because you were getting on. And for someone that had been in such a bad way . . .' He trails off. 'So, I decided I wouldn't, which was a tough one because I know how close you two were. And I am sorry if that wasn't the right thing to do.'

I manage a smile.

'Plus,' he sighs. 'Roman never wanted me to.'

I sit up. 'But why? Did he – did he mention anything that happened? Something bad, that would cause him to run like that?'

He shakes his head. 'I asked, Lizzie, believe me, I asked.' His voice is soft and calm. He always had this way of slowing my heart and my racing thoughts back then, simply by speaking, by listening to me and by reacting to the things I found impossible or terrifying, as if they had an end – as if they would one day be a loose end, tied, and forgotten. 'I told him he should reach out to you, but he wouldn't.'

'But why?'

Ramesh shakes his head. 'I stopped asking that after awhile. I don't know. But I am sure Lizzie James hasn't left Roman Meyers's thoughts once in twelve years.'

Ramesh pauses and pushes back on his chair, turning away to the shelves behind him, and I'm relieved. My eyes are misting, the mound in my throat hardening, and I swore I would not cry here, today. 'Where is it?' he mutters to himself, running a hand along a row of binders. 'It was here, Roman took it out. Bet he's mucked up the system.'

The way he is speaking of Roman in the present tense, as if twelve years haven't passed, as if he never disappeared, as if I'm fifteen again and he's grumbling about Roman losing his paperwork, as he always did, is dizzying.

'Ah. Here we go.' Ramesh pulls open a folder and passes it to me with a smile. 'Our trip.'

'*Scotland?* Are there . . . photos?'

Ramesh nods. 'Yep. Loads.'

'Oh my god.' I laugh, my hand at my mouth. 'I forgot you took these.'

'Oh yes,' Ramesh smiles. 'And please ignore my ridiculous haircut. It's not until you look back on something like this that you realise how many things have changed. There are some bad fringes in there, some very, very bad sweatshirt choices.'

I am barely listening, I am flicking through the binder, past text and leaflets and printed emails between people arranging the trip and a certificate of the grant The Grove received from a charity. Then I turn the page. Photos – a mosaic of them, covering the page. I can hardly breathe. I want to see his face, just as much as I can't bear the thought of it.

There's Ramesh, grinning at the entrance of The Grove, among suitcases and backpacks, the class on the platform at the train station – and I see myself instantly, standing awkwardly, hands at my stomach, beside Jade and her white-blonde hair. No sign of Roman.

There are images upon images of scenery – green hills and high cliff-tops – and a lot of Mitchell Geddes and Kai Browne, the confident ones, who I remember hijacking Ramesh's camera and holding it high above their heads, looking up into it, with ridiculous expressions. So many smiling faces. Masks. You'd have never guessed.

I turn the page. It's him. Roman, laughing hysterically, his smile huge and white, eyes scrunched, a floppy maroon beanie hat pulled down on his head, his hair escaping from its edges, a mad mass of curls.

It's involuntary. I laugh – a burst. And my hand flies up to my mouth.

Ramesh laughs too.

'Oh my god,' I say. 'Look at him.'

I turn the page, and then another, hungry for more, but then stop. Because there we are. Frozen in time. Roman and me, together. In fact, there are a few. Not just of us, but a class photo of us walking on the beach, a group photo of us in the hostel, décor straight from the seventies, rooms that all smelled of musty church halls, all of us eating sloppy beige food around a big table. There's one of us all posing on the top of a cliff, another of a group of us eating ice cream, half of our faces just visible at the back, my hair windswept, Roman's cheeks the colour of candy floss. There we are. Undeniable. Out in the fresh air, in the open. Together, side by side, at all times. And this one. This one I can't take my eyes off. It's the way I'm looking at Roman, who seems to be mid-chat, and I'm laughing – really laughing, mouth wide, cheeks pink. I wish I could remember what was so funny. I wish I knew what he was waffling about. Aardvarks. How Paul McCartney died years ago and the one we all know is actually an imposter. McFly and how, OK he'll admit it, the album I gave him was 'sort of decent' but nothing trumps old school The Smiths or Mary J. Blige. Veggie burgers. *Balls.* Of course balls.

'This is . . . surreal.'

Ramesh nods and sips his tea. 'Photos can be stirring. Moments caught in time, in a picture. Still quite an incredible concept.'

My skin tingling beneath my top. 'I haven't seen his face for years. Not that he probably looks like this anymore.'

Then it dawns on me that Ramesh knows exactly what he looks like. He knows exactly who he is – Roman as a man; an almost thirty-year-old man.

'Well, he's taller, if you can believe that,' Ramesh smiles. 'Hair's a bit calmer, still got those ol' cheek bones . . . still got the *cheek*, too, of course.' Ramesh chuckles, leaning back on his chair. 'Had a bit of a beard when he first turned up, too, but he'd sorted that out by the time he left.'

'And is he . . . is he OK? Is he . . .' My voice, tight and tiny now, trails off. The more he speaks, the more the vision of Roman as a man, in present day, grows and becomes more real and I just want to know – I want to know everything. I want to know he's OK – *really*. I want to strike a line through the worries that have been plaguing me and dragging me further and further down since his letter found me. I want everything Ramesh has. 'I mean, where's he living? What's he doing? Where is he?'

Ramesh presses his lips together, and it's the way he pauses, then leans forward, slowly, bringing his hands together on the desk that makes my heart sink to the pit of my stomach. 'I . . . I really don't know, Lizzie,' he says. 'He isn't married or settled down, but then I doubt we ever expected wife, kids, mortgage, nine to five.' He ducks to look me in the eye. 'He gives nothing away. And I think that's the way he likes to keep it.'

Tears fill my eyes now, and how quickly they do surprises me. This feels hopeless. Another dead end. Ramesh watches me, and I think he's going to speak again, but he doesn't, and quiet falls over the room. Wind gusts against the windows, and autumn leaves drift to the ground through the glass. I look down at the binder in my lap, at the photo of Roman looking down at me, me hysterically laughing, nothing but sea and sky and the world behind us. *Tongue.* That's where we were. And of course he got way too much joy from the name of that town. I remember how he kept saying it, kept saying how one day we'd bring Sea Fog here because it fit our 'criteria'. It had everything. We ticked them off in our minds as we sat on that cliff, beside the building site, a field of half-finished wooden lodges. Barely any people, *check*. Somewhere far away, *check*. Somewhere that could definitely accommodate a wood-burning stove, *check, check*.

'I feel free here,' I remember saying to him, as we sat looking out to endless angry ocean and perfect, clear blue sky. And I don't think I've felt as free since. The feeling of having so much good waiting for me, that I just had to get through this and there it'd all be. The feeling of having as many clean slates as I wanted, because nothing was too much to ask for from a world this powerful, this beautiful and vast. And yet, here I am, as free as I have ever been, but unable to move, to see beyond the cloud and the fog – fog that has been thickening slowly, every day, since I lost Hubble. Since I lost Roman. And now sitting here, miles from work where I should be on a Monday morning instead of making up doctor's appointments . . . it just feels cruel. Cruel that he was here – *right here*. That he knew where to find me – has always known – but has never even tried.

My vision is blurred from the tears, and I know Ramesh has seen. He takes a deep breath. 'He went to your grandad's funeral. Well. Tried. I'm not sure if you knew that.'

I shake my head. It whooshes with my pulse. 'I did, but . . . I didn't know if that was really what happened.'

Ramesh nods, his hands balled together on the desk. 'He came down for it. Couldn't do it. Saw you across the churchyard and . . . just couldn't bring himself to. He ended up here, and—' he shakes his head. 'Broke down. We went back together, later. He laid something at the grave, and then he left.'

My heart falls from my chest and settles in my gut. 'What? Why would he not come and see me?'

'I don't know.' Ramesh shakes his head sadly. 'But . . . your grandad's death affected him far more than I think anyone realised.'

I can't speak. 'He and Hubble were close, Roman thought the world of him, I—' My hands shake, and Ramesh gestures towards the filmy mug of tea in front of me on his desk. I pick it up and drink some. It's cool and bitter, and I wish I hadn't.

'Roman needed help,' Ramesh says. 'He was eighteen, in a toxic environment, and after many years with us, his programme with us had come to an end. Your grandfather's death was the final nail, I think, if you like. And I think he needed to leave, Lizzie. Something physical. To move from the circles he was in, from people taking advantage of his mental health, from . . . *using*.' Ramesh watches me for a moment. 'Look, I'm going to go and see about getting us some fresh tea,' he says, rising from his seat. 'Take a breather. You're OK?'

I nod.

Ramesh smiles, then steps out of the room, leaving the door pulled to. Silence. I dry my eyes and look down at the open binder in my lap. I place my finger on Roman's face. He was there. He was at Hubble's funeral, he was there, he could *see me*. But he couldn't let me know. Why? And the way Ramesh had said, 'Using.' *Using.* My stomach gurgles and cramps and I want to run to the toilet. That's not who he was. He was recovering. He was. He was getting better. He was better than me, most of the time, the most level-headed of us all at The Grove. It was just his mum. It was Ethan – Ethan and his dodgy circle, smoking, giving him stuff to help him sleep. He *was* getting better. Nine months and I'd have finished my first year at college, got my qualification and could've applied to take the second level elsewhere – anywhere. It was up to us. As long as we were far, far away from here.

Ramesh returns a few moments later, as I'm gazing down at an empty space in the binder on my lap, and a blob of something – old glue – in the gap.

'That was one of you two,' he says, placing down two fresh mugs of tea and settling back in his chair.

'Was it?'

Ramesh nods, gulping down a mouthful. 'Roman asked if he could have it. He took that and some other things from there, a leaflet for something in the town we stayed in. You know, as souvenirs.'

I put my fingers on the space. 'What was it of?'

'Just you two, on a bench. Smiling. He said you never smiled for cameras, always hid your face.'

Then there is more silence. Rain begins to spit against the glass and through the slats of the blinds, I can see the sky has turned to smoky grey.

Ramesh's phone rings, and he diverts it. He looks at me and brings his hand to his chin. 'When I said I didn't know where he is,' he utters, swallowing, 'I wasn't lying. I don't. But I do have a number – a mobile.' He pushes a pink Post-it note across the table. I reach out to take it, but Ramesh's fingers don't lift from it, fingertips pushing it to the desk. He clears his throat. The way his eyes seem sloped at the corners and the way his lips are now tightly closed, make me dread his next words. 'Roman forgot his credit card. He booked a plane ticket at my desk and he left it here.' His brow furrows. 'Charlotte called the mobile a few times, but no joy. Eventually he called us after he'd realised he'd lost it, and Charlotte posted it out to him. This is what she remembers of where she posted it to.'

I glance down at the words written above the number in looping blue ink. 'Friar Medical Group, Berkshire,' I murmur, my brow furrowing involuntarily. I look up at Ramesh.

He looks at me sadly. 'It's a hospital,' he says.

'A hospital.' My words are whispers. My chest tightens. My stomach contracts. 'What's he doing at a hospital?'

'I don't know,' Ramesh says. 'Although Charlotte is sure he said he works there.'

Relief trickles through my body and I find myself letting out a long breath, as if I'd been holding it all along. 'Right. I'll get in contact with them.' But Ramesh hasn't moved a muscle. His hand still holds the Post-it note to his desk, and he's still looking at me worriedly, like he used to all those years ago. When he wouldn't take my 'I'm fine' for an answer.

'Look, I don't know much,' he says, 'but . . . I got the impression he's under care of some sort.'

'Care? What, you mean, he's . . . sick?'

Ramesh holds a hand up, his lips parted, as if he was about to speak and thought better of it. 'I mean, he . . . he seemed well. But he mentioned doctors, in passing a few times. And I noticed he set alarms for meds. Three or four.'

'Three or *four*?'

I close the binder, which feels as heavy as a rock now on my lap. Medication? Hospitals? I feel the blood drain from my face.

'As I said, he seemed OK,' jumps in Ramesh, ducking to meet my gaze. 'I just would rather you have all the information if you're looking for him. I asked Charlotte if she remembered where his flight was to or where he might've been going, but she said she never asked and he never told. Lizzie? Are you OK?'

I nod, but I'm not. My head is racing, galloping at speed, and nausea is rising from my stomach to my chest.

There doesn't seem to be much more to say now. We make small talk, Ramesh and I, about the new layout of the rooms, the weather, and old therapists and teachers I remember to lift the mood. It does little though, to disperse the dread that has begun clouding around me. When I leave, Ramesh promises he will pass Roman my details if he calls 'before I get to him', and places his hand on my back in the way he used to – when he was worried I might just crumble.

I walk to the train station, hood up against the rain, barely flinching as it sprays my face. I take the route we used to, past the large, old houses of Hillingbrook, past the post office, the Spar and the Chinese takeaway place we must've bought a tonne of chunky salty chips from, and for the first time in a very long time, I walk past the park; the park in which Hubble fell to the ground that terrible night. Alone. While I slept, while everyone danced and drank at Auntie Shall and Uncle Pete's reception.

Sinking into a window seat on the train to London, I stare at the Post-it in my hand. I can't call him. Text maybe? No. Not a text after all this time. I'll call. Just not right now.

I unlock my phone. A text from Priscilla:

How did it go? I'm not in today. Called in sick.

I type back that I'll call her later, but I can't shake the unease that Priscilla is off. She never takes sick days. Even when she is sick.

Then I open an internet browser, and in the search bar I type in what Charlotte remembered of the address. 'Friar Medical Group. Berkshire.'

The train lurches and rocks, like a boat on rough waves.

It comes up instantly – a website, and news articles about a new post-natal ward, about a £50,000 refurbishment, a skydiving surgeon raising money for its cardiology wing, the opening of a new hospice. The Friar Medical Group. It's a group of hospitals in the south of England – two of which are in Berkshire, and one of which is where Roman is.

'Hi, you're through to the phone of Roman Matias, I am probably busy, asleep, or dead right now, so leave a message after the beep. If I'm either of the first two, I'll get back to you. If I'm the last one . . . I'll certainly have a good go.'

BEEP –

Chapter Seventeen

9th March 2005

Hubble speaks to the receptionist. He says he's Roman
Meyers's grandad and the woman on reception smiles sadly
at him – a smile that says, 'you poor thing. What must you
be going through?' I hang back behind him, trembling; it's
this whole place – the bleeping, the smell of disinfectant and
hospital dinners, people being wheeled by, hunched, as if they
are damaged inflatables, bowing and sagging into themselves.
This is a place for sick, old people that need to be cut open
and fixed. Roman isn't like them. He is sad. He is lonely. He
needs love and for his mum to stop drinking and cook him a
meal, ask him about his music and the books he's reading, talk
to him about his day. He doesn't belong here. So, why is he
here? Why did he do this? How could he? How could he do
this to himself? To *me*? He said he'd never leave me. Oh, god,
shut up. How can I ask that? I'm selfish. I am a selfish, horrible
human being.

Hubble puts his arm on my back and says, 'He's in the
Thomas Ward, Lizzie. Bay two. Bed four. The lady says it's
at the back by the window.'

We walk with speed, the wards quiet, except for the
squeaking of trolley wheels and the jangling of buckles on
coats and shoes as visitors walk purposely to their sick loved

ones. This doesn't feel real. He doesn't belong here. The anger rises in my chest like lava as we walk, and it sits in my throat.

We arrive at the entrance to bay two. There are four beds. All men. Two are old – seventies, eighties, one hunched over a Zimmer frame, the other sunken and grey, asleep with his mouth open, tubes snaking from his nose. And the other is a small Asian man with yellowing skin and bruises on his face, who sits on the edge of his bed, staring out of the window. The other bed – bed four, Roman's bed – has its curtain drawn around it.

Hubble's hand lands softly on my back again. 'I'll wait here,' he says. 'Or do you want me to come with you?'

I want to run. I want to bury my face in Hubble's chest and hide and tell him to take me away. From everything – from Mum, Dad, Nathan, Auntie Shall and Uncle Pete, school, social workers, The Grove . . . all of it. This whole mess. I want to be fixed. I want this all to go away. I didn't ask to be born. I didn't ask for any of this. I can't take much more. I won't.

'Darling? Are you sure about this?'

I nod. Despite myself, I nod. 'I'll be OK. I want to.' Because this is my only chance to see him. Dad thinks I'm at The Grove. Ramesh thinks I'm at a dentist appointment. No questions will be asked, and nobody will know. Dad banned me from seeing Roman last week, before and after school hours. He found out about Mum and Clark getting engaged and I chose that same evening to get home half an hour late, after Roman and I fell asleep watching films in Sea Fog.

He practically spat it at me as I walked in. 'You've proved you can't be trusted when you're around him,' he growled, 'and if you think for one minute you'll be seeing him before or after school, then you're bloody mistaken. Try it. I dare you.'

When I tore up the stairs and locked the bathroom door, my chest caving in, choking, drowning, I heard him crying downstairs, deep sobs. And I didn't care. I wouldn't care if I never saw Dad, or even Mum again in this moment. I just want to run away. Now. I wish we could. I wish we were at an airport now, me and Roman, or at a service station, on our way to the rest of our lives. Instead of here, in this building, full of sick and dying people. God, I hope he's OK. I need to see him. I need to know he is alright.

I walk slowly across the ward, past noisy breathing, the bleeping, the inflating and deflating of a blood pressure machine, the scratching of a pen on a clipboard in a nurse's hand. And now I stand face to face with the green flecked curtain that surrounds Roman's bed; which guards him.

'Think he's still sleeping, my love,' says the nurse with the clipboard, all rosy cheeks and white teeth. 'You here for Roman?'

I nod, rigid to the spot.

'You can go on in,' she says, and she smiles that sad smile again. The one the lady on reception had given Hubble. The 'poor unfortunate teenager' smile.

My hand trembles as I pull back the drape and for a moment, I can't see where the curtain ends, or splits. But then they part – just a sliver. I freeze. It's him. My friend. Asleep. Peaceful. I step inside and turn to see Hubble standing tall, hands in the pockets of his beige trousers. I close the curtains. It's just me and him now. Pain that feels like hot solder soars through my chest. A long sting of sadness and anger, all mixed together, bubbling, rumbling inside me. My legs are desperate to collapse. I want to sink to the ground and scream, 'Why aren't you listening? Why don't you care? This is Roman. Roman Meyers. This is my best friend. He is so clever and he knows so much about so many things, and despite everything he wants good for people and for the world. Why would you let this happen? Why doesn't anyone fucking care?'

But I am silent, besides the breath hiccupping in my throat. I grip the bottom of the bed and stare at him. He's on his back, his chestnut hair brushed out of his face. Pale. Beautiful. His lashes feathery and criss-crossing, his lips so pink and parted ever so slightly. Just asleep. Like he looks when we fall asleep in Sea Fog and I wake up before he does and stare at his forehead, wishing I could watch his thoughts like a movie.

I move to the chair at his side and sit down in it. I see his hand, open, above the blanket at his side. I move my chair slowly across the shiny floor and reach out and hold it. It's warm. Smooth. Nibbled nails, scratches of old purple polish on the thumb. I bring his hand to my face. It doesn't have its smell – the Roman smell, of cigarettes and lemon shower gel. But he's here. He's alive. I take Roman's hand in both of mine on the bed and stare at his face. I'm sorry, Roman. I'm so sorry you're so sad. I wish I could do something. I wish I could take it away. I wish I could fix all this.

He looks so young lying here. I always see Roman as a man; so tall, so strong in build, that it's hard to remember, sometimes, that he isn't even two years older than me. He's brought himself up – 'dragged' himself up as he said – and he's savvy and street smart and he likes the things older people do. But he's a kid. He's a seventeen-year-old *kid*. Two people made him seventeen years ago, and now he lies in a hospital bed on his own. Their child. Their baby. How can they sleep at night? How do they live with themselves?

His finger twitches in my palm. He stirs; sniffing, letting out long breaths, eyelashes bristling. I stop breathing. I don't know what to say to him. I don't know what to do.

His eyes open. Slowly shutting, then opening again. He stares at me, then weakly, his beautiful pink mouth smiles.

'Hey, J.'

'Hi,' I say. My lip is quivering, and I am shaking from head to toe. I try to stop, to steady myself. Roman sees. His eyes narrow, and his nostrils flare. I think he's going to speak but he doesn't. He just looks at me, as if the world has ended. As if he has never been more sorry.

'Roman, are you . . .' I can't continue. He says nothing either, just tightens his hand on mine. Then I try again. I open my mouth. 'Are you in p— are . . .' And I can't. I can't. I burst into tears, my hand flying up to hide my face.

'Lizzie,' he says. I hear the creak of the bed and moving sheets. He groans – his stomach, maybe? Does it hurt after? I don't know and I don't want to ask. He's sitting up now, and both of his hands hold mine.

'Don't– don't do that again,' I say, words morphing instantly to sobs. 'Please. Please, Roman.'

'J, I . . .' He looks away, turning his face. I hear his breath quiver. He strokes his thumb across my knuckles and I squeeze his hand tighter.

'Whatever it is, we can sort it together,' I say, tears running. 'You just ring me. Come round. B-bang on the door. Anything. Please, Ro. *Please*. We can sort it. It's us remember? And we can sort anything.' I hear him take a deep, shaky sigh and when I look up, he's looking at me. Roman is crying, tears sliding down his cheeks and onto his baggy hospital gown.

'I'm sorry,' he whispers, and quickly, violently rubs the tears off his cheek with the back of his forearm. 'I'm sorry.'

'No. Don't say sorry.'

'But I hate seeing you cry.'

Then there's quiet, between us both. We stare at each other, across the sheets, crying quietly, in the stillness of the ward. Our grips tighten on each other's hands. There're so many unspoken words, but there's no place for them here. Not now. My best friend is in a hospital bed because he didn't want to be here, on this earth, anymore. He didn't want to live. He could have succeeded. And I would have woken up in a world where he didn't exist. No Roman. And nothing seems to matter anymore. Other than him. Other than us together, behind this curtain, hearts beating, blood pumping. Here.

I bring his hand to my lips. 'I love you,' I whisper, and I kiss his knuckles. 'I have never told you that, but I do. I love you.' I know if he ever needed to hear those words, now is the time. That's more important than my fear of saying them, to this boy I've known nine months; my fear of him taking it the wrong way or thinking I'm too heavy. He needs to hear it. He needs to know. Because I wonder when it was that Roman last heard those words.

He pauses, as if thinking about what I've said, then lifts one of his fingers from our grip and strokes my cheek. 'Me too,' he says. 'I love you, too, J.' His face is wet with tears. He bites his bottom lip as if to stop more.

'Just don't leave.'

He shakes his head. 'I won't. I promise I won't.'

'I'm here,' I tell him. 'Always. No matter the time, no matter how old we are.'

I reach over to hold him, and I lay there, across the bed, across him, my head on his chest, his arms tight around me. We lay there like that for a while, and it's oddly calming. The quiet ward, the curtain around us, protecting us, and the window on our right, looking out to nothing but blue sky. Just us two, here. Just us, and the sky.

Roman cradles the back of my head. 'I'm so glad you're here,' he whispers against my hair. 'So glad.'

'I'm so glad you're here, too.'

'I'm sorry,' he says again.

I shake my head. 'No more sorrys,' I tell him, eyes fixed on the bluest sky, my cheek against his chest. Warm. His heart beating, strong. Still here.

We listen then, as Roman lightly draws circles on the top of my arm, to the distant mumble of a hospital TV, to the birds outside through a small crack in an open window, to a nurse speaking quietly to another, to the pouring of water from a jug on the other side of the curtain. Calm slowly shrouds us both, like mist.

'How was the dress fitting?' he whispers after a while.

'Awful,' I croak. 'Shall wants the bridesmaids to change into red sequin dresses for a performance at the reception.'

Roman makes a noise in the back of his throat. '*Performance*. Is she having a laugh?'

'I know,' I whisper. 'And she wants us to sing backing. Me and the other bridesmaids, in a line. Like it used to be when she worked on the cruises.'

Roman stretches. 'So, you'll all be like the von Trapps?'

'Yep,' I sniff. 'And I'm finding it so hard to remember the lines. My brain just won't. I don't sing, I don't perform. I never have, for god's sake. Walking down the aisle is scary enough.'

Roman nods slowly. 'Have you told her?' he whispers. 'That you're struggling to—'

'I did, so did Hubble. She just said that my behaviour was giving her stress-eczema and made me feel bad.'

Roman shakes his head. 'God,' he breathes. 'What a balls-up, eh, J? What a bloody balls-up.'

I look up at him with misty eyes, inches from his face, and I say, 'It's always balls with you, isn't it?' and Roman smiles and says, 'always.'

Chapter Eighteen

'Did it ring at all?'

'No, just straight to voicemail.'

'So, it's off. Dead?'

I nod, hand in the biscuit barrel. 'Must be. I've called a few times and it's never on. I did send a text.'

Katie stops drying the plate in her hands, a checked tea towel scrunched in her fist. 'Did you?'

'I just said hi, that it was me, and if he could – if he wanted to – he could text or call me. Told him I just wanted to know how he was, that I got the letter, that there was no pressure . . .'

'And I take it you got no reply?'

'Nothing. It's not been delivered and last time I called, the phone was still going straight to voicemail so,' I laugh, chomping a bourbon cream in half, 'perhaps it's time I accept he doesn't want to be found.'

Katie starts drying again, shaking her head as vigorously as the tea towel circling the plate. 'I don't think that at all.'

'I'm starting to,' I shrug. 'Anyway, is there any more of that cheesecake left? The mood I'm in, I just want to eat until I have to be cut out of the house by firemen.'

It's Thursday at half-past seven, and of course, I'm here at Dad's with Nathan and Katie for dinner. It's the only thing that feels safe at the moment – the only thing I can trust to be exactly what it is. Tonight has been a little different, though, but still, being here, leaning across the kitchen counter, elbow-deep in biscuits, the kitchen windows steamed up from home-cooking and chatter, is as close to content as I can get right now. Dad's girlfriend, Linda, is here too because she and Dad are off to Menorca at midnight, and where Dad is usually marvelling at his latest crumble combination as if it's a newly discovered antidote to a deadly childhood disease, he has spent most of this evening pacing the house, mumbling to himself, about boarding passes and hotel transfers, sweating with stress.

'So, are you going to go to the hospital?' Katie pats my arm. ''Scuse us, Liz.' I duck my head as she reaches up and puts clean, dry plates away in the cupboard above.

'There're two. They're both in Reading. We just don't know which one he works at.'

'You could call them.'

'I'm going to.' I hear Linda and Nathan burst into laughter in the next room. 'I'm going to call both, and just ask for Roman Meyers. Well, Roman *Matias* as he is now.'

'What's that?'

It's Dad. In the doorway, reading glasses on the end of his nose, plane ticket print-outs inches from his face. Dad needed glasses for years before he got them. I remember the way Mum would nag him about it, insistent on booking him an optician's appointment, and he'd grumble, bat her suggestions away with his hand. It was two weeks after Mum left him that he came home in glasses. He did that when she left; did so many of the things she had wished he would for years, as if that would convince her to come back. As if it would mend everything and make up for everything he dwindled.

I straighten. 'Nothing, Dad. You OK?'

'Nothing?' Dad smiles, tight at the corners. 'Didn't sound like nothing.'

'Girl talk,' Katie jumps in with a smile. 'Coffee, Charlie?'

Dad looks at me for a moment, and then shakes his head. 'I won't, darlin', thank you. Already got the jitters about this flight, I don't wanna add fuel to the fire.'

'You'll be fine, Dad.'

'I can't find the bloody return flight number.'

'It'll be on there.'

'Oh, Christ, he isn't boring you all about that bloody Trip Advisor review, is he?' Linda wraps her chubby, freckly arms around Dad's round tummy from behind him. Her pink, smiling face appears over his shoulder. 'I told you, relax, or we're going to have a horrible time.'

When Mum and Dad announced they were getting divorced, my mind shot forward like it's supposed to before you die, but the reverse. I saw my future. As a bridesmaid at their second weddings, two bedrooms, two Christmases that never ever felt the same so each heavily overcompensated with gifts nobody really wanted, Sunday night drop offs, the parent at the door, and the parent in the car nothing but markers to run between. And then there was the vision of an evil step-mother with long flowing blonde hair and a constant smirk on her face. I was right about most of it. All except Linda. Linda isn't an evil step-mother. She is gentle, kind and sixty-seven per cent Hattie Jacques. She has the biggest boobs I have ever seen and is so short and wide, that hugging her is extremely satisfying. Like cuddling a pillow. She looks like a 1950s housewife all of the time with her neck scarves and high-waisted A-line skirts, and she bloody loves ballroom dancing. And Dad. She loves Dad, every inch of him. I said that once with Mum in ear shot.

'Every *inch*? Well he sure has a shit-tonne of those, doesn't he?' she'd said.

But then, she was never going to say anything else. She's never forgiven Dad for what he did. He's never forgiven her for leaving him.

'Seven cossies, I've packed. *Seven*,' grins Linda, squeezing through the kitchen and picking up a tea towel. 'He can't quite believe it.'

'But that's one for every other day,' I say. 'That's wise.'

'Thank you!' she says, her chubby arm shooting up to point across the room at Dad. 'Tell that to bleedin' Mr Baggage Allowance.' Dad doesn't hear her, though. He's too busy muttering under his breath, as he scrolls through his phone.

'I still can't find it,' Dad grumbles, and Linda rolls her round eyes.

'It'll be on the ticket,' shouts Nathan from the other room. 'Don't worry about it. Just get your stuff together and get ready to go.'

'Is Nathan taking us, love?' Linda asks Katie, who slides a pile of washed and dried side plates into the cupboard.

'No, I am. He's going to do the pick-up.'

'Good plan,' winks Linda. 'Get *him* to do the dead-of-the-night drive.'

'Exactly,' grins Katie.

'For Christ's sake, where is this damn bloody flight number? You'd think they'd make it simple, wouldn't you?' Dad is so flustered, he's tomato-red. Beads of misty water sit on his forehead, which is so furrowed, the deep, dark grooves look like troughs.

'Dad, I told you, it's—'

'Dizzy, I am telling you—'

'*Give*.' Linda tuts and holds her arm out. It jingles, as clusters of gold bangles and chains sway, glittering together at her wrist. Dad gives up with a sigh and hands over the pile of papers.

'It's all so bloody complicated,' mumbles Dad, his dark greying hair unruly, but still shiny from this morning's gel.

It dangles in front of his eyes. Dad has always had a lot of hair. Thick and dark. I've never really liked it long, though. It just reminds me of all the times he'd bumble around the house, depressed, reeking of last night's drink and sweat and old sheets, barking things at Nathan and me, screaming at Mum down the phone. I remember almost looking forward to the meetings we'd have with my social worker, or with Ramesh about my progress at The Grove, because he'd make an effort then. He'd brush his hair, flatten it with gel, and put on aftershave like all the other dads you'd see at parents' evening or school plays. I looked for safety everywhere back then, in the tiniest things, anywhere I could. It was either that or give up. So, I held on. I stared out into the pitch-black darkness and looked – *hoped* – for just glints; tiny specks of light to show me all was not lost. That there was light to come.

'See, I think they get too cocky these days,' Dad carries on now. 'They put everything on there; internet addresses, Facebook bloody names, hashtag whatsits, but no flight—'

'Got it. Right, Nathan, note this down, love,' calls out Linda. 'MH1723. You'll need that for when you pick us up.'

'Hang on, Lin,' shouts Nathan. 'OK, I've got a pen. Say it again.'

'Where did you find that?' gawps Dad, eyeing Linda as if he is quite sure that she's lying and somehow etched the number there herself when he wasn't looking.

At eight, we say goodbye as Katie leaves to take Dad and Linda to the airport, and for the first time in a really long time, Nathan and I find ourselves alone. Just us, two cups of tea and a box of old paperwork at the kitchen table; the table at which we sat through everything; through those seemingly endless childhood years, night after night, all of us gathering together. Before we fell so easily and quickly apart.

'Jesus this is old. Look at this.' Nathan holds up a Thames Water bill that looks as though it was printed on a screen printer and delivered by a small boy on a promise of a goose for his family. Nathan and Katie are going to start renting the house from Dad when he moves in with Linda in a couple of months, so have been spending every waking moment recently, gutting old cupboards, and emptying the loft.

'And this,' laughs Nathan. 'This is from when Dad worked at Fry's. I don't even think you'd been born yet. And look,' he says, holding up a small curling brown envelope. 'This is Mum's payslip from when she worked at the aerobics studio.'

'Which is now an American restaurant.'

'Says it all,' Nathan grins, slumping back into his chair. He brings his mug to his lips. 'I just don't understand how there's so much stuff. I even found Mum's hairdryer and rollers in the back of one of the wardrobes, her hair still in some of them.'

I bring my shoulders up to my ears. The back of my neck prickles with goosebumps.

'What?' says Nathan. 'It's not like they're a dead person's.'

'I dunno.' I shudder. 'It's just weird, isn't it? It feels like another lifetime. Like those people – *that* Mum with the rollers and *that* Dad working at Fry's – it's like . . . were they even real? Were they ever even together? They're completely different people to the Mum and Dad we know now.'

Nathan stretches, leaning back on his chair. It creaks as he does. His arms are huge, and I find it amazing that those are the same arms that used to struggle helping me up and over Hubble's garden wall when we were kids, the same skinny arms that would wrap reluctantly around me on bad days, struggle to pull me to standing from the bathroom floor when the panic would get so bad, I'd throw up the entire contents of my stomach until I was exhausted and bruised. They're also the same bandy arms that would shoot out as he shook a fist in the 'wanker' sign behind Auntie Shall's back after she'd tut and say to Dad, 'She's fifteen, Charlie, it's called *hormones*. You don't see me laying down and dying and *I* had a full hysterectomy last November.'

'Well, I suppose it's 'cause they *are* different people, Liz,' says Nathan now, papers in hand. 'Nobody stays the same, do they?'

'No,' I say. 'I suppose they don't.'

Then there's silence for a while, as together we continue to sift through the mound of musty, dusty papers, sipping tea in the dim light of the kitchen, nothing but the soft amber under-counter lights on. I like the dark nights that come with Autumn. They remind me of the bonfire nights we'd have as kids, Dad barbecuing sausages, face lit by the fire, Mum lighting sparklers, lamps glowing through the windows of the lounge where we'd bundle afterwards for warmth in front of the fire.

'They were that gross couple, Mum and Dad, weren't they?' Nathan says, cutting through the silence. 'The pet names, the PDAs . . .'

'God, yeah.' I toss an old handful of business cards into the recycling box on the floor beside us. 'Made me want to spoon my eyes out. The snogging . . .'

'And the arse-grabbing.' Nathan laughs, and passes me another pile of letters. 'Chuck anything that isn't important or a photo.'

I hold up a crumpled page of A4. 'Keep? A school trip letter for you from 1996. Way back when Emma Bunton was in power.'

We laugh and Nathan motions for me to sling it in the box on the floor. 'Nah. Bin.'

I unpeel an old envelope, next. World cup football stickers. Years ago, Mum would buy three packets of them for Nathan every Wednesday evening after night-school, and I'd get an issue of *Shout* or *Smash Hits* magazine. It was like she felt guilty, for stepping out of her usual Mum-and-wife shoes, for focusing on something other than us, and she needed to bring home gifts to show us she still cared. 'They were happy, once, weren't they, Nate?'

'Who, Mum and Dad?'

'Yeah.'

Nathan nods. His eyes don't shift from the papers which move as if on a production line through his hands. 'I mean, I know they had their issues. When Dad had that . . . well, whatever it was with that woman at the scouts. I don't ever think they – *you know.*'

'Ninette,' I say. 'Ninette deGrassy. And I dunno, you know, I think something might have *gone off.*'

Nathan grimaces. 'Maybe. That was a bit of a dodgy time, though, wasn't it? Mum was studying, barely home, obsessed with that fucking weird plastic personal trainer guy.'

'Jean,' I smile, tearing a bunch of receipts into strips. 'Face like Kryten off *Red Dwarf* and hands like sweaty turnips. Ugh.'

'God, he was the worst,' Nathan laughs. His cheeks have always gone taut, like apples, when he laughs properly. 'Totally up his own arse.'

'He was the pits.' I ditch the next piece of paper. Junk mail, advertising a new local restaurant that no longer exists.

'But yeah, I just think they had a slump, then,' says Nathan, custard cream between his fingers. 'And every couple has slumps, don't they? Those times where you question what the hell you're both doing it for because it's more arguing than it is anything that even resembles joy. But I dunno. Dad and the money. That changed everything.'

I nod. 'She forgave everything else. Like when she heard that he'd told Fiona in the Co-op that he wished she was more like her, more *spontaneous*, and someone thought they saw them snog in the car park. Do you remember when Mum emptied that massive tub of koi carp food into his suitcase?'

Nathan bursts out laughing after a mouthful of tea, and quickly covers his mouth.

'Yes!' he says, composing himself. 'And she put it in the driveway, and put the luggage tag on it, saying . . . what was it, again, Liz? What did she write on it?'

'Slag. Simply "slag". As if she was his destination.'

Nathan and I laugh, stomach-tightening, rosy-cheeked, *real* laughter; the sort that warms you through like hot soup after being caught in the rain; the sort of laughter that feels precious, because it's shared, and understood by only the two of you. And I realise this is the first time I have laughed properly, for weeks. It has lifted a weight I had no idea was even there, and it's not until I feel it lift, that I realise just how dragged down I have felt the last few weeks. It's as if the digging I have done into memories, all the excavating, and delving, and all the energy I have put in to finding Roman, to the thinking and worrying, has bit by bit, utterly drained me.

'She put up with a lot,' says Nathan. 'But the gambling . . . she couldn't come back from that. And I don't think I could ever blame her.'

'I can't imagine how that was,' I say. 'It was everything she'd worked for, every penny she'd saved our whole lives. To check your bank balance, and see nothing.'

'He was addicted, though, Liz. Completely.'

I fray the edges of an old council tax bill in my fingers. Gambling. *Gambling*. It still feels like we're talking about someone else. Not Dad. Not my dad. A gambler. An addict. So far gone, he didn't care who he hurt to get the money. He just knew he had to, and when he did, his moment would come: he'd make it all better, he'd give us the life he wanted to, full of bigger, better things. We'd have it all. He just didn't realise we already did. He didn't see it until it was too late. 'I know,' I say. 'And Mum. She was no saint, I know that. She had the affair and that was all really fast.'

Nathan's sausage fingers hold his mug of tea at his lips. 'And then they broke up . . . and broke down.' Nathan laughs lightly, his eyes downturned just a tad, at the corners. He meets my eye. 'They lost it didn't they, Liz? Both of them. Properly lost it.'

'Yeah.' I give a slight smile. 'I remember it well.'

Nathan watches me, as my face flashes with heat, then he smiles and says, 'How could we forget right?'

And that is that. But the look – the meeting of our eyes across the pile of old papers, dated way back to when we were just kids at this table – is warm. Because there was a time nobody could mention that period of our lives without it feeling as though the words were catching on something raw – an open wound. You'd see the winces, the swallows, every time Clark, the man Mum left Dad for, was mentioned at a Thursday dinner, or when Mum would mention the mortgage they would've been able to pay off early had Dad not gambled away their life savings on the horses, each withdrawal slightly bigger than the last. He'd been out of work, and in true Dad style, he didn't want a soul to know we'd had to scale back on food shopping or cancel our yearly family holiday. He always wanted the world to think he had the perfect life – that he was Charlie James, scout leader, self-employed extraordinaire, a man without a care, a man with money, and work coming out of his ears. A man who had the life everyone dreamed of. He'd always been the same – so much more concerned about what people we chatted to twice a year at a neighbour's barbecue thought of him, than us, his flesh and blood – the people who loved him most. He kept up appearances the way people kept up a rigorous gym routine. It was exhausting. All of it was. Mum, Dad, and all their lies. The anxiety and depression that crept in slowly like fog, eventually draining the very colour of who I was. The shattering of our family. Life without Hubble in it. But now, there is none of that. It's acceptance. Relief. The sort that comes from going through something together and being out the other side, unscathed. It's over, it's done, and now, it's so far behind us, that it's just something we can look back to from the safety of the world we made despite it all.

And it flies out of my mouth.

Falls.

Straight out and onto the table in front of us.

'So, I'm trying to find Roman.'

Nathan's face drops, slowly, with the realisation and the replaying of the words in his head.

'Wh– you're trying to . . .'

'Find Roman. I got a letter from him, Nathan. Old. Like, twelve years old. I think it got lost or something but I don't know.'

Nathan stares at me, papers still in his hands.

'So, I'm trying to find him. Trace him if you like.' I give a laugh. I'm nervous. My palms are cold and clammy, I can tell as I reach for my mug, but I don't take my eyes off my big brother.

Nathan stares back at me, still, not moving. He exhales, as if being deflated.

'Jesus,' he says, leaning on the table with his forearms. 'I haven't heard that name in god knows how many years.' Nathan pauses. 'Have you . . . got close?'

I shake my head. 'Not really, no. But I'm hopeful. I have his number. But I just keep getting his voicemail. His voice . . .'

Nathan's eyes widen. 'How did that feel? Hearing him.'

I shrug, but then, despite myself, my face breaks into a grin. Heat spreads across my ears, in the way it used to when Nate

quizzed me on boys at school. 'Weird,' I say. 'But sort of . . .
like I have my ear to a time portal, or something. He sounds
different, but the same, all at the same time.'

'Like Roman at seventeen, but with extra bass?'

I laugh. 'Yeah, I suppose.'

Nathan clears his throat. 'Can I . . . see the letter?' I show
him. The letter shakes ever so slightly in his grip, and his
hand stays over his mouth as he reads. He stares for ages, then
eventually, looks up at me. He hands it back.

'Well.' Nathan swallows. His face is pale, the colour of
dishwater. 'Didn't see that coming.'

I take a sip of tea. 'Me either.'

Nathan looks at me across the table, and I know he's there
now, where I have been for weeks. Suddenly rushing backwards, as if on a track, fragments of memories flying together,
to make whole scenes.

'Look, shall we call it a day?' stretches Nathan. 'There're
hundreds of papers and it's only nine. We could put a film
on, make some popcorn . . .'

My heart tingles with warmth. 'Yeah. Why not?'

'Cool.' Nathan shoves all the paperwork into a pile, quickly,
and I stand and make my way to the kettle. 'I'm going for a
piss,' he announces. 'Popcorn's in the cupboard. Two minutes
in the micro on full. I'll stick on *John Wick*. Got the blu-ray.'

When Nathan leaves the kitchen, I throw a brown bag of
popcorn into the microwave and turn it on. I hear the toilet
door close upstairs and attempt to neaten the pile of paperwork in the centre of the table as the kettle rumbles. There
are receipts, magazines, pamphlets, letters from lawyers, from
gas companies, there are business cards, there are invoices.
Years and years of documents; decisions, hobbies, milestones,
opportunities. I push everything into as neat a pile as I can
manage and slide it to the middle of the table. I dab away

crescents of tea left by our mugs and swipe biscuit crumbs from the table into my hand.

And it's then that I see something.

A piece of paper poking out from beneath the flurry of papers.

A4, like so many of the others in the pile, but it's unmistakable.

And my heart is hammering before I even move, before I even edge forward and slide it out. Because I know what it is. I can't believe it, can't process it, but still, I know. I know before my mind can even catch up.

The pile scatters all over the table like the fanning of feathers, as I pull out the page.

There at the top of the piece of paper in my hand – the piece of headed paper – are three gold-brown letters.

And then I know.

Then I remember.

DDC.

This is Dad's. Dad worked for DDC. It's his headed paper.

Chapter Nineteen

4th December 2005

'Are you in pain, P?'

'A little. But it's normal, the doctors say.'

I stand at the side of Priscilla's bed. The room is dark for half past four, but winter's dark sky is slowly closing in, and the only light in the bedroom is the light from Priscilla's tiny pink TV. My eyes sting, my cheeks are puffy and sore, and I can hardly breathe. I try to hold it together. For Priscilla, for everything she has been through, because it would be selfish not to. But I can't. I try. I do. But I burst into tears, the ball in my stomach contracting, bending me double. It hurts. It really does.

'Lizzie?' Priscilla sits up. 'Oh, Liz, what? What is it?'

And I tell her. I tell her Roman is gone. I tell her he's taken the money we saved for the day we'd leave together, and he's disappeared. He isn't picking up his phone, because it's on his bed. The bed in his empty, echoing bedroom, and his mum, a drunken, sobbing wreck, has no idea where he is. 'He's gone, Lizzie,' she just kept saying, tears at the edges of her eyes, her lip quivering with anger, arms pulling her baggy cardigan tight around her as if it was the only thing keeping her upright. 'He's left me. His stuff . . . it's all gone. And there's nothing I can do. He's really gone.' Gone. Gone. Roman has gone. And this is not a bad dream. This is my life.

Priscilla's eyes fill with tears and she pulls back the duvet. 'Get in,' she says, and I do – coat, boots, and all – and she wraps us both in it, her arms around my neck. We cry together, tears soaking hair and shoulders and cheeks. My tears are for everything. For myself, for Mum, for Dad, for how broken we all are. I cry for Priscilla – for having to do this at sixteen. The pain, the heartbreak, the termination itself. I cry for Hubble. I cry so much for him. I have never missed someone so much that it made me ill, sick to my stomach, and I just don't know how I am meant to stand looking at that coffin with him inside, under the lid, in the deep blue shirt he always wore when we went out to dinner, alone. Without Roman. Because he's gone. And that's what most of my tears are for. For him. Angry tears, sad tears, tears of desperation. Because I know – deep down I know – he isn't coming back. And lying beside Priscilla, in her bed, beneath the duvet, she holds my face, as if holding me together at the seams, and I melt down. Everything inside me breaks. Something dies. Hope. Light. Something good. It dissolves.

'I'm here,' she whispers. 'I am here, and I am not going anywhere, ever. I promise you, I *swear*, with everything I can.'

I can't speak. I can't even nod. I just sob. That's all I can do.

'I've got you,' says Priscilla, holding my shaking shoulders, her words hiccupping over her tears. 'And you can trust me. Even when everyone else lets you down, you've got me. I've got you. We've got us. Always.'

Chapter Twenty

Ever since I found that letter on Dad's kitchen table yesterday – ever since I found that headed paper, with the DDC logo at the top and a scrawled, quick invoice of Dad's written on it; a page *identical* to the piece of paper Roman's letter was written on – I have been thrown here, to this uneasy place. I don't know where to go, or what to do. I just know I don't want to be here. I want my home. I want to feel safe. And I may be opposite Priscilla, at lunch, in the autumn sunshine, bundled up in the warmth of my coat by Camden's cobbled canal, but I can't shake this constant desire to 'get out', to run . . . but then, where do you go when it's your own mind that you're trying to escape from? I could run from here to Fiji, and it would still be right with me.

Priscilla stares across the table at me. She holds out the half-empty bottle of ketchup.

'No, thanks. I can't eat.'

Priscilla nods once, her mouth twitching nervously at the corner, making a perfect dot in her cheek. 'Lizzie, there may be an explanation.'

'I know,' I say. 'But I don't think there is.'

'What do you mean?'

I don't say anything. I just look at her across the table and bring my shoulders to my ears. The steam from our sweet potato fries dances between us, wisping into nothing.

'Eat something,' says Priscilla. 'Just something little. You said you didn't eat anything for breakfast.'

I didn't tell Nathan. I couldn't, in the moment. I stood, frozen to the spot, the piece of paper in my hands, the popcorn, popping like gravel pinging against a windscreen behind me. Then Nathan had creaked down the stairs and past the door.

'Don't even think about opening the Revels and giving me all the coffee ones,' he'd said, and I'd quickly folded the piece of paper in four and slid it into the back pocket of my jeans. I carried on as normal. I sat beside him with tea and a buttery bowl of popcorn and pretended to watch the film. Pretended to be relaxed, snuggled there on Dad's old squishy sofa. But inside, I was spiralling. Why? Why did Roman have Dad's paper? How would he have got it? Roman and Dad barely spoke, barely saw each other, so how did Roman ever come to write this letter to me – this desperate, cryptic letter written twelve years ago – on paper that would sit in my dad's work rucksack or scattered in his van? *How?* But then logic keeps pulling me back and sitting me down, making me look at this with a calm, realistic head, and with a mind that isn't looking for the negative, for the deceit, for secrets. Roman probably grabbed the paper while visiting – maybe he didn't have any of his own. Maybe he ended up with a scrap of it after I did a doodle for him – he loved my doodles and drawings more than anyone, he marvelled at them as if they were wonderful, as if they were proper *art,* the way I'd stare at my Mimi's paintings as they came to life the longer you looked at them. He asked me to draw him things and I drew on anything I could find. Maybe I drew something for him on some headed paper and picked up more than one piece without realising. Maybe he found some at Hubble's. We were at Hubble's all the time. It was our haven. He was. Dad sometimes stayed there when he couldn't bear to be at home, especially after Mum had been to collect her things, so maybe he left some there, along with work clothes and a toothbrush. Maybe that's where he took it from, because things are never as bad as they seem. That's what they say, anyway, isn't it? And so, I've tried. I've tried to look at the logical reason, the realistic reason. But still, my stomach churns and aches, as if it knows more than I do.

'I think you should try and speak to your dad,' says Priscilla, fanning away a dozy fly that attempts to settle on my sandwich. 'Put your mind at rest.'

'I'm not calling the hotel.'

'But you can't sit and worry yourself sick with this for over a fortnight, Lizzie.'

'I can't call him, P. I can't.'

And a part of me wants to. But he's just got the new iPhone and treats every foreign country as if it's a place that crooks go to sharpen their craft – every street and marketplace outside the hotel complex is a danger zone – so he and Linda have left their phones at home, switched off. We have the number for the hotel, for emergencies, should, god forbid, something bad happen within the next fourteen days, and he's emailed a couple of times from the internet café by the hotel, but I can't have this conversation with him on a hotel phone, or via email, hundreds of miles away. I want to see him when he tells me he knows nothing. Because now I can't get his face out of my head – that smile he gave me when he walked in on Katie and me talking about Roman – tight in the corners, his shoulders tense, rigid.

'Liz?' I look up. Priscilla is staring at me, fingers entwined holding the knee of her crossed legs, her back straight. She releases her grip and puts her hands on the table in front of us. I see her swallow. 'When I saw Roman's brother, he – he told me something.'

My heart immediately speeds up. 'What?'

Priscilla sighs and brings a hand to her temple. Her eyes are closing, her lids settling shut for longer than usual, and I know that face. Priscilla's regretful face; the face she'd wear when she'd pull me into the school loos to tell me she'd screwed up or done something she wished she hadn't – like the day she'd nicked her dad's car keys and reversed it off the drive into the brick wall, or when she'd gone on a date with Joshua in sixth form but he was so shy he didn't speak to her the entire night so she kissed his older brother as he walked her home and let him feel her boobs. The morning in the P.E. loos when she told me she was pregnant.

'I didn't tell you,' Priscilla says now, voice shaking at the edges, 'because I'm a selfish bitch and I didn't want to dredge up old memories. Old shit.' Priscilla squeezes her hands together on the table, her knuckles white. 'Roman lived with Ethan. At Edgar Fields.' She reaches forward and grabs her drink, holds it up, and says, 'God, I'm making a bit of a habit out of this wine at lunch thing, but . . . screw it,' and downs a mouthful. I can see her hand is trembling.

I stare at her. My palms are tingling, and my pulse is hot and whooshing in my ears. 'Y-you're . . . sure?'

She nods, lips pressed together. 'Yeah. Positive. Matt told me.'

I nod slowly. 'So, was Ethan the—'

'Ex-con. Yeah,' she laughs, a burst of sarcastic angry laughter, and swishes the drink around in the glass. 'Ethan Sykes doing time. Who saw that coming? Apart from . . . well, everyone.'

Priscilla's eyes shine and instinctively, without even thinking, my hand flies across the table and lands on her wrist. 'Priscilla . . .'

'I'm OK.' She sniffs, and puts her other hand on mine and squeezes. 'Actually, I'm not. Things are . . .'

'What?'

Priscilla shakes her head and takes a deep breath. 'At home. Things are tough, Lizzie. It's me. All me. I'm picking fights, I'm being a total bloody nightmare to live with.'

'I'm sure you're not, P—'

Priscilla shakes her head. 'I am, Liz. I'm completely ruining it.'

'You know you can talk to me. About anything.'

She smiles, weakly. 'It's my stuff,' she says. 'I'll sort it. I will. Honest.' And I know after sixteen years of knowing this woman, the pleading look in her eye, that she wants me to leave it now. A ball of guilt aches in my chest. All of this will be pulling up old weeds for Priscilla, too. I didn't stop to think about her really, and looking over at her now, I could cry. This is not just my past. This is hers, too.

'I'm just sorry,' she says, ruefully.

'For what?'

'For not telling you.'

I shake my head. 'No. Don't be, Priscilla. I get it. I do. But . . .' I lower my voice. 'You know I wouldn't have gone looking for him, don't you? I wouldn't have dragged you across the country, looking for him, for Ethan Sykes.'

Priscilla hesitates. 'I know that, but I *want* you to find Roman, Lizzie. I know you're meant to find him. I know you have to.'

'I want to find him too,' I tell her. 'But you come first, Priscilla. You always will.'

Priscilla shakes her head and brings a bent knuckle to her eye. 'You motherfucker,' she laughs. 'Don't make me cry off this incredible eyeliner, I look bloody good today.'

Back at work, I struggle to keep my eyes open, and will the hours away until home time. Cal rattles on about Eva, first girlfriends, supermarket curry sauces, and how the work system is as flawed as life itself, and I nod, chat, try to laugh and joke as much as I usually do, but my mind continues to stew and unravel and run, run, run down dark holes that make me surer than ever, that I can't trust anyone or anything. Everything feels so unknown, as if all things and all the people I have ever known could be that wizard behind the curtain.

Ethan Sykes. Why the hell would he live with Ethan of all people? He acted disgracefully towards Priscilla. Pretended he barely knew her, that she was some sort of desperate teenager with a crush, and not someone he chased and pursued, someone he spent a night with, someone he created a life with. He intimidated people, created nothing but trouble for the world, and he was why Roman ended up in that bed. He is why Roman got hold of the stuff he took, and why I almost lost my best friend. Him going to Ethan . . . it feels like a betrayal. He promised me he'd give it all up, that he'd stop seeing him, stop disappearing with him to dark, dodgy corners, to meet dark, dodgy people, and yet he chose to take shelter with him. Him and not me. Why not me? What happened to push him so far away, that he would choose somewhere like Edgar Fields, with someone like Ethan Sykes, instead of me, after everything we navigated, and everything we planned?

I don't trust Dad. I don't trust Roman – something I realise I have continued to do, even after he disappeared. I don't trust the memories, stories, reasons, explanations, moments . . . I don't trust anything.

And I am so tired.

This PC/D: Lizzie Laptop/Roman/
Roman signed in on 01/12/05 23:57
Roman: Are you getting my messages?
Roman: Liz . . . . . . are you awake?
Roman: lizzie?????
Roman: You appering offline?
Roman: appearing^
Roman: I need to talk to you. Please please please let me know if you see this.
Roman: lizzie
Roman: j??????
Roman: :(
Roman: You're obv in bed. Dw. Gonna try n sleep.
Roman signed out on 02/12/05 00:01
Roman signed in on 02/12/05 03:03
Roman: I'm sorry Lizzie.
Roman: I am so so sorry.

Chapter Twenty-One

'Hello there, this is a message for Lizzie James. This is Stephanie Akenzua calling from Borough of Camden College regarding the appointment you missed today in relation to the Access to HE Art and Design course you were interested in. If you'd like to reschedule your appointment, you can contact us on the form through our website, or call me directly, by using my extension which is 561, and we can hopefully fit you in some time soon. We hope to hear from you. OK? Thanks. Bye.'

If Auntie Sharon talked as much about things that actually matter as she does about waists and thighs and the hidden evil of potatoes, I think she would at least be invited to some sort of Amnesty International summit, solving famine or the ever-dwindling rights of women.

'Minna, I have honestly never seen a waist like it,' she says, for what has to be the seventy-ninth time in about ten minutes. Minna – a really lovely woman who has just finished telling us about the £870 she raised for a children's hospice – glows red and sort of shrugs, smiling embarrassedly. Auntie Shall reaches across from lounging back on the cushioned cubes in the middle of the dressing room and pats Minna's midriff. 'Were you born with it?'

And I can't help it. I laugh. Right there. A burst, as my tits are being squashed into a silvery crepe skirted dress by one of the wedding shop assistants.

Shall swings round and glares at me. 'What?'

'Nothing. Just, well, was she *born* with her stomach or did she buy it from Superdrug?'

All the girls laugh, and Auntie Shall tuts. 'She knew what I meant. Didn't you, Minna, sweetheart?'

Minna laughs nervously and lays her hand, flat to her stomach. 'I take after my dad. He's a beanpole.' She looks at me and pulls at the belt around the dress identical to the one I'm being levered into, except in gold, and says, 'this sash is lovely, isn't it? Very elegant.'

'Oh, I hate people like you,' exclaims Auntie Shall, throwing her arms in the air. 'I look at a chip and that's it, I've put on a stone. But I bet you eat lots of chips, don't you, Minna?'

'Um, I don't act—'

'Carbs and sugar and *poof*,' titters Auntie Shall, 'it just . . . well, *vaporises* due to that lovely fast metabolism you must have. Not bloody fair, is it?' And she turns to look at me. Only me.

'Sorry,' I croak to the assistant still stuffing my tits in the dress. 'I really don't think this is working. I don't feel comfortable. My boobs . . . if I could get the bigger size.'

The dress isn't working. This whole bridesmaid thing isn't working. And I suppose that's what you get for being the last-minute bridesmaid. This is the second dress fitting I've been to and both times, they've started without me. 'Oh!' Livvy had said, as I arrived at some dress shop in the back arse of nowhere by the skin of my teeth, summoned by a rushed, last-minute text. 'Lizzie! Sorry, we thought we'd get started. Limited time and everything.'

Katie has looked crestfallen both times, too. When I got here today, she was still dressed, coat and everything, waiting by the entrance. 'Shall told me she called you,' she whispered, and I had shaken my head and told her not to let it bother her. But it is bothering me. It doesn't feel right, and it probably doesn't look right, either. My irritation at being constantly left off group texts before Katie adds me herself, and always arriving in the middle of fittings and 'last-minute drinks' at places I know you have to book, is probably very obvious in my face every time I walk in. And my back is up. I can feel it, constantly tense, shoulders always up by my ears, no matter how hard I try to relax. Because there is no fighting it – I am not wanted here. I am the human equivalent of the cold deckchair on the end of a perfectly made-up Christmas dinner table.

Livvy walks in the room now, tapping away on her phone. She looks at Minna, then at me, then back down at the screen in her palm. The last couple of times I've seen her, she's seemed quite stressed – harassed is the word Katie used. But then arranging a wedding is stressful, and she hasn't given herself much time.

The assistant pulls at the back of the dress again, then stops.

'Please could you—' I start.

'Bigger size,' she says quickly.

'Yes, please,' I say. 'If you don't mind.'

The assistant dashes off through the curtained changing room area and into the main shop. Katie, an image in silver, the material falling down her legs in perfect crepey lines, stands beside me. She presses her lips together as we lock eyes, and we both let out a giggle.

'Any blood left in your old girls?' whispers Katie.

'Pass,' I reply. 'Well, I can't feel them anymore, so I'm guessing no, but who knows? Stay tuned.'

Katie laughs, and so does Minna, and I carefully peel off the dress from my chest. Livvy looks up from her phone, her face pale and stony, her mouth, closed and downturned. I smile.

She doesn't catch it – she's already looked back down at the lit-up screen in her hand.

'How are you feeling about the silver?' she asks, eyes still fixed on the screen.

'Me?' I say.

'Mm.' Her index finger taps and swipes on the phone in her hand.

'It's really nice,' I say, and find I feel on edge. I hate that I still feel inadequate in her company. I always have. Ever since we were kids, and Auntie Shall would make her do things she knew I struggled with in front of distant aunts and uncles. We started gymnastics classes together at age seven and after the fourth lesson, I ended up in tears in Mum's car because I still couldn't do a simple front roll like the other girls. Auntie Shall and Livvy sat silently in the back seat as I hiccupped tears. The following week, Auntie Shall got Livvy to show Hubble and Mimi how many cartwheels she could do in a row and then she asked me to do one, knowing full well I couldn't. I hid in the bathroom afterwards and cried, my face so hot and red with embarrassment, I had to use a cold flannel to cool my cheeks down. Hubble found me, and told me gymnasts always have bad joints, and faces that fall off like melting wax once their slicked-back, tight buns are taken out.

'Do you think you'd prefer the gold?' asks Olivia tightly.

'Um.' I look at Katie. We've pissed her off. Or *I've* pissed her off, that's more likely. 'No. Well, I don't mind. They're both nice.'

'Well? Gold or silver?' Her words are so sharp, so tight at the ends.

'Either,' I say. 'I really do like both.'

Katie's eyes widen a little, and she shrugs. I look at her with raised eyebrows, telepathically asking 'what the hell was that?' and start to peel down the dress, but I stop. It's done up tightly at the back and if I split it, I will have to pay for it and I do not have that kind of money. It's a beautiful dress. It really is. Everything Olivia has chosen for this wedding is beautiful. She has exquisite taste. But the price is overwhelming to me, and when I saw the price of this dress alone, I could hardly bear to touch it. I will never forget the pain on Auntie Shall's face when she thought I'd jammed the zip of one of the sequinned gowns she had hired for the bridesmaids to try on for her entrance 'show' on the night of her vow ceremony. If that was anything to go by, I did not want to be ruining a dress worth this much, knowing it'll be coming out of her purse. She'd love that. She'd never let me forget it. So, I just stand in this awkwardly quiet room, half-dressed, the gown cutting into my waist, and I wait. I hold my hands in my lap and look at Katie out of the corner of my eye. I twiddle my fingers, I sigh, yawn, clear my throat, and go to open my mouth, to say something – anything to fill this drab, horrible silence – when Olivia jumps in.

'Do you want to actually be here?'

I am so taken aback that at first, I am sure she is talking to someone else.

'M-me?'

Her eyes lift towards the ceiling. 'Yes, you, Lizzie.'

My lips part. No sound comes out at first. Heat creeps up my neck, and onto my cheeks. 'Sorry,' I say. 'Yes. Of course I do.'

But I don't. I don't want to be here at all, yet I am trying. I really am. For Dad. For Olivia. For my family. Although in this moment, I don't know why. All I do know, is that it's not for me. None of it.

'Then I wish you'd stop taking the piss out of it,' says Olivia, her cheeks flashing pink. 'This is my day. This is my wedding. And I would appreciate it if you didn't stand there taking the mick as you try on £400 dresses that I will be paying for.'

'Well,' chimes in Auntie Shall, folding her arms. 'That your uncle and I will be paying for, actually.' She's staring at me, eyebrow cocked, as if I am a dog that has just shit on the carpet. She's enjoying this. And I wish I had a smart answer. A formulated, sensible, smart response, but I can find no words. I am stunned. I have shown up to every fitting, every meeting, even when given a mere half hour's notice. I was there, at the magazine evening, circling dresses and telling Olivia over and over how lovely she would look in everything. I was the forgotten bridesmaid and I have been acting like a chosen one.

'I haven't been taking the piss,' I say, voice wobbling slightly. 'Honestly, I haven't, Olivia, and I'm sorry if you—'

She gives a little laugh, her cheeks now the colour of pome-granates. 'You *are* taking the piss, Lizzie. Making smart little remarks, smirking away to Katie . . .'

'I haven't been,' I say to Olivia, my voice louder now. 'I have hardly said a word tonight—'

'Oh, don't start acting as if I'm some sort of Bridezilla nut job who's being totally bloody unreasonable, because I'm not. I've been so calm during this whole process, despite the pres-sure I am under—'

'I'm not. I never said anything of the sort, and I think you've handled everything perfectly. I was just pointing out that I've barely said a thing and I haven't been taking the piss and I'm sorry if you feel that I have.'

The shop assistant appears, a larger dress in her hand, and starts unfastening me. She smiles a tiny, sad smile at me before disappearing behind me. A tiny sad smile that says, 'yes, this happens all the time, but honestly, if you've been in the game as long as I have, love, you learn to take it with a pinch of salt. Even the murders. Water off a duck's bollocks, that.'

'Olivia,' says Minna sweetly, clearing her throat. 'Did you . . . take a look at those hair pieces I—'

'I just *wish*,' cuts in Olivia, standing up so we're now face to face, only a few feet apart. 'That every time we're all together, you didn't feel the need to make fun. You know, make jokes, make everything a piss-take, act like you'd rather be *anywhere* else . . .'

'What?' I shake my head. My mouth is open and nothing – not even air is coming out. 'I'm sorry, but . . . I'm just making conversation, Liv. Having a laugh.'

And I see Katie now, in the corner of my vision, her phone still in her hand, hanging at her side, and her mouth open with worry.

'But this isn't a laugh. This is my *wedding*.'

'I am quite aware of that Olivia.' My voice is loud now – irritated – and my throat feels as though it's swelling. I will not cry. I will not cry, standing here, like this, tits out, being hoisted out of a dress as if it has become another layer of skin. 'I know this is your wedding. That is why I'm here. Every single time you ask me to be somewhere, I turn up, even when you forget me—'

'Oh, I don't *forget* you,' snaps Olivia, arms flailing at her sides. 'It was once.'

'And I am always here, regardless,' I say again. My eyes are shimmering with the threat of tears now.

'And then proceed to make fun of everything, *disapprove* of everything, act like your being here is a favour to us all—'

'That is not what is going on.' It's Katie. Standing beside me now, her voice loud – louder than I have ever heard it raise it.

'It is exactly what's going on!' Olivia replies, eyes wide. 'I'm sorry, Katie, you're a lovely girl, and I know she's your sister-in-law but . . . well, it's not like this is the first time, is it?'

For a moment, I can't speak. My pulse booms in my ears. But then, 'What?' croaks in my throat. Nobody says anything. '*What*?' I say again.

Olivia's shoulders sag and she cocks her head to one side. 'I just thought that after Mum's vow ceremony, you'd be making more of an effort, that's all.'

'I am making an effort.'

'You didn't want to wear the dress, at the last shop. You made such a fuss—'

'I didn't, I just said I don't feel comfortable in skirts above the knee—'

My words are lost, as Olivia runs over them, her voice raising. '. . . and I'm standing there, thinking *really*? You're doing this? Again? You're making a fuss, having to be different, all eyes on Lizzie.' Olivia scoffs a laugh. Anger fizzes in my stomach, in a fiery ball. 'Creating drama, once again, like you did then, and like you're doing now—'

'I have never!' Words fly out of my mouth at speed, as the shop assistant pulls down the dress and leaves me there, in bra and knickers. But I don't give a toss. I do not care an iota. The room is still and silent now. Everyone stares. 'I have never in my life created drama for anyone, not now, and especially not then—'

'Right,' huffs Olivia, shaking her head, then turning away and snatching up her phone from the stool. Shall is watching as if it's an episode of *Birds of a Feather*. She is enrapt. All she needs is her dressing gown on and a cigarette, and she could be there, on a Sunday evening in 1989, on the sofa, watching TV.

'I'm sorry you see it that way,' I say, straightening. 'I really am. And I'm sorry that the pair of you are still convinced I ruined your vow ceremony, Auntie Shall. I'm sorry that after everything that happened that night – to poor Hubble – that is all you take from it. *Your* day. *Your* night.' Auntie Shall's eyes widen, as if I've mentioned something forbidden. 'But if you had perhaps taken two minutes out of your day back then . . . to take me to one side, to talk to me like a real human being, to ask me how I was, instead of treating me like . . . like I was trouble, or a bloody leper it probably wouldn't have ever happened. I wouldn't have *ruined* your day.'

'So, it's my fault,' Auntie Shall says, shooting a look at the bridesmaids behind her, eyes flashing. 'My fault that you ruined my day and my *silken shoes*, that you couldn't control yourself, my fault—'

'I'm sorry what happened, happened,' I cut in, my face raging with heat. I stand my ground. I don't move, despite wanting to run; despite the fact all eyes are on me, here, in my underwear, barriers collapsing around me like the sides of a wooden box. 'But I'm not sorry for being ill. I'm not sorry for who I was.' My heart hammers in my chest. The shop assistant is by my feet, asking me to step into the new dress. I shake my head. 'No, thank you,' I mutter, looking down at her. 'Not right now. Not today.' And I turn around and pick up my jeans from the changing booth behind me.

'Oh!' says Auntie Shall. The sound is an amalgamation of an 'oh for God's sake' and a 'ha! Told you so, knew it, she always does this.' 'So, you're going, are you? You have a nerve, you do. Not a sodding *clue*.'

Olivia says nothing. She just watches me, her cheeks blotched pink, her eyes fixed on the floor, phone to her chest.

'Yes,' I say, pulling my jeans up and buttoning quickly, tears wobbling at the edges of my eyes. 'This is meant to be a happy time. I don't want to be the reason it isn't.'

'Fine.' Olivia slumps down onto the cushioned cubes beside Auntie Shall and continues tapping away on her phone, sniffing, and I don't know whether she's crying or not. I can't see her face. It's silent in here now, bar the odd throat-clear and cough, and the whispering of other assistants to the bridesmaids, animatedly asking, 'so is that feeling comfortable?' because nobody knows what to do with their faces.

I pull on my boots and go back into the changing booth for my coat and bag. I stand for a moment, with the curtains closed, and gather myself. I'm shaking, from head to toe, and although tears threaten to spill from my eyes and shine the spotlight even brighter on me, I feel relief. As if a cloak I've been wearing heavily upon my shoulders has been blown away in one gust. I take a deep breath. My heart slows. I catch a tear with my index finger, my lip wobbling, but swallow the rest down. I stare into the mirror, and look myself in the eyes, right through to every version of me that got me as far as standing here. I look at the sixteen-year-old girl that lives inside, somewhere deep down, but still has her fingers tightly around my wrist. Scared. Scared to stand up for herself. Scared to step over the threshold of a college, to attend a simple meeting. Scared to visit her grandad's grave – so scared that the week after his burial was the last time, because the sight of the dead flowers and that one, single, green, white-budded plant had broken her heart too much to face it again. I nod to her. She doesn't need to be afraid anymore. It's over with. We are strong enough to look it all in the face. We are strong enough to walk away.

When I step out of the booth, Katie is standing waiting for me, fully dressed, boots, coat, and handbag.

I stare at her. 'Kate?'

'Oh, Katie, you're not going?' Olivia says, her eyes snapping up. Her face is pale, her eyes, cloudy. 'Tell me you're not going.'

'Nathan's coming to get us,' she says sharply. 'And actually, yes. I would like to go too, please. I don't feel comfortable.'

Olivia shakes her head and looks down at her phone. She says nothing else. And that, is that.

Minna and Kirsty look up and smile sadly as we leave, and as we step over the threshold, I hear Auntie Shall say, as if talking about a naughty child, 'She's always been the same. Always has to be about her. Did I ever tell you about Pete and I's vow ceremony? Did I? It's jealousy, I think. Pure jealousy.'

Chapter Twenty-Two

27th November 2004

I stand beside Roman on the edges of the gravel by the entrance to the church. Joanne, Auntie Shall's best friend, faffs with Shall's enormous up-do and sprays it with blasts of hairspray, into the crisp winter air. Roman lights a cigarette and looks down at me beside him.

'The dress is disgusting,' he grins. 'But you look beautiful, J. *Amazing.* Seriously.'

I'm hardly listening. My heart feels as though it's swelling, filling my throat, and my eyes won't focus clearly – *why* can't I focus? I don't want to be here. I don't think I can do this. I can't.

'Tux looks good, right?'

I nod. It's all I manage. Because it does – *he* does. The trousers are a bit creased, and his bow skewed, but Roman looks incredible in his black tux. So striking. Like a man and not a boy.

'Not bad for a *scummy kid,* eh?' he says, blowing a smoke ring. The smell of hot ash is making me want to be sick. I step away, eyes fixed on the ground, trying to remember the exercises Cassie taught me at The Grove because this is a panic attack. It has to be, though I've never felt quite like this before. *Focus on one thing in your line of sight or close your eyes*, Cassie said.

So, I do. I stare at the church window, though it's blurred in my vision – in, two, three, four, out, two, three, four.

Olivia looks across the gravel at us. Her friend, Sian, another bridesmaid, Joanne's daughter, whispers something to Olivia, her breath creating clouds in the cold. They giggle over at Roman and Sian waves, all fingers. He smiles back at them; gives them that flirty, stupid smile where he bites his tongue, and winks.

'*What*?'

'Nothing.'

Roman puts on his silly Sean Connery voice. 'You're not jealous are you, Ms James?'

I feel funny. Everything feels funny, like the world is tipping to one side. I need to get out. I need to go. It's cold out here, but I feel hot under this fur collar. Red hot. Roman's hand lands on my arm. 'J?' he ducks. 'Are you OK?'

'I . . . I feel weird,' I say, pressing my hands to my chest. 'I don't— I can't . . . God, I'm gonna pass out.'

Roman tosses his cigarette to the floor, and steps in front of me. 'You're OK,' he says, lifting his hands to hold my arms. 'You're fine.'

'I'm not. I feel dizzy.'

'You're fine, Lizzie. I'm here. I look a massive twat in a tux, but I'm here.' He laughs, although it's a nervous laugh. Not his real one. 'Deep breaths, OK?'

I can't even nod. I can't even gulp down enough air. My head feels as though it's a tightly twisted spinning top, finally let go.

Sian goes into the church first, as rehearsed. Joanne waits to go, hovering at the entrance, hands together at her chest holding yellow flowers.

I'm next. But I can't. I swear I can't. I can't walk down that aisle. I can't have everyone staring at me. My legs wobble and my gullet does that thing again – where it starts to close, or at least halves in size. I told Dad. I told him I couldn't do this, even Hubble tried to tell them, to let me sit with him, in a pew, that it was bad timing, that I had only just started college which was big enough, that I'd not long been on the tablets, that I needed to take small, steady steps. But they wouldn't listen. Dad, Auntie Shall . . . either of them.

'Lizzie!' squawks Auntie Shall across the churchyard, the small mustard and cream posy in her hand held tightly to her waist.

'I . . . can I—'

'Can she have a minute, please?' calls over Roman, his hands not letting me go. 'Lizzie.' He crouches. 'Easy breaths.'

'I feel so weird, Ro. Like . . . I'm going to be s . . . s-sch-sick.'

Roman watches my face. His brow furrows. 'Liz,' he says, voice low. 'Did you . . . did you have anything at the house?'

'What?'

Roman's eyes widen. 'The champagne, Lizzie. You said at your dad's house they had champagne. Did you have any?'

'For fuck's sake,' I breathe, 'I'm not *drunk,* Roman. I had one. Barely even th-that. Someone left half a sm-g-glass in the garden—'

'But . . .' Roman leans in. 'The meds—'

'I'm seriously going to be sick. My head, Roman. It's spinning—'

'J, you can't drink on meds. The tabs you take . . . you can't.'

My heart stops. My eyes snap up to look at him. I try to focus. 'I didn't even think, I— I was nervous. It was one glass. I . . .' I stop as sick pushes its way up my chest. I swallow hard. I can't believe I was so stupid. An idiot. I'm a reckless fucking idiot.

'It's OK,' says Roman. 'You're just having a panic attack, and the drink's probably made it all feel worse. You'll be alright, it'll pass. Trust me, I know. Let's get you some water, OK? Maybe think about sitting down—'

'Lizzie!' squawks Auntie Shall again.

'Sorry, can I just get her some water—'

'No, you cannot! Lizzie? *Lizzie!*' Shall turns towards Olivia and screeches at her to get Dad, and I call out to her not to, but I don't think they hear. I can hardly inhale, let alone speak clearly. My heart is going to explode. I'm sure of it. I'm going to stop breathing. Or I'm going to be sick. Or faint. Or all of them.

'J . . .' Roman is practically squatting now, in front of me, holding my arms, looking into my eyes. 'J, I'm going to get you some water from the café across the street, OK?' I nod and hold onto his hand. Roman's fingers tighten around mine. 'The panic will pass soon, remember? Then we'll just be left with you acting a bit like Liam Gallagher at the 1996 Brit Awards with any luck, and who doesn't enjoy a bit of that?'

'Excuse *me!*' Auntie Shall grabs my shoulder. My head swirls, but I focus on her. I try.

'She needs a minute.' Roman stands tall beside me. 'Give her a minute and she'll be OK.'

'No!' she screeches again. 'The ceremony has begun, you stupid child. Don't you *dare* try to dictate to me what's bloody best.'

Then she takes one look at me, quivering on the gravel, my chest rising and falling the way someone's might mid-cross-country-run and spins around, growls with gritted teeth, '*Now!*' and storms back towards to the church door. She says something to Joanne, who nods and step-together into the church. She straightens Olivia in front of her, her hands on her shoulders, then looks back at me, hoping, I suppose, that I'm not about to ruin the order she has hammered into our brains over the last few months.

Roman watches me, like someone does a ship too close to an iceberg; with hope that it'll miss and be alright, but body steady and ready to act if it isn't. I look up at him.

'Lizzie? Can you—' he starts.

'I have to,' I say, nausea rising.

'Don't. Not if you can't.'

I glance back over at Auntie Shall and Olivia, both staring at me, rigid with the cold, both swaying slightly in my vision. I think of Dad. I think of him waiting for me, in the suit he was so paranoid looked too big on his slowly-shrinking frame, the way he watched me all morning, in the same way Roman is looking at me right now, just waiting for me to crumble, and I swallow. I lie. 'I think I'm starting to feel better.'

Roman nods. 'You're sure?'

The organ plays loudly, I can hear Auntie Shall ranting, squawking, beneath the long, sombre chords.

I nod at him. He holds out his hand and I take it. Together we walk to Auntie Shall, my legs wobbling, the world still tipping ever so slightly, my stomach churning with what feels like hot acid. Sick. I feel so sick.

Auntie Shall practically pushes me down the aisle, as if I am a carriage on a track. I hate letting go of Roman's hand, but I pretend the flowers in my hands are him. I pretend they are keeping me anchored, upright and safe. I don't look anywhere but ahead. I just need to get to the end of the aisle; I need to get to the front. Then I can sit down, then I can find Hubble and squeeze myself next to him. Or I can sneak out and lay on the grass somewhere. I can drink water and vomit. I can go home to my bed, cocoon myself in the covers. I just need to get this done with, walk to the end of this aisle, wait for Olivia, who should be behind me now, and then for Auntie Shall. That's all I need to do. A minute or two, at most, and I can go.

I trip over my feet, but I don't go over. I skip, almost, and I don't think anyone notices, or if they do they don't show it. God, my head . . . it is spinning. It's like my brain is going to spin so much it'll propel out of my skull and slap on the church floor in front of us.

I see Dad. He smiles at me, then his brow furrows. He mouths something. I force a smile back and look to the altar. Step, together, step, together. Almost there, almost there. Uncle Pete has turned now and he's smiling at me. I force one back but god, I feel sick, and everything sounds like it's underwater. Is this how drunk feels? I have never been drunk before, not even tipsy. Why did I do it? *Why* did I drink the champagne? I didn't think. I've been taking the tablets a little while now, and it's become a habit so fast, like brushing my teeth, like washing my face, that I just didn't even consider it. I just wanted to join in, like everyone else. Have something for the nerves, like Joanne did.

A hand. A wave. It's Hubble. Relief floods me as I lay my eyes on him. He's sitting in the second row, just behind where the bridesmaids will be, and I keep my eyes on him – soft smiles and safety – as I pass him. Seconds later, I join Joanne and Sian at the altar. My arm touches Sian's and she moves away as if she's just touched a turd. But my breathing – now I've done it, now I've made it to the altar in one piece – is getting easier, my throat not as tight, my chest not as tightly wound. It's just the nausea and my head, which feels like it has a spinning top inside. Even the smell of the flowers is making me want to vomit. Swallow. Swallow it away. 'It's a tiny half hour out of your whole, entire life,' Mum would say if she was here. 'It'll be over before it's begun.'

I'll be OK. Of course I will. The hardest part is over.

Olivia appears, and shortly after, Auntie Shall arrives at the altar, taking Uncle Pete's hands, and we all sit as the vows begin. The vicar waffles, we sing a hymn, and although my head spins and my stomach churns, I am holding it together. I honestly think I'm going to be OK. But then . . . I'm not. I am going to be sick. I really am going to be sick. It pushes like an about-to-erupt volcano in my chest and I gulp, my hand flying to my mouth. Instinctively I stand. I won't be seen if I run around the outside of the pews and out of the doors. I need to get outside. I need to throw up. But Joanne grabs my wrist.

'Lizzie,' she whispers through a tiny gap between her lips, her eyes wide. 'What're you doing?'

'I'm going to . . . be sick,' I whisper back, hand at my lips, pulling my hand from her, but she doesn't let go.

Then Shall ducks, strides forward. 'Sit down,' she hisses, her mouth pulled into a fake grin. The vicar, smile fixed, eyes me then continues talking.

'Please,' I say, breaking free from Joanne's grasp and striding past her. 'I'm s-sick . . . I'm . . .'

Auntie Shall stops me. I hear the shuffling from bodies on pews. She's making a scene now. She should have let me go. Nobody would have seen, nobody would have known, or cared.

'Lizzie, sit down *now.*'

'I'm going to be . . .'

'Are you . . . are you *drunk?*' Auntie Shall whispers, her hand at her chest, eyes wide.

'Please.' I gulp hard, my body convulsing as vomit forces its way up my throat. Auntie Shall strides back, eyeing me like I am a wild animal on the attack. And it's too late. My body has won. Right here, at the altar, in front of a church full of people, in front of a vicar, in front of a man with an obscenely large video camera and tripod, and Jesus himself, I vomit. Not once. Not twice. Three times. On my dress. On my flowers, which without thinking, I shove in front of me to catch it, because I so badly don't want anyone to see. And a third time, onto the shining wooden floor of the church, and onto Auntie Shall's shoes. I hear her squeal before I hear the church doors squeak open in the distance.

'*Charlie!*' echoes around the church, but before Dad can even get to me, I'm running, dress gathered in fists at my side, towards the doors, where Roman is standing, fingers on the handle, blue skies and bright light breaking through the crack behind him. And we run, Roman in a tuxedo, me in a dress the colour of winter catarrh. We run from the church, through the town, and through backstreets and garages, gasping, Roman laughing, both of us holding onto lamp posts and fences to slow ourselves as we take corners. We only stop when Roman takes off his jacket and gives it to me to wear.

When we get to the park, we collapse against a huge oak tree and slide so we are sitting on the ground by its gnarly lumpy roots. Dusty mud covers our shoes, and when I wipe my eyes, make up smears all over the back of my hand – a smudge, like a milky way, of shimmering black mascara and pink blush. I can't imagine how we look, sitting here like this, but nobody says anything for ages – we just sit, beneath blue sky and the spindly, naked branches of the tree, waiting for our cloudy breaths to slow. I wait for my mobile to ring – Dad, irate, or Hubble, worried. But it doesn't. It's lifeless.

'Feel better?' Roman asks finally.

I nod. 'Yeah.'

'Puking is what you needed. Get it all up.'

'It's all over me,' I say weakly. 'And probably your jacket now.'

'Sound,' says Roman with an amused smile.

I can't believe that what happened just *happened*. How will I look at them again? How will I ever, ever look any of them in the eye? I have ruined it. I ruined their big day. I want the ground to open up, suck me inside it. I want to run away.

'And you say you can't run,' Roman chuckles, beside me, still breathless. He turns to look at me, waves of hair dangling over his beautiful eyes.

I smile, barely there. 'Yeah. Who knew?'

'You flew. *We* flew.'

I close my eyes and lean my head against the rough grooves of the oak tree. 'But I shouldn't have done that, Ro,' I tell him. 'I shouldn't have run from her.'

And he just shrugs and says, 'Yes, you should. You should run from her and never look back.'

Chapter Twenty-Three

'I'm afraid I can't give out further information, for confidentiality reasons.'

'But I know he works there. The other Berkshire hospital – Hynsondale – that's closed, isn't it?'

'It is, Madam.'

'So it has to be this one. And I know he was working with you over there, or at the very least, *did*, until a few weeks ago, because a friend sent him a package there, to you at The Hartland.'

'I'm sorry, and I understand your frustration, but our staff is made up of many volunteers, doctors, and therapists, and then there are the patients, of which we can have up to seventy-two at any one time. All I can tell you is that our website has a staff page of our resident staff members, so if I can direct you—'

'I've looked already. He isn't on there.'

'Then I'm afraid I can't help you. You may wish to email our head office and they could see a way to assist—'

'Listen, I'm sorry. Jill? It was Jill, wasn't it? Look, I know for a fact that Roman Matias was working at your facility around six weeks ago.'

'Madam, as I said, because this is a mental health facility, and we have lots of high profile, voluntary patients, confidentiality at The Hartland is of paramount importance and I can't assist—'

'It's . . . sorry, it's a mental health facility?'

'Yes. It is indeed. Hello? Hello?'

'Hi. Sorry. I— OK. Look, please could you run his name again? Through your . . . what was it? Staff database?'

'I'm afraid it's still not finding any results.'

'Could you perhaps—'

'Miss James . . .'

'He may be under Meyers. Or are you able to just search for *Roman?* It's an uncommon n—'

'*Miss James.* Could y— please, if I may. Are you one hundred per cent sure that your friend is indeed a staff member here and not . . . a patient? Hello? Miss James?'

Nathan knows. I know he does. It's the way he won't meet my eye, the way the tips of his ears are red, like they always are when he's embarrassed. Or guilty. We sit opposite each other at the greasy spoon at the top of the road from work, two cans of Coke between us, so cold, the tins were tight like drums with pressure when they were first placed down by the silent wait-ress. He pushes the ring pull of the can around and around with the tip of his index finger, his eyes quickly and routinely looking at me beneath dark lashes, and then back at the Coke can.

'It's um . . . nice of you to think of this,' he says with a stutter. 'Us meeting for our lunch breaks. We don't do it enough.'

'We don't,' I say, then bend down to the handbag at my feet. I pull out the folded piece of paper and put it onto the table between us. He swallows then, and after a pause, he opens it for just a second, then places it back down. I jump in before he can say anything.

'This is Dad's headed paper.'

Nathan, as red as a strawberry now, a sheen of sweat dappling his forehead, roughly rubs his mouth with his hand. 'I know,' he says, simply. 'I know it is. I should've told you. That the paper was his.'

An old lady, unsteady on her feet, fist clutching a walking stick, squeezes by our table. She knocks over our ketchup bottle which bangs loudly on the wooden surface. I stand it up again. A man dashes to open the door for her.

'You knew right away, didn't you? As soon as you saw Roman's letter.'

Nathan blows out a long breath. 'I wanted to tell you, but I dunno, Lizzie. I shit myself, I suppose. I had to digest it myself before I came to you. It threw me.'

'Threw me too,' I tell him. 'I found a blank piece when you went up to the loo. And I remembered. Just like that.'

Nathan deflates with a noisy sigh. 'I thought you might. There's loads of that stuff. Katie and I used it for scrap paper at uni, there was so much of it.'

I don't say anything. I just watch my big brother, red and bumbling, wondering what's going to come next. Bracing for it. But whatever it is, I am ready. Ready to know all these truths now, that keep making their way to the surface, like fat. Strong enough.

An old Carpenters song hums through a boxy radio on the counter. Nathan presses his lips together. 'I needed to gather myself, go back there, to when it all happened, get my own head straight before I could talk to you about it. It's been a long time since everything.' Nathan's voice is deep and bassy as he drops it a fraction more in volume. 'See I always thought Dad played a part.'

'Really?'

Nathan brings his thumb to his mouth, resting the nail between his teeth. 'The day before Roman disappeared, I saw him. Dad, coming out of Roman's house.'

My insides feel as though they have plummeted downwards, the way they do on the drops on rollercoasters. 'W-what? Are you . . .' I can't even finish my sentence.

Nathan is pale now – almost grey. 'I couldn't get hold of you,' he whispers. 'You were in hell, you were a mess, Liz, you know how it was after Hubble died, you were . . . crushed. And you just went off, one afternoon, and you were gone ages. I was worried. I was always worried back then. So, I went for a walk to try and find you. I went to Roman's first, thinking you'd be in that caravan or wandering about, eating chips or something . . .'

The waitress appears at the side of our table. 'Two bacon,' she mumbles, before plonking a shiny, crusty roll down in front of each of us and walking off. Nathan raises his hand in thanks. I can't move or speak. I am rigid, my head, swirling, pumping, the walls closing in.

'But I didn't see you. I saw Dad. Coming out of his house.'

'What did you say to him?'

Nathan raises a shoulder. 'I didn't say anything. Not right away. I don't know what I thought. But when he disappeared . . . that's when I approached Dad about it. At first, he denied even going to his house but then he just said Roman was ill. He was struggling. And he'd been looking for you too, and that's when he found him in a state.'

'In a *state*? What does that mean?'

'I don't know. He was out looking for you and found Roman in a bad way, I suppose and—'

'I would've been at P's,' I snap. The tension between us is palpable. I can't shake this feeling of betrayal. That's how it feels. That all along, my brother knew this, while I cried myself to sleep, called police stations and hospitals and The Grove, desperate for anyone to tell me where Roman had gone. It was the not knowing. It was feeling as though I wasn't good enough for him to stay. I let it whittle me down, let it talk me out of my dreams; out of college when I'd only just started, out of fresh starts and happiness. But all along he knew. He knew that my dad had barely spoken to Roman in over a year yet was seen coming out of his house just twenty-four hours before he left. That was a big thing to sit on. Huge.

Nathan watches me, eyes watery, unblinking with worry. 'You were at P's,' he says. 'I went there after.'

'So why was Dad there? Why was he inside Roman's?'

'I don't know,' says Nathan quietly. 'But the caravan wasn't there anymore, 'cause that's where I was hoping you'd be.'

I remember. I remember dashing there, when it got to almost an entire twenty-four hours of calls going straight to voicemail. I was sure I'd find him, maybe in a bad way, maybe at that place again, dark and sad and wrapped in a blanket, on that narrow brown sofa. And we'd talk about it, make plans, pull hope from anywhere we could like we always did, and I'd be frightened – terrified – that he was so down again, and of what he might do, of what he might take. But he'd be in Sea Fog. He'd be there. Safe. But that day, Sea Fog had gone and instead a stretch of discoloured stone, shielded from the sunlight for all those years, was all I found. 'So, he knocked at the house,' carries on Nathan. 'Dad said Roman's mum's bloke had sold the caravan.'

'What?'

Nathan raises a shoulder to his ear. 'Sold it and legged it with a load of cash.'

I open my mouth to speak, but just strained sounds come out. A tiny part of me had always hoped that somehow, some way, he'd managed to do what he always said he'd do when we were free – towed it far, far away, and just kept going, until he found where his heart wanted to be.

I shake my head, backtracking on everything Nathan has just spilled out on the table between us. 'What did he mean when he said Roman was ill? W-what does that matter? What does it even *mean*? Why mention—'

'The drugs,' Nathan cut in. 'He mentioned the drugs. And that Roman was in a bad place.'

'What do you mean the drugs?'

Nathan shakes his head, his mouth pressed together with irritation. 'He said he found him wrecked. Off his face, Lizzie, in a bad way, upset, and he was worried for him. He sat with him, talked to him—'

'But . . .' My face screws up and I shake my head. 'But the drugs weren't that much of a problem. Not really. Not after what happened. I was with him when he got rid of them after he got home from the hospital. And OK he might've done the odd thing with Ethan, with his mates, like *lots* of teenagers do—'

'*Lizzie.*' Nathan stares at me. He takes a breath, eyes shutting and opening slowly. 'Lizzie, he was an addict.'

'He wasn't an *addict*.' I scoff a laugh, shake my head. 'He was depressed, sometimes, really low, and yes, he sometimes took things, but . . . then he'd be fine, he'd be more than fine.'

'I'm sorry, Lizzie, but no child goes to a day centre, for rehabilitation, for therapy, for years, for nothing. I know he had other troubles but . . . Lizzie, he was an addict. A junkie. That's why he was there. With you.'

I swallow down tears. I can't speak. *Junkie* hurts. It burns in my chest.

'I'm sorry, Liz,' he says, face softening. He reaches forward and holds my wrist, gently in his shovel hand. 'I'm sorry. I know I didn't know him like you did. I'm just telling you what I think you need to hear . . .' He trails off. I nod at him and wipe away tears with the cuff of my jumper. 'And I'm sorry for not telling you about Dad. Back then and any time after that.'

I see the way his eyes shimmer, and the pink tips of his ears and I realise, in that moment, how much that year affected us all. Not just me. Not just Dad. All of us. Everything changed so quickly. Our family was torn into shreds, our foundations, collapsed. And he was just eighteen. He wouldn't have got through that year unscathed either.

I put my hand on my brother's. 'It's OK,' I tell him, although it doesn't feel that way, not at all.

After a while, Nathan starts to eat, but I can't. I tear pieces of fluffy bread from the sides of the roll and chew, but I can't swallow them. Because the walls aren't closing in anymore. They're falling away, like a set, crashing, and shattering, leaving only reality – leaving only the truth. And it hurts to look at it, like looking at the sun.

'Is there anything else,' I ask thickly. 'Has anyone else been lying to me?'

Mid-mouthful Nathan shakes his head and makes a muffled sound. He looks hurt, but I wonder if his chest feels as heavy, as crushed, as mine does. If his world feels as much of a sham as mine does right now. 'Of course there isn't. I promise. Dad said he just talked to him. And that was it. None of us mentioned it again and after that, nothing. I'm not hiding anything else.'

'And you believe that? That nothing else happened.'

Nathan leans forward on the table, forearms resting on the wood. 'I did,' he says. 'Until I saw that letter was on Dad's paper. Now I just . . . I dunno.'

'I think Dad helped him leave.'

Nathan's brown eyes widen. 'Why, though? Why would he do that?'

I look at my brother, the worried crinkles by his eyes, his brow furrowed with concern, his gaze fixed on me, the little sister he has always tried so hard, in his own way, to protect, and my heart twangs. Nathan was one of the only reasons I felt guilty for planning to run one day, with Roman. I used to imagine him going into my bedroom, to toss me a new CD, to see if I wanted to watch a film, like we always did, the pair of us cross-legged on my little single, and find me not there, my stuff gone. The thought of his face, the colour draining at finding an empty bedroom, empty wardrobes, stopped my heart. No matter how much I wanted to run away back then, he was one of the only reasons I wanted to stay.

'I don't know,' I tell my brother now. 'Maybe Dad wanted to get him away from me. He didn't like Roman. He even resented Hubble giving him the time of day . . .' The words catch in my throat.

'He's a father, Lizzie. He worried about you. He worried whether The Grove was even good for you. He wanted you back at school, everything back to normal.'

I don't say anything. I just twist and tear the edge of my roll, my eyes fixed on a spot on the table.

'Are you going to talk to him?'

'When he gets home,' I say quickly. 'But we're going to a hospital first. In Reading.'

Nathan looks at me, can of Coke inches from his mouth. 'A hospital?'

'I think we've found where Roman is,' I tell him. 'And I would rather hear it from him first.'

Chapter Twenty-Four

24th August 2005

We sit amongst colour, Hubble, Roman and me, the pinkest pinks and the greenest greens. The air smells of honey and lavender and carried on the breeze is the faint smell of coffee from the tea room across the path. It's beautiful here. Like a safe pocket of the world as Mother Nature intended it to be, in the middle of chaos. You would never know it's here.

'Bored yet?' Hubble asks.

Roman, beside me, shakes his head. 'No,' he says to Hubble. 'No, sir. Definitely not.'

Hubble smiles, eyes scrunching at the corners. 'Good,' is all he says, then there is silence again, between us three, here on the cool stone bench beside one another, me in the middle, Hubble on my left, Roman on my right. It's a hot day, 'bloody unbearable' Dad called it this morning, hunched over his toast in the dark of the kitchen, slinging down the slices after messy bites, as if simply holding it was too much effort. But there's a breeze here, in the gardens of Fort Manor. There's air. Hubble comes here a lot, meeting his friends, Angie and Jim, for lunch, and when Mimi was alive she'd go too. I have never been before. Sitting here, lost among all this colour, among the rustling of leaves, the trickling of water, and the calm of distant voices, I wonder why it's taken me sixteen years.

'It's sorta nice,' says Roman, hands clutching the grey stone of the bench at his sides, arms straight, 'to be somewhere else. To be away from everything.'

Hubble nods. 'It's important you are from time to time,' he says. 'Even if it's just an afternoon, a change of scenery, a change of air . . . it does wonders, I think. Especially somewhere like this.'

I smile up at Hubble and he leans, touching his arm to mine.

'It was a good idea,' I say to him, 'bringing us here.'

'Well, I did think you might be bored.'

'*No*,' Roman and I insist at the exact same time, and the three of us laugh. I wish every day could be like this – this easy. I wish Roman could stay with me, with Hubble, every second of the day, so I know he's safe. So I know he isn't taking anything or getting into any trouble with Ethan and his mates. He doesn't talk about them anymore, not since the hospital, but I know he still sees them. Perhaps, just not as much. Still, I wish I never had to say goodbye to him, so I know he isn't lonely, in that bedroom, within those tinny, damp walls of Sea Fog. So I'm right there – *we* are, Hubble and me – should he ever feel again, like there's no point to his being here. Because we'd show him there is. There are so many.

'Great masterwort,' Hubble says, a hand gesturing towards a mass of pink flowers and herby green leaves beside Roman. Its flowers bow and sway with the weight of bees landing and taking flight from its centres. 'Or Astrantia. That's its other name. One of the first things I ever planted when me and your nan moved into our first house, that was.'

I gaze at the plant, its flowers are like Catherine wheels with large petals fanning out at its sides, but tinier ones spraying from the inside, like the seeds of a dandelion.

'They're really pretty,' I say softly and Roman leans over, lowering his nose so it touches a flower.

'OK, so you don't smell as nice as you look, dude,' he winces with a smile, and Hubble laughs and says, 'I'm sure they'd say the same about you, if they could.'

I close my eyes and lift my face to the sun, and listen to the buzzing of bees, to the chirping of birds, to Hubble quietly explaining to Roman about great masterwort – about its hardiness, how although it looks fragile, it is strong; stronger than most, even those that look as though they could easily brave a storm. It can survive in the coldest frosts, in gale-force winds and blazing sun. 'Through it all, it keeps living,' he says, and it's then I feel Roman's fingers touch mine.

'We thirsty? Hungry?'

I open my eyes at that, and see Hubble is standing now, hand digging deep in his jeans pocket for his wallet.

'I'm OK, thanks, Hubs,' I say.

'You sure?' he asks, white eyebrows raising. 'Don't want an ice cream or something?'

I pause, and of course nod as quickly as I can. 'Um, *yes*,' I tell him with a grin. 'Definitely want ice cream if that's an option.'

Hubble lifts his chin. 'You, Roman?'

'I'm fine. But thank you.' Roman says no to everything Hubble offers, even though he might really want to say yes. It's politeness. It's pride. When we're at his house together, the pair of them play an almost well-rehearsed game; a dance, if you like. Hubble offers Roman something, Roman declines, Hubble nods then brings it anyway, whatever it is – tea, toast, a roast dinner – then Roman enjoys every moment, and thanks him, *always* more than once.

Hubble strolls slowly across the path in the direction of the tea room, and Roman and I sit in silence for a few moments, following one another's gazes, to the sky, to birds flitting, perching on branches, on the edge of the stone fountain, pecking at the shallow pool of water, to passers-by, to flowers. Then, eventually, to one another.

I smile gently at Roman. His curly eyelashes bat slowly. 'It's so nice here,' I utter, and he nods, but says nothing else. I can feel it. Something there, something swelling inside his mind, weighing him down, passing shadows across his face.

'Mam seemed upset this morning,' he says, quietly. 'She found some old photos of me. At nursery, and when I was at primary school, and she was crying. A lot. Sort of made me feel like crap.'

'Why?' I ask gently.

Roman shrugs, his eyes staring at the ground, hands still grasping the bench. 'Things were better back then, J. We were, I dunno, happy. *Happier*, anyway.'

I nod. 'Feels like another life, sometimes, doesn't it?'

Roman nods and steals a glance at his side, at me. 'I just think if I wasn't like this, maybe she wouldn't—' He stops, shakes his head. 'I mean, it can't be easy, can it? Having a son whose head's like a fuckin' rollercoaster, you know? A son who does stupid, selfish things and doesn't even go to a normal school or do normal things—'

'No,' I cut in. I duck to meet his eyes. 'Roman, what she does is nothing to do with you.'

'How can it *not* be?'

'Because . . .' I stare at him, my mouth open, gaze unwavering willing him to stay with me, to listen, to believe me. 'Because I know plenty of people who know you, and love you, and spend time with you and . . . we don't do what she does. You just make us happy.'

Roman swallows hard, hand covering his mouth. I want to reach out and push his hair behind his ears, to twist it around my fingers, to kiss the top of his head. But I don't. I don't move, but I don't take my eyes off him. 'Sometimes,' he says in the tiniest voice, 'I feel like I ruin things, Lizzie. Like I'm bad for people.'

I tell him he's not. That he's the opposite for me; that like holidays and sunshine and laughter, he is good for me. Because it is true. He makes me feel healthier. I feel nothing but warmth around him; nothing but light.

He holds my hand and we sit for a while, once again surrounded by all those colours and the smell of warm syrup and coffee, and when a man walking by trips on an uneven paving stone and tries to pretend he didn't by doing a very theatrical footballer's run, we giggle until we are laughing without sound, without breath, behind our hands. We lean on each other, eyes closed, happy tears at the corners. Our hands, still holding.

'Oh, *I* see,' Hubble says, approaching with a plastic bag and a Styrofoam takeaway coffee cup in hand. 'Laughing at some poor unfortunate swine who almost fell arse over tit, are we?'

Then he pulls two white chocolate Magnums from the plastic bag in his hand.

He hands one to me, and the other to Roman with a smile. 'Eat up. Before they melt.'

'Thanks, Hubble,' Roman says. 'Thank you.'

Chapter Twenty-Five

The Hartland isn't at all like I imagined – not in the slightest.
In my mind's eye, I'd seen the usual: a concrete tower, beiges
and greys, the clinical smell of disinfectant mixed with vats
of mince being cooked for lunch, the mousy squeak of the
wheels of trolleys, people rocking in corners, distant shouting,
nurses in tan tights wielding big syringes. In my mind, I'd
seen Roman appearing in amongst it all, in a white coat and
an even whiter smile, like Dr Drake Ramoray from *Friends*.
Like those doctors on the posters of private hospitals who
advertise on the tube. I didn't expect this. A house that looks
as though it plays regular host to murder mystery weekends
or is owned by the sort of bloke who wears pastel colours and
checked trousers and gets whipped by his secretary on the
weekends.

'Who knew hospitals could look so . . . idyllic?' said Priscilla
as we arrived at the top of the sweeping, stony drive. 'I mean,
seriously, if Chris and I pulled up here on a mini break, I
would be over the moon. It's beautiful. And listen.' Priscilla
closes her eyes. '*Silence*. Seriously, if ever my kidneys fail—'

'It's a mental health hospital, P.'

'Well if ever I need an asylum.'

I raise an eyebrow.

'It was a joke,' she says, linking her arm through mine. 'A bad one. Sorry.'

Priscilla and I had come up to Reading on the train. 'It's only a ten-minute walk from the station. Plus, Chris needs the car,' she'd text last night. What she hadn't realised, though, was that 'the ten-minute walk' was at first along a speeding main road with a tiny footpath that wasn't really a footpath, just a kerb, which she screamed the whole way along as lorries roared by. One had even honked us, probably an attempt to bring to our attention our utter disregard for basic safety, and the sound was so loud, we both screamed and threw our arms around each other as if shielding each other from death.

'This may not have been the best route,' shouted Priscilla into the wind and gusts of exhaust fumes, her hand firmly squeezing mine behind her. She didn't take her eyes off the phone in her other hand, held high up in front of her, the polite Google Maps lady's calm rasps completely lost in the screeching and rumbling of speeding vehicles. 'We should have got a taxi.'

'Oh, *should we?*' I shouted back, eyes scrunched against clouds of exhaust and dust. 'I seem to remember suggesting that. I did, didn't I? Actually, I vaguely remember suggesting it about seventy-five seconds ago.'

'Shut up, Lizzie! Keep left!'

'Yet all you did was mention how we were both going to die of high cholesterol if we didn't walk more.'

'For Christ's sake, keep left, Lizzie! Concentrate!'

'Which is hilarious really, Priscilla,' I shouted over the roars of cars and lorries, 'considering we are practically dancing with death right now.'

'Forty yards!'

'Goading it, even. *Mugging it off,* as you would say. Staring it in the face and cackling loudly.'

'Just thirty more yards, Lizzie. Thirty'

When we finally got to the safe turning of Beaufort Way, a road with speed bumps, a pub, a library and a secondary school, it was like that end scene in *Heathers*, where Christian Slater has blown himself and the school up, and amid the chaos and madness, Winona Ryder just floats out, blackened and burnt, but with the sort of face belonging to someone who's just had a hot stone massage, and calmly lights a celebratory cigarette. There was silence, people carrying babies and shopping bags, a couple sitting outside a café drinking coffee, and there we were, throats hoarse from screaming, our hair windblown, and our shoes covered in mud and exhaust dust. Then Priscilla stopped and lit a cigarette, and when she looked at me, we both broke down in fits of giggles.

'So,' Priscilla says now, looking up at The Hartland; grand, with smooth, thick pillars and walls the colour of sand. 'Should we buzz?'

I take a deep breath. 'Yeah. I suppose.'

Priscilla smiles gently, long, silky hair dancing in the breeze. 'It'll be alright, babe, you know,' she says. 'Whatever happens, whatever we find—'

'Say if he's really ill or something,' I blurt. I look to my side at her. 'Ramesh said he took tablets when he saw him. Several.'

'You don't know he's a patient.'

'I know that, but what if the tablets are because he's ill, and he's sending old letters, volunteering here, volunteering at The Grove to . . .' I can't finish my sentence.

'To what?'

'Make amends before it's . . . too late, or something'

Priscilla jerks her head as if she's been slapped. 'Jesus. Lizzie.' She presses her lips together. 'Look,' she says, 'you're bound to be going around and around in circles, trying to piece this all together.' Priscilla reaches out and touches my arm. 'But the danger of that is that you can piece it together the complete wrong way. Put two and two together and get . . . *eighteen*.'

I nod once, eyes to the gravel, chin to my chest.

'Chris takes three different tablets, at the moment. He's not dying. Neither is Katie, and I know she takes that pill once a day for her low blood pressure.'

'I'm just worried that . . .' I exhale a long, tight breath. 'I'm worried I'm going to find something I wish I hadn't.'

'Lizzie,' says Priscilla, her hand giving my arm a gentle squeeze. 'We've got this. I promise.' Priscilla straightens and eyes the front door. 'Buzz.'

I pause, but I know she's right. I have to. It's time. I tread up to the top step and push down on the cold, brass intercom button. Moments later, instead of a voice from an intercom, a woman, short and rotund, in an immaculate skirt suit, pulls open the heavy chestnut door, a big brass knob smack bang in the centre. She's my mum's age, perhaps a little older, and she has short hair the colour of wheat, that is sort of standing on end.

'Another half hour until visiting, but if you have your forms, you can come on in and wait,' she says warmly, and I can tell by her voice – the slight, Irish twang – that it's the woman from the phone. 'Unless you have an appointment, that is, then I can take you straight through.'

She takes us both in, her eyes scanning us subtly.

'Um. N-no,' I start. 'I– are you . . . Jill?'

She nods, gold, ropey hoops in her ears swinging. 'Yes.'

'We spoke on the phone. I'm Lizzie James, I—'

'Yes!' Jill's mouth bursts into a wide smile that blushes her cheeks pink. 'Of course. You're trying to find your friend. Please. Come in.'

Inside, The Hartland looks more like a hospital. The ceilings are still high with ornate, decorative coving, plums, and leaves, carved into the wood, and the light surrounds are the same. There's even a chandelier in the reception area, the glass slightly yellow with age, but these little footprints, traces left from when this place was a house for a privileged family, complete with a library and oppressed daughters, is offset by stark injections of present day – a rumbling vending machine, the deep, low song of the reception phone, and makeshift signage of laminated pieces of A4, with bright green clipart arrows printed on them.

'I won't be a moment, and then I'll be with you,' says Jill, circling the beech counter, and taking a seat behind it. She types something into a computer, then picks up the phone.

Priscilla squeezes her leg into mine. 'You OK?'

I nod my head.

'Wonder if she's calling him,' she whispers with an excited grin.

I barely manage a smile. My chest is tightening with nerves. The vision of Roman appearing in the entrance beside the reception desk, tall, filling the doorway, prompts a flurry of butterflies; him ducking to let Jill know he got her message, and *yes, Jill, what is it*? And her nodding, gesturing to me, sitting here, frozen on this chair, and his face, when he sees me . . . frozen, too, eyes widening, as it registers on his face. Or him, in a hospital gown, surrounded by nurses, his eyes bruised, his face full of shadows like it was on that hospital bed. 'Oh god I don't know about this, Priscilla.'

'It's going to be fine.'

'Seriously, P, I feel like I'm gonna shit myself.'

'Oh, Lizzie, you won't—'

'Seriously, if you mention being on first name terms with my bowels or whatever I will—'

'Miss James?'

Jill is standing now, and beside her, is a short brunette, with rosy cheeks and an eyebrow ring. She is smiling at me. 'Miss James, this is Harriet, one of our volunteers. She's going to try to assist you.'

'Hiya,' says Harriet. 'Do you mind if we step outside?'

'In theory, I'm not really allowed to say much.' Harriet pulls an electric cigarette from her jacket pocket. 'Patient confidentiality, you know.' She raises her shoulders and her eyebrows at the same time. 'But Jill told me when you called, that there was a girl asking for Roman, and . . .' She sucks down on the electric cigarette and blows out a mist of appley vapour. 'Sorry, girls, do you mind?'

We both shake our heads, and she laughs. 'Did that a bit backwards, didn't I?' She has a West Country accent and a jolly face, and as much as she seems lovely, I'm having to resist grabbing her shoulders and shaking her, making her stop with the giggling and the small talk, and *talk* – tell me why we're out here, on the gravel.

'You're Lizzie,' she says, looking at me, arms at her side, fleece zipped to the neck.

I nod, although it isn't a question. 'Yes.'

She smiles, cheeks mottled pink from the cold. 'Did you get the letter?'

Priscilla immediately turns to look at me. I hear a small gasp in her throat.

'Yes,' I say urgently. 'I did. Roman's letter, you mean. The letter w-with . . . the Christmas stamp.'

I stop. Because she's nodding and grinning at me, teeth, crooked, and two dimples like perfect prod marks in her pink cheeks.

'I sent it,' she says.

I look at her blankly.

'I sent Roman's letter,' she says again, the smile on her face beginning to fade. 'To you. It already had the stamp, everything else, I just stuck it in the postbox. And I don't know if I should've but . . . well, I did, but now you're here I'm starting to feel a bit better about it.'

I look at her, opening my mouth to speak but she cuts in.

'Sorry, I probably sound unhinged,' she says, with a chuckle. 'I'm a volunteer here. Have been for many years. Used to work the odd Saturday, after my son passed, but ah, I dunno . . . gets under your skin, this place, becomes part of you. Now I'm here most days of the week in some capacity.' Her eyes scan my face. 'I don't know how much you know.'

'Not a lot,' I say, and she bows her head, lips together, as if considering her words.

'Roman was a patient.'

It's not like it wasn't what I was expecting, but her words are like pins to the heart. It stings in my chest. 'Well, *is* I suppose you'd say. With Roman, he comes and goes. Has done for as long as I've been here which is what, five years now? So *is*. Was. I dunno which, until the next time. I always hope,' she ducks her head as if it's a secret, 'and in the nicest way, that I never see him again when we say goodbye. But,' Harriet doesn't finish. She just sighs and says, 'You know.'

Rain begins to patter down, and Harriet holds her hand out, motioning to the curved Perspex smoking shelter on the drive, at the side of the house – it's the type they have in school yards for bikes and looks totally out of place before such a beautiful building. We walk with her and duck under it. The rain taps on the roof – that satisfying steady, clip-clopping sound of fat rain drops, quickening, and multiplying.

'You grow very fond of people,' says Harriet. 'They become friends. Friends that you want to see better, see fixed, see them off out in the world again, getting on, finding happiness. And Roman was the first one I got to know. A favourite, I suppose, although I know many would say that.' She laughs to herself, scratching her nose with her thumb. 'Same age as my son, he was, when I met him, and we just got along. Though, it's hard not to get along with him, isn't it?' She looks up at me, head cocking ever so slightly to one side. 'You alright there, flower?'

I nod, trying to stop my teeth from chattering with nerves and hot anxiety which are both building up inside my chest like a rising fountain.

Harriet sucks on her electric cigarette and exhales. 'It's hard to believe sometimes that someone that *cocky*, that full of beans, could end up back here, time and time again, but . . . well, it doesn't discriminate, does it? It takes who it takes. Long as you're human and you've got a brain, you're up for grabs.' A lump sits in my throat. There are so many words in my head; so very many swirling around, like papers in a windstorm and I am reaching for them. But I can't get hold of one.

'When you say patient,' starts Priscilla, her voice hushed and low. 'I mean, is it—'

'Drugs?' I ask. 'Is it drugs? Is it depression? Is he . . . *sick*?'

There is silence for a beat, and Harriet sighs. 'I'm sorry, girls. I can't go into details of it – wouldn't want to. I shouldn't even be doing this but as soon as I heard Jill on the phone, mentioning Roman, I had to ask. When she told me, I even . . . well, I did a right *dodgy* and did 1471 on your number.' She lifts her shoulders quickly, as if she's just let slip a secret. 'Wrote it down and everything. But Jill said she knew you'd come. That she'd in not so many words told you Roman was a patient and I thought, if it's meant to be, she'll be here.' She raises her eyes to the sky and smiles gently. 'Jill and I are both very fond of him. I told her I was sending the letter, so I think we were both hoping, secretly, deep down—'

'Does he know you sent it?' I ask. 'Did he ask you?'

Wind swirls through the shelter, and Harriet brings her fleece down over her fingers.

'Roman left the letter in his room when he left in June. He always leaves something – it's his thing. I once told him my son loved poetry. When he left, he'd left a book of poetry on his bed; poet had the same first name as my boy. I once told him in passing that I loved carrot cake, and . . .' She chuckles. 'You can guess what was on his pillow in a cake box when he left.'

That's Roman. The Roman I knew. I told him once, that one of my happiest memories was being in a rainy car after flying kites with Hubble and Mimi, and Mimi had given us all a Wispa bar, which we had dipped in plastic flask mugs of tea. After that, Roman often left a Wispa bar in my school bag, whenever things were particularly bad, when my anxiety made me shake and vomit and killed every morsel of my appetite. To make sure I ate, even if it was just chocolate. He never forgot anything. He held onto little things, as if they were huge, defining things. 'Because they are,' he'd say, 'more than where you were born, and who your parents are.'

'Anyway, we'd talked about you, one day in the garden just before he left. Just over there. Of course, I knew about you before that – he always talked about the centre, you, his mum, and your grandfather—' She stops herself, slotting the electric cigarette back into her pocket. 'Anyway, that letter. He said he always carried it around with him, always had, wanting to send it. But the more time had passed, the harder it had been to post.' She pauses, watches my face. Her eyelashes are so fair, they're hardly there at all. 'And that was it really,' carries on Harriet. 'Few days later, he left, sessions were up, and off he went, as he always does, into the world somewhere.' She clears her throat and shoves her hands into her pockets. Chill tingles at my neck, but my cheeks are red hot with nerves. 'And I found it. The letter. It were on his bed. I took it as a *go on, Harri. Send it.* So, I did.'

The pieces of the puzzle, like the play pieces on Jumanji, move and slide together, some of the picture coming into focus.

Then it's quiet between us. Rain continues to pop and spit against the misty Perspex glass, and the sun just manages to push through the purple-grey clouds.

'How is he?' I ask. 'Really? Is he . . . is he well?' And I mean it in every sense. How is he? How is the boy who is now a man; the boy who saved my life every day that he showed up to be at my side? What does he look like now? Does he still listen to The Smiths and know every word to every Mary J. Blige song? Is his mouth still ridiculous and huge, and does he still do that smile where he bites his tongue? Does he still say 'twat' for every other word and paint his fingernails in weird colours and patterns using markers? And does he still have that way – that way where he makes you feel like everything he says is a cold hard fact. Where he makes you feel like he understands the world more than anyone else on the planet but nobody is ready to listen yet?

'He's . . .' Harriet grimaces, as if she's trying to find the right words. 'Well, he's Roman. He's charming, hilarious, offensive, let's himself get away with nothing. But he's . . . well, he's better than he has been in the past.' She watches me, searching my face for a reaction, something to go on, but I can't speak. 'In this job, you generally see two types of people. People that look at things face on and get better, and people that don't want to look it in the eye, not really, and they bolt. Run from it.' She looks to her feet, then back up at us. 'Roman is the latter. I think he's spent his whole life running.'

'From what?' I ask, my eyes blurring.

She shrugs her shoulders, and sniffs noisily. 'That's his story to tell,' she tells me. 'All I know is that if he knew I was standing here, with you, with his *Lizzie*. Well, I think we'd have to peel him off the ground.'

I am staring at her, the woman who has all the answers I've been dying to know for what feels like my whole life, hanging on her every word, and I feel like I am about to melt into a heap. I want to cry. I want to laugh, with relief, that he's alive and that we're getting closer and closer, the gap between us closing like a bridge being built, slat by slat. I want to see him. I want to wrap my arms around him and hold his face in my hands.

'Bloody hell.' I look beside me at Priscilla. Her hand is at her mouth, the way it is when she watches a sad film. 'Fuck me hard,' she whispers into the silence, and we all laugh. And it's like they say, there's a fine line between the two, because the laughing tips me over the edge into tears.

'Oh, love.' Harriet steps forward and puts her arms around me. She squeezes me tight. Tears catch and sit on the thick fuzziness of her fleece. She smells like the lavender fabric conditioner Mimi used. 'Goodness,' she wobbles, pulling back to look at me. 'I'm shaking. I dunno why *I* am shaking, bloody cheek of me.'

After a moment, she lifts her sleeve back and peers at a black leather watch at her wrist. 'Oh, girls, I've got to get back, I'm sorry.'

And suddenly I want to grab her by the lapels and tell her to stay with us. Stay and tell me everything about him. Tell me it all. I want to soak it all up, revel in it, bathe in it.

'You've been amazing,' says Priscilla, folding her arms. She's shuddering, her nose, red at the end. 'And I know that you're going to say that you can't say anything, but—'

'But where is he?' nods Harriet. 'The truth is, I don't know. I really don't. Information like his address, his number, that's at his discretion, and I really would be breaching—'

'Is there anything?' I say, my voice is pleading – desperate, even. 'Anything at all?'

'The coast,' she says. 'I know he spends a lot of time at the coast. He likes to move around, take a lot of holidays. But he talks about his place at the coast a lot. Scotland, I think . . .'

'Where in Scotland?' asks Priscilla, eagerly. 'North, south?'

'As I said, girls, I really don't know. He showed me pictures once and I remember thinking he was mad, being out on a bloody cliff in winter, little chalet thingamabob, nothing for miles, but it takes all sorts, as they say.'

'Do you remember anything else he said?'

'Priscilla,' I say. I want to tell her to stop pressing – there's no need now.

'I'm sorry,' Harriet says again, shaking her head. 'It's in Scotland, and it's by the sea. That's all I know.' She looks again at her watch and cocks her head to one side. 'I've gotta make a move, lovies.'

We thank Harriet again, and watch as she trudges across the stony drive.

'Jesus Christ.' Priscilla blows out her cheeks. 'Are you OK?'

My cheeks are tingling, my heart racing, every cell in my body, fizzing. 'Yeah,' I nod. 'I am.'

Priscilla smiles. 'God, I feel like we're close now, Lizzie. Really close. I just wish we knew where to go now. I mean, Scotland's massive, and the coast . . . well, that's bloody broad, isn't it? I just— what?' Priscilla stops and takes in my face, her eyes narrowing. 'What? Why are you looking at me like that? Liz?'

'Because I think I know where he is, Priscilla,' I tell her, my cheeks stinging with how much I am smiling. 'And if I'm right, it's where he said he'd be all along.'

Chapter Twenty-Six

27th November 2005

I told them I couldn't do it. Even Hubble tried to tell them, to let me sit with him, that it was bad timing, and I wasn't in the right frame of mind to be in a place full of people, to walk down an aisle, all eyes on me. Dad, Auntie Shall. Nobody listened.

My bedroom door clicks. I look up. It's Hubble, his crisp white shirt still perfectly pressed, the point of his navy-blue tie between his fingers. 'Found a straggler,' he says with a small, barely-there smile. He pushes the door so it opens wider than a crack and light from the landing brightens the dim haze of my bedroom. Roman, dicky bow wonky at his neck stands beside Hubble, hands in his tuxedo pockets. After Auntie Shall and Uncle Pete's vow ceremony had finished, Dad had found Roman and I in the park. He'd bowled towards us, car keys dangling in his hand at his side, suit jacket swamping his frame.

'The state of you,' he'd muttered, as if only to himself as he approached. He stared only at me, pretended he couldn't even see Roman, although Roman stood at the sight of him, dusting the dirt from his trousers. 'Come and get in the car, Lizzie.'

'Dad. I'm . . . I'm really sorry, I—'

'You're to go and get warm. A hot shower. And get that stuff off of your face.' *Stuff.* Stuff he'd said looked 'stunning' on me just a couple of hours before. Before I had ruined everything for everyone. 'Have an early night. We'll talk in the morning. I think it's best you avoid the scout hut for the reception. Your grandad will be leaving after the meal to look after you.'

I'd waved at Roman as we pulled away, who'd mimed that he would text me. Dad said nothing on the way home, and when he let us in the house, he strode off to the kitchen, leaving no chance for words, from either of us. I went to my room and closed the door. I heard the front door close downstairs a few minutes after.

'Alright?' Hubble asks me now and I give a nod. I haven't moved from my bedroom, from sitting, hugging my pillow on my bed, skin still unthawed from sitting in a frosty park.

'I'll be popping back to the reception now to pick up my coat, then I'm going home,' he carries on. 'Your dad should be back a bit later, so don't take the mick.' Hubble gives a small smile, then leaves us, shutting the door slowly behind him.

Roman stands for a while at the foot of my bed, hands in pockets, head ducked. His eyes drift around the room. 'Nice,' he says, eyeing the posters covering my wardrobe doors. 'Very . . . Lindsay Lohan Freaky Friday.'

I smile. 'Thanks? I think.'

He bends to sit at the bottom of the bed, slouching forward and knitting his fingers together, his forearms leaning on the thighs of his ridiculously long legs. 'I've been wandering, waiting for the house to be free so I could knock, see if you were OK,' he says. He turns to look at me. 'Are you?'

I pause, pull the sleeve of my long pyjama top so the tips of my fingers are only just visible. My face is still itchy with the amount of foundation Auntie Shall's make up artist pasted on this morning, and my curls still stiff with hairspray. 'I don't know. I'm mortified. I can't believe that it happened. I can't believe I *did that*.'

Roman shrugs. 'I told you, it's not your problem, and not your fault.'

'It was just the champagne. I shouldn't have had the bloody champagne. But I was nervous, wasn't I? About the aisle, about the reception . . .'

'J, we've been over this. Nobody would blame you—'

'But they think I was drunk. Dad does. So they all probably do. They'll all be thinking I cared so little about their day that I actually got *pissed*. Nobody will believe it's the tablets, that I didn't realise—'

'Well, fuck them, J, OK? Seriously. Let them believe that. What does it matter?'

I shake my head and cover my face with my hands. 'I just keep thinking of her face. And my dress. Shall's shoes. The *video*.' I look at him through my fingers. 'And what about the performance?'

'What about the bloody performance?' Roman rolls his eyes.

'She wanted to be like Jane McDonald,' I tell him, 'singing and making Uncle Pete fall in love with her all over again and stuff, like she did on the cruise ships. She wanted all of us as backing singers, like she had back then, and she bought me a dress for it. And I ran.'

'You were sick, Lizzie. You were ill, and you were forced down that aisle. Of course you ran.'

I groan and drag my hands through my hair. 'I am so embarrassed, I can't think straight.'

Roman looks to his side at me. 'J, seriously, you did nothing wrong. You told them. You told them you didn't want to walk down the aisle, time and time again, that you didn't want to do the song, that you felt sick. It's no wonder you felt the way you did. Champagne or no champagne.'

'I know.'

'And I know you're getting better but a *performance*? I mean, come on, Lizzie, it's ridiculous, for anyone. A joke. Something out a film.' Roman shakes his head, his face screwed up. 'You go out there, and ask anyone, weeks into recovery or not, if they wanna walk down an aisle, let alone get on a stage and re-enact, I dunno . . . Cliff Richard and the fucking Shadows or some shit. You see what they say.'

We stare at each other across the bed. There's a beat. Then I snort and burst out laughing. And so does Roman. I double over, burying my head into my duvet, laughing so hard my stomach aches, the sound of Roman's laugh making me laugh even more. My cheeks are tight and hot, and tears — happy, joyful tears — wet my bed sheets. I love this laughter. I really do. It makes me feel alive. It warms me through like sunshine.

When I get my breath, I raise my head from the bed, curls gathering now in a mass on my head. Roman is lying back on the duvet, hands on his stomach, his face inches from mine. He smiles, and slowly, hesitantly, reaches a hand up to my face. He runs his finger down the bridge of my nose. The skin on my arms tightens with goosebumps and I don't breathe. I can't. Instead, air and words stay trapped in my throat, fluttering like butterflies. I am frozen. I can't look away, but I also can't bear looking at him this close, all at the same time.

Roman's eyelashes bat slowly, chestnutty curls falling away from his face. 'Hi,' he whispers.

'Hi.' I barely mouth it. Barely breathe.

Roman edges closer, just a tiny bit, so our noses are almost touching. I can feel his breath on my face. He's going to kiss me. I think he's going to kiss me. And I want him to.

There's a low hum. Roman's eyes close, and he laughs. 'Phone,' he says, getting to his feet.

I sit up, my cheeks glowing with hot embarrassment. I don't know where to look. I don't know what to do with my hands.

Roman talks woodenly and quietly into the phone. It's all 'yes', 'no' and 'alright, then'. Then I hear him say 'bro'. It's Ethan. It has to be. I can just tell by the way he's speaking, the way he's standing, slouching and awkward, the way he does when he's with him and his little gang. He changes shape almost, into someone else when he's with them.

'Ah, bugger.' Roman hangs up the phone. He holds it in his hand, at his mouth, lips parted. 'I uh . . . I've gotta shoot, J.'

'Why?'

'Mam,' is all he says. Then he gives an awkward smile and says, 'Plus. Don't fancy being here when your dad gets in.'

I don't say anything about Ethan. I don't say anything about just now or tell him I want him to stay with me. I just say, 'OK. I'll text you,' and settle back against the headboard, legs crossed.

'Cool,' he says.

'Cool,' I say.

His eyes linger on me for a moment, then he strides across the room in one step, ducks and kisses me on the forehead. 'See ya, Cliff,' Roman grins, inches from my face. 'And remember, if Jane McDonald starts giving you shit, keep on running.'

Chapter Twenty-Seven

'Let's have champagne; just a glass each. To celebrate. And also,' Priscilla leans across the counter and whispers, 'it'll help settle our nerves.'

'Why? You're not a nervous flyer.'

'No, I'm not,' says Priscilla, nudging my arm. 'But *you*. You on a plane, Lizzie. It's . . . huge.'

I nod. She's right. It is huge, but the truth is, I hadn't thought much about it. I knew where I needed to be – where Roman was – and I just simply took a breath and booked the tickets. Fear barely had a say. 'My stomach is in knots, I'll admit, but I'm ready for it.'

Priscilla smiles proudly. 'Well, I don't know about you, but my stomach is in knots thinking about actually *getting there*. I can't actually believe we're going to do this.'

'Me neither,' I say. 'Now, where's that barman? I need something strong enough to make Phil Mitchell wince.'

'I'll just have one. Being the driver for this adventure, and all.' Priscilla laughs, and rifles through her handbag, pulling out a tiny circular tin of lip balm. She pats it onto her lips and I look down the length of the bar, eyes glancing at the clock on the wall every few seconds, as if it is even possible that an hour could accidentally fly past and we'd miss our flight.

'So, we'll get into Inverness about eight,' waffles Priscilla, eyeing herself in her compact mirror, 'pick up the hire car, and drive to the hotel. It's about two hours. And I got a four by four. 'Cause you know, it's cold, it's hilly – is hilly the word? Or is it mountainous? Fuck, I've only ever driven as far as Nuneaton. I hope I'm gonna be OK.'

The barman appears, dark eyebrows raised.

'Two glasses of champagne, please,' I say. 'One small, one big.'

This week has been the longest of my life, waiting for today – Friday. For the day that Priscilla and I fly to Scotland, to the lodge park I am positive Roman lives. In a tiny village near Tongue, in the Highlands, where all of us at The Grove went for that school trip where for a few days, we were all set free. That place that fit the criteria for our other life – barely any people, somewhere far away, with nothing but sea and sky for miles and miles – as if you could well be looking out to the very end of the world. I'd known the second Harriet mentioned Scotland, the second she mentioned a cliff, in winter. Instantly, I saw us, sitting high up on that bench, being battered by winds, watching the angry turquoise waves crash and foam, the half-built lodges shells, waiting, ready for new lives to play within them. I knew that's where he'd be.

Priscilla knocks back a mouthful of champagne. 'Thank you, Lizzie,' she says.

I smile, surprised. 'What for?'

'For letting me come.'

I clink Priscilla's glass. 'I wouldn't want to go on a plane or to the middle of nowhere with anyone else. It would always be you. Every time, P.' And I mean it. Priscilla is a source of light to me – she has been from the moment I met her. Even during the darkest, most hopeless times of our lives, when I am with her, when we are together, there is light. Glimmers, bursts, and sometimes, only little sparks, barely there but *there*, nonetheless, reminding me to hope. Reminding me that there are better times ahead – better days – because she is there. Because I have her.

Priscilla nods, her lips pressed together. 'I meant for letting me come along for the ride. For letting me help you find him, for letting me butt in.'

I crinkle my brow. 'Shouldn't I be thanking you?' I ask. 'You've been my sidekick in all this. Actually, *I've* been more of the sidekick. You have been Sherlock. Living and breathing Sherlock.'

Priscilla laughs, then looks down into her glass. 'I needed this, Liz. A distraction.' She doesn't say anything else, and while it's quiet at this bar, amongst the loud hubbub of rushing commuters, ambling time-killing holiday makers, and tannoy announcements, I ask her something that's been niggling at me for weeks really, and ever since she told me about Ethan, on the cobbles by the canal.

'Are you OK, P? I mean. Are you really OK? How is every-thing . . . with you and Chris?'

I expect her to raise her eyebrows, widen those huge eyes of hers, laugh, and do her infamous, over-exaggerated gesture of the hands, and say, 'What, me? *No!* Oh, I'm fine. *Fine!* I'm just tired! You know me, I'm always happy.' But she doesn't. She stares at me, eyes unblinking, glass at her chest in her hand, and shakes her head. 'No,' she says. 'No, I'm not OK. Not at all.'

I nod. 'I've wanted to ask, Priscilla. I have. But I know what you're like. You only talk when you're ready and I've tried to—'

'I know,' Priscilla says. 'And I know you've known for weeks, that things aren't right.'

'You speed up,' I say. 'You always speed up when things are tough and—'

'I know, I know. God, Liz. This whole thing is a mess. It's . . . I mean, me and Chris are fine, I love the man to death, he's wonderful. A saint.' Priscilla pauses and looks at her lap. 'It's me. All me. I'm pushing him away, Lizzie. He . . .' She brings her hand to her forehead and presses her fingers against the skin. 'He wants a baby and . . .'

'You don't.'

'No,' jumps in Priscilla, looking back up at me. 'The thing is, Lizzie, I do. I really do.' Priscilla brings the champagne flute to her mouth and takes another mouthful. 'And OK, yes, he was mentioning trying for a baby two years ago, and then I was dead against it, and he was fine about it. Chris is . . . he's never put pressure on me. He might mention it, joke about it, say something like "you don't *have* to take it, you know" when I take a pill, but he's always said if I never want children, then that's fine.' Priscilla closes her eyes, as if gathering herself. She opens them again. 'But last year, we went to see Perry's daughter's new baby and he talked a bit more seriously about it in the car on the way home. And I told him we'd start trying. Soon. But I never took a pill after that.' She pauses and looks at me. 'I was hoping to surprise him. But . . .' She doesn't finish. She puts down her glass on the bar and brings her hands together, at her nose, as if in prayer. 'It hasn't happened. Nothing. Not even a day late, not once.'

'Priscilla,' I lean in. 'It can take a while. I'm certainly no doctor but look at Eva and Cal. Three years of trying and—'

'Say if . . .' Priscilla shakes her head and dabs at her eyes with the pads of her fingers. 'Lizzie, say if that baby was my only chance, and I blew it.'

'No,' I utter. 'You don't – that's not how it works, P.'

'How do we know, though?' she asks, dark-with-mascara tears now steadily sliding, one after the other, from her eyes. She takes a small square napkin from the bar and dabs at her cheeks. 'How do we know that the baby I was pregnant with at sixteen wasn't the only baby my body was going to make. That Ethan's baby wasn't the only one written in the stars for me and I . . .' Her words catch in her throat. 'I got rid of it. Just like that.'

I hold her hands tightly and open my mouth to speak, but the barman appears at our side and picks up Priscilla's empty glass.

'Can I get you another drink?'

'Two orange juices. A little champagne in mine, please,' I say quickly, and he walks off. 'P,' I whisper. 'Have you been to the doctor?'

Priscilla shakes her head and says, 'I already know. I know what it is. They told me. After the termination, when I had all those problems. It was on a sheet they gave me. That . . .' Priscilla pauses, voice wobbling. 'That it can sometimes, in very rare cases, cause infertility.'

'In very *rare* cases, Priscilla,' I say, but she's already crying, hands hiding her face. 'Look, you did the right thing, back then. Do not for a minute beat yourself up about something that was right for you.'

Priscilla looks at me, lifting her shoulders to her ears. 'I just can't shake this feeling that I'm being punished.'

'No. No, Priscilla.'

'And now I'm going to have to explain it all to Chris, aren't I? Everything. That I got knocked up at sixteen and I've probably ruined our chances of having kids, just like that.'

'You didn't do anything *just like that*, Priscilla—'

'At some random party,' Priscilla's angry words run right over mine, 'with a boy that treated me like I was something to be used and thrown away. I'm an idiot.'

My heart throbs. I want to tell her she doesn't know that, that it's the worst-case scenario, and making a mistake at sixteen, at *any* age, doesn't define anyone. It's a mistake. We're allowed to make them. And no god, no force in their right mind would punish a woman, a good person – anyone – for something like this. But she is crying again, and I can do nothing but wrap my arms around her and tell her everything will be OK. Because it will be. We haven't come this far to be shaken now. And Priscilla is steel. We are.

Two hours, two more drinks, and a Burger King meal each later, Priscilla has made me promise that the subject is to be left in London, and we are on the plane, fifteen minutes into our journey to Inverness. On our way to see Roman. *Roman.* My friend Roman. I want to say it out loud. I want to say it over and over again. I want to tell every single person on this plane.

'I could eat another one,' I say, rubbing my stomach.

'Another what?'

'Whopper,' I say to Priscilla, as a flight attendant walks by with her trolley of puffed up Pringles and miniature cans of coke.

Priscilla pauses, then bends, losing herself in giggles. '*Whopper*,' she squeaks. 'Do you . . . do you remember?'

'What?' I laugh, as she bends, dragging down on my arm, juddering with giggles beside me.

'It's what we called Mr Reed's dick,' she laughs, hysterically, as a man a few seats away, looks up from his laptop, and scowls.

'P, *shhhhh.*'

'Don't you remember?' whispers Priscilla, eyes wide. 'Oh, come on, of course you do.'

'Priscilla, I do, but people can hear—'

'When he came into school in those cycling shorts and you could see it. Like a damn marrow with a beating heart, it was so big. And we drew it in your maths book and you . . . you drew it . . . with arms . . . holding dumbbells . . . and *breeze blocks*.'

The man on the laptop, tuts and huffs, as we explode into fits of laughter.

Bursts of light, up here, in dark, autumn skies.

Chapter Twenty-Eight

2nd December 2005

Roman finds me on the bathroom floor, knees under my chin, my back against the bath, the lights off. He opens the door and stands in the doorway for a moment, hesitating, before pulling the door closed behind him and crossing the room, boots scuffing on the tiles. He sits beside me, back against the bathtub, long legs in front of him.

'Nathan let me in,' he says. 'Cold arse?'

'A bit.'

'Generally what happens when you sit on the floor of a bog.'

'I felt like I was going to be sick,' I tell him. My voice is deep and hoarse but tiny, and it echoes around the cold, empty bathroom, barely sounding like my own. All the crying. All the heartache, ripping through me like a storm. 'I just needed to be somewhere cool and dark.'

Roman shuffles so our hips touch. 'Like a slug,' he says, putting his arm around me.

'My face looks like a slug.'

Roman laughs. 'Give over.'

'It does,' I croak, laying my head on his shoulder. 'It's swollen. Like a big bollock. From the crying. I think that's why Dad's gone away to his cousins'. He says it's to talk to them about Hubble, explain what happened, talk about the funeral but . . .

me crying; he doesn't know what to say to me. He can barely look at me.' I choke on the words.

Roman squeezes me into him. The whirring of the extractor fan on the wall stops, and besides the drip-dropping of water, there is pure silence. Neither of us says anything. We just sit, side by side, in the darkness, the sounds of Nathan and Katie moving downstairs, opening the fridge, closing the living room door, turning up the television, echoing through the floor. It reminds me of when I'd lie in bed and listen to Mum and Dad downstairs when I was younger, when they were together, when I felt safe. I feel safe now, here, with Roman.

'Tell me,' I whisper into the darkness, 'things will get better.'

Roman swallows. 'They will.'

'Promise me.'

Silence.

'Roman?'

I lift my head from his shoulder. The only thing lighting the room is the moon outside, shimmering through the frosted glass of the bathroom windows, but I can see his eyes are watery. I can see the shadows on his face.

'What's wrong?'

He looks at me. 'Sorry,' he says. 'I just . . .' He blows out a breath, his cheeks puffed out, and brings the heels of his hands to his head.

'Ro? What is it?'

Roman closes his eyes and brings his hands down so they're hiding his face. 'It's . . . H-Hubble, man,' he says, his voice cracking. 'This is so hard, J. It's not fair. I . . . miss him. He should be here. He should be right here and—' Beneath his hand, Roman sniffs, his voice breaking and I feel like a thumb is pressed on my heart, bruised as it already is. Roman misses Hubble. He loved him. Like I did. It's been six days since I've been able to call him, to hear his voice, to nuzzle my nose into his flannel shirts, to smell his lovely smell, to hold his crepey, strong hand, to watch him make mince and mash, humming to the radio, using patterned, chipped dishes and pots he and Mimi got on the happiest day of their lives, forty years before, and the longing in my gut is sickening. I miss him. I miss him so much my bones ache and I want to scream. I link my arms around Roman's, and in a heap on the dark bathroom floor, we huddle together, foreheads pressed together. We listen to the silence and the sound of each other's breathing, and we sit like that for ages, head to head, limbs tangled. I don't know what to do. I don't know the way out of this. How will we ever smile again, without him?

'Shit.' Roman wipes his eyes roughly with the back of his hand. His eyes open slowly, his dark lashes fanning so close to my cheeks that I feel them. He shakes his head, forehead still pressed to mine. 'I feel like everything's changing,' Roman says, his voice so quiet, it's barely there. 'And I'm— I'm scared, J.'

I push a loose wave of hair away from Roman's eye. He's beautiful. He really, really is. 'Don't be scared,' I whisper to him, even though I am too. Terrified. 'I'm here.'

He stares at me with deep blue eyes. They shine like marbles. 'You,' he murmurs, the corner of his mouth twitching a smile. 'You're . . . something.'

'Something?'

His breath tickles my lips. His eyelashes catch on mine. 'Perfect,' he whispers.

And like we've done it a million times before, in every version of ourselves, in every universe, I kiss him. I kiss Roman Meyers. I press my lips softly to his; those pink, perfect lips, and feel the warmth of them on mine. So close. Closer than we've ever been. He leans forward, kissing me back, and like something has interrupted us, we draw back, suddenly, lips inches apart. Roman looks at me. I look at him. My heart thumps in my throat. I open my mouth to speak, but the second I do, Roman's lips are on mine, parted now, his hand holding the side of my face, his fingers in my hair, hungry, both of us melting together. And I fall away from myself. I'm free in this moment. Nothing else exists. And I don't want him to stop. I don't want this to end.

Roman Meyers is kissing me.

More.

We are more.

Chapter Twenty-Nine

It's just like I remember. Rugged, dark and moody, and utterly, utterly beautiful. Other-worldly, really. A place of nothing but stretches of landscape, and hills that look like a watercolour, the houses in the distance, dotted upon them like tiny white Lego bricks. Priscilla drives slowly, with both hands on the wheel. At the next turning, we will be there. We will be at Cliff Acre Park – the now finished site that me and Roman sat beside when they were only half-built. We will be there, where we always promised to be when we met again. We will be there, at the end of the world.

'That *view*,' says Priscilla, as we wind, close to the cliff edge, an endless stretch of rough, angry sea beside us, like wide open arms, welcoming me back. Priscilla looks at me quickly, then back to the road. 'We OK?'

I nod. And so does she. Then she reaches over and squeezes my hand.

'Fuck,' she says.

'*Fuuuuck*,' I say. Then we both burst out laughing.

'I feel a bit sick, you know,' laughs Priscilla. 'Like I might shit myself.'

'Oh? Oh, it's nerves,' I sing. 'I know your bowels *so* intimately, Priscilla, you'll never ever *shit* yourself.'

Priscilla shoves my leg and laughs loudly – that infectious pneumatic drill of a laugh that's been part of the soundtrack of so many of our memories together. 'Shut up,' she says 'Oh, look. Are they lodges? Those little dots. Do you think that's it? The park?'

As Priscilla turns the car left, it all comes into view. It's as if I have been winded; a punch to the stomach, and all the clocks in the world have stopped ticking. Everything slows, and I feel like I am stepping into a memory – a place that is sharper and crisper than the memory itself. Everything is the same. The cliff where we sat on that bench is just ahead, and just beyond it, I'm sure I can see the lodges like tiny bricks on the horizon – on the grassy heath that was once a building site.

'This is it,' I say, the tension building in my chest with each breath, like strong wings fluttering against my chest. 'God, Priscilla, this is definitely it.'

We are so far from home. We are so far from everything that is safe, and it's not until I stepped on the plane, saw the world below getting tinier and tinier as we rose into the sky, that I realised how stuck I have been, living in what is a tiny, barely-there speck on this earth. Dormant, even, because living is something I haven't done for so long, not really. And I want to. As I felt us take off, home moving further and further from me, and now, as I look out to endless ocean and endless sky, I realise I *really* want to. I want to see places and do things and feel *terrified* but do it anyway. I don't want to hide anymore. What's that quote? The one about wanting to see the world, as much as you can, before it goes dark. That's what I want. Because there is no darkness now. I left that behind twelve years ago. I want to start living in the light, where I can be seen.

'Don't look down,' winces Priscilla, fists clenched around the steering wheel as we pass a sheer, stomach-flipping drop to nothing but jagged ocean below. 'Take more than the AA to save our arses if we fell down there now.'

'Yeah, try not to kill us before we get there, P,' I smile. 'I'd prefer not to die never knowing.'

I open the window halfway, and cold air laps in, whipping our faces. I remember this; the smell of the salt and the way the air felt new and clean, like it had been made just for us. I remember the greens – a kaleidoscope of them – and the hills of thistley grass that looked as though it would leave scratches on your skin if you laid upon it. I remember the view that knocks the wind from your lungs. And I remember exactly how I felt. Free. Hopeful. Healthy.

'This is it,' Priscilla says, tapping a fingernail to the sat nav's screen. 'See.'

Priscilla is always calm, but I can tell by the way her hands squeeze the wheel, the way her shoulders are up by her ears and her eyes are barely blinking, that she's nervous. The way she'd get before she did a presentation at school or knew she would be seeing Ethan Sykes at a party. He was the only boy ever to do that to her. She shrunk around him.

Priscilla clicks the headlights on. The November sky is dimming now, beginning to cloud with the smoke of the night, and the lodges are silhouettes, growing bigger as we approach. One of them in the distance is Roman's. One of those lodges is where Roman lives. I know it now, inside, in my veins and my gut, that we're in the right place. Maybe it's hope. It feels like much more.

We arrive at the entrance. A wrought iron gate, and a burgundy sign, bordered in gold and with a small lamp above it, dimly lighting the words, 'Welcome to Cliff Acre Park'. Priscilla pulls in, the nose of the car inches from the gate. It's shut, and doesn't open automatically, like I expect. Through the railings, there is a steep path, just wide enough for a car, and at the top, a brick chalet, posters and leaflets in the window, but it's in darkness. A reception, perhaps, for guests to check in.

Priscilla kills the engine and undoes her seatbelt. We stare through the windscreen, then at each other.

'It . . . it looks shut,' I say.

'But there're lights on.'

Priscilla's right. The street lamps that light the path beyond the gate are on, dim against the dusk.

'I'll try the gate.' Priscilla gets out of the car, skipping over to the entrance. She pulls hard on the railing. It doesn't budge. Through the window, she turns back and shrugs, mouthing, 'It's locked.'

Now my heart is sinking.

Priscilla gets back into the car, slamming the door behind her and bringing her arms around herself. 'Jesus, it's *freezing*.' The pair of us look out at the locked gate again, in silence. She leans forward, cupping her hands around her eyes and looks out into the darkening night. 'Maybe there's another way in.'

'Where though, P?'

Silence again.

There's tension now, between us both. The hope that surrounded us and bounced off us so tangibly, like electricity is slowly turning into sizzling, hot tension and panic. We've come all the way here – all the way to the end of the world, alone – all because a stranger told us the person we are trying to find lived in Scotland, in a chalet. This is the white rabbit again, and we have chased it for hundreds of miles – hundreds of miles to a dead end.

A car pulls behind us, gradually slowing and then stopping. The headlights fill our car with yellow light. Both of us turn to look through the rear window. A figure gets out of the car – a large, dark, four by four. And all I am thinking is that this is the part where we get murdered. This is when we get murdered and people all over crow about how two young women shouldn't be in the Highlands in a bitter cold seaside town in November, alone, on a cliff-top, with nothing but useless mobile phones with barely-there signal and half a Spar shop tuna sandwich between them.

The figure approaches the car, his engine still running behind us, headlights still on. Priscilla clicks down the lock on her door. There is a bang as all the locks shut into place at once. The figure is at the window. It's a man. He bends and knocks on the glass. He must be Hubble's age. His face is a mix of concern and irritation.

Priscilla presses to slide open the window.

'If you're going to sit with your rear out like that, put on your hazards,' he says. 'This road is narrow and if there's passing traffic, we won't see you.' He has a thick Scottish accent.

'Oh, I-I'm sorry,' says Priscilla, her saleswoman phone voice springing into life. 'I didn't realise I was jutting out.'

'It's a narrow road.'

'We're not from the area.'

'Aye. Right.'

He looks at the gate, then at me, then again at Priscilla. He rubs his chin with thick, chubby hands. They're gnarly from arthritis or gout or something similar, and at his wrists there is blue checked material jutting out from under a huge dark wax jacket. I smile at him. He doesn't smile back. Again, the news article and 1453 *Daily Mail* comments about how women should never be on cliff-tops alone, saying we brought it on ourselves, flash through my mind.

'You after a place to stay?'

'No,' I say quickly, and it alarms both him and Priscilla. 'We are staying in a hotel,' I say, softer this time. He nods once.

'It's closed.'

'Sorry?'

'*This,*' he says, eyes rolling in irritation. 'Cliff Acre. It's closed. Season runs March through to October.'

'Oh,' says Priscilla. 'We were hoping to get in.'

The man laughs and says, 'You can't. Ain't no night life round here, girls. It's shut.' Then he steps away from the car, says, 'Put your hazards on if you're gonna stay here,' taps the roof of the car and then mutters something about staying safe. When he drives off, he toots his horn twice and raises a hand, and disappears up the creeping hill at speed, as if he does this every day and doesn't have to think twice about hill starts and how not to career off the sides into the blisteringly cold ocean beneath the roads.

There's silence between Priscilla and I.

'I can't believe—'

'Lizzie,' says Priscilla. But I can see she is searching her head for words. 'Look, this ain't over, babe. We'll sort it. We'll sort something.' Then she clicks open the car door. 'I need a wee.'

'Can't you wait until we're back at the hotel?'

'No, I'm literally gonna piss myself. If you see Farmer Giles, send a smoke signal.'

She shoves the hazard button and gets out of the car. She ambles over to the sign, wind whipping her face, and moves behind it, into the bushes. She disappears, pops her head out, puts her thumb up, and disappears again.

I can't believe this. I cannot believe we were so stupid. To just get on an actual *plane*, to rent a car and come all this way, to a town we have no idea about, except for a glorified silly school trip which is mostly a blur. We should have written or something, found some sort of phone number, we should have thought about this. But we didn't. Not enough. We got too caught up in the whirlwind of it all, after meeting Harriet; after getting so close. I rode my emotions all the way here.

To Scotland, to Tongue. Where me and Roman were, twelve years ago.

But he isn't here.

Roman isn't here.

Maybe we missed the boat. Maybe we left it too late, and the life in which me and Roman meet again, is out there, playing out, without us in it.

Priscilla clicks open the car door and pulls it open wide. She stands there looking in at me, her mac open at the waist, flapping in the bitter wind that has picked up outside. 'There was an intercom,' she says, breathlessly, her eyes wide. 'And I spoke to someone. A bloke. It's closed to holidaymakers. But not residents.'

Priscilla gets into the car, quickly, shutting the door, not buckling her seatbelt, and as I open my mouth to speak, the gate in front of us begins to open. Priscilla turns to me; she's grinning a dazzling white smile.

'I've found him,' she beams, starting the engine. 'The man I spoke to says Roman is a resident. And he's home. You were right, Lizzie. You were right.'

This PC/D: Lizzie Laptop/Roman/
Roman signed in on 22/06/05 21:01
Lizzie: Hi Ro.
Lizzie: You hiding offline? Are you there?
Roman: Hey J
Roman: I am. Looks like you found me.
Roman: Been waiting for you :)

Chapter Thirty

Roman lives at number eighteen Cliff Acre Park. He's alive. He's here. I've found him.

Number eighteen is the furthermost lodge, at the highest point of the cliff, and the closest to the edge – the edge of the cliff, where we once sat, and looked out to endless sea and sky.

'If you fancy the beach, drive down to the car park. Don't be tempted to use the footpath you can access by Roman's. Gets very slippery,' said Freddie, the man who Priscilla spoke with on the intercom. He was tall, round, with a wide smile that made his eyes close. In his sixties, I'd guess. He and his wife, Saskia, a small, giggling, gutsy woman with beautiful long blonde hair, live in number four, and told us proudly they were wardens of the park. Priscilla had done most of the talking, while I stood outside the car, gazing around the park, digging deep for air in my lungs, unable to find a single word.

'And he's home? We're old friends and, well, it's a surprise,' Priscilla had beamed.

'Yep, he's home, my love, last time I checked.' They directed us to Roman's lodge, all hands and arms, and I was glad Priscilla was listening, because I couldn't hold onto a single word they were saying – it was like they were oiled, just passing in one ear and out of the other.

'They brighten the place up,' Saskia had told us. 'Him and Barney.'

'*Barney?*' Priscilla had gawped, and Freddie had laughed. 'His mutt,' he said, and my body filled with warmth, like pouring treacle. He has a dog. *Someone to love him in all of his ugliness.*

We'd got back into the car, and Freddie had leaned into the window and told us the code to the gate, so we can 'come and go as we please'. It amazed me how trusting they were, but as we drove off, I saw Freddie knock on a neighbouring lodge's window and wave. This tiny little nook in the middle of a sleepy coastal town, battered by the seasons, is probably the sort of place where doors are left unlocked, and everybody knows each other. 'It's a family. A big family.' Freddie's words.

It was easy to find Roman's lodge.

'Follow the road round until it ends, and that's Roman,' Freddie had said. 'He's got the best views, the most peace and the coldest winds.'

And it is peaceful. There are minutes between the last lodge we saw and Roman's. It's on its own. And it looks out to the end of the world, which roars and crashes beneath us.

It's only seven o'clock but it's dark, and from inside the hire car, under the deep, indigo sky, stars sprayed across it like paint, the end of the world looks like exactly that.

'Do you want me to get out and just go and see—'

'No, no.'

'I don't mind coming to the door with you, babe. We can knock and I'll run before he—'

'No, Priscilla,' I say. 'No. I'll be fine. I just need a moment.'

'Course,' nods Priscilla, and other than the distant roar of waves, there is silence.

We've been sitting here for the last ten minutes or so, staring at the back of Roman's lodge and the small, grey path which circles the side of it, around to Roman's front door. And sitting here, already, I know more than I have ever known about Roman as a man; Roman in his next life. He has a dog named Barney, he drives a Range Rover in bottle green, which has a tree-shaped air freshener hanging from the rear-view mirror, and he has blinds up in his lodge. Beige ones, and tonight, dim lamplight glows behind them. Roman is behind them, too. Roman is home. He is just feet away.

When we first pulled up, we saw the lights on, steam rising and wisping from the small metal chimney on the side of his lodge, and the excitement had surged through us like an electric shock. We screamed. Then laughed and screamed some more – a release of everything built up inside us. But now, the excitement has gone, and it's like everything is still – as if the clocks have once again stopped. We made it. We found him. And now, I get to see him. I get to look at him, talk to him, and not just in made-up conversations in my head.

'After this,' I say to Priscilla in the quiet of the car, 'I don't get to dream up answers that make me feel better. And I'm scared.'

'Scared is OK.' Priscilla reaches over to hold my hand. 'Scared means that you're on the edge of something happening. Of change.'

'I hate change.'

Priscilla laughs. 'We all do. But we love it, too. The whole human race is in a love-hate relationship with change.'

'Say he tells me to fuck off.'

'Lizzie, as if—'

'Or say if he doesn't want to see me, for whatever reason, and all this was a waste of time?'

Priscilla puts her hand on mine. 'Well, if he does, then we have this, Lizzie, don't we? We have this trip, and this crazy memory. We have me and you. Always.' Moonlight reflects in Priscilla's eyes. 'Now. I promised you a long time ago that you weren't ever getting rid of me. That I'd be beside you, behind you and in front of you dragging you the fuck along when you need me to.'

I laugh, my voice is thick, and there are tears at the edges of my eyes.

'And that, my friend,' laughs Priscilla, 'is where I'm about to be. In front of you, dragging your arse up that path.'

We look at one another. 'Go and knock, Lizzie. Get out of the car and knock. There's nothing between you now. No parents, no dragon-arse aunties, no social workers, no hospitals. Just you and Roman. You two.'

And I know that she is right. It is time. It is time for answers. It is time for us to meet again.

I click open the car door.

'Do you have signal?' asks Priscilla.

'Yes,' I say, checking my phone. 'Three bars, no internet, though.'

'Text me. Have a text ready on your phone. An 'I'm OK', or one word or something, and press send the second you know it definitely *is* Roman, and that you *are* OK with me leaving, and I'll go back to the hotel. The second you need me to come and get you, just call me. I'll wait up.'

I nod. 'OK. Thanks, P.'

'And I'm gonna wait here for a while,' she says. 'OK? Even if you send the text. I'll wait for half an hour or something.'

I push open the car door. 'OK.' Then we pause and Priscilla leans forward, throwing her arms around me. I hold her tightly. My Priscilla. My lovely, lovely Priscilla.

'I love you,' I say.

'I love you too, Liz,' she says. 'Shit loads.'

I don't feel the icy winds or the spray from either the sea or the beginnings of rain, as I walk the path to Roman's lodge. I am shaking, but I am warm. I am where I am meant to be in this moment.

I turn the corner, Priscilla now out of sight. And I stop, dead, at the sight of it all; of Roman's home. *A porch*. Roman has a porch. The wraparound porch we talked about, looking out to the sea, and I feel like I am stepping into a dream. Into a life that's been waiting for me all this time, somewhere out there, in the universe.

I count my shaking breaths as I step up to the front door. I hear the muffled sounds of a television. Audience laughter.

Here goes nothing. Here goes everything.

And I knock.

An explosion of deep, excitable barks. *Barney*.

Then a muffled voice, too quiet to make out the words. And footsteps. Heavy, steady. I stand back, phone in my hand, thumb hovering above 'send'.

The door opens.

And he fills the frame. Taller. Broader. But I know. It's the eyes. And it's the mouth.

I press send, and look up at my friend – my friend Roman Meyers.

Chapter Thirty-One

I don't know how I thought it would be. I have imagined this moment so many times; many versions of it. I have imagined a thousand different scenes starring me and Roman; one, five, twelve, thirteen, twenty and even thirty years forward. In some it was awkward, in some I screamed at him, in some we flew together, and in others, I didn't recognise him at first, or he didn't recognise me. In most, it was awkward, stuttery, talking all at once, and then not at all, and the desperate searching for a reason to leave, get away – like when you're cornered by an old school friend in the supermarket.

But like most things, it's never how you imagine.

As soon as I saw his face, I wanted to cry tears of joy. Happiness – this sudden, fizzing happiness, filled me from my toes to my brain, like a champagne bottle, just opened. And then I could barely speak.

Roman, at first, spent a couple of seconds with that 'yes?' face on – the sort of face you have on for the person that stands on your doorstep with a clipboard and a fixed grin. That raised eyebrow, shut-mouthed smile, a corner upturned, eyes unblinking. Then, it registered. I saw the exact moment that it did, like a penny landing with a clang. His face dropped, his mouth fell open. His whole body, sort of sagged. It was like watching a slow-motion video of someone who'd just been booted in the stomach.

And as if I had been rehearsing, I said, 'Hi, Roman.' It was relaxed, almost amused, almost cocky with a, 'so, are you just gonna stand there, then?' confidence. But I was none of those things. I was elated. I was heartbroken. All at the same time.

Because it was Roman.

Older, manlier, broader, more chiselled. But Roman. Roman Meyers, standing in front of me, on the cliff which we sat on twelve years ago, planning our lives, planning what we'd do and who we'd be when we were free.

He opened his mouth to speak. But he didn't. Couldn't. His hands flew up to his head and he held his skull, staring wide eyed at me; as if he'd just witnessed a near-miss. As if I was that boat manoeuvring through the waves, too close to an iceberg.

'Hi,' I said again, thinking for a moment that he didn't recognise me, or thought the years had stamped on me, wiped the floor with me, and he was shocked at the sight of me. I had played out this scenario so many times. I knew this part. He thought I was Lizzie but then I had aged so badly that he was too scared to say my name in case it wasn't me and instead some very old lady looking for a Tupperware party or something and had got the wrong door. So, I went to say my name. I stepped forward, just inches between us both now, and had, 'It's me. Lizzie,' on the tip of my tongue.

But then his lips parted, and with his hands holding his forehead, his chest rising and falling, he said my name. In a whisper. 'Lizzie.'

And beneath the stars, like a thousand searching torches, suddenly, I was in his arms, and he was holding me, tightly against his chest, and that's where we stayed, on the wraparound porch, swaying side to side, the waves, rumbling, crashing beyond the darkness.

He said my name again, louder, and then, 'Oh my god,' and, 'Jesus, I can't believe this,' and at the sound of his voice, which was the exact same, just in a deeper note, butterflies broke free in my stomach. And I told him I'd never forgotten that sound. Then I looked up at him, and said, 'So. *Tongue.*' And he'd laughed, and so did I. Muffled, hysterical laughter, our arms still wrapped around each other, faces buried – both of us knitted together, under that endless sky.

Then the rain began.

Fat, noisy drops, so cold they stung my scalp.

And when we pulled back to look at each other, I couldn't work out if they were rain drops or tears on his face. I knew what they were on mine.

Roman smiled, and squinting to look up at the sky, he laughed, and said 'Welcome back, J. Do you want to come in?'

Steam rises from our mugs, and dances between us. Roman made tea the minute we got inside, and as he stood in the kitchen, he seemed to forget how. I watched him from my seat at the small, square kitchen table, Barney laying at my side, as he took out mugs, swapped them, then put them back. He'd then got one out. Then two. Then boiled a kettle that had nothing in it but a trickle.

And I started laughing. So did he. He held the sides of the kitchen counter and looked over at me, grinning that grin that always exploded onto his face.

'You've forgotten how to make tea,' I said. 'Do you want me to do it?'

'I'm a twat,' he said, laughing. 'I'm all over the shop here.'

'Me too,' I said.

'And no. You sit. I can do this.'

Now, at the small, square table, in the warmth of the teak lodge, we sit in the dim light of the kitchen. Just us. Me and

Roman. Twelve years on. Rain clatters down. The TV in the next room, mumbles. It's us, opposite each other, questions hanging in the air around and above us like clouds, but both too winded to ask the first one – both too stunned. So, we just gaze at each other and then our teas, fiddling with the mug handles, and not looking around the room, but just giving the impression of it, with the movement of our necks and heads, turning our faces, to pass the time.

'I'm . . .'

I look up from my tea. He's looking at me, smiling gently.

'I . . . I guess I'm speechless,' he says. He is still so beautiful, his smile still transforms his face, his eyes still flash with something at all times. Cheek. Worry. Amusement. All of them.

'Y-you're here. You're actually here,' he says. 'Lizzie J. In my kitchen.'

I wrap my cold, shaky hands around the mug. 'And I'm here. At Roman M's table. In *Tongue.*'

Roman smiles. His Adam's apple bobs in his neck. 'God. I never thought I'd ever . . .' He trails off. He can't speak.

'Me either.' I look skyward, to the high, wooden ceiling, and in and around Roman's home. It's beautiful. It's small, and cosy, and full of books, and weird trinkets and instruments. It has him all over it. 'I like it,' I say. 'It's very *you.*'

'Thanks.' Roman slouches back on his chair. He gazes at me, thick eyelashes slowly batting. 'Got the wood burning stove.'

'Have you?'

'In the other room.'

Then there's silence again. There is so much I want to say – but it all just sits in my chest, crammed, and blocked; a huge mass in my throat. I'm guessing if it was any other type of reunion – the type between two old school friends who just fizzled, who moved away, promised to write and never did, then this might be the sort of reunion full of, 'how the devil are you?'s and 'what are you doing here?'s. But it isn't like that. It feels nothing like that. It's as if the last twelve years have been geared towards this moment – like we both knew, on some level, that we were always headed here, and now we have arrived. Sitting still within it, this moment; soaking it in, before things have to move, have to change again.

'I tried calling you.'

'Which number?'

'Ramesh—' I start.

'It's an old one. Pay as you go. I'm rubbish with phones. Don't like them.'

'Ah.' Simple. The simplest of answers.

More silence now. The fridge whirs behind us. Barney pads out of the room.

'I've thought about this,' Roman utters. 'Hundreds of times. And you think you know how you'll feel or what you'll say, then it happens, and . . . god,' he chuckles to himself, 'I— you . . . you look exactly like you.'

'So do you,' I laugh.

'You still have the lone dimple.' Roman leans forward and touches my cheek. 'The lone, orphan dimple lives on.'

My cheeks heat at his touch.

'And you still have that mouth,' I say. '*Too big for your face,*' we say together. Our laughter trails off, and there's quiet between us again. The rain hammers the lodge and a sombre, newsreader's voice mumbles from the television next door.

'I feel like I'm dreaming,' I say. 'Like, I'm going to wake up any moment or something.'

'Well if that's what this is,' says Roman, with a smile, 'let's hope we don't.'

Then I start from the beginning; from the letter that I held in my hands, on that sweltering tube carriage, back in July, to now, and everything in between. The hours speed by, and as the silent early hours creep in, Roman falls asleep first, and I lay there, beside him on the sofa, watching him, counting his eyelashes, and imagining, like I did back in that caravan, what answers and secrets are playing out beneath the skin, beneath the skull, and in that brain of his.

This PC/D: Lizzie Laptop/Roman/
Roman signed in on 27/05/05 22:11

Lizzie: been calling you.

Roman: I know J. Sorry. lefft my phone hERe

Lizzie: where've you been?

Roman: ooooout :P

Lizzie: I meant where did you go?

Roman: chill

Roman: popped out with ethan baby.

Lizzie: why are you being weird?

Roman: im not

Lizzie: you are. you're typing weird. you called me baby.

Lizzie: are you OK?

Lizzie: Roman???

Roman: I am.

Lizzie: I thought you said you wouldn't see him anymore. after last month.

Roman: I'm fine lizzie

Lizzie: I'm just worried. I'm obviously going to be after what happened.

Roman: I know. But pls stopppp.

Roman: I'm fine

Lizzie: you're still being weird. Have you done something? please tell me the truth.

Roman: No! I promise. I swear. I'm fine. Just a bit drrunk

Lizzie: ok

Roman: Don't sulk with me J.

Lizzie: I'm not.

Roman: don't make me paint you another willy in a fur coat

and monocle. Just because you aren't at the grove anymore
doesn't mean I can't paint you penis masterpieces in art
therapy

Roman: i will not hesitate

Lizzie: shut up.

Roman: to prove that all penises are not sad ugly grub worms
like you think they are

Lizzie: Shut up!

Roman: Hahahaha. I can feel you smiling from here.

Roman: Meet me tomorrow before school?

Lizzie: Ok. 8:15? by post box?

Roman: yeh. I'll call you.

Lizzie: you better.

Lizzie: See you in the morning.

Chapter Thirty-Two

'What are you, the robber from *Home Alone*?'

'This is Scotland, J. It's freezing.'

'But fingerless gloves?'

Roman laughs, grabbing one of my hands, and says, 'And there are actual eyes on your gloves. *Raccoon* eyes. Like that's normal.'

We've been awake since eight, after four awkward, uncomfortable hours sleeping, sitting on the sofa, one at each end, under a thin blue throw. Roman got up first, and I woke to the distant clinking and rumbling of the kettle in the other room. It was dizzying, waking with him there; as if I was dreaming, or had woken up, age fifteen, after a nap in Sea Fog on Roman's mum's driveway. Things felt even better this morning – I had that fizzy holiday feeling, where the day ahead is a clean slate, and only yours to fill. I kept looking at him, over my tea, and I caught him doing the same. We kept laughing, like kids, kept grinning at each other in the silence, shaking our heads, eyes widening in disbelief.

Roman took our mugs back to the kitchen and found me in the doorway of the porch, looking out to the sea, Barney at my side.

'We could go for a walk. Unless you need to—'

I shook my head. 'No, that sounds perfect. Can you give me an hour? I'm gonna go back to the hotel, see P, take a shower, put on some clothes.' I pulled on my hair. 'Sort out my hair so I don't look like Meatloaf.'

Roman laughed. 'Ten points if you can tell me his real name.'

I crossed my arms. 'Pete um . . . l . . . s . . .'

'Clue: It doesn't rhyme with loaf.'

'Then I'm stumped.'

I'd called Priscilla who answered the phone after half a ring and was at Roman's within fifteen minutes. He walked me to the car, hands in pockets, ducking his head in the way he used to back then, where his hair would dangle down and hide his face. His hair is shorter now. Still wavy, still messy and deep chestnut brown, but nowhere near long enough to fall over his eyes. Priscilla squealed when she saw him, jumping out the car and putting her arms around him. They both laughed and hugged for ages. Priscilla kept holding his face and saying, 'Fuck. *Fuck!* You're a man. A huge, massive, grown man.'

We went back to the hotel, and I showered and got dressed, while P sat on the loo and quizzed me, her mouth moving at the speed of light, answering her own questions, speculating excitedly about the day me and Roman would spend together. She packed my bag as I dried my hair.

'Just in case,' she said, stuffing a canvas tote bag with pyjamas, my make up-bag, a toothbrush, and a cardigan, 'you want to stay again.'

She dropped me back at the lodge and then told me she was going half an hour out of town to a second-hand book shop, then going back to the hotel to 'read and eat everything'. 'But call me any time and I will shoot back,' she'd said, kissing my cheeks. 'I'm proud of you,' she said, and I told her she was the greatest friend a woman could wish for – the type I used to dream about when I was a lonely nine-year-old and read *The Babysitters Club* books in awe.

Now me and Roman, wrapped up to the necks in coats, hats pulled down to our eyebrows, traipse up the hill we sat upon all those years ago. The wind sweeps into us, as if playing a game to see who it can knock over first, and Barney runs ahead, mouth open, as if grinning and in total ecstasy at being outside, in the fresh air.

'Just a bit further,' says Roman, breathlessly, into the wind. 'Just up here.'

My cheeks tingle, and my hair, from the bottom of my hat, whips around my face.

'This feels like country mouse and city mouse,' I puff, treading uphill. Roman turns and looks at me and laughs.

'Who's who?' he grins.

'*Ha-ha.*'

'Come on, J. Put your back into it.'

Roman turns, walking backwards, then takes my hand and twirls me under his arm, the way dancers do, until I'm facing the way he is. 'Look at that,' he says. And there it is stretching out ahead of us, dark, powerful, beautiful, and endless until the horizon.

I smile, overpowered by the beauty, by the memory, by the wind. 'The end of the world,' I say.

Roman looks at his side to me, and after hesitating, says, 'Told you we'd be back.'

For a moment, we stand side by side, looking out, in silence, the way we did on that school trip, with all that pain and mess left behind at home, and this day – in the future, where things were brighter – nothing but a distant dream. An impossibility, almost.

Then Roman turns, lets out a loud whistle, and carries on walking up the hill. 'Barney! Come on, boy!' Then he stops and says, 'And you, City Mouse. Little bit further.'

We keep walking, and I stop, every now and then and look behind me, at the unfurling view, that gets larger, more breathtaking with each step. When we reach the top, both of us breathless and red-cheeked, Roman gestures with a hand to the ground. A rectangle of concrete, like a grave stone, where our bench once was.

'The bastards took it away,' he says.

'No!' I say, standing upon it and looking down at my feet. 'How dare they!'

'But they can't take this away,' smiles Roman. 'Nobody can take this away.' He stands tall, looking out to the ocean, and distant cliffs. The sea roars and sways for miles and miles ahead of us – a floor of deep blues and greens, boats, tiny, like models on the horizon, seagulls swooping, like kites above it.

'The piss-angry sea,' I shout against the sweeping winds. I open my arms, as if greeting an old friend. 'I've missed you!' I shout and Roman laughs and outstretches his arms too.

'The piss-angry sea welcomes you back!' he shouts. 'Piss-angry sea has been waiting!'

We both laugh, teeth white, cheeks tight, and stinging, out here in the cold, and we stand, beside one another, Barney sitting at Roman's side, ears and fur blowing in the bluster. I feel high. *Alive.* I want to throw my arms around him. I want to scream. I'm here. I made it. I followed the white rabbit. I said yes to adventure, to facing the truth. I didn't turn away and run. I was scared, but I came anyway, despite it. And this feels so right, this moment. Me and Roman, back beside one another, being battered by Mother Nature, not a single other soul around. Just us, like we planned; planned as lost kids with the odds against us.

And then it comes out of my mouth. Because this really would be such a perfect moment, if it wasn't for all the questions hanging over us like black clouds. Because this isn't a reunion of fizzled friends. He disappeared, and I had to find him, search for him, to get here. I need answers. I do. And up here, the world at our feet, I feel brave. Up here, I'm not afraid anymore. I am ready for the truth.

'Why did you leave?'

Roman looks at me, quickly, as if shocked I asked. His smile fades, and he opens his mouth to speak.

'Where did you go, Roman?' Wind fills my ears, whooshing, like metal sheeting being waved, like being plunged underwater. 'Why? Why did you leave?'

Roman's face has changed. It's pale, etched with sadness, darkening with shadows.

'Lizzie, we should talk about this later. It's bloody freezing up here—'

'No, I want to talk about it now.'

And he doesn't try to persuade me like I expect. He just nods – once, like a bow. 'Let's find somewhere quiet. Then we'll talk.'

✉

We are the only ones in the café. It's part of a small hotel, near the seafront. It's a bit dated and shabby, but the restaurant is bright and warm, and smells of hot bacon. Roman and I sit opposite each other, at a small scallop-edged pine table by a radiator we've laid our hats and gloves on. Barney slumps half under the table, his warm belly heavy on my feet.

'Things were bad, Lizzie. Things were . . . really grim. Mum's bloke was back, the drinking just got worse, I was—' He stops and looks up at me. 'Using again.'

My stomach tightens. I don't react, wanting him to carry on.

'I was drowning.' He stops again and rubs his face.

'I didn't know—'

'I didn't want you to,' he says. 'You were the one good thing in my life. You were . . . everything.'

My heart stops at those words, and heat creeps up my back, to my neck, and ears. He still disarms me.

'And you were getting on, J. You were better, and god, that's all you wanted. More than me. More than anyone.' Roman's eyes don't leave my face. 'And you did it. You were back in school, starting *college*, you were . . . *alive* again, and I just couldn't be the reason you fell off track. 'Cause you worried about me, Lizzie. You always worried so much about me, and when I went down, so did you—'

'So, you just disappeared. A week after Hubble died, you *leave* without telling me?'

'Things were worse than you knew.' Roman's voice cracks, and his eyes plead with me. A waitress walks by the table, and he waits for her to pass before he carries on. 'When Hubble died, I . . .' He just presses his temples with his fingers and closes his eyes. His face is white. 'My mam's cousin . . . it was a way out of that house, away from her, away from her bloke, that parasite. And I kept saying no. That I couldn't leave, couldn't leave her, but in the end . . . I couldn't stay.' Roman breathes in sharply, shaking his head. 'The day of your Auntie Shall's vow thing, after we legged it, and I left your house . . .' He stops and looks at me, waiting for a prompt, a nod that I remember. I do. Of course I do. We were on the bed and I thought he was going to kiss me. Then Ethan called him and he left – summoned by him, like he always was. 'I walked back home,' he carries on, swallowing hard. 'And Sea Fog was gone. I went inside and Mum was out of it. But he . . . Mum's bloke, he was sitting there counting his fucking money. He'd sold it. All my stuff was inside and I just . . . I lost it, Lizzie.'

'Oh, god,' comes out of my mouth almost silently. My hands fly to my face. 'Your stuff. Your clothes . . .'

'Clothes, CDs, laptop. Everything. Everything that was mine. And the plant pot. Our money, Lizzie. I brought it inside to the caravan. I didn't trust him not to find it in the porch of the house, but . . .'

'Oh, Roman.'

He rubs his eyes, the way he always did when he spoke in group therapy – as if to push the tears away. 'I needed to leave, Lizzie. I needed to run away. And leaving without saying goodbye to you was . . .' Roman's eyes fill with tears and he drags his hand through his hair, hunching over the table. 'I was desperate. I was terrified. Everything I touched I broke—'

'My dad,' I say, firmly, anger rising in my chest. 'Did my dad warn you off? Did he force you to leave?' Roman was vulnerable. He was desperate. It wouldn't have taken much pushing to make him go.

Roman's eyes widen; his whole face drops. He goes as pale as snow. 'N-no. Why would you— I—'

'The letter you wrote me. It was on his headed paper, and he kept it in his van. I know he went to see you.'

His skin has gone a shade of grey now; sallow. 'Lizzie, have you asked him?'

I shake my head. 'No. I'm asking you.'

He lets out a deep breath and leans back on his chair. His arms fall limply, defeated, at his side. 'He came over one afternoon. He found me. I was wrecked.'

'Wrecked?'

Roman pauses. 'High. Out of it.'

'The painkillers again.' A sting flashes across my chest. 'I mean, I knew you did stuff, with Ethan sometimes, but—'

'I had a drug problem, Lizzie.' Roman pauses to look at me, then smiles, sadly. 'You just never saw what everyone else saw.'

'So, I was, what, ignorant? *Naïve?* Stupid?'

Roman shakes his head. 'No. No, not at all, J, no. You saw me. You saw *me*. Past all of that. In spite of it all. You made me feel normal. Like a normal seventeen-year-old boy.'

There is a burst of laughter from behind us. I turn. Two waitresses behind the glass counter of cakes are giggling, looking down at a phone in one of their hands. I turn back to Roman, who is watching me, nervously. 'What did Dad do,' I ask, 'when he found you?'

'You really . . . you haven't spoken to him?'

I shake my head.

Roman looks down into the mug of tea he hasn't touched and leans forward, wrists resting on the table. 'I broke down on him. I told him I couldn't stay, that it was too much, too hard to live there anymore. And he helped me. I told him about my mum's cousin at the farm, and he said he'd help me leave.'

'Of course he did—'

'No,' cuts in Roman, eyes flashing. 'He loved you. The guy . . . his eyes just lit up, talking about you. As if you were the most precious thing. This *masterpiece* or something. He wouldn't have wanted to hurt you, Lizzie. Never.' Roman ducks to meet my gaze. 'Don't blame him. He helped me. He was kind. He stayed with me, cleaned me up, made me a drink, we talked. He bought me clothes – all the things I lost in the caravan. He was good to me.'

I don't react. It sounds like kindness. It does. But I can't help but think it suited Dad as much as it suited Roman. My heart settles in the pit of my stomach.

'Lizzie, he owed me nothing. He'd just lost his dad, for Christ's sake, face down in the park, and I was the last person he should have been helping but . . .' His eyes fix on my face, unblinking for a moment, then he turns away, looking to the misty windows on the other side of the café. He says nothing else.

'So, he helped you.' My voice is tiny, like a child's.

'I begged him, Lizzie,' he says softly, not looking at me.

'And he helped me. He gave me another chance. He picked me up the next day, and I left.'

Nobody says anything after that, for ages. We drink our tea. We watch a family come in, two teenagers, a boy and a girl, a mother and a father, stiff in tight, puffy coats, and faces pink and weather-beaten. The father gets up and goes to the counter, standing back admiring the cakes, and the teenagers slump at the table. The boy stares out the window, head resting on fist, finger drawing a face on the misty glass, and the girl looks around the room – her large eyes stop on me and Roman for a second. She smiles when I do.

Roman meets my eye across the table.

'It's a lot to take in,' I whisper.

Roman nods. 'That letter,' he says. 'I grabbed the paper from the van. I was gonna send it. I was. But every day that went by . . . I just couldn't do it. So, I kept it instead, as a reminder. Proof or something. Of us. Of me and you.'

'I wish you'd sent it. I'd have known you didn't want to leave me.'

Roman's nostrils flare and he looks away. 'I tried. I tried to come back – the funeral, I came down, but I— I couldn't. I waited until later. I went back with Ram, left a plant for him. I always hoped you'd see it or something, and know, somehow.'

I can't speak or look into his eyes. I know I'll sob if I do.

Roman lowers his voice. 'Not a single day has gone by,' he says, and he says nothing more.

Answers. I have the answers I have longed for for twelve years.

He lives here, near Tongue, when he isn't travelling around, 'following his nose', with the money his dad left him.

He has used The Hartland for ten years, coming and going. No longer for painkillers, but 'for his head' – nightmares and panic attacks and insomnia. 'Some things I can't get past,' he said. I asked him about the meds. He takes two types of anxiety medication, and three different types of vitamins.

He stayed at Edgar Fields with Ethan, who got out of prison for drug possession and GBH. He was the only friend he had left. Roman stayed with him for two weeks, before he realised Ethan had no intention of getting better. Roman left with nowhere to go – that's when Roman went to his dad's. He was desperate. He had nothing left.

His Dad died. He was left everything.

And he left me because he was ill. More than I ever saw, and ever knew. Because I didn't want to. Because *he* didn't want me to. Instead, I saw him; his best version. I didn't see addiction. I didn't see struggle. I saw straight through, to him. To who Roman really was.

The waitress drifts by the table a few times, eyeing our empty mugs, our empty, silent gazes. Roman stretches, sitting up in his chair. 'The sun's coming out,' he says, hands pushing into his pockets, looking out of the steamed-up window.

I stare at him. My cheeks are wet, and stinging. Roman looks at me, and I see his eyes flash as he registers my tears. He puts his hand on mine. 'I'm sorry,' he whispers. 'Leaving you was—'

'No more sorrys,' I say, squeezing his hand. It feels the same. Strong. Warm. Safe. 'No more.'

After a while, a woman comes to collect our cups. Roman goes to the counter to pay, queuing behind the mother with the teenagers. I wait for him outside, filling my lungs with damp, salty air, cleaning and cleansing my insides. When Roman comes out he stands beside me. I reach down and hold his hand. He looks quickly at me, surprised almost, but tightens his hand around mine. Birds swoop above us, and the sun breaks free from the clouds. Roman and I squint up at the sky, as he points out the different birds.

'I'm waiting,' I say from beside him, 'for a fact about bird balls or penises.'

Roman bursts out laughing. 'That sounds like a challenge.'

We take a slow walk back to the lodge, holding hands all the way, towards the end of the world.

Chapter Thirty-Three

Hubble used to say the answer to everything is obvious. We just make it complicated or impossible because sometimes the answer isn't what we want to hear or see. We detour, purposely going around in circles, dragging our feet, or even standing still, because we don't want to get to the end of the road, to the answer, to the truth, to closure. We're too afraid. We aren't ready.

Tonight, I lay in Roman's bed, and he, on the sofa. It's gone two o'clock. I fell asleep quickly at eleven; the way you do after a day of being by the sea, drunk and drowsy on sea air, and exhausted from walking uphill. But I woke, wide awake, 'bolt upright' as my mum would say, at half-past one. And now I can't sleep. My brain is spinning in my head, my ears, noisy, with my pulse, and the wind we left outside.

I thought I would feel free; I thought the puzzle would slot together, and a weight would lift. The fog would clear. But it hasn't.

Because something isn't adding up.

Something won't leave me alone, tugging at my sleeve.

He knew.

Roman knew about Hubble. How did he know he'd died in the park? It took me two years to learn that's where it really happened. Did I mention it, that sleepy, dizzying night I got here?

My mouth is dry and I feel nauseous. I need water.

I slide quietly out of Roman's bed, and pad down the hallway, my footsteps nigh on silent on the carpet. The lodge smells of wood and rosemary. Roman has a plant of it in his kitchen. I remember Hubble and Roman together, looking at the plants in the garden, and Hubble telling him about the meaning of the name, or what was best to plant in certain weathers. I remember being embarrassed, worrying Roman was bored, but he never was. Instead, he'd ask questions, and tell me things later on, proudly, as if they were his own learned facts.

The lodge is in darkness. If I'm quiet enough, I can get a glass of water without waking him. He always slept like a corpse and fell asleep as if knocked out – no gradual fading.

I get to the sink and pick up a mug from the draining board. I cringe, looking over my shoulder to the sofa, still and shrouded in darkness, hoping not to wake him, I turn on the tap and fill it with water. I turn, full mug in hand, and that's when I catch sight of the light through the blinds; just a glimpse of orange light. It's the porch light. Not the blinding, white automatic one – the soft, orange light we put on yesterday evening, as we ate soup, and watched the sun go down from the wooden deck. I rush over to the sofa. Roman isn't there – no blankets. No sign of Barney either. I walk to the window, pulling up the blind a crack. He's right there, his back to me, a huge, heavy blanket over his shoulders. Barney is a few feet away, curled up by the tall, robot-like outdoor heater. His sandy fur sways like wheat in a field but he doesn't move. It must be freezing out there. I glance at the clock on the kitchen wall. It's half-past two now.

I grab my coat from the kitchen table and put it over the T-shirt and pyjama bottoms I'm wearing. I leave the mug on the table, and push down the cold handle of the door. At the sound, Barney looks up, and his tail wags, smacking against the decking. Roman swoops round. My heart sinks. The look on his face is the one he'd wear on days when we were at The Grove. Days he would barely speak, or spend most of his time with Ramesh, one on one. The face he had on in that hospital bed – pale, his cheeks red blotches, his eyes watery and glassy and wide, as if he's sitting trying to work out an impossible conundrum and won't allow himself to sleep until he knows.

'I-it's freezing out here J,' he says, stumbling over the words. 'Go. Go back in.'

I don't. I lower myself next to him on the step. 'What're you talking about?' I say, voice trembling as the cold stings my legs. 'It's lovely. I might sunbathe.'

I laugh, nerves rising in my chest, and pull my hood up over my head. Roman says nothing, and goes back to looking ahead into the blackness. It must be minus five, at least. The heater behind us takes away the sting in the air.

We sit in silence. His breathing is fast and noisy.

'Bad dream?' I ask.

'Seriously, J, it's freezing out here, go inside.'

'And leave you out—'

'Lizzie, please.' His words are harsh and urgent. But I don't move. He moves his hands to his face so they're covering it.

'Roman?'

He brings his long, strong legs up and bows his head. He brings the blanket higher over his shoulders and hides his face away.

'Roman, what is going on?'

'I can't do this.'

I stare at him. 'What?' My heart starts to hammer. The waves crash and thunder below us.

'I can't. I just can't.'

'You can't do what?' It's barely a whisper. I knew it. I knew there was something else. I knew this was too good be true. I felt it, like you do in the air before a storm.

'I'm sorry,' he says, his voice squeaking at the end. 'Jesus Christ, I am so sorry.'

Bile rises in my throat. What is it? What's he going to say? I want to grab him and shake him – I want to grab his face and pull it out from hiding and make him look at me. I want to scream at him to just say the words.

'Roman, what is all this about?'

Silence.

'*Roman?*'

Silence again. He brings his arms further above his head as if he is trying to disappear into himself beside me. Roman inhales deeply, sniffing, breath trembling. Blood rushes to my legs and I can't help it. It explodes from my chest, firing out of my mouth. 'Fucking hell, Roman, please answer me!'

Barney, I see, in the corner of my eye, tilts his head, inches off the decking floor, as Roman lifts his head, quickly. His cheeks are wet. His eyes are wild, as if fire roars behind them. 'I thought I would be able to,' he says, his voice wobbling, his teeth gritted. 'When the moment came and I actually saw you, in front of me, years later, that I would have the words. That I would know what to say, how to explain . . .'

I say nothing. I look at him, trying to remain calm, trying to remain open. An ear. I don't want him to close off. Because Roman does that. He closes off like he falls asleep – sudden; a shutter slamming.

'And it's killed me. It's eaten me alive and . . .' He stops and drags his hands through his dark hair and lets out an exasperated sigh. 'And I am still lying. I lied. Because I don't fucking have the words. There is no way of making this better. And I can't do it. I can't.'

'Roman, what are you talking about?'

Roman stares at me. His mouth is such a tight line, the colour has drained. He closes his eyes. He looks childlike – like he's still seventeen. Frightened of the world. Despairing of who he is. He turns to me and puts a hand to my face. 'I lied to you.'

The words are barely there – trapped in his throat. They come out in croaks and sharp breaths.

And now I feel sick. My stomach swirls and churns with what feels like lava.

'I lied to you yesterday, in the café,' he says. His hand has moved from me now. They're holding his bent head. He stares at the ground. 'I lied about why I left.'

'About what? What do you mean?' My voice is cold now. Urgent.

'I left because I ruined your life,' he says, breaking into sobs. My face is contorted. I have no words. I don't know what's happening. I don't know what to say. Then he says the words, and everything – like a gentle, flawless unravelling – slots into place.

'I am why Hubble died,' he says, shoulders shuddering. 'I was why he was in the park. *Me*. Hubble is dead because of me.'

I stand, as if an electric shock just shot through my body. 'What?' I'm shouting. My voice cuts through the wind, and the black, lifeless night. '*What?*'

Roman shoots to his feet. He lunges for my hands. I fly down the steps onto the grass. I can't see anything beyond my nose. My socks fill with icy water.

'Lizzie, please listen to—'

'*What* do you mean?' My voice is loud, but breaks. My chest is caving in. My world is imploding.

Roman grimaces, as if in pain. 'When I left yours, after the vow ceremony, I— I met Ethan,' Roman says, lips, trembling.

'He was selling. A-and I said he should stop, that I didn't wanna help anymore; that we'd piss someone off, that the money wasn't worth it—'

My heart plummets to my stomach. *Selling.* The money he'd appear with, tens, twenties, for our plant pot. From dog walking. *Dog walking.* 'I wanted to leave, Lizzie. I wanted to leave but these blokes turned up. In the park. And . . . he must've seen. From the bathroom window, when he got home.'

I can't listen to any more. I can't. I fly towards the door.

'Lizzie, please.'

'Get out of my way,' I growl. My hands tingle with heat at my sides.

'I'm sorry. I'm so sorry. I would have never . . . if I'd known Hubble was gonna get involved I wouldn't have— but he did.' Roman's voice cracks and breaks. 'Please, Lizzie.'

'Roman, get out of my way.' Tears come then as he holds my shoulders. The way he used to. The way he did when he calmed me, counted my breaths with me, brought me back to earth. I want to hit him. I want to scream at him, for bringing my poor, poor grandad – the kindest heart, the most gentle, gentle heart – out into the cold, at night, to that park.

'I was with him,' Roman speaks desperately, rushing his words out. 'I didn't leave him. I stayed with him, in the ambulance, and . . . they said he was going to be OK. It was just . . . he got involved, Lizzie, but he was just trying to help me. They all legged it. The blokes. Ethan. We . . . Hubble and I . . . we walked together but he kept stopping, kept holding his chest— Lizzie, *please*, listen to me.'

'Get out of my way!' I scream. Barney jumps to his feet and lets out the beginning of a bark. He watches Roman, paws still on the ground.

The waves roar beneath us.

Fine drizzle soaks our faces.

I storm inside, pack my bag, and within minutes, I'm standing, shivering in the car park, sobbing on the phone to Priscilla. Roman tells me to wait inside, where it's warm and safe, but I ignore him. He looks as though he's deflating, bent with pain. But I don't care. The anger, the betrayal is drowning out the part of me that cares. Hubble. My poor, poor Hubble.

Priscilla arrives in minutes, still in her pyjamas, her eyes ringed with sleep.

I get into the car, and pretend to not see Roman, standing, watching me from the path, Barney, staring sadly into the darkness, at his side.

We drive away, and I leave him. I disappear into the night, and destroyed, heartbroken, when he needs me to stay the most, I leave him.

I leave him just like he did me.

Chapter Thirty-Four

28th November 2005

I run. I run and run, the hood of my coat up, hiding my tears. I run the whole way. My lungs are collapsing. My heart is giving out. It hurts for it to beat. I'm going to be sick. This is not real. This isn't my life.

Roman doesn't answer the front door straight away. Neither does Lindsey. I bang and bang. I shout through the letterbox. Nothing. I dash back down the path. The park. He might be at the park.

'Lizzie?' Spinning around, I see Roman, standing in the doorway of his house, his eyes swollen, his hair a mess and on end, a blanket over his shoulders. I fly up the path to him. I hold onto the wall to steady myself.

'T-they wouldn't let me come.' My lungs are giving out. I can't speak. The world is lurching. It's breaking in two, right down the middle. 'I ran. I . . . Hubble . . . h-he died.' Roman's face falls. The colour drains from his skin and I see it – the moment he breaks. And I fall to my knees and sob. He holds me up. He tells me everything's OK, but for the first time, I don't believe him. Pain sears and slices through my heart. The noises I make sound nothing like me. They're screams and roars and come from my stomach. I sound like someone whose world has ended; like someone in agony.

Roman shushes me. He holds the back of my head to his chest and sways. 'Shhhhhh. It's OK. It's OK,' he says, but I can hear in his wobbling voice, he is crumbling too. He carries me as he steps backwards. I have no strength to hold myself up anymore. I hear the rattle of the latch as the door closes. The house falls silent, and in the hallway, after barely a step across the threshold, I crumple, sagging against him, the noises howling from me are so alien, I am sure they are coming from someone else's body. Someone else's heartache.

Roman tells me over and over that he's there, that he's got me, swaying me, shushing me, between his own tears, and somehow, we are on the floor. A crumpled heap, Roman's back against the foot of the stairs, my arms around his neck, tangled up in each other, wrapped in a blanket that smells of him. I cry until I am depleted, until there is nothing left in me; no life. After for ever, I look up at Roman, his cheeks, pink and shining with wet. He says nothing, but kisses my head, and leaves his lips there, against my hair. I close my eyes, blanket tight around me, cocooning me in his lap, and hope that when I open them, I'm not here. I'm not anywhere. This has all gone away.

We listen to nothing but one another's heartbeats, laughing children, passing cars.

I keep my eyes closed, and so does Roman, and for a moment, it's so silent, so still, I think he's asleep. But then he says, 'I'm sorry,' against my head. 'I am so sorry, Lizzie.'

Chapter Thirty-Five

'Lizzie?'

I say nothing.

'Babe?'

I hear the rustling of a plastic bag. I pull the duvet further and tighter over my head and shuffle further downwards. My eyes are swollen, and I feel empty, as if my heart is shrinking. I am despairing – of everything, and everyone, and every memory I have ever had. I feel lost. I feel betrayed by the world.

'OK, so that weird little corner shop doesn't have much,' says Priscilla, energetically, 'but I've got Kettle Chips, sausage rolls, two pasties – one chicken, one veggie – a Yorkie bar. Erm, what else have I got here?'

I listen, staring beneath the thick hotel duvet. If I was feeling happier, if I wanted to talk, I would've asked why? *Why* on earth have you bought me a lunch fit for an ogling scaffolder on a frosty rooftop? But I don't. I make a 'hmm' sound instead and stay where I am.

'I've also got a scotch egg, French Fancies, and two Dr Peppers.'

'Hmm,' I say again.

'Fancy anything?'

'No, thank you.'

'How about a cuppa? I got some more teabags from reception.'

'No, I'm OK.' My voice is muffled from beneath the duvet.

More rustling. 'Ah!' says Priscilla. 'Crunchie?'

I say nothing.

'*Crunchie?*'

I pause. 'Yes.'

'OK,' says Priscilla, amused. 'Open up. I'm coming in.'

Light floods in as Priscilla yanks back the heavy duvet and stands for a second, looking at me, curled in a foetal position, like a shrimp, my knees as close to my tucked under my chin as I can get them. I haven't showered. I haven't brushed my teeth. I haven't eaten anything or slept for a single moment. I'm still in my pyjamas from Roman's, yet it must be at least midday. I look up, slowly. Priscilla looks flawless in a pair of skinny jeans and a thick cream roll neck jumper. She smiles at me, and hops into the bed, pulling the duvet back over our heads.

'Hello,' she says, holding the Crunchie between our faces.

I take it. 'Hello.'

Then she puts her arms around me and pulls me to her chest. She rests her chin on top of my head and pulls me close. She smells fresh, like perfume and cocoa butter.

'You smell nice,' I sniff, my voice thick and raspy.

'Miss Dior.'

'Misty what?'

Priscilla laughs. '*Miss Deee-orrr.* As in Christian Dior. Idiot.'

We lay under the duvet, in silence for a while. Priscilla watches as I unwrap the Crunchie. She seems happy when I start eating it, as if she's pleased I'm doing something normal, instead of crying and talking and swearing at the air.

'How are you feeling?'

'Awful, Priscilla,' I croak. 'Sad. Gutted. Lost. Angry.'

Priscilla nods then holds my elbow of the arm holding the Crunchie bar. She bends and bites off a lump. 'I think you need to go back and see him. Talk,' she chomps.

'No, Priscilla.'

'I know this is rough, babe, and I know it's a lot to take in—'

'P, he lied. He lied to me. Hubble was . . .' I can't speak. I shake my head. 'He might never have died if it wasn't for Roman.'

Priscilla looks at me sadly, her huge brown eyes wide, her mouth, slowly chewing. 'I know it's awful, but Roman wasn't the reason we lost Hubble, Liz, you know that.'

'But, Priscilla—'

'Hubble died because he had a massive heart attack that the doctors said could've happened at any moment. Picking up a heavy box, putting out the washing . . .'

'But it wasn't any of those things, was it?' I say. 'Roman was the reason. Him, spending time with Ethan, helping him, despite everything, despite *you*, he put himself in danger for Ethan, stood next to him on seedy little deals with god only knows who. Drugs, Priscilla. He promised me he—' The words lodge in my throat. I can't speak.

Priscilla sighs sadly, then looks down to the Crunchie in my hand. She bends and bites another lump off. I do the same. Between us, we finish it, then push the duvet from our heads and sit up, beside one another, leaning against the large, grey quilted square of headboard.

'I know this is probably not what you want to hear, because it is shit . . . it *is*,' says Priscilla, 'but I think this is all bittersweet in a way. Because you and Roman . . . you two and Hubble, you were all sort of meant to be. You all saved each other, if you think about it.'

Brushing Crunchie crumbs from my lips, I look at her.

Priscilla draws in a deep breath. 'I know it was hard when he left. But a part of me was . . . glad. *Selfishly*, I was glad – for you. Because he was worse, Lizzie, worse than you could see. And you were getting on. You were so much better. And I was getting *you* back. My girl. My mate Lizzie.'

Priscilla holds my gaze, pink lips pressed together, chest rising and falling. The heater on the wall clicks and rumbles. Seagulls squawk their seaside cries outside. The weatherman on the small hotel TV gestures to the sun drifting across the map, all hands, raised eyebrows, and smiles.

'You need to go back. Talk to him.'

My heartbeat whooshes in my ears like crashing waves, and for what feels like ages, I don't take my eyes off the telly, my eyes glazing over, blurring the screen. 'I just feel like everything's a mess,' I say, bringing the duvet over my legs. Priscilla pulls it across to her and shuffles closer to me. She rests her head on my shoulder.

'Was a mess,' she says. '*Was*. But it's done.'

We sit up in bed, beside one another, for what feels like ages – just like we did for years, as kids when we'd pass Maltesers and crisps between us, figuring out the world while watching *Hollyoaks* and *Girls in Love* in our pyjamas.

'I feel stupid, that I didn't know how bad he was. The drugs, the circles he was in. He was so 'together' around me, P.'

Priscilla shrugs. 'Sometimes people give the best version of themselves to other people. Because it's easier; it's easier to rescue someone else. It's so much harder to do it for yourself.' Priscilla sits up. 'And I don't know a lot, but I know that he loved you. The kid loved you and did everything he could to help get better. Probably *still* loves you. I knew it, we all knew it.'

'Hubble knew it,' I croak.

'And he died helping him,' sniffs Priscilla. 'Roman didn't ask for that. It was Hubble who took it upon himself to help, because that's who he was. OK, it was bad luck, bad timing.

And think about what might have happened if he hadn't intervened. Ethan was trouble. Everyone he knew was trouble. Well. Almost everyone.'

I look up at her and see her lovely face – her lovely warm Priscilla face, with huge brown eyes that she dries now, with the cuffs of her jumper. Then she reaches forward and catches my tears on her fingertips.

'What time's our flight again?'

'Eleven. We'll have to leave about half six, seven latest.'

'Can I take the car?' I ask. 'To sort this out, go and see him.'

Priscilla nods, eyes brightening. 'Of course,' she says. 'Go. Go and have your goodbye.'

Chapter Thirty-Six

4th April 2001

Hubble sits the cyclamen plant next to Mimi's stone. He stands back and dusts down his jeans, then moves to stand beside me. The sun beats down, and we both hold our hands up to our faces as shades. We stand and look at where Mimi has lain for a year now.

'Do you know what the meaning behind the cyclamen is?'

I shake my head, my eyes settling on the white buds, and its tiger-print-like, cabbagey green leaves.

'It's a symbol of departure,' says Hubble, placing his hand on my shoulder. 'That all things must end someday. A symbol of *goodbye.*'

I bring my shoulders to my ears. 'Well, that's depressing.'

'Is it?' Hubble asks, straightening and turning his face to the sun. 'I don't think so.' Hubble pauses then squeezes my shoulder gently. 'We don't always get to say goodbye. Sometimes you'll be holding the balloon, and it's pulled from you. Or you drop it, without realising until it's too late. And it's gone. That's it. You can't get it back.' Hubble bends and pulls a stray weed from the ground. He tosses it behind us and straightens again. 'But if you're the one that lets it go, then you should count yourself lucky. You get to prepare, you get to say goodbye. You get to close the book.'

A plane bumbles across the sky, high above, and Hubble and I follow its path, hands still shading our foreheads. When it disappears, we look back down at Mimi. The flecks in the marble of her headstone glitter, just like her earrings used to in the sunshine as she painted, or picked vegetables to sketch in late summer.

'Goodbyes are a privilege,' says Hubble, putting his arm around me. 'They are one of life's gifts, not punishments.'

Chapter Thirty-Seven

It's a beautiful day at the end of the world. The sky is one clear sheet of endless blue, peppered with tufts of skittery cloud, and the air is pure and crisp. Gulls screech overhead, and the day is so clear, I can make out distant rocks jutting out from the sea, like the backs of resting whales. The sea is calm today – it whooshes and fizzes, instead of roars.

I find Roman, lounging back, leg bent on his porch with a book, Barney at his side. He stands as soon as he sees me, the book hanging at his side in his hand, his index finger slotted between pages. I'm still, at the foot of the path. We stand, eyes fixed on each other. He's searching my face – he wants to know what he's up against.

'You should put socks on,' I say, eyeing his bare feet.

Roman's face floods with relief. He looks to the ground. 'Why?' he asks. 'Because I'll catch a cold or because you hate feet? The things we were born with that allow us to actually *move*.'

'Both,' I say. 'But yes. Mostly because I still hate them.'

Roman smiles weakly, as if despite himself. 'I didn't think you'd come back.'

'I didn't think I'd come back either.'

We smile, neither of us saying anything, as we slowly close

the gap between us. We stand opposite each other. A breeze blows around us, crunchy auburn leaves circle our feet.

'I shouldn't have left,' I say.

'Isn't that what I'm supposed to say?' Roman's face doesn't flinch – his eyes are serious and shining with sadness.

'I'm so sorry,' he says.

I shake my head. 'Don't,' I tell him. 'Just tell me. Tell me what happened.'

'OK,' Roman says. 'But come and sit with me. Just for a moment.'

And on the porch we dreamed up all those years ago, we sit, looking out to sea, and he tells me. He tells me that after he left my house, he met Ethan in the park, but when they got there, there was a gang of older guys waiting for them. There was a fight. All Roman remembers is Hubble shouting saying he'd called the police, as he pulled Roman off the ground. Everyone scarpered, Ethan too, and Hubble told Roman to come inside, but he kept stopping, holding his chest. That was it – the moment everything changed. He fell against Roman, who held him, and lowered him to the ground, just metres from Hubble's back garden gate. He called the ambulance. They stayed on the phone with him.

'I talked to him all the time, Lizzie. He couldn't speak, but . . . I stayed with him. I talked to him, about everything, about anything. I didn't leave him. Not once.'

Roman said he melted down in the ambulance and had to be restrained and calmed down. He told them it was all his fault. He told them he'd got into a fight. He told them to call the police on him.

When they got to the hospital, Roman told them they had to call Charlie – that everyone they needed to notify was at the scout hut, where Auntie Shall and Uncle Pete were having their vow ceremony party. Dad arrived through the doors first, then

Pete and Shall. Dad flew at Roman – shook him, screamed at him, held his fist inches from his face. Roman says he expected it. He took it. *Wanted* it even, because he deserved it. Shall squawked and screeched at him, she told him he would 'go down for this'. Pete said nothing.

'They asked me to leave, the doctors,' says Roman. 'But they told us that it was nobody's fault, and that he was stable. The next I knew, was you banging on the door the next day, telling me he'd died.'

And that was the moment. The moment he knew he'd betrayed me. That he'd ruined my life. He wanted to die, because he blamed himself.

'I was a mess. I've never felt so desperate in my life as I did that week,' he says. Then Dad had found him, shivering, sick from no sleep, from the sheer weight of living with what he did, his mum and her boyfriend passed out downstairs. Dad couldn't turn away. He helped him. He saved him. He gave him a second chance. He set him free.

'A therapist once told me,' says Roman, now, his hand folded round mine, 'that I didn't need your forgiveness. I needed my own. And I think that's always going to be my problem, J. That's what I can't get past. I will never be able to forget that night.'

I press a tissue to my wet cheeks and squeeze my fingers around Roman's hand. 'Well if you feel you need mine,' I say, 'you have it.'

We sit together, watching the calm waves, the distant boats, and soaring birds. We sit there, together, under that endless blue sky until the sun begins to go down. We drink tea, we talk, we laugh, we remember and sing the songs we used to love. We laugh until we hold our stomachs. We sit. Just us. Just us, the sea, and the darkening autumn sky. And I don't want to move from beside him. I don't want to let go of his hand.

'I thought I ruined it,' I say, head against Roman's chest like a pillow, his chin resting on my head. 'At first, I thought I was why you left.'

'You?' asks Roman. 'How would you have ruined anything?'

The sun glitters on the ocean turning the waves to jewels. My head rises and falls with Roman's breathing. 'That night,' I say, softly. 'In the bathroom.'

Roman tenses. 'When I kissed you.'

My cheeks pulse with embarrassment. 'When I kissed you, you mean.'

Roman laughs and pulls back, turning so he can see me. 'There's no way that could've ruined it,' he smiles, 'when it's all I'd wanted to do for, well, what felt like sixteen centuries. Seventeen-year-old boys are hardly subtle, are they?'

I burst out laughing and bring my hands to my face.

'But we were *banned* remember?' says Roman, mockingly. 'Not allowed to have relationships with one another. As if we weren't depressed enough already.'

I nod, still laughing. 'You called Ramesh a heart-Nazi.'

Roman bursts out laughing. 'God, I did, didn't I? Jeez. Poor Ram.' He relaxes back on the bench, tightening his arms around me once more. His hand hasn't let mine go. Not for a second. 'Some of my happiest memories are of The Grove, though, you know.'

'Mine too.'

'And in Sea Fog,' says Roman.

'Of course, Sea Fog.'

A bird screeches across the sky, and Roman leans back ever so slightly, his arms not moving from around me, to get a better look. I can hear his heart now I've turned my face. It's steady. Strong, like a drum. He settles back down.

'I've been looking at camper vans, actually.'

'Really?'

Roman nods, chin skimming the top of my head. 'About time we commenced the hunt for the perfect fudge, isn't it?'

I smile, eyes closing as the wind blows a warm swirl of air from the outdoor heater in our direction. It smells of dust and sea salt.

'And chips. Massive fuck-off, salty ones. In the paper,' I say, 'and not served in those offensive polystyrene things.'

Roman laughs. 'I will find you a chippy that deals with only paper, J. And you can doodle those little people on the chip forks. Like you used to. Remember you drew the one of Morrissey, then I used him and his face melted off?'

I laugh, cheeks stinging, stomach juddering under my jumper. 'Shame,' I say. 'Poor Melted Morrissey.'

'He deserved better.'

'Debatable.'

The sun sits, half-dipped in the sea, like a perfect semicircle now, the way it does in films and on calendars, and I wish I could freeze frame this moment. I don't want time to move. I don't want to leave.

My phone vibrates in my pocket. I sit up to read the message. Roman stretches and sits forward, forearms resting on his knees beside me.

'Priscilla,' I say.

Roman nods, his hands knitting together.

I lock my phone and slide it back in my pocket. When I look up, Roman is looking at me. I see the light catch his eyes, the way sun glints on water, and my heart sags, as if sighing in my chest. A part of me longs to throw my arms around him. A part of me longs to, more than anything, kiss him again, to stay here like this, by the sea, up here, world at our feet, for ever. A part of me wants just to run with him. Drive with him under the stars until we reach somewhere we'd like to explore, for fudge and chips, running for our lives, just a little later than planned.

A part of me wants this. A part of me loves him, and always will. And that part wants to stay, right here. With him. Never letting go again.

I get to my feet, and Roman mirrors me, standing slowly. We're face to face on the porch, clouds swirled with pinks and purples stretched high above us, and the sun, just a hump now, peeping from the waves behind us. Nobody says anything for a while. We just look at each other, as if taking one another in, remembering everything we can, in case life doesn't grant us a chance again. Because the biggest parts of us know. The biggest parts want to let go. The largest, strongest parts know it's time.

'Can you not stay another night?'

I shake my head. 'I can't,' I say. 'Work.'

Roman nods once, inhaling deeply, his pink lips pressed together, muscle in his jaw pulsing.

'Plus, I have a wedding next weekend,' I tell him. 'I'm bridesmaid. Well . . . actually, I'm not sure I am anymore, it's all a bit fraught.'

'Interesting,' smiles Roman. 'Not the bride this time, then?'

'Absolutely not. That'd be Olivia.'

Roman's eyebrows lift and he rubs his chin. '*Shit*, Olivia? Shame I don't still have my tux.'

'The black or white?'

'Your choice,' Roman says. 'Always.'

I look up at him and can't help stepping forward to close the space between us. I bring my hand to his face – his face, that's still the same, despite the lost years – and I want to say so much – so many things that I could never put into words. I want to thank him. I want to tell him that he meant more to me than any person ever has. I want to tell him he saved me, every day. I want to tell him I'm proud of him, and that a part of me will for ever be for only him. But I don't. Instead

I reach up on tiptoes and kiss his cheek. 'I've missed you,' I tell him. 'I have missed you every day.'

Roman smiles, eyes glistening, and he wraps his strong arms around me. 'And you were always the best thing in my life,' he whispers into my ear. 'Nobody ever loved me like you did.' And against his chest, tall and unwavering, I close my eyes. I breathe him in. I want to remember this. I want to be able to replay this moment when I feel alone in the world, so I'll remember I'm not. I want to be able to replay this when I have not got a single ounce of faith in myself, so I'll remember that I am brave. I want to be able to close my eyes and be right here, when I'm old, and grey, and my body aches, when years and years have grown between us like oceans, and remember what it was like to love, and let go. I want to remember the butterflies. I want to remember the hope. I want to remember the moment we said goodbye for the rest of my life.

And there we stand, Roman and me, in our goodbye. Ready to let go, to go back to our other lives – our real lives. Ready to let this one play out, somewhere out there, among the stars, in time and space, with no guarantee we'll ever find it again.

The sun is barely a sliver as I leave; just a glow, breaking through the ocean. Roman walks me to the hire car, with Barney ambling along at his side, never more than a few feet away.

'You know where to find me,' he says as I stand at the car's open door, him on the other side.

'I do,' I say. 'Meet you there someday.'

'It's where I'll always be.'

✉

This PC/D: Lizzie Laptop/Roman/

Roman signed in on 24/04/05 20:19

Roman: Tomorrow's gonna suck without you J.

Roman: And the next day . . .

Roman: And the next day, and the day after that.

Lizzie: ditto.

Lizzie: i'll miss you Ro. it's been a blast.

Roman: And a pleasure :)

Roman: You'll come meet me after you finish school won't
   you?

Lizzie: course. try and stop me.

Roman: Good.

Roman: Now go do great things J. Change the world. Show
   those fuckers who they're dealing with :)

Chapter Thirty-Eight

The automatic doors part and I step over the threshold and into the busy reception area. There are walls of posters and art, and twirling stands of brochures and leaflets. A man, around my dad's age sits behind the reception desk on the phone. Beside him is a woman with hair the colour of white sunshine, who is explaining something to a boy in baggy jeans with a heavy rucksack. Both of them hunch over a form on the counter, the woman circling things with a red pen as he nods. I unzip the bag at my hip, to check I remembered my questionnaire for the career advisor. Yep. There it is. Just beside my sketchbook. The sketchbook, finally out of its black tissue paper, and finally with a few drawings in its fresh, blank pages. I could never start it back then. It was as if I knew I'd never see the end of the course; as if I knew I wasn't ready. Not like now.

I stand in the queue, looking through the large window behind the reception desk. It's alive out there. Bustling. There are scatters of people, some standing in groups, chatting, cans of Coke to their lips, mouths in smiles, lips moving quickly. There are some walking purposefully to classes, bags over shoulders and across chests, and there are some on benches, writing, reading, scrawling. Young people, older people. Teen boys, teen girls. All together. All here for one thing. All to learn. All to steer their lives onto the path they want to travel.

'Hello there, can I help at all?'

The man has hung up the phone, and looks at me from behind the counter, brows raised.

'Hi,' I say. 'I have an appointment. At eleven. It's with a career advisor.'

'Sure,' he smiles, looking down at his computer. 'Can I have your name, please?'

'Lizzie James.'

The man nods, typing quickly onto his keyboard with ringed fingers. Then he turns to me. 'Great,' he says. 'All booked in. You'll need to take a left out of here and follow the signs for W Block. That's the art department. Is this regarding the next study year?'

'Yes,' I tell him, and he nods once, rifling through a drawer at his side. He hands me a thick brown envelope.

'A couple of our course guides for next September, and a feedback form.'

'Great. Thanks.'

'Anytime,' the man says. 'Welcome to the college. Let us know if you need anything else.'

Chapter Thirty-Nine

Olivia answers the door in a towel turban, and a black silk robe that just skims the floor. The house is silent behind her. No bridesmaid slumber party, no music or distant family members emerging from the kitchen diner with wine glasses and mini quiches in hand, cheeks ruddy with tipsiness. Just Olivia, skin bare and glowing, face shining with moisturiser.

'I'm not staying,' I say quickly. 'I just wanted to see you. Before tomorrow. Before the big day.'

Olivia nods, mouth fixed with a grin. 'OK,' she says. 'Come in. I've just made some camomile tea.'

The house is empty and cold, and every surface, bare and shining – the whole place smells of Dettol. With all the adventures Olivia and David go on, with all the things they do, the travel and the classes, the stark, clinical walls in which they live never cease to shock me. I always expect artefacts and postcards, shelves of weird wooden instruments and coral from far away beaches. But there is none of that. It's a blank canvas. Soulless, even.

'Did you get the text? Of the itinerary for tomorrow? Times, and things . . .'

I nod. Nothing more.

'I know it's controversial,' says Olivia, pulling a small white cup from a wooden mug tree, 'but I just wanted the evening before to be peaceful. The last few months, arranging this thing have been so full on, the thought of having to be around lots of people, not sleeping in my own bed . . .' Olivia trails off, sliding a rounded white teapot across the counter and pouring its contents into the mug. It stinks. Of dusty tights and pot pourri.

'I get it,' I say. 'I think I'd be the same.'

Olivia looks up at me and smiles, embarrassment flashing across her face. 'Tea for you?'

I shake my head. 'No, thank you.'

Olivia gives a nod and wraps her hands around the mug on the counter. She leans against it and looks down into the murky liquid.

'Livvy,' I say, and she looks up, cheeks pink, white teeth nibbling her lip. 'I'm sorry if things were said that probably shouldn't have been at the dress shop the other day.'

Olivia shakes her head. 'It's fine, Lizzie, let's just forget it.'

'No,' I say. 'Let's not. I don't know about you but I'm over brushing things under the carpet.' Olivia's skin turns slightly pink and she gives a stiff nod. 'It happened,' I say, 'and things were said that really needed to be, but perhaps they were said in not quite the ideal place.' I give a wry smile, and Olivia looks down into her tea, her shoulders tight and raised, ears pink against the soft white towel swirling her head.

'I don't blame you,' murmurs Olivia. 'I don't think I realised that you were ill. Anxiety disorders, depression, all of it. I didn't get it. I was young.'

'So was I,' I say. 'But your mum wasn't.'

Olivia looks up, lips pressed together. She stares at me, then nods. 'I know,' she says. 'She should've known better. They all should've.'

The dishwasher behind her beeps, and Olivia turns, staring at it as if she's never heard it make such a sound before, and fusses with dials on the front longer than she should. She doesn't know what else to say – she feels awkward, I know that. There's a tray on the breakfast bar, set with a sandwich on it and a book, opened face down. I need to tell her now. I need to tell her and leave, so she can continue with her evening – the quiet, calm night-before-the-rest-of-her-life that she was enjoying before I interrupted.

'Olivia, I'll be there tomorrow,' I tell her, as she faffs around, pulling open the dishwasher door. 'But I won't be a bridesmaid.'

She spins round. 'What? No, Lizzie, you have—'

'I don't want to,' I say, fingers fumbling at my lap. 'We aren't really that close, and we needn't pretend to be. And I think if you were honest, you'd prefer I wasn't your bridesmaid either.'

Olivia stands and holds onto the edges of the counter. And I brace myself. I wait for the argument – I wait for the hurtful words, the words that tell me I've ruined her wedding, just like I did her mum and dad's, when I drank 'a bottle of' champagne, because I was a tearaway teenager who had no respect and knocked about with scummy council estate dwellers (Auntie Shall's story only of course, and plucked straight from the depths of her arse). But then she looks up at me, her eyes softening. 'I'm sorry,' she says, 'for what I said.'

I nod. And she doesn't argue. She doesn't tell me we *are* close, and that she loves me, and that of course she wants me to be her bridesmaid. She just asks, cheeks still pink, 'Will you still come for the whole day?'

'If you want me to.'

'Of course. I can sit you with Nathan and Katie.' Olivia brings her shoulder up, the silk of her robe shining in the bright kitchen spotlights. 'Katie and I talked. She said she didn't feel comfortable, after the argument. I can't say I really blame her.'

'Oh,' is all I manage. I push down hard, the instinct to apologise.

'Katie was Mum's idea anyway, so we could have a family member . . .' She looks up at me, sadly. With shame. With apology. 'So, it'll be three bridesmaids now, I suppose. My two best friends, and David's young niece.'

'As it should be,' I say, and Olivia sips her tea.

When I leave, I tell Olivia that I want to pay for my dress – for anything they've paid for, for me, and she whacks the suggestion away in the air, as if it's a swarm of gnats above her head. 'No,' she says. 'No, don't worry yourself about that,' and I get the impression she can't wait to get me out of the door and off her driveway.

I walk home through the park – down the path Roman and I walked down, time and time again, talking about music and conspiracy theories, and the best things we'd ever eaten. I walk by the back of Hubble's house and stop to take it in for the first time in twelve years. It has a loft conversion now, a shiny, dark grey cladded box jutting from its roof, and there are blinds at Hubble's old bedroom windows now. They are pulled almost to the bottom, like eyes, falling asleep.

I walk until the stars come out, and when I get home, I draw them. A whole page of clear deep purple sky, with twinkling planets and stars and meteors, tearing across the sky like celebratory fireworks. A whole universe, before a pile of blank pages. A whole universe of colour.

Chapter Forty

'So, did she freak?'

'Not at all. She was relieved I think, P.'

'Did she at least say sorry?'

'Oh, yeah,' I say. I turn to the window of the café beside me and duck to see beneath the large letters embossed on the glass. Nobody's here yet. 'She didn't even try to defend it or to defend her mum. But then, how could she?'

'Good,' says Priscilla. 'Oh, hang on, Liz, I've got to get in a lift. I might lose signal.'

'Are you at the hospital already?'

'Yep.'

'You're nice and early.'

Priscilla sighs down the line, but there's a smile in her voice. 'I'm really nervous.'

'It's going be fine, P. I promise you.'

On the way back from Scotland, Priscilla and I talked in whispers while the rest of the flight slept or read. It was 9 p.m. and we were exhausted, and with our coats as blankets, pulled up to our chins, we talked through everything Priscilla had been bottling over the last year – the last twelve years. Priscilla said she was going to tell Chris about Ethan, and about her pregnancy at sixteen. She said she wanted it out in the open.

She planned on telling him the next day, in the morning, after sleeping on it, formulating exactly what to say, but when she walked through the front door, she told me she burst into tears on Chris at the sight of him, and told him everything, right there, in the kitchen, her shoes and coat still on. And of course, he was amazing about it – she said she couldn't have wished for a better response. First thing the next morning, Priscilla called their doctor, and they sent her for blood tests, and Chris for a sperm assessment. Today, they are getting the results. Just like that. Months and months of worry and panic, eased with the truth.

'You know,' says Priscilla. There's the sound of lift doors sliding open on the other end of the phone. 'I'm bloody proud of you.'

'Thanks, Priscilla. I feel happier that I did it. Lighter.' A waitress walks by my table, two plated piles of chips in each hand.

'Seriously, Liz. To stand up for yourself, to know your own mind and heart enough to do what you did. To walk away from a situation you didn't want to be in, regardless of what people might think. It's really brave.'

'No, it isn't. You're brave, P. Facing the thing that's been scaring you the most. For years.'

'Just like you did last weekend, eh?'

I laugh. 'Then we're both brave,' I say.

'Sherlock and Watson reincarnated,' Priscilla giggles, and I smile so much my cheeks sting. 'Oh, Chris is calling, I've got to go.'

'Let me know how it goes. Text me.'

'I will,' says Priscilla. 'And do not forget to update me on what eighties throwback your Auntie Shall rocks up in today. I better get pictures of Madonna tits, and Pat Butcher shoulder pads.'

Priscilla hangs up, and I duck again to look across the road to the church. There are a few guests now, standing in the churchyard, smoking, chatting, backs already breaking in heels as high as skyscrapers. A pearly wedding car pulls up. It's David, impeccable, in a dark grey suit and dusky pink tie. His mum stands beside him, her hand on his back. She's a tiny woman with a smooth, square bob and a skirt suit the colour of limes. His best man nervously paces the gravel, looking down at his phone, then stands at the edge of the circle, as if contemplating running, just like Roman and I did once upon a time through that gate.

I wait in the café, sipping my water, scrolling through my phone, until I see Nathan and Katie arrive – Nathan, a vision indeed, in baby pink, and Katie, in a fawny-coloured crepe dress, her hair in a neat, not-a-hair-out-of-place up-do. I watch them chatting, greeting distant family members I can barely remember the names of, until they go inside.

It's a little early, but I'm ready to go. I screw the top on my water, pick up the small potted cyclamen on the table, and head for the frosty churchyard. I should manage to have a few minutes with Hubble before the ceremony starts. To clear any dead flowers and November leaves. To tell him I know.

To say hello. And goodbye.

'The pink is . . . questionable.'

'Oh, be quiet.'

'I mean, I never thought I would see you in actual baby pink but then again, these things are sent here to surprise us.'

Nathan tuts and brushes a hand down his trousers. 'You're going on like I'm wearing a bloody Mr Blobby costume.'

Katie leans across him from her seat on the pew. 'I said he looks like that Screech from *Saved by the Bell*.'

'Which is a huge diss,' grumbles Nathan, as I burst out laughing beside him.

'It wasn't meant to be an insult,' grins Katie. 'It's just very nineties, that's all.'

The pew behind us fills up, and I lower my voice. 'Plus, isn't the guy a bit weird now?'

'Who, Screech?' whispers Nathan out the side of his mouth, eyebrow raised.

'Yeah,' I nod. 'Does all sorts of dirty stuff now. He even had a video out where he put his finger—'

Katie makes a snorting noise, like she's trying to stifle a laugh, and Nathan puts his hand on my leg and ducks his head. 'Shut up,' he hisses, smiling. 'We're in a bloody church.'

'Oh. I am *sorry*, Cliff Richard.'

The church looks glorious, today. It really does. On the end of every pew, there is a posy of pink flowers, and cream, organza ribbon, and at the altar, there are tall, ornate candle holders, flickering with fat candles, and they too are decorated with the same pink flowers and ribbon. It looks brighter than it did the day I struggled to walk into it, all those years ago; the place I puked in, not once, not twice, but three times, all over its shining wooden floor, my flowers, myself, and Auntie Shall, of course. It was a mess. Everything was back then. And so was I, in a way. But I got through it. I healed and kept holding on, as hard as that was sometimes, through it all. And I'm glad I did. Comparing that version of myself to the one, here, on this pew, lighter, confident, unafraid and out the other side, I know now I have never felt more together. Old threads, severed. Loose ends, tied.

A hand lands softly on my shoulder. I know who it is before I turn around. He's wearing the same black suit he's had for as long as I can remember. He smiles, his eyes scrunching at the corners as he does, and he sits beside me. The pew creaks, and his chubby leg presses into mine.

'Hello, darlin',' Dad says. 'Alright?'

I haven't spoken to Dad properly in almost three weeks. I called him Thursday when he landed in London and told him I knew – he cried on the phone. So did I. This is the first time I've seen him or spoken to him since.

'Bloody cold out there,' whispers Linda, brushing her hand over her bum before she sits down. She looks amazing, and just totally Linda, in a black and white polka dot halter-neck dress, a furry cream shawl, with a matching fascinator. 'Hi, Lizzie, love,' she winks, leaning over and squeezing my wrist. 'You look fantastic.'

'As do you,' I say. 'So do you, Dad.'

Dad smiles proudly at Linda, who reaches into her bag and takes out her phone. She starts tapping away on it. The church falls quiet, as the organ rings out a final note of a song.

There's quiet; the shuffling of feet, whispers, the odd cough.

'You look a picture, my girl,' Dad whispers.

'Thanks, Dad. Do you like the trousers?'

'Love 'em,' he nods. 'I used to have something similar myself.'

'Back when King Henry was in power?'

Dad lets out a chesty laugh and nudges me. 'Keep that cheek up your sleeve,' he says. Then it's quiet again, and I see him at the side of my vision watching me, the way he would when I was a child, when I'd be painting or fiddling with Playdoh. Admiring, almost. Pure love.

'Lizzie,' he says, his voice a deep whisper. More and more guests filter into the church, and I see Nathan and Katie wave to someone across the aisle. 'Are we—'

'Dad . . .'

'I'm sorry,' he says. 'I'm just so sorry.'

'Dad, you don't need to apologise.'

'I do, darlin'. Back then we . . .' Dad brings his chubby hand up to his mouth. 'We let you down. We try, you know, as parents, to do the right thing – *the best thing*. And we get it wrong. And we did, back then, your mother and I.'

Nathan stands and chats to the someone across the aisle, miming with his mouth and hands, but I don't take my eyes off Dad, whose face is reddening, whose eyes are watery.

'We put on this all-seeing, all-knowing mask for our kids, and most of the time . . . we keep it up,' he whispers, sniffing, knuckle rubbing the end of his nose. 'But sometimes it slips. We lose it. And you see that we're human, and that we don't have a bloody clue, really, we're just as scared as you are. More so. And I'm sorry.'

'Dad . . .'

'I'm sorry that when you needed us we were too busy messing about, acting like spoiled teenagers to see that our child needed us.' Dad's thumbs fumble in his lap. 'You needed us to have that mask on, to be strong for you. And you didn't get that, Liz. And I will always be sorry.'

'*Dad.*'

'And about Roman . . .'

'Dad,' I say, loudly, although it warms me hearing Dad say his name as if it's that – a name and not a forbidden, dirty word. A woman in front of us in an obscenely large hat turns at the sound of my voice and looks at us as if we are vermin. Dad looks at me, stifles a schoolboy smile.

'It's done,' I whisper to him. 'It was another lifetime ago.' Then I kiss Dad's cheek and say, 'I love you, Dad.'

He squeezes my hand as the organ strikes up and everyone stands, an echo of shoes squeaking and scuffing on the dark wooden floor.

And I watch – bridesmaids, one by one, floating down the aisle, step-together, step-together – until Olivia appears, gliding, as she always does, in a dress almost identical to one we all bookmarked in *My Bride* magazine that night at

319

the restaurant. She looks beautiful as she drifts by, like a dream, like a heroine from a movie. I crane my neck. A tiny red-headed girl holds the long, lace train – little Lilly, David's niece. She looks excited, happy. Right where she belongs.

Everyone cranes their necks to try to see further down the aisle; to see Olivia and David meet at the altar, but I catch someone across the aisle waving, behind me. I rise a little on my toes, to see who it is, beneath the very elaborate, teal hat. My heart jumps. It's Mum. Mum and Clark, side by side. Clark doesn't see me, he's looking forward, face formal and serious. But Mum's looking right at me. Her face explodes into a grin. 'Hi, darling,' she mouths, then blows a kiss.

Dad leans in, then. 'Who're you waving at?' he asks.

I smile. 'Mum.'

His eyes widen, then he pauses, gives a nod, and turns, stretching his neck to see her. When he does, she simply holds a hand up in a wave; just a little, lifting her hand to wiggle her fingers, before both turn and face the front of the church. Nathan nudges me and gives a victorious smile. 'See,' his smile says. 'Things are changing. Things are better now.'

The doors of the church are still open, and golden sunlight from the outside pours through, lighting the aisle. I can just see the gate from where I sit. The gate Roman and I stood by, on the gravel, all those years ago, him in his tux with the skewed bow, me in that dress. The gate we ran through together – flew through, like two birds dying to be free.

A pregnant lady walks by, a toddler on reins, zigzagging in front of her. An elderly man with gelled white hair and a newspaper under his arm, pauses by the gate, craning his neck to see inside. He walks away, the sunshine on his face. A bus. A man, face contorted and angry, rambling into his phone. Then, two teenagers, chatting, laughing, drifting by the gate;

neither looking up to take notice of anything but one another.
If I squint, it could almost be us.

The music stops.

We all take our seats.

The church doors close.

This PC/D: Lizzie Laptop/Roman/
Roman signed in on 03/06/04 21:37

Roman: Hey, it's me. Roman. The boy with the big gob from The Grove.

Lizzie: hiya. just added you :)

Roman: Cool :)

Lizzie: was nice to meet you today Roman M.

Roman: Cool to meet you too Lizzie J.

Acknowledgments

Like raising babies, it takes a village to bring a book from a niggle of an idea and 'can I do this? Can I really write this story?' to a finished, shiny novel you can hold in your hand and I am lucky to have had the help from a small village of wonderful people. (Here is where I start breathing into my brown paper bag, sure I will miss someone crucial and they will forever hold an acknowledgment-page-shaped grudge.)

First, thank you to Juliet Mushens, my brilliant agent, who made my author dreams come true one wet and rainy morning in January in Soho. You got this book, wholeheartedly, and you got me, and everything I was trying to do with Lizzie and Roman. Thank you for absolutely everything, and of course, to the whole team at Caskie Mushens, too, for your cheerleading and endless hard work.

Thank you to the entire incredible team at Trapeze and Orion, and of course, to my editor: the dreamy, funny, talented and relentlessly hard-working, Katie Brown. For 'knowing' and loving Lizzie and Roman as much as I do. For helping me elevate this book beyond anything I could have imagined. For making me delete my 'shit's. For the Mini Eggs. For it all. Working with you is such magic.

Thank you to my writing clan. Where would I be without

you? Gilly McAllister, Hina Malik, Becky Williams, Laura Pearson, Stephie Chapman, L D Lapinski, Hayley Webster, Lynsey James, and so many more of you on Twitter who have kept me going. Thank you.

Now for some non-writerly nods. (This is where I start crying and thank *God* you can't see me at my keyboard, right now.) Pat, you always knew I would. Michelle, I wonder if I would be here without that Jimmy 'Shoe' belief we never let go of. (We did it!) Grace and Sally, my over-the-road and round-the-corner buddies, thank you for looking after my babies so I can write in peace, and most of all, for looking after me. To every friend who has stuck by me, through the good, the bad, the ugliest times: thank you from the bottom of my heart. You are why I write about friendship. You know who you are.

To my Nan and my lovely, lovely late Grandad. I couldn't have written about the impact of wonderful, loving grandparents if I didn't have any myself. Thank you for your love.

Bubs, my little brother, my best friend, for believing I would do this more than I ever did, (and for casting all my characters for me with an undiscovered-casting-director's eye.) I could not have done this without you.

Dad, thank you for showing me from the second I could understand that there are no stupid, unreachable dreams, and that jobs didn't have to feel like work if you loved what you did. That was invaluable.

Mum, through every high and every low, you never ever once stopped believing in me. Thank you for it all. There are no words.

And like saving your Yorkshire puddings until the end of a roast dinner, I saved the very, very best until last. Ben, my three babies: my whole entire world. Thank you for the happiness you bring me every day. I love you.

Author Q & A

Catriona Innes interviews Lia Louis

The book begins with a letter . . . is this what came first in your writing process?

I knew there was going to be a letter very early on in getting the idea for *Somewhere Close to Happy*, but it was actually one of the very last things I wrote. I wanted it to be short, but at the same time, carry a lot of mystery and prompt questions from the reader, so I kept putting it off (until I had no choice but to sit down and just get it written!)

✉

It deals with these mental health issues in such a realistic, relatable way. How much research did you do?

For most of my life, I have suffered intermittently with anxiety and depression – as a teen and also, as an adult. I spoke to friends who I knew were comfortable with discussing certain mental health struggles they'd had, but I wrote mostly using my own personal experience. It was cathartic at times, but I have to admit that it also had the opposite effect some days, where writing a certain scene or having to 'dig deep' into a memory would leave me feeling emotionally exhausted. I like to think that's what makes it feel realistic and relatable though and for me, if others can relate, or it helps someone feel less alone or understood, that's completely worth it.

The characters - even those who have smaller roles – are so 3D. What character development did you do? Do they all have huge back stories that the reader doesn't know?

I think their 3Dness is a lot to do with how long I have been writing Lizzie James and her family (eight years, on and off, give or take!) She was such a strong voice in my head, as were her family, but it took me ages to decide what sort of story she should be telling. All of the false starts I had with Lizzie James – scenes and chapters and a whole book I scrapped some years ago – served as practice and a way of really finding out exactly who they were before I finally started what became *Somewhere Close to Happy*.

It takes a long time before we get to meet Roman in present day . . . so much so that we're absolutely dying to meet him (yet are already in love with him). Were you tempted to bring him in earlier?

I can't tell you how excited and desperate I was to write the present-day Roman scenes! Weirdly, one of my original book ideas actually opened with Lizzie and Roman meeting again for the first time in twelve years, but in hindsight (and with a little more experience now!) I don't think that would have ever quite worked as a whole book.

✉

You manage to balance the light with the dark so expertly. This can be tricky when dealing with such heavy subjects - you don't want to look like you're poking fun at them, yet humour is how so many of us cope with the tough times in our lives. How did you find writing the funny parts?

I loved writing the funny parts. They were the perfect anecdote and light relief to some of the harder, sadder scenes I had to write. I find humour to be a life-line during difficult times, and I really wanted to show that although someone might be really up against it and struggling, they are not totally defined by that one thing. They are still 'them', can still laugh and joke, and I wanted to be sure I did that realistically, without belittling or making fun of their struggles or experience.

✉

The ending is happy, but not *everything* is tied up in an expertly tied bow. Was this deliberate? Did you write lots of different endings and this is the one that felt the most real?

I knew from the very beginning that I wanted it to end the way it did. Although the fairy tale lover inside of me toyed ever so slightly with the idea of them running off into the sunset together, in my heart, I knew the only ending that made sense was this one. I wanted them both to finally have the closure they so badly needed to be able to fully live their lives once and for all. Whilst Lizzie's journey was about finding Roman, it was more about finding herself and facing her fears. In the beginning of the book, she was living quite a lonely, confined life, and by the end, had become her own hero, getting on planes, standing up to family members and starting college.

✉

Priscilla and Lizzie's friendship is so real, is it based on any of your real-life friendships?

I am lucky to have a small number of friends who I feel I can be 'warts and all' with and that was exactly what I wanted Lizzie and Priscilla's relationship to be – the sort of friendship where nothing at all prompts any sort of judgement, only love and acceptance. I think those friendships are very rare, but when you find someone like that – someone that loves you for everything that you are, even those vulnerable, flawed pieces you're scared to show the rest of the world – it is a very special and powerful thing.

✉

It places real emphasis on the power of the friendships we make in our formative years – do you think the friends we make in our teens stay with us, somehow, throughout our lives, even if we no longer see them?

Absolutely. In our teen years, relationships are so intense and full of firsts – those first true belly butterflies, first kisses, first staying-out-too-lates, first fights – that naturally, they get under the skin more than perhaps friendships in adulthood do. There's something about 'coming of age' with someone that knits you together in some way, even if those people are no longer in your life. Those first friendships and relationships shape who we come to be.

Credits

Trapeze would like to thank everyone at Orion who worked on the publication of *Somewhere Close to Happy* in the UK.

Agent
Juliet Mushens

Editor
Katie Brown

Copy editor
Laura Gerrard

Proof reader
Linda Joyce

Editorial Management
Charlie Panayiotou
Jane Hughes
Alice Davis

Audio
Paul Stark
Amber Bates

Contracts
Anne Goddard
Paul Bulos
Jake Alderson

Design
Lucie Stericker
Joanna Ridley
Nick May
Clare Sivell
Helen Ewing
Janette Revill
Sidonie Beresford-Browne

Finance
Emily-Jane Taylor
Jasdip Nandra
Afeera Ahmed
Elizabeth Beaumont
Sue Baker
Victor Falola

Marketing
Lucy Cameron

Production
Claire Keep
Katie Horrocks
Fiona McIntosh

Publicity
Alex Layt

Sales
Jen Wilson
Victoria Laws
Esther Waters
Rachael Hum
Ellie Kyrke-Smith
Frances Doyle
Ben Goddard
Georgina Cutler

Barbara Ronan
Andrew Hally
Dominic Smith
Maggy Park
Linda McGregor
Sinead White
Jemimah James
Rachel Jones
Jack Dennison
Nigel Andrews
Ian Williamson
Julia Benson
Declan Kyle
Robert Mackenzie

Operations
Jo Jacobs
Sharon Willis
Lisa Pryde